Look what people are saying about The Mighty Quinns...

Conor

"...a dangerous world of murder, presenting strong conflict and terrific characterizations. Very highly recommended."

—*Wordweaving.com*

Dylan

"...a great hero, yummy sex and a fascinating family."

—*The Romance Reader*

Brendan

"...a gem, loaded with suspense and sexual tension."

—*Romantic Times*

Liam

"*The Mighty Quinns: Liam* is perfect reading for any summer day!"

—*WritersUnlimited.com*

Brian

"...a grade A hero."

—*Wordweaving.com*

Sean

"*The Mighty Quinns: Sean* engages the reader's emotions—and funny bone—from the very first page."

—*Romantic Times*

Dear Reader,

The editors at Harlequin and Silhouette are thrilled to be able to bring you a brand-new featured author program beginning in 2005! Signature Select aims to single out outstanding stories, contemporary themes and oft-requested classics by some of your favorite series authors and present them to you in a variety of formats bound by truly striking covers.

You may notice a number of different colored bands on the spine of this book. Each color corresponds to a different type of reading experience in the new Signature Select program. The Spotlight books will offer a single "big read" by a talented series author, the Collections will present three novellas on a selected theme in one volume, the Sagas will contain sprawling, sometimes multi-generational family tales (often related to a favorite family first introduced in series) and the Miniseries will feature requested, previously published books, with two or, occasionally, three complete stories in one volume. The Signature Select program will offer one book in each of these categories per month, and fans of limited continuity series will also find these continuing stories under the Signature Select umbrella.

In addition, these volumes will bring you bonus features...different in every single book! You may learn more about the author in an extended interview, more about the setting or inspiration for the book, more about subjects related to the theme and, often, a bonus short read will be included.

Watch for new stories from Vicki Lewis Thompson, Lori Foster, Donna Kauffman, Marie Ferrarella, Merline Lovelace, Roberta Gellis, Suzanne Forster, Stephanie Bond and scores more of the brightest talents in romance fiction!

We have an exciting year ahead!

Warm wishes for happy reading,

Marsha Zinberg

Marsha Zinberg
Executive Editor
The Signature Select Program

Kate Hoffmann

The Promise

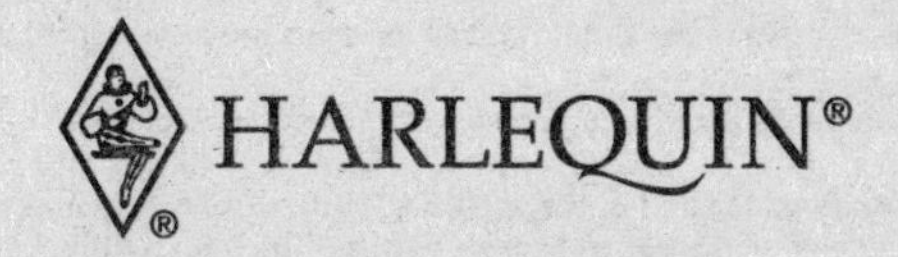

TORONTO • NEW YORK • LONDON
AMSTERDAM • PARIS • SYDNEY • HAMBURG
STOCKHOLM • ATHENS • TOKYO • MILAN • MADRID
PRAGUE • WARSAW • BUDAPEST • AUCKLAND

ISBN 0-373-83644-9

THE PROMISE

This edition published by arrangement with Harlequin Books S.A.

www.eHarlequin.com

Printed in U.S.A.

Dear Reader,

So many of you have written asking about future Mighty Quinn books and I'm happy to say that your requests have been taken to heart. I never intended the Quinn family to have such a long publishing life, but I'm glad they have.

This is the story of where it all began. Writing *The Promise* has given me a chance to write something completely different form the short contemporary novels I'm known for. When I traveled to Ireland about eight years ago, the country captured my writer's imagination. The magical beauty of the landscape filled my head with ideas for stories and the people were so warm and welcoming that I immediately felt at home.

I hope you enjoy reading *The Promise* as much as I enjoyed writing it. And who knows, there may be even more Quinn stories looming on the horizon.

Happy reading,

Kate Hoffmann

THE MIGHTY QUINNS MINISERIES

HARLEQUIN TEMPTATION

847—THE MIGHTY QUINNS: CONOR
851—THE MIGHTY QUINNS: DYLAN
855—THE MIGHTY QUINNS: BRENDAN
933—THE MIGHTY QUINNS: LIAM
937—THE MIGHTY QUINNS: BRIAN
941—THE MIGHTY QUINNS: SEAN

HARLEQUIN SINGLE TITLE

REUNITED

To Tracey and Jaye for making my mornings brighter.

And with special thanks to Grainne Burke
for her help in making this book authentically Irish.

PROLOGUE

County Cork, Present Day

FLUFFY WHITE CLOUDS hung in the sky, the sun's rays slanting through them to cast the green hills in a divine light. A slender woman looked down on Ballykirk harbor, the brisk wind snatching strands from the tidy knot of hair at the nape of her neck. She drew a deep breath of the salt-tinged air then closed her eyes and let memories of her childhood wash over her like the evening tide.

Fiona McClain Quinn hadn't stood on Irish soil in many years, not since the day she'd left with her husband and family for the promise of a new life in America. She could barely remember the woman she'd been that day, dressed in her Sunday best, just twenty-five years old and already the mother of five boys.

She tried to imagine herself as a young woman, her hair long and dark, her skin smooth and her body so slender. Life had been simple then, an endless horizon stretching out in front of her, all her dreams just waiting to be realized. Images whirled in Fiona's mind, flashes of the past interwoven with the hopes she'd kept hidden deep in her heart.

Fiona had been born to do great things, to make a difference in the world—at least that's what her mother had always told her. It hadn't happened in Ireland, so she'd set off for America, sure that her destiny awaited her there.

A tiny smile touched her lips, the optimism of her youth now merely an amusing recollection. She glanced over her shoulder and watched as her eldest son, Conor, a man of thirty-seven, perched on a boulder with his two-year-old son, Riley, tucked between his legs.

Her eyes met Conor's and held for a long moment. He nodded, as if he could read her thoughts and sense her melancholy. "It's a beautiful spot," he called.

"Yes, it is," Fiona murmured, her words swept away by the wind. She turned back to the sea, back to her memories. When her daughter, Keely, had first suggested this trip, Fiona had been reluctant to agree. But the more she'd thought about it, the more she'd realized that Ireland could be both an ending and a new beginning. She and her husband, Seamus, were grandparents now and it seemed as though all the years they'd spent together—and then, the years they'd spent apart—had passed in the blink of an eye. Would the rest of her life fly by just as quickly?

She'd navigated through the previous thirty years, searching the shifting currents for something to cling to, the part of herself that had been lost since her impetuous youth and had drifted just beyond her fingertips. Who was Fiona McClain Quinn? After fifty-six years, she ought to know. But standing here, in the spot where her fortunes had taken such an unlikely turn, Fiona was forced to wonder if she'd lived the wrong life, a life meant for some other woman. If she'd turned down Seamus Quinn's proposal of marriage all those years ago, where might her life have taken her?

Fiona turned away from the setting sun and walked back to Conor. "It's greener than I remembered," he said as she approached.

"It's the light," Fiona explained. "It filters through the clouds to make all the colors seem more brilliant. Especially the green." She leaned back against the rock. "We came here the day we left. Your cousin, Maeve, took a picture of us standing right at this spot."

"Odd. I remember the green, but I don't remember that day," Conor said.

"You were barely six years old. And the twins weren't even a year. But your father insisted we come here just once more before we left Ireland forever. He wanted this sight—the sea, Ballykirk below us, the hills behind us, and the sun shimmering off the water—as his last memory, to hold close to his heart."

Conor's expression brightened. "This is Oisin's Rock, isn't it?"

"You do remember," Fiona said, laughing softly.

"Your father used to tell the tale over and over again, and you boys never seemed to get enough of it." She bent down and pointed to a chipped area near the base. "When you were little, you came up here and tried to crack the rock to let Oisin out. You were certain your Mighty Quinn ancestor was still in there somewhere."

Conor rested his chin on the top of Riley's head, the boy's nearly black hair brushing against his father's cheek. "I don't remember," he said. "It's been a long time since I've heard one of Da's tales. Tell me. I'd like to pass it along to Riley one day."

"Well, most of your da's stories were well embellished, but people around this part of Ireland believe the tale of Oisin Quinn is true." She drew a long breath and tried to recall the story as Seamus had first told it to her all those years ago. "Oisin Quinn was a strapping lad, strong and stubborn, with thick arms and raven-black hair. He was good of heart and pure of mind and loved by all who knew him. Many years ago, this part of Ireland was ruled by a kind and benevolent king, King Tadhg, who cared deeply for his subjects. Life was good. The forests were filled with game, the seas teeming with fish, and the land so rich a man could grow food for ten families. But armies from the neighboring kingdoms often invaded, their leaders coveting this land and all it promised. Tadhg's soldiers fought them back, simple farmers and fishermen often joining in the fight, for they had just as much to lose."

Riley's eyes, wide and curious, were fixed on her face as she spoke. "As time passed and Tadhg grew older and more feeble, the people of his kingdom began to worry. He had no son to succeed him and a kingdom without a king would quickly lapse into chaos and despair. Oisin and some of the men from other villages asked for an audience with King Tadhg and they told him of their concerns. The king, in his wisdom, told them that when he died, they would rule themselves."

Fiona reached out to brush a strand of hair from Riley's eyes, her fingertips sliding over his rosy cheek. "Freedom in Ireland had always been a fleeting dream, Riley, even back then. But Oisin knew freedom meant a better future for everyone and he promised King Tadhg that he would fight with his very last breath to keep it."

The breeze off the sea freshened and Fiona wrapped her coat more tightly around her, slipping her hands into her pockets. "It wasn't long before King Tadhg died and the first armies gathered at the borders of his kingdom. His people were ready and they fought them back, but not without considerable loss of life. Again and again, the armies invaded and Oisin fought, with a spear and a cudgel, wielding both with superhuman strength. Soon, the enemy began to fear him, his feats of courage becoming legend throughout the land. They thought he might not be a man, but a god, sent by King Tadhg's spirit to protect his people. Years passed and many battles were fought and won, but gradually, the people began to tire of the wars and talked about surrender. Oisin stood firm, remembering the king's words. One day, an enemy army gathered in the hills above Ballykirk. Oisin tried to rouse the men of the village to battle, but no one wanted to fight. So Oisin took his spear and his cudgel and came out to this very spot, determined to protect his friends and neighbors. The soldiers came and he fought, one man against a vast army. Again and again, he drove them back, killing many soldiers and striking fear into the hearts of those who retreated. He never slept or ate, standing guard, day after day, year after year, fighting all who challenged him. He grew old and people tried to convince him to surrender, but he'd made a promise to the king and was determined to honor it. And so, the village was safe for a long time, the armies afraid to invade. One day, the townsfolk wandered up this hill to thank Oisin Quinn for his protection. But when they arrived all they found was this stone, huge and imposing, and shaped very much like the crouching giant of a man that Oisin once was. But Oisin was nowhere to be found. Some thought he'd been killed long ago. Some believed he'd wandered off. But as his friends examined the rock that had never been there before, they realized the rock was Oisin. He'd been magically transformed so that he might guard Ballykirk for centuries to come, never to grow feeble and weak, never to fall to an enemy sword. And though the rock has been worn by the wind and the rain, if you look carefully, you can still see the face of Oisin Quinn."

"Do you believe it?" Conor asked.

Fiona reached out and took Riley from her son's arms. "It was the first story your father ever told me. I was just a little girl, but even as a boy, he could weave a fantastic tale. I never doubted him for an instant." She pressed her lips to the top of Riley's head.

"Are you happy you came, Ma?"

"I am. Keely and Rafe were right. We needed to come back." Keely's husband, Rafe Kendrick, had arranged all the details of the trip and paid for the tickets and accommodations. Fiona couldn't imagine the cost of bringing sixteen adults and two children across the Atlantic, much less putting them up in a fancy hotel for a week. But she was glad she'd finally agreed to make the trip.

"Nana."

Fiona nuzzled her grandson's cheek. "And what do you think of Ireland, Riley Quinn?"

"Up, up," he said, reaching out to Oisin's Rock. "Go up."

She chuckled and hugged the two-year-old tight in her arms as she stared out at the landscape. "I thought it would all seem so unfamiliar. But the moment I breathed in the air and felt the grass beneath my feet, it came back. It's as if I just left yesterday. Where have all the years gone?" She shook her head. "I haven't been able to bring myself to visit the cemetery yet. Money was so scarce that I couldn't afford to come back for the funerals. When my mother and father were buried, I was miles and miles away. When my grandmother was buried, too. I've carried that with me for so many years. It's time to say goodbye."

"I've heard so much about the Mighty Quinns. Tell me about your family," Conor said. "I just barely remember my grandparents. Did I ever know my great-grandparents?"

Fiona shook her head. "I didn't know your great-grandfather. His name was Aidan McClain and he was a doctor. My father barely remembered him, but my grandmother, Maura, used to talk about him all the time. She said he was a sensitive man. I took it to mean that he was troubled because there were always whispers when it came to a discussion of his life and death. He was killed in a car accident when my father was just a little boy."

"I do remember Nana McClain," Conor said.

"Maura Sullivan. She came from a very prominent family in Dublin. Her father was also a doctor."

"And what about Da's grandparents?"

"Ah, now there was a story of a true Mighty Quinn. Jack Quinn fought for freedom in Ireland, just like Oisin Quinn did hundreds of years before. He was wounded in the civil war and your great-grandfather Aidan saved his life."

Conor took Riley from Fiona's arms and swung the little boy up onto his shoulders. Then he took Fiona's hand and tucked it into the crook of his arm. As they hiked back down the hill to Ballykirk, Fiona recalled what she knew of Jack Quinn and Aidan McClain, of the history that had brought their two families together, intertwining their destinies for three generations.

But as they walked and talked, she could only wonder at the details of lives lived so long ago, details that she and her children and their own children would never know. How many promises had been made and then broken, how many dreams imagined, then shattered? These hills, this land and this sea, this sun and this wind, had watched it all.

And only Ireland knew what was legend and what was fact.

PART ONE
AIDAN'S PROMISE

CHAPTER ONE

Dublin, June 1922

THE NIGHT WAS WARM and the scent of the river hung in the air. The damp had settled deep into Jack Quinn's bones as he stumbled in the darkness toward the Ha'penny Bridge. He gulped in a deep breath, trying to keep his head clear and his legs under him.

The gas streetlamps had gone unlit, the streets of Dublin deserted. Soldiers of the Free State forces patrolled the city, shooting at anyone who looked like an IRA insurgent. Ireland was at war with itself and Jack was in the midst of it. He winced as he sat down to catch his breath, his back braced against a stone wall along the quay.

The bullet wound in his side stung and when he touched the spot above his hip, his fingers came away sticky with fresh blood. Christ, he'd never held a gun before he'd joined in the fight and now the pistol shoved in his waistband was the only thing between him and a long prison term. What did a fisherman from County Cork know about guns?

He groaned softly as he stood, fighting off a wave of pain and knowing that he had to keep moving. Though he'd been willing to fight for Irish freedom, he never thought he'd be killing fellow Irishmen. The same men who'd fought side by side in the Easter Uprising of 1916 were now firing upon each other. And the British stood in the background, pulling the strings as they always had.

He sank deeper into the shadows of a building. The bullet had caught him just after dusk and since then, Jack had kept himself hidden, slowly making his way across the city to the River Liffey. All he needed was a safe place to hide, to nick a bit of sleep, before he completed his task and found his way out of Dublin.

Jack reached for the oilcloth packet he'd tucked in the waistband of his trousers. He'd come to the city three years before, full of both himself and his political ideals. It hadn't taken him long to get caught up in the cause and now he'd become a valuable asset to the IRA, a fearless smuggler, comfortable on both land and sea.

He'd learned to navigate the city as he'd navigated the waters off the Irish coast. He was first given the task of recruitment, spending time in the pubs along the coast, searching for young fishermen loyal to the cause. He'd developed a network of both men and boats that could be called on to sneak weapons into the country.

But since hostilities had escalated, he'd been a soldier, working with a small group of men in raiding government supply depots. One gun or one hundred, it was all another step toward a true republic. What he did branded him as a traitor to the Irish government, but as a Republican, he refused to recognize a government that still bowed to British rule.

Recently, Republican forces had seized government buildings, city neighborhoods and, in some cases, entire towns, determined to undermine the treaty that the Free State politicians had made with the Brits.

Jack had killed his first man three months before, in the days leading up to the IRA occupation at the Four Courts. He'd been caught in a raid, the Free State forces bursting into a small factory that they'd used to cache their weapons. It had been self-defense, but that didn't make the killing any easier to stomach.

Jack closed his eyes and tipped back his head. There were times when he was ready to trot back to County Cork, to leave the cause to its own ends. By sunset tomorrow, he could be back in Ballykirk, steering his father's fishing boat around the little harbor, the salt spray cool on his face, the smell of war gone from his nostrils.

But he'd left that all behind, his family, his work, a girl he loved, to fight for a dream that had finally seemed close enough to touch. He didn't want to raise his children in an Ireland without a future. Maybe he had been too idealistic, too caught up in a goal that might never be achieved in his lifetime.

Jack scanned the street. He had to keep moving. If he didn't, he'd pass out and wake up with a rifle muzzle pressed against his head. The bombardment at the Four Courts had begun at sunrise, the British-backed government determined to teach the Republicans a lesson. How many of his friends had died that day? How many had been arrested? He cursed softly, then pressed on. It was no use thinking about it right now.

Jack kept to the shadows of the buildings along the river, resting in doorways and alleys, gathering his strength and fighting back waves of nausea and pain. In the distance, shots cracked and men shouted, breaking the tense silence of the city.

A pile of toppled crates gave him cover to observe the north end of the Ha'Penny Bridge. He reckoned it would be his best shot to get across the river. The other bridges had been blocked to prevent carts and motorcars from passing, but the Ha'Penny had been left to a pair of uniformed soldiers who lounged against the rail, smoking cigarettes.

Crossing the bridge would be impossible. He stared across the water to the far side. If he could slip into the river unnoticed, he could swim across and crawl up the quay on the south end of the bridge. He wrapped his pistol in the oilcloth pouch, took a deep breath and then ducked down low as he ran. A few moments later, he was in the water. He slowly stroked across the river in the dark, the pouch in his teeth, his side aching with each movement.

As a fisherman's son, he'd learned to swim at a young age and had always felt at home both in and on the water. Though the river was foul with garbage and scraps of civilization, Jack tried to imagine that he was crossing the harbor at Ballykirk, the salt water clean and clear.

He found a foothold on the quay and crawled up and out of the water, then swung over the rail and dropped silently onto the pavement. Jack wiped his hair back from his face, ready to push on.

It took him nearly an hour to make the short walk to the boardinghouse, situated in a street lined with run-down buildings. He watched the facade for a long time, considering his options. It had been nearly three years since Jack had arrived on Aidan McClain's doorstep, fresh from the country. And though they'd rarely seen each other since then, the moment Jack had found himself in real trouble, he'd known where to turn. Aidan would help him, of that he was certain.

They'd been the best of friends since the day they'd begun school together in Ballykirk—Aidan, the shy, intelligent boy from a prominent family and Jack, the rowdy son of a fisherman. Aidan's father was one of the wealthiest men in County Cork and Jack's father struggled to put food on the table. Aidan dressed in the finest clothes and Jack wore the same pair of shoes until the soles were worn through. But Jack was strong and quick with his fists, the kind of friend a sensitive boy like Aidan needed.

Over the years spent wandering the hills around Ballykirk in search of boyish adventures, they'd developed an unshakable loyalty to each other that surpassed social standing and material wealth. Their lives had diverged in the past five years, Aidan turning his energies to the study of medicine while Jack had slipped into the shadowy world of the IRA and gun smuggling. But they shared a bond that could never be broken.

Jack shifted, knowing he had to find help soon. He watched an old man weave drunkenly down the street, past the boardinghouse. Jack had been surprised that Aidan had chosen such a shabby residence considering his father's money could buy much more luxurious accommodations.

He stared up at the window of Aidan's room, noticing the sash was open to catch the evening breeze. If he were quick about it, he could climb up the porch roof and be inside in short order. But before he did, Jack took a moment to reconsider his decision. Normally he wouldn't have involved his friend in political affairs, well aware of his feelings on the Republican cause. But regardless of his politics, Aidan could be trusted, more than any other person Jack knew. He reached to scale up to the porch roof.

To his surprise, once inside he saw the room was empty, the bed still neatly made. He crossed to the washstand and dumped the contents of the jug into the bowl. Scrubbing at his dirty face, Jack wiped away the grime clinging to his face. Then he stripped off his sodden shirt and prodded at the seeping wound in his side. It hurt like hell but Jack was fairly certain it wasn't fatal.

He grabbed a washrag from the bar on the stand and swirled it in the bowl of water, then pressed it to the wound. The doorknob rattled and Jack quickly stepped to the other side of the wardrobe and held his breath. The door opened, a match was struck and a small oil lamp illuminated the room. He waited a moment, then moved toward the slight figure standing near the bed. "Aidan?"

The young man jumped, then spun around, the lamp raised as if to fend off an intruder. "Jack? Jaysus, you scared the piss out of me. How did you get in here?"

"The window," Jack said. He pointed to the framed photo of Aidan's mother, sitting on the table next to the bed. "I wasn't certain I had the right room until I saw that."

Aidan regarded him uneasily. "I—I didn't know you were still in Dublin. I haven't seen you in months. What are you doing here?"

"I got the note you left at Skelling's Pub at Christmas. They could have told you where I was, but they're a wee bit suspicious of well-dressed strangers."

Aidan's attention fixed on the pistol that Jack had set next to the washbowl. "What have you gotten yourself into?"

"You needn't ask," Jack muttered.

Aidan brushed a lock of pale hair from his eyes, his focus on Jack's face. "Why did you come here? You know I don't want any part of this."

"I needed your help," Jack said. "You're the only one I can trust." He stepped forward into the flickering light. Gritting his teeth, he held up his arm and pulled the rag from the wound. "I got myself shot, I did."

"Christ, how did this happen?" Aidan asked, his expression etched with concern.

"Are you blind? There's a war going on out there."

"You should have stayed in Ballykirk," Aidan said. He shook his head, then slowly approached Jack. "The Irish are ruling Ireland. It's called Home Rule if you're not aware. I can't see why that's not good enough for you." He nodded at the bed. "Sit. I'll take a look. I've certainly patched enough bullet wounds over the past month to make easy work of yours."

"Thanks," Jack said. "I didn't know where else to come. I couldn't risk going to hospital."

Though they were the same age, Jack had always felt like an older brother to Aidan, watching over him when the bullies might find an excuse to pummel him. Now it was Aidan's turn to take care of Jack.

Aidan grabbed another rag from the stack of clean linens, then disappeared with the empty jug. When he returned to the room, he drew the lamp closer and squinted at the wound. Carefully he dabbed away the blood.

His arm raised above his head, Jack fought the pain. "So you're a doctor now, are you?"

"Not yet. But I'm on my way. Between my classes and my hours at hospital, I've been working in private practice with Dr. Edwin Sullivan." He glanced up at Jack. "You've lost a fair amount of blood, then?"

"I'm shot, you dumb gombeen. And I've been leaking steady since it happened," Jack muttered.

The corners of Aidan's mouth curled slightly. "Haven't changed much, have you?" He turned away from the bed and grabbed his grip, opening the black bag and retrieving a roll of gauze. "It's been a fair bit of time since I've patched you up. It wasn't my father who convinced me I'd be a fine physician. It was you."

"As I recall, I took most of those beatings defending you."

"This isn't a cut lip or a black eye, Jack. It's a gunshot wound. Maybe this will be enough to convince you to go home."

Jack shook his head, gritting his teeth. "I can't. We're so close."

"You could fight forever and it will make no difference. The British are not schoolyard bullies. They're not going to get scared off and let Ireland go."

Jack's temper flared. "When are you going to open your feckin' eyes, Aidan? The Republicans hold Ennis and they're fighting in Limerick right now. We've got an army in Cork. If we could get the whole country behind us, we could drive the Brits out for—" A sharp pain sucked the air from his lungs and Jack cursed. "All right, we won't discuss politics."

"I'm just worried about you," Aidan murmured, glancing up at him. "I'm afraid the next time I see you, you'll be lying dead on a stretcher, a bullet through your skull."

"Then you'll have to bring me back to life. You're a good doctor and you owe me for all those times I saved your arse from Jimmy Boyle." Jack looked around the room. "When are you going to make enough money to find yourself a proper place to live? I live better and I don't have two shillings to rub together."

"I like where I live," Aidan said. "No one bothers me, no one cares when I come and go. It has...privacy."

"It's no place to bring a lady," Jack said.

Aidan smiled uneasily. "I have no time for ladies," he replied, "nor the interest."

"So am I going to live? You can tell me the truth, Aidan. I've always been able to count on you for the truth."

Aidan shook his head, laughing softly. "There's never been real truth between us," he murmured, his expression unreadable.

The comment took Jack by surprise. "How can you say that? You've always been able to tell me anything."

Aidan drew a sharp breath. "Have I?" His words

were more accusation than question. He stared at the rag, now soaked with Jack's blood. "There are some words that just can't be said aloud."

"What is it?" Jack reached out and touched Aidan's arm, concerned by the stricken look on his friend's face. "You can trust me," he murmured. "Whatever it is, it can't be that bad."

Aidan stood, then crossed the room and busied himself with rinsing the rag in the washbowl. "All right." He took a deep breath, his shoulders rising and falling, then turned to face Jack. "I've wanted to say this for so long and now that I have the chance, I can't seem to get the words out." He sighed softly, then met Jack's gaze. "What if I told you I loved you? That I always have and I'm afraid I always will. I love you, Jack."

Jack moaned softly. "Aw, mother of God. I'm dyin' then? You can say it plainly. I don't want it to come as a surprise."

"No. The bullet went clear through and the bleeding's stopped. I—I was just telling you how I feel. You wanted the truth."

Jack stared at him, confused by Aidan's odd proclamation. "Well…I love you, too. You're like a brother to me, Aidan. You always have been."

Aidan shook his head, then slowly crossed to stand in front of Jack. He'd always been much smaller than Jack, but now he seemed so frail, so vulnerable. With a trembling hand, Aidan reached out and touched

Jack's face, smoothing his palm over Jack's beard-roughened cheek. "You don't understand. I'm in love with you. Not as a brother, and not as a friend. As a…a man."

Jack brushed his hand away, chuckling softly. "Stop joking."

"I've wanted to tell you for a long time, but I was afraid. I've always felt different, but I thought I was alone. Then, after I got to university, I realized I wasn't."

Through the haze of exhaustion and pain, Jack began to hear what Aidan was saying, but he couldn't seem to understand. He shook his head. "Stop," he muttered. "I'm in no mood for a laugh."

"You have to hear it because it's the truth. And I want to trust you with the truth. I thought if I just got away from you, away from Ballykirk, these feelings would go away. But now I know, they're never going away. I think about you all the time, and I wonder how I can bear to—"

"What's this?" Jack jumped to his feet, shoving Aidan aside and putting as much distance between the two of them as he could. He'd always known Aidan was different, but he'd never once considered that Aidan was—Christ, what was he telling him? "Jaysus, Aidan, enough with the joke."

"It's not a joke," Aidan murmured.

"Have you gone mad? You're telling me you're some kind of pervert and I'm to believe you."

"That's just what society calls me," Aidan said, his tone desperate. He reached out to Jack. "There's nothing wrong with it. If you felt it, you'd know it wasn't wrong. How can it be if it's love?"

Stunned, Jack stared at his friend, unable to speak. Aidan wasn't joking, he was dead serious. What the hell was he supposed to say to that? Jack had never once suspected that Aidan's feelings went further than friendship.

With a low curse, Jack crossed to Aidan and grabbed his lapels, giving him a hard shake. "Take it back. Say that it's not true." Jack let go and Aidan stumbled back to the bed, rubbing his chest. "The church says it's wrong. I say it's wrong. The government can toss you in jail for it."

"Jack, please, I want to explain."

"I don't want to hear it. It's disgusting, it's unnatural and it makes me sick to think that you'd be involved in it."

"I'm still your friend," Aidan said. "But I can't change how I feel."

Jack held out his hand in warning, his fingers clenching into a fist. "Stay away from me. Don't ever come near me again or I'll beat you to a bloody mess."

Aidan slowly rose to his feet. "You have to understand."

He reached out for Jack, but Jack raised his fists. Part of him wanted to beat Aidan, to destroy whatever it was inside him that made him have these feelings.

"We are not friends," Jack sneered. "You're as good as dead to me now."

"Please," Aidan begged. He stepped closer, ignoring the threat. But that only provoked Jack's anger. He drew back his arm and punched Aidan in the face. Aidan slammed back against the wall, then crumpled to his knees, his nose bleeding.

A sob tore from his throat. "Do you think I like what I am?" he asked, blood dripping down his chin. "I hate that I feel this way. Every day I wake up and think, today I'll be different. Today I'll meet a woman and I'll fall in love and my life will make sense. But I'm tired of waiting to become something I'm not."

Jack stared in disgust at Aidan, his cowering figure making a pathetic sight. How many times had he stood up for Aidan when the bullies had called him names? How many fistfights had he endured to protect Aidan's disgusting secret? "You make me sick. I can't look at you and not see what a lie our friendship has been."

Aidan scrambled to his feet, grabbing at Jack's hands, his expression desperate. "I'm sorry, I'm sorry," he begged. "I didn't mean anything I just said. I'm trying to change, I am. You can't tell, Jack. Swear to me, you won't tell."

After grabbing the oilcloth packet and his pistol, Jack yanked open the door. Then he reached out and grasped Aidan's shirt, drawing him forcibly forward. He pressed the pistol beneath Aidan's jaw. "You breathe a word to anyone I was here, *I* swear, I will kill you."

"I—I won't. I promise. Just let me help you. You can stay here as long as you like. I'll leave. We won't ever talk about this again. I'm going to go back to hospital. You can stay until morning. You need some rest, Jack."

Aidan scurried around the room, gathering his medical supplies and refusing to meet Jack's gaze. Jack turned away from him and walked to the window. Though he wanted away from Aidan as fast as he could run, Jack had to consider the offer. He knew he was in no shape to be back out on the street. He hadn't slept in two days and he hadn't eaten since early that morning. At least he'd be safe here. "This doesn't mean I take back what I said. Either you're my friend or you're a—a—Christ, I don't know what to call you."

"The medical term is homosexual," Aidan murmured, "but if you're looking to insult me you might call me queer or fairy."

God, just the thought of it made Jack ill. "Well, you can't be both, a fairy and my friend."

"I—I know that now," Aidan said. "You'll be safe, I promise."

Jack heard the door close behind him and he let out a tightly held breath. He'd been a damn fool not to have seen it before. Aidan had always worshiped him as a kid, hanging on his every word, playing the needy victim. He'd always made excuses to spend more time with Jack. Jack had assumed Aidan's family life had been unbearable, but now he knew differently. It seemed as if their whole friendship was based on nothing more than Aidan's dirty little secret.

Jack let his shirt drop to the floor, then set his pistol back on the washstand. The sun would be up in five hours. He'd leave as soon as the city began to stir. If he was lucky he'd be able to take care of business by his deadline and get out of Dublin without a hitch. If he kept fixed on the task at hand, he wouldn't have to think about Aidan's revelation.

AIDAN SLIPPED out the front door of the boardinghouse and looked up and down the empty street. A stray dog scampered into the alley, his head hung low. Aidan's heart slammed in his chest and he fought back tears of humiliation. He'd never expected Jack to turn on him. They'd been friends for as long as Aidan could remember and Jack's loyalty had been the only thing in his life he could depend upon.

The words Jack had hurled at him still rang in his head, the humiliation more than he could bear. He'd heard insults before—words like pervert, queer boy, fairy. Sometimes they'd been insults from strangers, but other times, they'd been terms of affection between the men he'd met in Dublin. Hearing such hatred coming from Jack's lips had been a knife through his heart.

In the years since he'd arrived in Dublin, he'd lived a double life, as a dedicated medical student and as a hidden homosexual. At first, he'd been frightened that someone would find out, but then he'd slipped into a complacency that had lulled him into believing he could keep the two worlds completely separate.

Aidan wiped the blood from his upper lip with his handkerchief and started down the street, his black leather grip clutched in his hand. He should never have confessed his feelings to Jack. How had he ever expected him to understand? Jack was a proper Catholic who'd spent most of his life in a provincial village, obeying the dictates of his parish priest. And though he'd thrown himself into dangerous work for the Republican cause, he was still naive about the ways of the world.

He turned back to look at the boardinghouse, his desperation growing. Maybe he ought to return and try to explain himself again. If only he could turn back the clock, fix his mistake and make his life safe again. He'd lived with the risk of discovery for so long that he'd begun to consider himself brave. But he'd never been tested, never been so close to danger as he was now.

All Jack needed was a few too many pints at the pub and the secret would be out. What if his parents heard? Aidan lived off his father's generosity; Eamon McClain's money made his double life possible. Would the money stop once they learned what kind of man Aidan really was?

A sick feeling settled into his stomach. He knew how impossible life could become. There were any number of young men of his acquaintance who'd had to turn to prostitution to support themselves once cut off from their families. He'd be expelled from medical college. And even if it didn't go that far, he could never build a medical practice as a known homosexual.

Aidan hurried toward the hospital, knowing he could find a safe place there, a place to think. Yet, even after all that had passed, he couldn't deny his natural inclinations. There was only one thing that could take his mind off his fear and only one place to find it.

The house belonged to one of his literature professors at Trinity and had become a gathering place for pretty young men and the elderly gentlemen who desired them. It was a place filled with art and music, intelligent conversation and thinly veiled seduction. He'd met his first lover there, and the second and third, as well.

He picked up his pace, keeping his head down as he walked, his anger growing with each step he took. "To hell with Jack Quinn," he muttered. If he'd been a true friend, then he'd have understood. But instead of understanding, he'd turned on him, like all those schoolyard bullies. He cursed the man he'd once considered a friend.

As he rounded the corner, Aidan was still lost in his thoughts. Two soldiers stood in front of him, blocking his way. They both held rifles, their fingers resting tensely on the triggers. "Where do you think you're going, boyo?"

One of the soldiers grabbed the grip out of Aidan's hand while the other pressed the muzzle of his gun into Aidan's chest.

"I'm a doctor," he said. "I'm on my way to hospital."

"At this hour?"

"I just went home to get some sleep and now I'm due back."

"How do we know you're tellin' the truth? We can't just let you pass."

"Check inside the grip. It's full of medical supplies. I work with Dr. Edwin Sullivan at the Charitable Infirmary on Jervis Street."

"How do we know you're not IRA?"

Aidan sighed. "I've pulled bullets out of legs and arms and bellies of soldiers just like you and I've sopped up their blood until my fingers have turned red."

The soldiers looked at each other, then shrugged, tossing the grip back to him. "Have you seen anyone about? We're lookin' for troublemakers."

"No, not a soul." Aidan began to walk away, then paused. "That's a lie," he murmured, slowly turning to face the soldiers. "There was a man who came to me for treatment. I'll tell you what I know, but I don't want to be a part of this. I was just doing my job as a physician—I didn't ask questions."

"Tell us more," the taller soldier ordered.

"I suspected he was Republican. He'd been shot and I bandaged his wounds. He had a gun and he threatened me. He—he hit me. I left him in my room at the boardinghouse. I'd assume he's still there."

"Where?"

"Number seven," Aidan said, pointing down the street. "Second floor, the door to the right at the top of the stairs."

"You say he's armed?"

"With a pistol," Aidan said. "But if you wait for a time, he will probably be asleep. This is all I can tell you. I don't want to be involved."

"How do we know this isn't a trap?" the soldier asked. "How do we know the room isn't full of feckin' IRA, all of them with guns trained on the door?"

"If that's the case, you'll know where to find me. I've done my patriotic duty, now. I have patients to tend to."

He started back down the street, praying that they'd accept his explanation. When he reached the next street, he stepped into a doorway and sank back in the shadows. Aidan swallowed hard, the impact of what he'd done hitting him full on. He'd just betrayed his only friend. But Jack couldn't be his friend anymore. He knew the truth and that made him dangerous.

Aidan's stomach roiled and he bent double and retched, his last meal spattering onto the toes of his shoes. As he straightened, Aidan wiped his mouth with the back of his hand. "Oh, Christ, what have I done?"

If he could get back to his room and warn Jack, he might have a chance at escape. There was a back door into the boardinghouse and a servant's stairway to the first story. He checked both ways, then hurried down the street, taking a route that would put him one street to the north.

He ran as fast as he could, but as he approached the boardinghouse, he heard a commotion out front. Keeping to the shadows, he circled around and came out on the far end of the street. In the faint light spilling from the front door of the boardinghouse, he could see a group of soldiers gathered, their rifles trained on a man lying facedown in the street. One soldier's gun pressed against the back of the man's head.

When they pulled the prisoner to his feet, Aidan could see it was Jack. They'd already beaten him badly and his face was cut and swollen. Aidan slowly backed away, then turned and ran, his feet echoing on the empty cobblestone street. He ran until his lungs burned and his head pounded, Jack's threat replaying over and over in his mind. *I will kill you. I will kill you. I will kill you.*

Maybe Jack should have shot Aidan when he had the chance, put a bullet in his brain and put him out of his misery. If Jack survived his ordeal and got out of prison one day, Aidan had no doubt Jack would seek retribution. Aidan's life would be over, his secret revealed, his revenge turned back upon him. But Aidan hardened his heart and cast aside his guilt.

He'd done the only thing he could. He'd protected himself from a man who might destroy him. It was the only choice to be made.

CHAPTER TWO

County Cork, Summer 1915

TWO BOYS STOOD on the edge of a cliff, staring out at the water, their faces damp with the mist that rolled off the Celtic Sea onto the shores of Southern Ireland. One was tall and lanky and the other smaller, more frail. Though Aidan McClain had prayed to the Blessed Virgin for longer legs and stronger muscles, the five Our Fathers and five Hail Marys he said each night hadn't had the expected results.

Luckily, he'd made a friend of Jack Quinn. Jack was tall and broad shouldered, a scrappy boy built for solving his problems with his fists. Aidan's mother called the Quinns "common" and he understood what she meant, but that didn't alter his admiration for Jack. It was understood around Ballykirk that anyone who bothered Aidan would have Jack to deal with. It was the mark of a true friend, Aidan mused.

"Why the hell are we here?" Jack asked.

"Right over there," Aidan said, pointing to a spot on the horizon. "Ten miles off Kinsale. There she went down. The cursed Germans, they sank her."

"The *Lusitania.*" Jack stared at the spot, his brow deeply furrowed. "They say a body came ashore the other day. My da saw it, but they took it away in a cart to the cemetery in Cobh." He peered over the edge of the cliff. "We could crawl down and look for more corpses. I never saw a dead body before."

"Your grandda died just last year."

"That's different. He was laid out on the kitchen table in his Sunday suit. He wasn't torpedoed by a German U-boat and caused to suffer a tragic death. He keeled over in the midst of his morning porridge."

"She was a grand ship," Aidan said. "I read in my da's newspaper that she weighed thirty-two thousand tons—the largest transatlantic passenger ship ever. She was on her way to Liverpool from New York City. Twelve hundred people sank with her, save those that have washed up on the shore."

"There could be a German U-boat out there right now," Jack said. "They could be looking at us through their periscope and taking aim."

Aidan laughed. "Sure and they'd waste a torpedo on a pair of gobshites like us."

Jack wrapped his arm around Aidan's neck and pulled his best friend into a headlock, wrestling him down onto the wet grass. "Who are you calling a gobshite, ya little mucksavage?"

Aidan flailed his arms, but he was badly outweighed. "Leave me be. Get off!"

"Give over."

"I will not," Aidan said, trying to wriggle out of his grasp.

"Give," Jack demanded.

Aidan went limp. "Fine. I give then. Now get off."

They tumbled apart and Jack flopped back on the damp grass, looking up at the feathery clouds in the sky. Aidan stared at his friend's face, raven-black lashes and brows against his pale skin, a wide mouth and strong chin. If God had made Aidan McClain small, why couldn't he at least have made him handsome like Jack? His hair was too pale and his ears stuck out too far.

"My da says this war is good for Ireland," Jack said. "It keeps the feckin' Brits busy with their own troubles. And the more that get killed, the less there are to come here and crack our skulls."

"Why do you hate them so much?" Aidan asked.

"And why don't you? You're Irish, too."

"But I'm not, really," Aidan said softly.

Aidan knew about the rumors. That's all they were around Ballykirk, idle gossip. But he also knew the truth of them. The man married to his mother was not his true father. Eamon McClain, the village physician, had been an old man when he'd taken a bride, the daughter of a well-to-do Englishman. She'd been sent away to Ireland, to work as a servant during her confinement. Turned out by her own family and with a child already growing in her belly, she'd been grateful enough to accept an old man's proposal of marriage. Even grateful enough to allow her only son to be raised a Catholic.

"It's all talk, that," Jack said, rolling over on his side to face Aidan.

"It's not. I know the truth. I'm not Irish. I'm English."

"You're Irish in your heart—" he poked him gently in the chest "—and in your soul and that's all that counts."

Aidan shrugged, then sat up, resting his chin on his knees. "I'm going to go fight, you know," he murmured.

"And why would you fight in their war?"

"It's not their war," Aidan explained. "It's the world's. If Britain falls, then Ireland won't be far behind. As soon as I can, I'm going to join up. I'd make a good soldier, I would."

Aidan glanced back at Jack, hoping for some sign of encouragement. In truth, he was afraid. Afraid he wouldn't be strong, or he'd die in the muck of some faraway land. But becoming a soldier was a way to prove to everyone that he was a man, a way to gain Jack's respect. After he went to war, Jack would consider him an equal. But even now, as he looked into his friend's eyes, he could tell Jack doubted him more than Aidan doubted himself. "You could enlist, too.

We're nearly fifteen. We could join up in a year or two if we lied about our age."

"My da says sending Irish boys to the front to fight for the Brits is wrong. England should live under the heel of Germany and see how it feels." Jack threw his arm over his eyes. "There's going to be war enough to fight here in Ireland. And I'd rather fight for my own freedom than for the freedom of a bunch of pox-ridden princes living in a palace in London."

Aidan stared at the toe of his boot. "You talk like there's going to be a revolution."

"Going to be? It's happening now. Maybe not in Ballykirk, but in Belfast and Dublin. They promised us Home Rule and then they took it away. If we want our freedom, we're going to have to drive King George's damn army out of our country. I want to be a part of that."

"So we'll both be soldiers," Aidan said.

"And what if it's over before you get a chance to fight?" Jack asked. "What then? Will ya fight for Ireland?"

"I suppose I'll go to university."

Jack scoffed. "What do you need university for? There's no university in Ballykirk. Or Kinsale."

"But there is in Cork and in Dublin, too. I'll go there."

"I've never been to a real city," Jack murmured. "I can't imagine what it's like. Crowded, I'd grant."

"You can come with me and see," Aidan said. "If

you studied, you could get in. You're a smart lad, Jack. You can be anything you want."

"My mam wants me to be a priest. Da has Declan to work the boat with him and I'm meant for the church. That's why they've let me stay in school so long. Da thinks if there's a priest in the family he can get himself gee-eyed every night at the pub, slap my mam around and still go to heaven."

"The church would be good for you," Aidan commented. "You wouldn't have to work the boat. And you'd be an important man. Everyone would listen to you. You're too clever to be a fisherman, Jack. You'd make a good priest."

He chuckled. "That's bollocks. I can't be a priest. What would I do with my wife?"

"Last time I looked, you weren't married," Aidan said.

"Ah, but I plan to. I'm going to go off to Cork and get a real job in a factory there, maybe be the boss man. I'm going to make fistfuls of money and I'm going to ask Molly O'Shea to marry me. And we're going to have our own cottage and we're going to do it every day of the week and twice on Saturday."

Aidan looked away, jealousy washing over him like a wave on the shore. He'd heard the boys in the village talk about what went on between a man and a woman, their descriptions crude and disturbing. He knew he ought to be interested in that sort of thing. But girls disgusted him. They saw him as nothing more than an easy future in the big manor house on the Skibbereen road, for Aidan McClain was the only heir to old Eamon's fortune and was considered a good catch.

Just the thought of crawling into bed with a woman made his stomach pitch and roll, like the boats on the bay below them. Aidan had come to the conclusion that he wasn't meant to marry, that maybe this was God's way of calling him to the priesthood. Perhaps he ought to take vows, then Jack would have more than just the Father, Son and Holy Ghost to keep him company.

"You like Molly O'Shea?"

"She's grand," Jack said. "I kissed her, I did. Behind the graveyard wall. I was just twelve and she ten, but I don't think she's forgotten it."

Aidan shifted uneasily. "I—I have to get back. My da is trying to teach me Latin and he gets angry if I don't study my verbs."

Jack levered to his feet, then pulled Aidan up after him. "I'll race ya back to the village," he said.

"It's nearly a mile!"

"If you're to be a soldier, Private Aidan McClain, you're going to have to march farther than a mile in a day. And if I haven't finished mending the nets by the time my da's boat comes in, he'll blister my arse."

With a wild whoop, Jack took off down the hill, stumbling over the rocks embedded in the ground. Aidan stared after him, wondering at his friend's confidence. How must it feel to know exactly who you were and what you believed in?

JACK DIDN'T HEAD directly to the docks after leaving Aidan. Instead, he wandered past the inn that Molly O'Shea's parents ran, hoping he might find her in the vegetable patch, tugging weeds or turning the soil. He found her just down the road, on her way to the market to shop for the evening meal. Grateful to snatch some time alone to court the prettiest girl in Ballykirk, Jack walked with her into the village.

There were plenty of local lads who fancied themselves good enough for Molly O'Shea. But she'd chosen to turn her attention toward Jack Quinn. She told him of a new book about roses her cousin had sent from Galway and a pretty piece of stone she'd found in the stream the day before last and a kitten that a local farmer had given her. And as they strolled, Jack felt as if they were in a world of their own.

"We went lookin' for dead bodies today," he whispered, eager to impress Molly with his bravery. "They're washing up all the time from that ship that sank."

"Did you see one?" Molly asked, her eyes wide.

Jack shook his head. "No, but I think I might have seen a U-boat just off the shore."

"My father says the war will be bad for business. With the English so worried about the Germans, they'll have no time to think about holidays in Ireland.

No one wants to get on a boat and come here. He says if the English are at war, it will hurt Ireland as well."

Political opinions varied widely around Ballykirk. The three pubs in town each catered to a specific group of patrons. Those who staunchly supported the Republican cause, like Jack's da, gathered at the Speckled Hound. And those who had their concerns about a complete break with Britain, drank their ale at Smiley's. Those who had no political inclinations at all and hated the inevitable fistfights that came with political talk frequented the Cart and Whistle.

"Do you think the Germans will invade Ireland?" Molly whispered, a worried look on her face.

"If they do, I'll join in the fight," Jack said. "But my da doesn't think it will come to that."

She sighed softly and stared off at a milk cow grazing in the meadow beside the road. "Good. I don't like war. It makes everyone so cross. What do you think I should name my kitten?"

Though Jack knew he ought to head down to the dock to await the return of the *Mighty Quinn,* he was willing to take the beating for a few more moments with Molly. As they approached the greengrocer, Jack noticed a small crowd of boys gathered near the rear of the tailor's shop.

"What's going on?" Molly asked.

Jack frowned. "I don't know." As they got closer, he noticed Jimmy Boyle in the midst of the boys and a knot of concern tightened in his belly. Aidan had said he was on his way home, but had he gone to see his father at the surgery?

"Stay here," Jack murmured. "I'll just see what they're about." He slowly approached and a few of the smaller boys noticed. Deciding that they weren't up to a beating that day, they grabbed their friends and ran off. Only then could Jack see the small figure curled into a ball on the ground. He recognized Aidan's shiny new shoes and his pale hair.

"Come on, get up," Jimmy shouted, kicking at Aidan. The boy was huge. He had at least thirty pounds on Aidan and a good ten on Jack. "Look at the pretty little lass, cryin' like a baby. Get up, baby. It's time to change your nappie."

With a low growl, Jack clenched his fists and launched himself at Jimmy. Hitting him full on from behind, Jack knocked the bully face first into the outside wall of the tailor's shop, then shoved him backward onto the cobbles. Jimmy barely had time to cry out before Jack began to pummel his shoulders and his head, Jack's hands coming back bloody.

The other boys shouted and tried to pull him off, and he heard Molly screaming in the distance, but Jack's fury overwhelmed him. Why were they always at Aidan McClain? Was it because his father had money and power in Ballykirk? Or was it because Aidan was weak and vulnerable? Jack didn't really care. He meant to make them pay for the pain they'd caused his friend.

He wasn't certain how long the fight went on.

When he finished, he went after some of the other boys, but they ran off before he could bring them down. In the end, Jimmy Boyle was left a sobbing mess, his nose and lip bloodied, a knot on his forehead turning purple. Jack gave him a good kick, then wiped his own bloody nose on the sleeve of his shirt.

"You touch him again," he warned, "I'll take your head off."

Jimmy stumbled to his feet and skulked off, cowering like an old dog. Jack turned to Aidan, the boy sitting on the ground, his knees pulled tightly against his chest, his face hidden. His clothes were dirty and his pale hair stood up in unruly tufts. "Come on," Jack said. "Let's see what they've done to you."

"Leave me," Aidan pleaded. "Just go."

Jack bent down and tried to look into Aidan's eyes. "They won't be back. Come on, I'll walk you home. We'll sneak in the kitchen and you can clean up before your mother sees."

He touched Aidan's arm, trying to pull him to his feet, but his friend lashed out, catching Jack with a wide punch to his jaw. Jack fell back, landing hard on the cobbles. "What the feck are ya doin'?"

Aidan scrambled out of Jack's reach, then hurried off down the road, his shirt torn at the sleeve and his trousers muddied. He looked back once and Jack could see the humiliation in his expression.

"Should we go after him?" Molly asked, standing at his side.

Jack shook his head as he watched Aidan's retreat. "He's embarrassed. He'll be fine—just give him his time."

Jack waited while Molly did her marketing, trying to stop the flow of blood from his nose with a pretty handkerchief that Molly had provided. They walked back out of town together, stopping so Molly could dab at his wounds with the corner of her apron. Jack's concern for Aidan ebbed as he gave himself over to Molly's careful attentions.

He spent the rest of the afternoon with Molly, helping her tend to the garden and carrying stacks of dried linens up the stairs to the guest rooms for her mother. The fight with Jimmy Boyle was forgotten. He'd never spent a more enjoyable afternoon and was certain when he left that Molly O'Shea was his girl.

Falling in love was so simple once a man found the right girl. Someday he and Molly would marry. Until then, he'd just have to find a way to convince his parents he wasn't meant for the priesthood.

CHAPTER THREE

JACK RAN DOWN the road, cursing the sun in the sky. He'd lost track of time and now he was in a fix. Since his fifteenth birthday, Jack had been expected to meet his father's fishing boat at the end of every day. He usually helped his older brother, Dec, unload the catch, then stayed behind to clean the boat and repair the nets.

When he spent his afternoons with Aidan, his friend was always careful to mind the time. But afternoons spent with Molly seemed to fly by so quickly. Too many times, Dec had been left to do Jack's tasks for him. At first, his older brother hadn't complained. But lately Dec had been in a wicked temper.

When Jack reached the dock, he found the boat clean and the catch gone. Dec would kick his arse if his father didn't beat him to it. Jack walked home slowly, trying to think of a proper excuse, knowing that he'd forgotten his responsibilities one time too many.

When he opened the front door to the cottage, Jack

found his father seated at the rough plank table, his siblings gathered around for supper. He looked over at his mother and she glanced at his da, then sent him a worried frown before turning back to her work at the hearth.

He knew the look in his father's eyes, the icy-cold glare that softened whenever Paddy Quinn had downed a few pints at the pub. Jack's father was a boisterous and bluff man when he was on the piss, but when he was off the drink, he was sullen and violent. Declan usually stepped in when his father's dark moods turned toward his mother, but Jack's older brother was rarely home anymore, preferring to spend his time with Gemma Maloney and her family. Two of Jack's three older sisters had escaped into marriages of their own, but nineteen-year-old Grace was still at home, along with Jack's younger siblings, Thomas, Niall and Sarah.

"Where were ye?"

"I—I was talking with Father Timothy," Jack lied. He had seen the priest on his way to Molly's and they'd shared a quick conversation. Jack would take care of the lie in confession at the end of the week. "I ran down to the boat, but the work was finished."

"Ye forgot the time again." His father shoved back from the table, his stool tumbling to the floor. Jack stepped back, knowing what was coming. He'd learned to take the beatings without protest. If he cried out at all, it only seemed to spur his father on, so he bore the pain in stubborn silence, knowing it wouldn't last long.

Mary Quinn reached out and grabbed her husband's arm, but he pushed her aside and started after Jack. Jack tipped his chin up and braced himself.

"Don't!" Mary cried. "It's not his fault that Dec has gone. You drove one son away, you'll not drive another from this house."

His father raised his hand, his arm trembling with pent-up anger.

"Please," Mary murmured. "Go down to the pub and have yourself a pint. I'll hold supper for you."

Paddy balled his fingers into a fist and, for a moment, Jack was certain that he'd get punched instead of slapped. "You're finished with school," he muttered, his jaw tight. "Tomorrow morning, you'll go out with me on the *Mighty Quinn.*" Paddy turned for the door and walked out without another word. When the door slammed shut, Jack's brothers and sisters breathed a communal sigh of relief.

Jack glanced at his mother. "Declan's gone then?"

Mary's eyes filled with tears and she nodded. "He and your da had a terrible row on the boat and when they docked, he said he was done with fishing. He's left for Cork to find work. He plans to marry Gemma. He won't be back."

Jack groaned. "I don't want to fish. I'll go to Cork with Declan."

"And I don't want to be a priest," Thomas whined.

As the next youngest son, Jack's future plans had now become his.

"You'll mind your da, the both of you, and there'll be no more talk of Cork. This family can't do without the money made from that boat and it takes two pairs of hands to run it."

"Half that money gets drunk up at the feckin' pub," Jack said. "I won't do it. I won't break my back so he can get pissed every night."

Mary reached out and slapped Jack across the face, his cheek stinging so badly it made his eyes water. "You will do it," she warned, her tone uncompromising, her gaze unyielding. "You'll do it for me and for Grace and Thomas and Niall and Sarah."

"I won't," Jack said stubbornly, his temper boiling over. "It's my life and I'll do as I please."

With that, he followed his father out the door. But he didn't head into town to the pub. Instead, he turned to the hills above the village. If he kept walking, he could probably walk all the way to Cork.

But Jack knew his life was here. He'd work the boat with his da, he'd marry Molly O'Shea, and he'd live out his days in Ballykirk. That was his lot in life and he'd have to learn to be happy with it.

"HABEO, HABES, HABET. Habemus, habetis, habent."

"Fine. Now the past indicative, active voice."

Aidan shifted on his chair and stared down at his boiled turnips as if they might help him with the answer. He'd been studying Latin for a year and still wasn't any good at it. *"Habebam, habebas, habebat, habebamus, habebatis, habebunt."*

"*Habebant. Habebunt* is the future." Eamon McClain shook his head. "We've begun far too late. You'll never know enough. We must double our efforts."

"Why must I learn Latin?"

"The study of medicine requires a working knowledge of Latin. You are lucky that I've decided to help you. I certainly have better things to do with my time."

"Yes, sir," Aidan muttered. "Thank you, sir."

Aidan might have been happy for the attention had his father chosen to teach him how to fish or ride or box. But Eamon had no interest in leisurely pursuits. He spent his days treating patients at his surgery and his evenings locked in his study with his books.

"Enough Latin for today. It's not proper conversation for Sunday supper." Louisa Winters McClain plucked her linen napkin from the table and spread it across the skirt of her elegant gown. Aidan was constantly amazed by his mother's stunning beauty. Louisa was just a year past thirty, her figure still slender, her features flawless. "Let's discuss literature. Aidan, have you read that book of Yeats poetry I bought for you?"

"Poetry? Bah," Eamon said. "A doctor has no use for poetry."

"But a gentleman does," Louisa. "And my son will become a gentleman."

Aidan winced inwardly. *My* son. Not *our* son. Though they'd never come out and told him the truth, Aidan had known for years. How could he not suspect? A beautiful young woman like Louisa Winters would never have married an old goat like Eamon McClain unless she'd been forced to.

He'd only seen his maternal grandparents once, on a trip to London. His father had attended a medical conference while he and his mother shopped and visited museums. They'd wandered into a pretty neighborhood near Kensington Square and Louisa had pointed to a beautiful town house. "That is where your grandparents live," she had said.

Aidan had begged her to climb the steps and ring the bell, but Louisa had refused and hurried him down the walk, insisting that they had other errands to complete before they returned to the hotel. The next day, they'd gone back at midmorning and stood across the street. After an hour, a well-dressed couple had emerged from the home. Louisa had squeezed his hand so tightly his fingers went numb and Aidan knew who they were. When he'd glanced up at her, he'd seen a tear roll down her cheek, and for the rest of the day he'd tried to put on a cheerful face.

Aidan poked at his meal as he distractedly listened to his stepfather's recitation of the day's cases. He remembered another thing about that trip to London. It had been the first time he'd realized the torture his mother had to endure to pay for her sins.

He'd slept on a small settee in the parlor of their hotel suite, but the excitement of the city had kept him awake late into the night. He'd heard them through the door to the bedchamber, the squeak of the bed, his mother's whispered protests, and the disgusting grunts of an old man slaking his lust on his pretty young wife.

The bile had risen in his throat and he'd fought the urge to vomit. Had he been a better son, Aidan might have burst through the door and protected his mother. But he'd been frightened of Eamon McClain, certain that the old man would throw the both of them out on the street.

It was a fear he'd carried around inside of him every day since then. If he failed in his studies, if he didn't keep a tidy appearance, if he spilled his water goblet at dinner—anything might bring an end to their comfortable life in the big house on the Skibbereen road.

"And how did you spend your afternoon, darling?"

Aidan slowly chewed his roast beef and pushed it past the lump in his throat. "Jack Quinn and I hiked up to Oisin's Rock."

Louisa shook her head. "I wish you wouldn't associate with that Quinn boy. There must be other young men who would make more appropriate friends."

"I like Jack," Aidan said. "He's nice to me. And now that he's working on his father's boat, we barely have an afternoon to ourselves."

"But he's..." Louisa searched for the word.

"Common?" Eamon suggested.

"I was going to say, uncultured. His family has no social standing in Ballykirk. His father is a drunkard and his mother is uneducated. I don't think she can even read. And those children run wild. Their clothes are unkempt and their hair uncombed. And I've heard Jack Quinn use foul language. A friend like that can do you no good."

Aidan bit his tongue. In truth, he was lucky to have Jack as a protector. He used to wait for Aidan at the front gate weekday mornings, even though it meant an extra mile on his walk to school, then returned home with him in the afternoon. But now, just the threat of Jack's furor was enough to keep Jimmy Boyle at a distance.

"Jack is going to be a priest," Aidan offered. "It will be good to have a priest as a friend, won't it?"

His mother snatched her napkin from her lap and dabbed at her lips. "And you think the Catholics have a golden road to heaven? It's that wretched Father Timothy who puts these ideas in your head."

"No, I—"

"We'll not bring up this discussion again," Eamon warned. "You know my feelings on this matter."

"And my feelings don't count?" Louisa asked. "My son is being brought up a Papist and I'm to sit by and watch while he's brainwashed by these silly country folk." She reached for the little bell she kept by her place at the end of the table. A few seconds later, the servant appeared with a tray. "Mr. McClain and my son will have dessert. I'll be retiring to my room with a headache."

Aidan didn't miss the possessive "my" in her reference. He watched as she flounced out of the room, her silk skirts rustling as she moved, then turned back to his cold turnips.

Eamon cleared his throat, then nodded at Maureen to clear. When she'd left the room, he fixed his gaze on Aidan. "Your mother doesn't understand life in Ballykirk. It does a person no good to be putting on airs. You're nothing more than an ordinary boy and don't ever believe that you aren't."

Aidan nodded meekly. "I don't think I'd care for dessert tonight. I want to study my Latin before bed."

"Suit yourself," Eamon said.

Aidan slipped from the table and hurried up the stairs. He passed the door to his mother's room, then paused and knocked softly. She called out his name, knowing it was him. When Aidan entered, he found her at her dressing table, the surface cluttered with perfumes and oils, paints and powders. She wore a silk dressing gown that cinched around her tiny waist.

"There's a good boy," she said. "Come here and talk to me."

When he stood at his mother's side, she slowly began to pull the pins from her hair, placing them in the palm of his hand. "Someday we'll be free from him," she murmured. "He's old and getting older by the day. We're young and we can afford to be patient. And when he's gone, we can begin to live our life the way we want to."

"And what will we do?" Aidan asked.

Louisa laughed as she picked up her silver-backed brush and began to draw it through her pale hair. "We'll travel. Perhaps we'll live in Paris or Rome. We'll buy ourselves a fine carriage and dress in the most fashionable clothes. We'll leave this bog of a town behind and make our lives exciting."

It wasn't hard to imagine how his mother had found herself pregnant and banished to Ireland at age sixteen. She'd always lived in a world of fantasy where she wore only Parisian gowns, where necklaces of rubies and emeralds adorned her throat. She fancied herself living in an English manor or a French château with a full staff of servants to tend to her needs. And she treated Aidan like her little prince, the only male she could ever trust.

"What thoughts are rattling around in that head of yours?" she asked, her reflection smiling back at him.

"Are you ever going to tell me about my father?" he asked.

She pursed her lips and began to brush her hair. "Your father is Eamon McClain."

"I know he's not."

"Your father is Eamon McClain," she repeated. "And that is all you need to know."

"Did you ever love him?"

"Eamon is my husband. A wife is bound to respect her husband, to obey him, to make a good home for him. I believe I've held up my part of the arrangement."

"I meant my real father. Did you love him?"

She stopped brushing her hair and stared at herself in the mirror, a faraway look in her eyes. A sigh slipped from her lips and brought her back to reality. "I thought I did. And I thought he loved me as well. And from that love came you."

"Why didn't you marry him?"

"Because he was already promised to someone else," she said.

Aidan's stomach twisted into a knot and he blinked back a flood of emotion. He shouldn't have asked the question if he wasn't prepared to hear the answer. Had he expected some fairy tale? He'd been born out of a sordid affair between a young girl of modest wealth and a man interested only in the pleasure he might take from her body. His mother had sinned and he'd be marked by that sin for the rest of his life.

"I—I'm glad you told me," Aidan said. "Now we'll never have to speak of it again."

Louisa turned in her chair and reached out to smooth his hair away from his forehead. "You are the only man in my life. We need no one else, Aidan, save the two of us. Do you understand? No one."

Aidan nodded. "No one."

"Good. Now run along to bed." She turned her cheek to him and Aidan kissed her.

It was only when he reached his room that he allowed himself to cry. He ran to the huge wardrobe and crawled inside, shutting the door behind him. His sobs were muffled by the clothes that hung around his head and he wiped his tears away with the leg of his woolen Sunday trousers.

Would he ever find a place to belong? If he did, then he'd be sure to never leave it for the rest of his life.

CHAPTER FOUR

JACK HOISTED the last of the nets onto the dock, then crawled out of the boat after them. The moment the *Mighty Quinn* had docked, his father had headed down to the pub, leaving the heavy work to his second-in-command.

"No wonder Dec bolted," Jack muttered. "Slave work for slave wages." He'd already hauled the catch to the local fishmonger and scrubbed down the hold. He'd have at least an hour's worth of work on the nets and rigging. By the time he got home, his father would be drunk, his mother exhausted and his dinner cold.

He'd only been at it three months and already Jack could sense the drudgery that lay ahead. He'd spent his time on the boat tiptoeing through every conversation with his father, afraid to set him off. Now Jack heard footsteps on the dock and looked up to find Aidan approaching, his schoolbooks slung over his shoulder and dangling from a strap.

"Are you almost finished then?" he asked. "I've brought some of my mother's tea cakes."

Jack straightened, working a kink out of his back. "I don't have time for tea cakes," he muttered.

Aidan frowned. "But these are your favorites."

"Damn it, I don't have time for cakes or hikes or running about with my mates from school. This is my life, Aidan. I work the lines and haul the nets and listen to my father's blather for ten hours a day while you're on the doss." Though he knew Aidan wasn't a layabout, it still felt good to take out his frustration on someone. Their lives had turned in two different directions and their friendship was irreversibly changed.

"I wish you could come back to school," Aidan said.

"What good is school to do me now? I'm bound to be a fisherman for the rest of my life."

"But we can still be friends," Aidan said.

"And how will that work? I'll wedge you in between supper at nine and sleep at half past." Jack glanced up at his friend, taking in Aidan's stricken expression. He managed a smile. "I'm sorry. I'm bushed and pissed off and I put a hook right through my thumb this morning and it hurts like hell."

"Isn't there something to do about it?"

"I can't bring Dec back and Thomas and Niall are too young. Between the two of them, they couldn't pull a net in, much less work the lines. It'll be all right."

"No, it won't," Aidan said, desperation evident in his tone.

"Is Jimmy Boyle bothering you again?" Jack asked.

Aidan shook his head. "I can take care of myself."

"I'm sure you can," Jack said, trying to bolster his friend's confidence.

"I miss you," Aidan admitted. "I don't have many friends."

In truth, Aidan hadn't any friends, save Jack Quinn. Besides his own physical shortcomings, Aidan had also become a target because of his father's position in town. Eamon McClain wasn't just the town doctor. He'd come from a wealthy Cork family and could easily have lived off his inherited wealth and practiced medicine for free. Even so, the old skinflint still required payment in advance for treatment and refused to consider any charitable cases.

"Did you see Molly today? Did she ask after me?" Jack asked.

"She ate her lunch with Will Calley. And she got a perfect mark on her sums test. She wore that blue dress with the white flowers and she mentioned she was going to visit her aunt after school."

Jack grinned, then tossed the nets aside. He crawled out of the boat and patted Aidan on his shoulder. "I'll talk to you later. I'm going to see if I can catch up with her."

"But I thought we could—"

"Sorry," Jack called as he jogged along the dock.

He ran all the way out of town, then headed down

the narrow dirt road to Dickie O'Shea's farm. Dickie's wife, Emma, was in poor health after the birth of her last child and Molly often went over to the farm to help her aunt prepare the evening meal.

He found some wildflowers along an old stone fence and yanked them out of the ground, then waited a fair bit down the road from the farmhouse. When he saw Molly walking toward him, he pushed off the wall and stood in the middle of the road.

"Well, if it isn't Miss Molly O'Shea," he teased. "I never thought I'd find you out for an evening stroll."

Molly's auburn hair fell in pretty waves around her shoulders, long lashes ringed her green eyes and her lips were the shape of a perfect cupid's bow. Jack used to believe she was the prettiest girl in all of Ballykirk, but now he thought she was the most beautiful in all of County Cork.

"My mam would not approve of you meeting me out here," she said, accepting the flowers that he offered.

"Ah, but I think she would. I can protect you from all manner of beasts out here—wolves, trolls, dragons and the odd runaway sheep." He took her hand and tucked it into the crook of his arm. "I will be a perfect gentleman. You'll have nothing to tell Father Timothy at confession."

"And what will you confess, Jack Quinn?"

"I've been thinking of my future. I'm a man now and I have to make plans. I want to take a wife and raise a family."

Molly's eyes went wide. "You're going to get married? And who would have you?"

He took a small measure of delight that she seemed genuinely jealous. "I haven't settled on one girl yet. But I'll be sixteen in a few months. It's not too early to start looking."

"My mam was married by the time she was sixteen," Molly murmured. "I'm not fifteen. By the time I'm old enough to look for a husband, you'll already be married."

Jack shrugged. "Maybe." He sent her a sideways glance. "Or maybe I'll wait for you."

A smile broke across her pretty face. Jack had kissed Molly once before when they were children, but he knew, instinctively, that this was the right time to kiss her again. He'd thought about it many times and wondered if, when the opportunity presented itself, he'd be able to perform. He drew a deep breath, grabbed Molly's shoulders, closed his eyes and pressed his lips to hers.

It was over too quickly and Jack kept his eyes shut, afraid to see her reaction. When he finally did open them, he found Molly staring up at him, a tiny smile curling her lips. "Was it good then?" he asked.

"I don't know. I have nothing to judge it against."

Jack groaned softly and pulled her to him again, concentrating on making the experience go a bit more smoothly. This time, the kiss was much softer and he made it last longer. Already he was learning from his mistakes. He'd be an expert by the end of next week. "There, now you have," he said.

"I think the second was better than the first," Molly murmured. She slipped out of his embrace and hurried down the road, then turned back to face him, her expression bright, her face flushed. "I'll be looking forward to the third."

"And I'll be kissin' you again, Molly," he called.

"That's jam on your egg," she said with a light laugh.

Jack watched as she ran off down the road. It wasn't wishful thinking. He'd make it happen and it would feel even better for her than it had the first time or the second time.

Father Timothy had warned the boys of the parish about following their lustful urges. He'd quoted scripture about the sins of the flesh and Jack had half expected to be struck down by the wrath of God if he kissed a girl. But now that he had, he realized that Father Timothy had probably never enjoyed the experience himself and couldn't speak with any good authority.

Kissing Molly O'Shea felt like heaven and, as long as she approved, he'd continue to kiss her whenever he had the chance, right up until the day they were married and after, as well. And as far as confession went, he'd keep this particular pleasure to himself.

JACK KNEW there was something wrong. As they were coming up on the dock, two men were waiting there.

When the boat drew closer, Jack recognized two of his father's mates from the Speckled Hound. "I wonder what they're about," he murmured.

"We'll soon find out," Paddy said from where he stood on the bow of the boat.

He hopped off the *Mighty Quinn* the moment it bumped against the dock, leaving Jack to tie up. At first, their conversation began in hushed tones, but then it grew lively and boisterous. "They've done it," Paddy cried.

"Jackie, come down from there and have a drink with us at the Hound," Mick Sheehan urged. "We've something to celebrate this day in Ireland."

"What happened?"

"A blessed rising."

"Easter Sunday was two days ago," Jack muttered, certain they were already pissed.

"Not that kind of rising, you eejit. A rebellion. Irish forces against the Brits. Johnny Bell's sister works at the post office in Cork and she says rebels have taken the GPO in Dublin. On Monday, Patrick Pearse stood outside the GPO and read a proclamation. He announced that Ireland was a republic and we have our own provisional government."

"Now is our time," Brian Doolin said. "The Brits are busy with their war. They can't put up a fight."

"Ah, this is good news," Paddy crowed. "Have you told the other boys at the pub?"

"They're all there. The crowd at Smiley's isn't

smilin' now," Brian joked. "Come on, leave the fish and let's get ourselves a drink."

The trio started off down the dock, leaving Jack to deal with the boat. But at the last minute, Paddy turned. "Come on, Jack. There's a pint waitin' for you at the Hound."

Jack blinked in surprise. He'd never been invited to the Hound. Declan had often accompanied his father there after a day of fishing, but Jack had assumed his father didn't consider him man enough to hoist a few with his mates. "I—I should finish—"

"Come," Paddy insisted.

Jack dropped the net he held and jumped off the boat. He tagged along after his father, Brian and Mick, unable to contain his pride. Paddy Quinn considered him a man now. And though he'd tasted ale before, he'd have to make sure not to drink too much. He didn't want to get bollixed his first time out.

The Hound was alive with activity when they walked in. The smoke from the pipes hung in the air, swirling in the sunlight that streamed through the small windows. Paddy pulled him over to the bar and called for two pints. When the glasses were set in front of him, he handed one to Jack and took the other. "To freedom," he said.

Jack forced a smile. "Freedom," he repeated.

Some of the men had gathered at a table and were discussing the details of the Easter Rising. Paddy pushed back from the bar and joined the crowd.

Jack knew it was a momentous day, one that he'd remember his entire life. A free Ireland. He'd heard his father talk about it for so long, endlessly during their time alone on the boat. Paddy Quinn believed it was the only way his children could build a good life. "It's not for me," he'd say. "It's for you."

For the first time in his life, Jack understood the significance. If he married Molly, he wanted to know that his future was his and his alone, that it didn't belong to the British. Though the news was hopeful, Jack understood that the Brits would not give up easily. They'd held tight to Ireland for far too long to let it go without a fight. Even as he watched the celebration, he wondered if there might be more troubles ahead.

CHAPTER FIVE

AIDAN WINCED as he tugged at the starched collar of his shirt. He was wearing his Sunday best, a wool tweed jacket and trousers his mother had had tailored in Cork for his sixteenth birthday. She'd insisted that he wear it to the church fair, even though summer was hard upon them and everyone else would be dressed casually—and in cooler clothes.

He'd looked forward to the fair for months, knowing that he'd get a chance to spend the entire day with Jack Quinn. Once he found him, he could toss aside his jacket and collar and have some fun.

Since Jack had started working his father's boat last winter, they'd met whenever they could, Aidan dragging his schoolbooks along and catching Jack up on the work he was missing. He'd also lent Jack a translated copy of *The Odyssey* that his mother had given him and Aidan was anxious to discuss the story with his friend.

As he walked through the crowd, he was ever watchful. Aidan knew the bullies would never dare attack at a church fair, but still he never let down his guard. Jack moved in a different world now, the world of adults, and the boys at school had become bolder without Jack's constant presence as Aidan's protector.

He could have used a protector at home, as well. Eamon McClain was set on sending his son to Dublin in the fall, to a private school which would help prepare him for university and, later, medical college. Aidan had begged his mother to keep him at home, terrified of the prospect of being out in the world with no one to turn to. But to his dismay, Louisa had agreed that a private school was a much more appropriate place for a young man of Aidan's social standing. He would need to learn to move with young men from Dublin's finest families. And so, at the end of the summer, he was off to Dublin.

Aidan spied Jack standing near a table lined with picnic lunches that were about to be auctioned off. He waved at him, and Jack immediately motioned him over. His friend was dressed in a freshly laundered shirt and canvas trousers, the shirtsleeves rolled up to reveal deeply tanned arms.

To Aidan's eye, he didn't look like a boy anymore, but a man. He'd gained at least an inch or two in height and his body had become finely muscled from the hard labor of his daily life, his shoulders more broad and his face weathered by the sun.

Lately, Aidan had become a bit intimidated by Jack, both physically and emotionally. Next to Jack Quinn, Aidan still looked like a boy, skinny and weak. And he often felt as if his friendship was merely tolerated by an indulgent older brother, as if Jack would much rather spend his time with his mates at the local pub. But once he and Jack had a chance to talk again, he was always reassured that nothing much had changed between them.

"Aidan!"

"Hello, Jack. You're looking well," Aidan said, smiling broadly.

"I don't have to work that damn boat today," Jack said, "so I'm a happy man."

"Are you going to bid on a picnic lunch then?" Aidan asked, pointing to the long table filled with baskets and boxes.

"I am," Jack said. "That lunch, there, in the pretty red basket. Molly made that and I have a pocketful of money to buy it. Will you share it with us?"

Aidan felt a twinge of jealousy as he realized the invitation was made out of courtesy and wasn't truly meant to be accepted. He'd wanted all of Jack's attention today. In four weeks, he'd leave for Dublin and he might not see Jack again for months. Spending the day with Molly O'Shea and enduring her inane prattle wasn't part of the plan. "No. I'd just be a third wheel."

"Her mother won't let us be together without a chaperon," Jack whispered. "You can be our chaperon. You're looking quite trustworthy in that fine suit of clothes."

Aidan shook his head, unwilling to allow his disappointment to show. "Naw, it's fine, it is. Have your lunch and we'll meet later. Look, Father Timothy is about to start the bidding."

Jack turned his attention to the crowd gathered around the small stage. Aidan slowly backed away and searched out his mother in the crowd. She stood at the fringes of the crowd, alone, refusing to associate with any of the townsfolk. Yet, she still insisted on making an appearance at public events, sweeping in like the Duchess of Ballykirk and flaunting her good fortune in front of one and all. Though Aidan loved his mother, he saw the hypocrisy in her actions. Louisa McClain considered herself a moral arbiter in Ballykirk, even though she'd come to town banished from her family in England and carrying an illegitimate child.

As Aidan stood beside her, he wondered at the sight they made, dressed in their formal clothes. She wore an exquisite ivory shift of embroidered silk, and strings of pearls that dripped off her neck. Her feet were clad in soft kid shoes, a sharp contrast to the serviceable footwear that everyone else wore. She carried a parasol even though she wore a wide-brimmed hat. "There's my boy," she said, drawing him closer. "Come, let's bid on a lunch. I'm famished."

Father Timothy, dressed in his long black robes, stepped onto the stage and motioned to the crowd to quiet. "Settle yourself now. We have some lovely lunches here for you to bid on. For those young men who are counting the change in their pockets, wondering how much it will cost to win lunch with a pretty girl, you'll be expected to share your meal in plain sight. We'll have no improper behavior at this fair." Some of the single men in the crowd groaned in protest. "We'll begin, then. This is for a new set of tires for my motorcar. I haven't been able to share supper with many of you because of the punctures, so be generous."

Father Timothy walked over to the table and selected the red basket, holding it over his head. "Miss Molly O'Shea has prepared this lunch. Come up here, Molly, and hold this basket for me. It must be a fine lunch to be so heavy. We'll begin the bidding at five pence."

Aidan glanced over at Jack, but his mother called out before Jack had a chance to speak. "Five pence!" she said.

"Mother, what are you doing?"

"I'm bidding on that pretty girl's picnic lunch," she said with an excited smile.

"Don't! I don't want to eat with her."

"Why not? I'm not asking you to marry her, darling. But you certainly should eat with the prettiest girl at the picnic and, from what I can see, she's the prettiest. It's your right."

"She's Jack's girl," he whispered.

Louisa scoffed dismissively. "Well, then he'll have to pay for her company if he wants her."

"Six pence," Jack called.

"Ten!" Louisa said.

"Twenty," Jack countered.

"Stop!" Aidan pleaded. "Mother, please."

"One pound," Louisa said. It was an exorbitant price for a simple picnic lunch. The crowd went silent and Aidan could feel all eyes on him and his mother. It was an insult, an arrogant bid, especially coming from an Englishwoman. He felt his cheeks flame with embarrassment.

Father Timothy blinked in surprise. "Well, would there be any other bids?" The uneasy silence had now turned to the low murmur of gossiping voices. "No? Then this picnic lunch belongs to Mrs. McClain and her son, Aidan."

Aidan glanced over at Jack. His friend's face was a stony mask of indifference. He tried to catch his eye, but Jack kept his attention fixed on Molly as she stepped down from the stage with her red basket. She looked furtively over at him, as if to apologize for their ruined plans, but his expression never changed.

"Here, darling, go give our money to Father Timothy. Then escort your pretty luncheon companion back here. We'll find a quiet spot to eat."

Aidan did as he was told. But as Molly walked back with him through the crowd, Aidan headed over to Jack. "I didn't want this," he said, his voice low. "It was my mother. You know how she can be."

"Right," Jack said, his jaw tight. He looked at Molly for a long moment, then turned and walked away.

"I'm sorry," Aidan said to Molly. "I know you wanted to eat with Jack and I've spoiled it for you."

She forced a smile. "Your mother's donation will help the church," she said in a sweet voice. "Jack will understand."

When they reached the spot where Louisa stood, Aidan's mother's delight at winning the auction had disappeared. She now maintained a haughty expression, carefully examining Molly O'Shea for the expected faults. Molly wore a pretty blue dress with lace and ribbon trim and her auburn hair had been intricately braided, but she had the look of country folk.

"And what is your name?" Louisa asked.

"I'm Molly," she said, keeping her eyes cast down. "Molly O'Shea, ma'am."

"And who are your parents, Miss Molly O'Shea?"

"You know who her parents are," Aidan muttered. "They run the inn."

"And how many are in your family?"

"There are eight," Molly said. "My da, my mam, four brothers, a sister and me."

"I simply can't understand why the Irish insist on such large families. It keeps you all on the edge of poverty." She sniffed, then shook her head. "Come along, then, let's find a place to enjoy this lunch."

They sat at a small table under a chestnut tree. As Louisa unpacked the basket, she continued to chatter on about the faults she found in the Irish people, in Irish politics, in Irish schools. When she'd finished with those subjects, she turned to a detailed critique of the meal, informing Molly that the bread was too dense and the ham overcooked.

If Jack Quinn didn't hate him already for stealing away with his girl, then he'd surely hate him now. Molly appeared to be near tears and she'd barely eaten a thing. Though Aidan had felt jealousy toward her before, now he could feel nothing more than pity. A naive young girl like Molly was unprepared to fight back against Louisa McClain's carefully aimed barbs.

As soon as the meal was finished, Aidan gathered up the remains and stuffed them back inside the basket. "It was a lovely meal, Molly," he said, drawing her to her feet. "My mother and I thank you. I'm sure you have friends waiting for you."

Molly grabbed the opportunity for escape, disappearing into the crowd, her basket clutched to her chest. Aidan breathed a long sigh of relief. "Was that really necessary?" he asked, staring out at the crowd.

"She's common," Louisa said. "She might be considered pretty here in Ballykirk, but in London, she'd barely be called ordinary."

He turned and faced Louisa, anger bubbling up inside of him. "Shut up, Mother." With that, Aidan followed Molly into the crowd, determined to make his apologies to Jack. He'd not risk losing his best friend because of his mother's behavior.

A WARM SUMMER BREEZE blew across the hills above Ballykirk. Jack held out his hand and helped Molly over a low stone fence, before they continued climbing higher. Molly had been granted a rare day of freedom, her work at the inn finished and her parents occupied with a group of pensioners on holiday.

"Are you planning to talk to me? Or am I meant to guess at your thoughts?" Molly asked. Jack picked up his pace and she had to hurry to catch up. "Aidan is your friend. If memory serves, you haven't spoken in close to a month. You can't continue to punish him for his mother's behavior."

"No true friend would have betrayed me like that," Jack shouted over his shoulder. "He knew I was keen to win your basket and he let his mammy shove him around. Aidan never stands up for himself."

He hadn't been completely alone with Molly since before the parish picnic and he was feeling insecure about the two of them.

"He was very sweet to me. And polite. He has fine manners."

"And you're saying I don't?" Jack asked. He cursed softly. "I can understand why you might fancy Aidan McClain. He's rich and he's smart and he can give you pretty presents. That's what all women want."

"I was nice to him because he's your friend. That's the whole of it."

Jack ground his teeth. Though he knew Molly had no interest in Aidan, it still stung to realize that she might be swayed by someone more "suitable" in her parents' eyes. Aidan McClain was considered the catch of the county. In the hierarchy that was Ballykirk, the O'Sheas ranked well above the Quinns, the McClains high above the O'Sheas. Molly's family enjoyed a comfortable life, although not one filled with extravagance.

"I have no interest in Aidan McClain," Molly insisted. "He's not for me. And if you're too thickheaded to hear that, then I'm better to talk to that rock over there."

"That isn't any rock," Jack said. "That's Oisin's Rock. That's my ancestor, that is."

"And now I suppose you'll charm me with another one of your tales. Well, I won't be hearing it today." Molly walked off in the opposite direction, her arms crossed beneath her breasts, her auburn hair whipping in the wind.

Jack watched her for a long moment, then ran after her. He caught her by the arm, spun her around and picked her up off her feet. Nuzzling her neck, he chuckled softly. "Don't be angry with me."

"Then don't be so bold," she said, pushing out of his embrace. "I won't have you pawing me."

"I'm going to do something great with my life,"

Jack said, throwing out his arms. "You'll see. I could go fight with the Volunteers. The men at the pub say it's only a matter of time before there's another rising."

"I don't want you to get mixed up in that mess," Molly said stubbornly, turning back to face him. "You could be hurt or even killed."

Jack grinned. "And then you could marry Aidan McClain and live with him and his mother in the big house on the Skibbereen road. You'll have pretty dresses and more hats than days of the week and he'll take you to the city in that shiny motorcar and you'll dine in a fancy restaurant."

"I don't want hats or dresses," Molly said, stamping her foot.

"What do you want?"

"I want you to stop being a ninny-hammer and go talk with Aidan. I don't want to come between the pair of you. Not for something as silly as a picnic lunch."

Jack reached out and grabbed Molly's hand, lacing his fingers through hers. "I'm going to marry you someday, Molly O'Shea. And there won't be anything that can come between us."

"And will you just turn up at the church and expect me to be there waiting, Jack Quinn?" Molly teased. "Or do you intend to ask me properly?"

"I'll ask," he said. "When the time is right."

He reached out and smoothed his palm over her cheek, then tucked a flyaway strand of hair behind her ear. Tipping her chin up, he kissed her, his tongue tracing along her lower lip. They'd grown closer over the past months and Jack was finding it more and more difficult to be satisfied with chaste kisses.

But for now, it would have to be enough.

CHAPTER SIX

A THIN FOG ROLLED off the water onto the shore, coating the moon with a haze. Jack shoved his hands in his jacket pockets and paced back and forth across the deck of the *Mighty Quinn.* He'd anchored offshore just as the sun had set and had been bobbing around for two hours.

Anti-treaty sentiment had continued to rise throughout Ireland. Since the Easter Rising two years before, the Republican movement had sputtered and stalled, most of the rebel leaders either imprisoned or executed. But in the past year, many of the remaining prisoners had been released in an attempt by the British government to arrive at some kind of political settlement. A convention in June of 1917 failed to provide a solution with both Sinn Fein and the Ulster unionists opposed to any further deals with the British.

Since then, the Irish Volunteers had begun to regroup, taking advantage of British preoccupation with the war in Europe. Soldiers loyal to the Republican cause had been forced to drill and train in secret due to increased government vigilance; but they were ready to fight, while Free State politicians were determined to maintain the treaty with the British at all costs.

Jack reached over and turned up the wick on the lantern, the flame brightening in the dark. He'd been ordered to light the lantern at precisely 9:00 p.m. A boat would come alongside him and they'd unload the guns into his hold. He'd then transport them fifteen miles up the coast to a small cove where another Republican crew would take the arms and move them inland.

No one had predicted the fog, or made contingency plans based on inclement weather. He squinted out into the darkness and tried to listen for the sound of an engine, but the fog seemed to carry sound in strange ways, distorting distance and direction.

Jack had always believed the talk at the Speckled Hound was just talk, old men tossing out their opinions on the cause of Irish freedom just to listen to themselves. But two months ago, he'd been approached by one of the older men in the village, Ned Duffy, a regular patron at the pub.

Ned had lived in Ballykirk all his life and for a long while had told no one at the Hound of his membership in the Irish Republican Brotherhood. Over the years, Ned had recruited hundreds of men in County Cork to serve the cause and Jack had been the latest. He'd asked Jack if he'd be willing to use his father's fishing boat to move "sensitive" cargo, insisting that Paddy Quinn be told nothing about the activity.

At first Jack had been reluctant, but then he'd realized that he was old enough to make his own decisions. At eighteen, he was no longer a boy and no longer under the control of his father. Even Aidan was out on his own, living in Dublin and attending university.

But Jack was forced to keep his involvement a secret. More and more of late, Paddy Quinn had been losing himself in the drink, and when he drank he talked far too much.

The muffled sound of an engine drifted over the water and a few seconds later, Jack felt the boat lurch. Slowly a lantern rose over the side of the *Mighty Quinn.* He hurried to grab the line from the other boat, then tied it off.

Jack helped a wizened old man onto the deck. From the calluses on his hands, he knew the man was a fisherman, probably out of Kinsale. The old man chuckled softly as he regained his balance. "I dinna think we'd be findin' you in the fog." He offered his hand. "I'm a friend of Ned's. Name's Davey."

"Jack." He shook the old man's hand.

Davey pointed over his shoulder. "My sons Jimmy and Johnny. They do the heavy liftin'. Boys, let's unload this cargo before the fog clears."

Jack watched as the two broad-shouldered fishermen hefted long wooden crates from one boat to the other. When everything had been secured down below, they climbed back onto their boat and Davey shook his hand again. "There'll be a double light at the cove. Land a hundred yards to the north. A dairy wagon will be waitin' to take the cargo inland."

Jack nodded, then watched as the larger boat was swallowed up by the darkness. He winched in the anchor, then started the engine. But the lights from the shore were no longer visible. He glanced down at his compass and steered north, knowing he could probably navigate the waters blindfolded if needed. But the fog continued to worsen and he was forced to steer out to sea to avoid running the *Mighty Quinn* aground.

After nearly an hour, to his relief, the fog cleared and he could see the faint lights from the coast. County Cork had always been a haven for smugglers and bandits and he felt a certain excitement in carrying on the tradition. But it was tempered by a healthy dose of fear. If he were caught with contraband weapons on board, he'd be thrown in prison and the *Mighty Quinn* confiscated. But he'd been arguing the Republican cause for years now. It was time to stop talking and take action.

He rounded Dursey Island and turned back inland, searching for the lights of Allihies. As he drew closer to the shore, Jack scanned the horizon for the lanterns, keeping his eyes open for patrol boats, as well. He dropped anchor as close to shore as he could get, then waited, lighting a second lantern in response to the two lanterns on the shore.

Ten minutes later, a skiff drew up beside the *Mighty*

Quinn. A single man climbed onboard and they silently loaded the crates into the flat-bottomed boat. Jack crawled in beside him, ready to help unload on the other end. When they reached the beach, he jumped out and pulled the skiff onto the narrow strip of sand. Cliffs rose all around them and men appeared out of the dark to carry the crates through the rocks and up to the waiting wagon.

"Where the hell have you been?"

The voice startled Jack at first, low and throaty—and feminine. A young woman stepped up in front of him, a lantern dangling from her hand. "You were supposed to be here an hour ago."

"The fog came in," Jack said, staring into her pretty eyes. He couldn't see much detail in the feeble light, but she had dark hair that had been pulled back from her face, tendrils whipped free by the wind and curled by the damp. Tall and slender, she wore knee-high boots, men's trousers and a rough linen jacket. "Your guns wouldn't do ya much good sitting at the bottom of the North Atlantic now, would they?" Jack said.

"Ned claims you can navigate these waters blind. Did he overestimate the talents of yourself?" she challenged, tipping up her chin. He could see more of her profile now and noted a perfect nose and full lips. She was young, no more than nineteen or twenty. An unbidden surge of attraction warmed his blood, and for a moment Jack was taken aback. He'd never noticed other women, so set on Molly O'Shea was he.

But this girl was an undeniable beauty, a modern woman, not a country lass.

"Have you been sent to scold me or are you here for a useful reason?" Jack asked, stifling a grin.

"I'm running this operation," she said. "And if we don't follow the schedule, we're bound to get caught by the sunrise. If you're not aware, we're waging war in Cork and Tipperary and it's becoming more difficult to move around freely." She turned to the man standing behind her.

"Then why don't we get to work?" Jack suggested. He walked over to one of the gun crates and grabbed a rope handle. "I can't carry this on my own."

With a low curse, she took the other end of the crate. "Jerry, help Robby with the next load." She started up the rocky path, straining at the weight of the weapons.

"I didn't expect to find a woman out here," Jack murmured, trying to take most of the weight himself.

She stumbled slightly and Jack waited for her to regain her footing. "And you believe only men can show concern for the future of Ireland?" she asked. "Someday, this country will be a place where both men and women live as equals. A woman will be able to do anything a man can."

"And then you'll be carrying this crate on your own, I suppose?" Jack teased.

"Some women might find that kind of talk charming, but I find it annoying," she said, tugging on the crate.

When they reached the top of the cliff, they carried the crate over to the wagon, handing it off to two men who were loading the guns in the false bottom of the wagon bed. "So how did you get involved in all this?"

She shrugged. "I had nothing better to do with myself, beyond getting married and having babies."

"Christ, you're a corker, you are," Jack said, chuckling. He held out his hand. "Is that the truth?"

"My father has been smuggling for the Volunteers for five years. He's been ill and I've taken his place." She wiped her hand on her trousers, then held it out to him. "I'm Siobhan. From Dublin."

"I'm Jack from Ballykirk," he said. Her fingers were long and delicate and he held on to her hand for a long moment before letting go. "Are you going to be all right then, Siobhan from Dublin?"

She nodded, a small smile curling her lips. "You'd better get back to your boat. I've work to do this night." She paused. "Be careful. And mind the patrols."

"I will. It was a pleasure. Perhaps we'll meet again someday." He walked back to the cliff, then made his way down to the beach, all the while wishing he might stay a bit longer. The skiff sat on the beach, empty now, its owner standing beside it. He crawled inside and Jack pushed the boat off the sand.

As they rowed out to the *Mighty Quinn,* Jack stared up at the two tiny lights high on the cliff. A few minutes later, they were extinguished and he imagined

Siobhan ordering the men on to their next task. He'd already decided that he'd volunteer his services to Ned Duffy again.

But he had no illusions that he'd ever see Siobhan again. Jack sensed that she was meant to do greater things with her life than haul smuggled guns up a cliff. And he planned to spend the rest of his life with Molly, raising a family and fishing the waters off Ballykirk.

"HOW DO I LOOK?"

Jack's younger brothers sat at the table, bowls of mutton stew in front of them. "What are you going for?" Niall asked.

"I don't know," Jack said, glancing down at the new white shirt he wore. "Do I look like the kind of man you'd wish your daughter to marry?"

"I don't have a daughter," Niall replied.

"Jaysus, must you take everything I say at face value, ya little gobshite?"

"Usually, you say exactly what you mean," Thomas countered.

"I'm going to ask for Molly's hand today."

"What would you do with her hand?" Niall asked. "Won't she be needin' it?"

"He's goin' to ask her to marry him," Thomas said, jabbing his younger brother in the ribs with his elbow.

"I'm going to walk straight over to her parents' place, rap on the door, and demand that her father give me permission to marry her."

"Are you afraid?" Niall asked.

"Afraid that he might say no," Thomas answered for Jack.

"Henry O'Shea doesn't agree with my politics. He's pro-treaty and I'm for the republic. He thinks Molly could do better than to marry a Quinn. And like every other father in town, he's hopin' his daughter will set her sights on Aidan McClain."

"Then why would you want to marry her?" Thomas asked.

Jack drew a deep breath. "A man has to start his life sometime and now's the proper time. She'll make me a fine wife, she will. And she loves me."

He strode out of the house, taking care not to get his shoes too dusty as he walked down the road to the inn. Had Aidan still been around, he might have asked him for his advice. But the rift between them had never been healed. Aidan had left for Dublin before Jack had had a chance to apologize.

When he reached the inn, Jack knocked on the front door. It opened and Molly quickly stepped out and grabbed his hand. "He's not in a good humor today," she whispered. "Perhaps you should come back tomorrow."

"No," Jack said. "It has to be today. I don't want to wait any longer."

"But he's already said I can't marry until I'm eighteen."

"That doesn't mean we can't make our plans."

Molly relented, giving his hand a squeeze. "He's in the front parlor reading the newspapers. Please, don't speak about politics."

Jack gave Molly a quick kiss on the forehead. "I won't." He stepped inside, leaving Molly to wait in the garden. He found Henry O'Shea seated in a comfortable wing chair, the smoke from his pipe curling up about the newspaper. Jack rapped softly on the open door, then snatched his cap off his head. "Mr. O'Shea?"

The old man slowly lowered the paper. "Jack."

"I've come to speak with you about something very important."

Henry reluctantly set the paper on his lap. "I think I know what you're about, Jack. And I'm going to stop you before you begin. I know you care for Molly and she cares for you."

Jack nodded. "I love her, I do. And I'd like to marry her…someday…soon."

"That may be. But I'm afraid I can't give you my blessing." He carefully refolded his newspaper as he spoke. "To be perfectly blunt, Mrs. O'Shea and I believe Molly deserves better. She deserves a man who can provide better than you can. Your father barely supports your family with that boat. How are you to support your own family as well?"

"I don't intend to be a fisherman my whole life," Jack said.

"It's not just that. My Molly has fancied herself in

love with you since she was a child. She's never once considered any other choices. Yes, she could marry you tomorrow if she wished, but I believe, given time apart, she might realize her feelings are not true love."

Jack felt his frustration grow. "And what if they are?"

"Then that love will last. Give her time. If she still wants you in a year, I won't stand in your way."

"A year?" Jack repeated, stunned.

"A year and a promise. I'm well aware you're mixed up with the Republicans, and you're doing things that could get you arrested. If you marry my daughter, you must give that up. I won't have you break her heart from the inside of an Irish prison."

"You mean to tell me how to live my life, as well?" Jack said, anger evident in his voice. Henry O'Shea might be Molly's father, but he had no right to meddle in Jack's politics.

"If that life includes my daughter, then, yes, I do."

"I could marry her now," Jack threatened. "We could marry outside the church. We'd leave Ballykirk and I could find work in Cork and you'd never see her again."

Henry slowly rose from the chair. "Do that and I'll disown her. Molly loves her family, and if you truly love her, you won't be putting her through that."

Jack cursed inwardly. He'd waited years for Molly already. "I'm not going to make any promises," he said. "The moment Molly will have me, I'm going to marry your daughter, with or without your damned blessing." With that, Jack walked out the front door of the inn, slamming the door behind him.

He found Molly waiting in the garden, sitting primly on a rustic bench, her hands folded in her lap. When she saw him, she jumped to her feet and hurried over, her eyes bright with excitement. "What did he say?" she asked, reaching out to lace her fingers through his. "Can we post the banns next week?"

"He refused me. He doesn't believe I'm good enough for you." Jack shook his head, cursing beneath his breath. "I can't stay here."

"Just wait a bit. He'll calm himself and then you can talk to him again."

"That's not what I meant. I'm leaving for Dublin, Molly."

"What?" Molly gasped. "Why? I'm certain I can convince him. I just need time."

Jack had been turning the idea over in his mind for days now. Ned Duffy had approached him a month ago about a larger role in the IRA smuggling operations and Jack had been sorely tempted. Over the past year, he had worked with fishermen up and down the western coast of Ireland and his experience had become a valuable asset to the cause. Now he was needed inland, to coordinate the shipment of guns overland to the Volunteer forces.

He'd turned Ned down, hoping that he and Molly might marry soon. But now, that didn't seem possible. It would be much easier to spend the year working for the cause than biding his time in Ballykirk. "He won't change his mind," Jack finally said. "And I can't stay here counting the days until he does."

"You don't love me, then?"

"I do. But Molly girl, you need to be certain you love me before you defy your family for me. And you won't know that until we've spent time apart." Jack drew her into his embrace. "I will marry you, Molly. And we will raise a fine family. But I want those children to be raised in a free Ireland. I can do something to make that happen—at least I can try—before I'm forced to put that part of my life aside for good."

"Why must you always concern yourself with politics?" she demanded, her voice thick with anger. "We're ruling our own country now. Why do you need more than that?"

"There's a place for me in Dublin. There's not a place for me here right now."

Tears flooded her eyes, falling freely down her cheeks. "This is all that silly prattle down at the pub. You listen to those old men and their tales of rebellion. I don't see them getting on a train for Dublin and taking up arms. Leave the battle to someone else."

"I can't."

"Go then," Molly said, shoving him back with her palms. "I won't say goodbye, because that will be the end of it then. I'll wait for you and you'll return and we'll begin again. Only we'll have wasted a year of our lives. And I'll never forgive you for that."

He bent down and touched his lips to hers, kissing her gently. "I'll think of you every day," he murmured. "You have my promise."

"And I'll hold you close to my heart," she said with a sob.

He kissed her once more before he walked away. Jack didn't bother to go home. It would be too easy to change his mind. Instead, he headed to Ned Duffy's place to offer his services. By sunset, he'd be on his way to Cork or Dublin or another spot in Ireland that he'd never seen.

When he didn't come home, his parents would wonder where he'd gone. But Thomas would be pleased. He would work the boat now with Paddy, spared a life as a priest. That responsibility would now fall to Niall, who had always been more suited to that profession in the first place.

CHAPTER SEVEN

AIDAN STRODE down the cobblestone street toward the boarding house, his jacket thrown over his shoulder, his black leather grip swinging at his side. He'd put in a long day at the library and now had the entire evening to himself. He'd been invited to the Friday-evening salon at Professor Campbell's town house and looked forward to putting a day of hard work behind him for some interesting conversation and attractive company.

He remembered the first time he'd been invited to attend. Aidan hadn't been sure what to expect. He knew the other young men who were regulars there and recognized they were all of a certain type—handsome in a pretty way, educated and refined...and slightly effeminate. He'd been afraid to accept the invitation, afraid it might mark him as different. But after his first evening, Aidan realized there were others like him, other young men who were more attracted to each other than to women.

His first lover had been an older student, a young man who'd lived most of his life abroad with his wealthy uncle. He'd been sophisticated, handsome and undeniably seductive, and Aidan had fallen in love immediately, only to realize a few weeks later that lasting relationships were not encouraged among this group of friends.

His life had changed so much since arriving in Dublin three years ago. He'd nearly forgotten Ballykirk. There wasn't much left for him there. His mother preferred to visit him in Dublin or meet him in London, taking the opportunity to spend more of Eamon's money. Rather than accompany his wife, Eamon wrote long letters, detailing medical breakthroughs he'd read about. As for Jack, the last time Aidan had spoken to him had been at the church fair.

Aidan had begun at least fifty different letters to him but had never finished one. Perhaps it was for the best. He'd been in love with Jack Quinn for as long as he could remember. But acting on that love would have been disastrous.

He rounded the corner and started toward the boardinghouse set in the middle of the block. But as he approached, Aidan slowed his pace. A man sat on the front steps, his elbows braced on his knees, a cap pulled low over his eyes. He shifted slightly, tipping his face up to the afternoon sun. Aidan gasped. "Jack?"

He glanced to the side, then smiled. "Aidan."

Aidan couldn't believe his eyes. Jack Quinn was the last person he'd expected to see today—or any other day for that matter. "I was just thinking about you. What are you doing here?"

"I thought it was time to see a bit of the world," Jack said. "Dublin was the best place to begin." He levered to his feet and smoothed his hands over the front of his wool jacket. He looked as if he'd slept in his clothes.

"How long have you been here?"

"A few months," Jack said. "I decided it was time to pay you a visit. I have a terrible thirst. Would you like to get a pint?"

Aidan nodded. "There's a pub just down the street." They walked together for a short time in silence before Aidan decided to speak. "Am I forgiven then?"

"Forgiven?"

"For the picnic lunch with Molly. We haven't spoken since that day. I understand why you were angry, Jack. I should have stood up to my mother."

Jack reached out and put his arm around Aidan's shoulders. "There's nothing to forgive. It's forgotten. That's the thing about best friends. Nothing can come between us."

Aidan smiled, glancing up at Jack. "And how is Molly?"

"She's grand. We're going to be married in a year's time. And how are your studies going?"

Aidan got the impression that Jack didn't want to talk about Molly and he suspected he knew the reason for Jack's holiday to Dublin. Henry O'Shea had always fancied himself a bit above the rest of the folks in Ballykirk. It was common knowledge that he hoped his daughter might marry "up" instead of "down."

"I've been very busy. In a few months, I begin work at the Jester Street Infirmary. I'm not to treat any patients yet but I'll serve as assistant to Dr. Edwin Sullivan. He's on the faculty of the medical college and an old colleague of my father's. It's quite an honor."

They stepped inside the Dancing Bear, a run-down pub two streets down from Aidan's boardinghouse. Aidan tossed money onto the bar, enough to keep Jack's thirst well quenched with Guinness. "What have you been doing here in Dublin?" he asked.

"Seeing the sights," Jack said. "Visiting the pubs, strolling the streets. Looking for work." He took a long drink of his ale then licked his upper lip. "So tell me, is it difficult? Your studies?"

Aidan nodded. "I have little time for anything else."

"What about women? I'm sure there are more of them to choose from in a city like this," Jack teased.

"I suppose there are. I haven't had time to look." It was a lie, but necessary to maintain the pretense. "Where are you staying?"

Jack shrugged. "I have friends," he said.

Aidan chuckled. "What kind of friends? You don't know anyone in Dublin."

Jack just shrugged again and Aidan dropped the subject. His mother had passed along a rumor that

Jack Quinn had gotten himself involved with the IRA. If it was true, then Jack was in Dublin for one reason only, to stir up trouble.

Aidan knew he ought to offer Jack a place to sleep, but the intimacy of the situation would have been too difficult for Aidan. He'd finally conquered his infatuation with his best friend. Now was no time to fall back into a part of his life he'd left behind. "Dublin can be a dangerous place," he warned.

"I'll be careful," Jack said with a wry smile.

They talked for a long time, catching up on the news of Ballykirk. Jack deftly avoided any talk about his political activities, and Aidan did the same when it came to his social life. But when they parted ways a few hours later, Aidan was left with a single realization. No matter how long he lived, his feelings for Jack Quinn would never die. And that secret would always stand between them.

JACK STARED at the newspaper, pretending to read as he sat on a small bench in Saint Stephen's Green. He preferred to set up his meetings in public places. It was easier to get lost in the midst of people than to find a completely private location in the middle of a busy city.

He'd been in and out of Dublin for two years and had slipped easily into a life spent procuring weapons for the Volunteers. Most were smuggled into Ireland by boat, many German made. Others were stolen from

British or Free State supply depots. It was Jack's job to get the guns into the hands of the soldiers who needed them, often requiring him to travel up and down the coast with the shipments.

He had no friends, only contacts without names and fellow soldiers in the cause. He hadn't seen Aidan since his early days in Dublin and knew that he couldn't get his friend involved in his new life.

Though he'd written a few letters to Molly, he didn't have a permanent place to live so there was no way she could write to him. He'd traveled to Cork three times in the past two months, but his business hadn't taken him near Ballykirk.

Jack Quinn had become a shadow, existing without a past or a future and he was beginning to enjoy it. His life with Molly seemed so far-off, as if it had never really existed at all. He'd thought about returning to her, but his contribution to the cause had become more important than personal matters. Besides, Molly had probably moved on, never wanting for handsome young men who paid her enthusiastic attention.

Someone sat down next to Jack on the bench and he turned, surprised to see a woman there. He was about to stand up and move on to another bench when he recognized Siobhan. She glanced over at him.

He turned back to his newspaper and spoke to her from behind it. "Jack from Ballykirk," he murmured. "We dragged a crate up a cliff one night near Allihies. Remember?"

"I wondered if I'd see you again," she said. "Since we're both in the same line of work, I suppose it was inevitable."

"You have a shipment you need moved south?"

"Fifty rifles and thirty-six pistols. The pistols are packed in sacks of wheat. They're hidden in a warehouse in the east end. We need to move them soon before the rats tear apart the sacks."

"How close is the warehouse to the river?" Jack asked.

"It's on the water."

"Then we'll take them out on the water," he said. "Tomorrow night. Down the Liffey and south along the coast. I've got a contact in Wicklow who can get them anywhere you'd like."

"Cork," she said.

"Cork it is," Jack replied. "Now, we'll work out the details later. Let's take a stroll. I don't like the look of that gentleman over there. He's watching us a bit too closely."

In truth, the old man was probably just staring at Siobhan. After all, she was the most beautiful thing within eyesight. Jack was willing to wager that she was the most beautiful woman in all of Dublin.

"I can't," Siobhan said. "I have to go."

"No, you don't." Jack tucked the newspaper beneath his arm, then took her hand and pulled her to her feet. "You'll spare a bit of time for an old friend." He grinned. He had precious few friends in Dublin. It might feel nice to carry on a normal conversation, one that didn't involve secrecy and intrigue and a healthy dose of distrust.

"We're not friends," she said, reluctantly taking his arm.

"You're one of the few people I know in this city. That makes you a friend. And as a friend, I should know your full name."

"Siobhan Burnett," she said.

He gave her hand a squeeze. "It's my pleasure, Miss Burnett. I'm Jack Quinn."

"Well, Jack Quinn, what are we going to do with ourselves now that we've met?"

"I haven't had a bite all day," Jack said, "and I'm as weak as a salmon in a sandpit. Would you like to have supper? I can't afford anything more than the local pub."

"A pub it is," Siobhan said, slipping her arm around his. "Malone's has a good Dublin coddle. Apple tart for dessert."

As they strolled toward Grafton Street, Jack felt himself relax for the first time since he'd arrived in Dublin. Though he didn't really know Siobhan Burnett, he knew he could trust her. They had history together and that was more than he had with anyone else he'd come to know in the city.

As they walked, Jack had a chance to look at her for the first time, beyond the lantern light that night on the beach. She was as beautiful as he remembered, if not more. Tall and slender, she carried herself with the grace of a dancer and the confidence of a man. She wore a fitted skirt and a tailored blouse and delicate kid boots that hid trim ankles. Her hair, nearly black, was pulled back from her face and knotted at her nape.

"How long have you been here in Dublin?" he asked.

"Not long. I travel between here and the west coast. My aunt has a home here, so I have a place to stay. I teach piano to young ladies to support myself."

"I've been repairing boats," Jack said. "Stitching sails and fixing engines. Enough work to keep me fed."

"And what have you seen of Dublin? It is the jewel of Ireland."

Jack shrugged. "I'm not one for culture. I prefer the pub to the opera."

Siobhan arched a dark eyebrow, her green eyes fixed on his. "You've never been to a museum, then? Or to a concert?" She sighed. "A culchie, you are, Jack Quinn. And you're proud of it."

"Then educate me," Jack challenged.

Her gaze flickered for a moment and Jack chided himself for being too familiar. After all, they were barely more than strangers. But from the moment he'd met Siobhan, he'd felt an easy camaraderie with her. She wasn't like any woman he'd ever known. Unfettered by society's expectations, Siobhan had stepped out of the traditional role expected of a young Irish woman and Jack couldn't help but admire her drive and independence.

He wanted to learn more, to see the world through her eyes, to understand her interests and her passions. And he wanted her to see him as more than a raw country boy, better suited to shine her boots than squire her around the city.

"And what will I get in return?" she asked, a teasing glint in her eyes and a challenging tilt to her chin.

"The great pleasure of my company," he said. "And a handsome escort with a fair wit."

"And a right chancer, you are, too," she muttered, shaking her head. "We should begin with the French paintings at the National Gallery. But I'd wager you'd prefer the dead and stuffed creatures at the Natural History Museum."

Jack chuckled. "Lead on. I'll bow to your wisdom on this decision as long as I'm fed first."

They picked up their pace, her hand tucked into the crook of his arm, her skirts brushing against his legs as they walked. Jack knew he ought to feel a wee bit of guilt for forgetting Molly so easily. But Molly was a girl and Siobhan was a woman. He felt affection for Molly, but with Siobhan, it was desire, pure and simple.

He wanted to touch her, to look into her eyes and take in the unique details of her face. He imagined kissing her and holding her in his arms. He'd been with just two women since he'd arrived in Dublin, both of questionable repute. But at least he knew what to do when the time might come.

Over the past months, he'd become a man who lived only in the present. And at the present, Molly was in his past. Siobhan was walking beside him, the sun gleaming in her hair, the color high in her cheeks. Today, she was his and he was going to enjoy every moment he spent with her.

CHAPTER EIGHT

THE OLD WOOLEN MILL was located in a run-down section of Dublin, the streets narrow and the air grimy with soot. The IRA used it as a central warehouse for gun smuggling, the guns arriving in large bales of wool and going out in the middle of the night in false-bottomed carts.

The owner of the mill was an ardent supporter of the cause, but Jack didn't completely trust him. He was a braggart who often wanted to be more involved than was practical. And he had the look of a drunk about him. A loose tongue could get them all killed.

"We'll move them out over the next three nights," Jack said. He glanced over at the two smugglers and then at Siobhan, who nodded. They'd been working together steadily for several months now and could read each other well. "Then we're done with this place."

"What do you mean?" the owner asked.

"Just a feeling," Jack said.

"Jaysus, a feeling? You're not going to get a safer spot than this. I've moved a lot of guns for you and this is the thanks I get."

Jack crossed the room and stood in front of the old man. The scent of whiskey was thick in the air. "If you're in this for the thanks, then I'd suggest you turn this into a home for the old and infirm. The longer we stay here, the greater the odds we'll be found. Do you have a problem with that? Or would you prefer to spend the next ten years in Mountjoy?"

"I'm not afraid of prison," the man said, his expression dark.

"I am," Jack countered. "After we move this shipment, Siobhan will give you the location for the next drop point."

They started for the door. But an instant later, the plank door burst open. Two soldiers, rifles aimed, stepped into the room, shouting and waving their weapons. Jack had a heartbeat to decide whether to throw up his hands or fight. He saw Siobhan duck behind a crate, and one of the soldiers raised his rifle in her direction.

Jack drew his pistol and aimed it. He'd been issued the weapon months ago and had never had cause to draw it. But now he prayed that his aim would be true.

The room exploded with gunfire and two more soldiers followed the first pair inside. Jack took cover on the far side of the room, wood beams splintering over his head. "Go," he shouted. "I'll keep them busy."

She stared at him, fear filling her eyes. "Where?"

"Duffy Street," he mouthed.

When she nodded, Jack reached over the crate and fired. Siobhan managed to crawl out behind the cover of the wool bales, the bullets hitting them with a soft thud. Jack risked a glance around the side of the post to see the owner of the mill sprawled on the floor, unconscious, a red stain on his shirtfront. The two smugglers had found cover behind an old loom, but had no means of escape. As soon as they ran out of ammunition, they'd be forced to surrender.

Jack drew a deep breath and steeled himself. But the moment he stood and tried to run, one of the soldiers followed after him, taking careful aim. Jack knew at that moment that he'd have to shoot or be shot himself. Time seemed to slow to a painful crawl as he pulled the trigger. The soldier crumpled to the floor and Jack threw himself into the stairwell.

He tumbled down the stairs, landing in the dank and musty cellar. The cellar held a hidden exit. Jack barricaded the door behind him and wriggled through the open window. He let it drop shut behind him. He shoved some empty crates in front of it before heading down the alley.

He knew every dark alley and narrow street in this section of Dublin. Moving in the shadows, Jack made his way east, back into the bustling center of Dublin, swallowed up again as an anonymous face in a crowd. It took him nearly an hour to reach the house, but by the time he got there, he knew he hadn't been followed.

He'd spent a few nights sleeping in the derelict house and knew that it had occasionally been used by the IRA as a rendezvous point. Set in the midst of a neighborhood of Fenians, Free State forces steered clear of the area, knowing an incursion would result in a hail of bottles and rocks.

The back door was ajar and he slipped inside. Dust motes swirled as he moved through the rooms, the sun slanting through the dirty windows and illuminating the tattered furniture. He found Siobhan curled up on the couch, her cheeks wet with tears. When she saw him, she jumped up and threw herself into his arms.

"I was so frightened you wouldn't get out." Siobhan skimmed her hands over his body. "Are you all right?"

He nodded, bending over to draw in a deep breath. He'd been too occupied to feel a trace of fear before, but now he had time to realize just how close he'd come. "What about you?"

Siobhan nodded. "They've got the guns."

"And I think they got Eddie and David, too."

She glanced around, the look in her eyes frantic. "We have to find a way to get word to Billy Brown. He's coming tonight to pick up the first shipment. They'll be waiting for him." She pushed away from the wall. "I'll go. They won't be watching for a woman. And none of the soldiers got a good look at me."

"No," Jack said.

She cursed. "Are you telling me what to do, Jack Quinn?"

He shook his head. "We'll wait. Once it gets dark it will be easier to move about." He reached into his pocket and pulled out a wad of paper money, meant to pay for the weapons. He let it flutter to the floor. "Billy will be waiting at O'Callahan's Pub until the midnight meeting time. He won't be difficult to find."

She stared at him for a long moment then nodded in agreement. "What will we do until then?"

Jack shrugged, raking his hands through his hair. An image of the soldier he'd shot flashed in his head and he pinched his eyes shut to try to block it out. "Sleep."

"You're mad. It's just past noon."

An uneasy silence descended over them, Jack's focus locked numbly on his dusty boots. "I may have killed a man today," he finally murmured. "When they burst in the door, the first thing I thought to do was take out my pistol. I shot one of the soldiers. He had his rifle pointed at me and I aimed at his chest and I pulled the trigger and I didn't take time to think. I just shot."

"You were defending your life, my life, the life of every man in that room. Any one of us would have done the same thing."

Jack looked up at her, his hands still braced on his knees. "But I'm the one who shot him. And if he dies, I'll have his blood on my hands for the rest of my days. I'll go to hell for it."

"We're fighting a war, Jack. Killing and dying are part of it all. If you're not prepared to do your duty, then you should go home to County Cork."

Jack slowly slid down against the wall, then buried his face in his hands, a flood of emotion overwhelming him. He'd known that the time might come when he was asked to take up arms, to aim a gun and shoot a fellow human being, even a fellow Irishman. And until this moment, he'd assumed that he'd be able to rationalize his actions as pure and noble.

But he didn't feel pure now. He felt dirty and sinful, as if the good left inside of him had disappeared the moment the bullet had struck the soldier's chest. He'd killed in order to protect twenty-three rifles and seven crates of ammunition.

"I don't know his name," Jack murmured. He pulled his hands away to look at Siobhan, surprised that they were wet with tears. "Don't you think I should know his name?"

Her expression went soft with sympathy and she crawled across the floor to sit beside him. Reaching up, she brushed his damp hair off his forehead. "Perhaps he's not dead," she said.

Jack drew a ragged breath. "Perhaps not." He wrapped his arms around his knees and forced a smile. "You consider me foolish then, to carry on like this?"

Siobhan placed her fingertips on his chest. "You have a good heart, Jack Quinn. A soul that longs to be free. That's what makes you a good soldier. You still remember what we're fighting for and you respect the price that is paid in sorrow and suffering."

"He could have a wife and family," Jack said. Suddenly he felt much older than his twenty-one years, the weight of the fight bearing down on him.

"I know, I know." Siobhan cupped his face in her hands and turned his gaze to hers. Jack stared into her eyes and felt her strength seeping into his body. He trusted her. Like him, Siobhan had refused to be hardened by the fight. With her, it wasn't just about driving the Brits out of Ireland for good. It was about her country, her people, and the bright future she could envision for Ireland.

"After we leave here, I'll try to find out what happened to him. There will be reports of the raid in the newspapers. I know one of the reporters at the *Independent*. I'll find out from him." She bent closer, pressing her forehead against his. "Until then, we have to keep our minds on the matters at hand."

Jack rested his arms on her shoulders, his fingers tangling in her hair. He closed his eyes, inhaling her scent, letting the warmth of human contact soothe the ache in his soul. And when he finally drew back, he found her staring at him, her lips slightly parted.

He'd fought his attraction to Siobhan for so long, his heart still back in Ballykirk with Molly. But he'd tired of the fight and he ached to surrender, to just let Ballykirk and his boyhood go, once and for all.

Jack gently touched his lips to hers, desperate for

this feeling of calm to continue. Since he'd arrived in Dublin, he'd thought of nothing but the fight, nothing that was soft and sweet and pretty and kind—except Siobhan. He'd found comfort in her presence. Now he wanted more.

He slipped his hand around her nape, drawing her closer, deepening his kiss, their tongues meeting, tasting. Jack waited for some sign of resistance, but Siobhan seemed to need this as much as he did. A tiny sigh slipped from her lips as she sank against his body and, before he could think, he pulled her down on the floor beside him, desperate to get even closer to her.

For an instant, he thought of Molly again, of the promise he'd made to return to her. But that vow had been made three years ago, by a boy who'd believed love would win out in the end. He knew better now. People had to take their happiness where they could find it, and right now Jack had found it in the soft curves of Siobhan's body and in the sweet taste of her mouth.

Her hands trailed down his chest and she slowly began to work at the buttons of his shirt. She brushed the faded fabric back and smoothed her hands over his bare skin. Somehow, Jack sensed that there would be no stopping once they began. Unlike his experiences with Molly, he and Siobhan were free of disapproving parents, overbearing priests and the threat of eternal damnation. If they chose to take pleasure in each other's bodies, there was no one to object.

Tomorrow he could be caught in the middle of another raid and be shot dead. Or arrested and sent to prison. Today, he'd feel like a man first and a soldier second. Drawing a deep breath, Jack fumbled with the tiny mother-of-pearl buttons on Siobhan's blouse. She brushed his hands away, then sat up beside him and finished the task herself.

She was the most beautiful thing he'd ever set his eyes upon. Deep green eyes and dark hair and features that were more striking than pretty. He held his breath, his heart slamming in his chest.

"I want you to touch me," she murmured.

Jack knew what went on between a man and a woman, but he sensed it was much more than the clumsy groping he'd experienced before. Then, it had been all about release, finishing the act as quickly as possible. He'd never had the chance to linger over a woman's body, to stir her passion and to read her response—and he was afraid he might not know what to do.

Siobhan shrugged out of her blouse, then slowly brushed the straps of her chemise off her shoulders. Jack sat up, bracing his hands on either side of her hips. His lips found the curve of her neck, the silken skin scented with rose water. He moved lower, to the soft flesh of her breasts.

The troubles of Jack's world slowly faded away as he explored her body, her slender arms, her perfect breasts, a waist he could span with his two hands.

They took their time, pushing aside clothing when it got in the way, both of them unafraid yet unsure of what came next. When she unfastened his trousers, Jack's body tensed. He was determined to maintain control, knowing if he didn't it would show his inexperience.

As she ran her fingers along his shaft, a shiver raced through him. Jack moaned softly, arching into her caress. It didn't feel like a sin, this pleasure they shared. It felt like the glory of heaven. She brought him close, but when he murmured her name, she slowed her tempo.

He'd assumed a proper lady was supposed to act like a trembling rabbit when faced with their first time, but Siobhan took as much enjoyment in the experience as he did. Suddenly he realized this might not be her first and only experience with a man. He wasn't sure how to feel, but in the end, it didn't matter. His need outstripped any doubts or insecurities he had.

She rose to her feet, brushing her hair back over her shoulders as she stood above him. Her chemise had gathered around her waist, her breasts bare. Reaching up beneath her skirts, she tugged her knickers down over her hips and kicked them aside. Then, without a word, she straddled his hips and sank down on top of him.

A moment later, he was inside her, moving, desire twisting deep in his core. Her hair fell around them like a curtain, shutting out the rest of the world, and all the worry and anxiety dissolved inside of him, leaving him with only the pleasure.

"I love you," he murmured, desperate to put words to what he was feeling.

"And I love you," Siobhan whispered, smiling down at him. "Just for today."

"For today," he repeated. Today was enough.

"YOU'LL WANT TO READ the Franklin paper on the treatment of pernicious anemia. I have it in my study. And I have the latest copy of the *New England Journal of Medicine*. A colleague in Boston sends them to me."

Aidan nodded as he picked at his roast beef. "Thank you. I'm anxious to see that." He ate dinner with Dr. Sullivan and his daughter every Sunday and Wednesday, and at first he'd enjoyed the good meal.

He'd worked with Edwin Sullivan in private practice and at the hospital for nearly three years and the elderly surgeon had done much to advance Aidan's prospects. Lately, he'd begun to suspect the meals were more than just a professional courtesy. Sullivan's daughter, Maura, had always been present at the table, retiring to her room after dessert. Now Edwin insisted on throwing them together at every opportunity—tea in the garden, a stroll after dinner, a piano recital of Maura's favorite tunes. It had become quite clear that Dr. Sullivan approved of the match.

Aidan glanced across the table to find Maura

watching him. She wasn't a pretty girl. She wasn't even handsome. Horse faced and clumsy, Maura was a bookish seventeen-year-old who rarely worked up the courage to speak in his presence. When she did, her stammer rendered her nearly incomprehensible.

Aidan ought to have felt pity for her. Her mother had died when she was just a small child and she'd been raised by her older siblings. Now that they were married with families of their own, she'd been left to fend for herself. She'd attended convent school and had been determined to take vows, but Sullivan had refused his permission.

"Maura, fetch us dessert. I believe Aidan has had enough of his dinner."

She jumped to her feet, sending him an uneasy smile. As she collected his plate, she brushed against him and he felt his blood run cold. He'd known for a long time now that women held no attraction for him. Though he'd tried to change his attitudes toward the opposite sex, Aidan had come to the conclusion that there was nothing to be done about it. He preferred the company of men. Men who also preferred men.

Once he'd accepted his choice, things had become much clearer. He had found others who shared his particular interests and soon had a circle of friends at Trinity who also lived in a shadowy world of hidden desires. His friends were poets and musicians, artists and scholars, men who valued beauty and culture and the pursuit of pleasure. With them, his life was no longer unsatisfactory.

"Maura made the dessert herself," Dr. Sullivan said as his daughter returned with the tray. "What are we having dear?"

"It—it's a pl-plum tart, Papa, with cl-clotted cream."

"Cook has been giving her lessons in the kitchen. My daughter can speak Latin, French and Gaelic, she can play the piano and sing a lovely tune, and knows her Shakespeare from front to back. But if she ever expects to catch herself a husband, she'll need to improve her talents in the kitchen."

Maura's face flushed red and she nearly knocked over her water goblet as she plopped down in her chair. "Papa, please," she murmured.

"I'm sure Aidan doesn't mind," Edwin said. "He's a practical man and he must know the value of finding a proper wife. A physician's life is made much easier with a good woman waiting at home. Maura's mother was a fine lady and a great help to me, God bless her soul." Maura and Edwin both crossed themselves.

"I'm sure she was, sir."

"Well," Edwin said, pushing back from the table. "I'm going to enjoy my dessert in the study."

"I'll join you," Aidan said.

He held out his hand. "No, no. You keep Maura company. I've got work to do." Edwin picked up his plate and kissed Maura on the way out of the room.

She and Aidan sat in uneasy silence for a long time, Aidan unwilling to encourage any romantic feelings on Maura's part by pleasant conversation. He turned his attention to the dessert and was quite surprised at how good it was.

"I—I know I'm not pretty," she murmured.

Aidan glanced up at her. Her wide brown eyes swam with tears but she'd plastered a smile on her face that belied her true feelings. "That's not true," he said.

"It is."

He sighed. "You could do more to make yourself attractive. That drab green in your gown doesn't flatter your hair and eyes. And the cut is far too severe for a girl your age."

"It belonged to m-my older sister," Maura explained.

"My mother wore that style six or seven years ago. There are plenty of dressmakers in Dublin who'd make you something more suitable. Ask your father to set up an account for you. And hire a lady's maid to do your hair."

"Why are you helping me?" she asked.

Aidan shrugged. "Your father expects you to marry. You'll improve your chances substantially if you make a few improvements."

"Thank you." She fumbled with her fork, then set it down. "Do you think *you'd* ever find me...attractive?"

"I'm not looking for a wife," Aidan said coolly.

"I understand."

Aidan dabbed at his lips with his napkin and dropped it beside his plate. "Tell your father that I'll see him at hospital tomorrow morning." He strode toward the door, then turned back to Maura. "Try Claire's on Connelly Street. Choose fine fabrics that will move as you do. Silk in pale colors will flatter your hair and eyes."

He walked to the front door and let himself out. But when he glanced over his shoulder, he saw Maura standing at the door. She smiled and waved at him and Aidan couldn't help but chuckle. He'd spent so much time listening to his mother prattle on about fashion, at least it had come in useful once in his life.

Aidan pulled his watch from his vest and opened the cover. It was nearly nine. The Sunday-evening salon at Professor Campbell's home would be well underway. He felt the need for some excitement. Perhaps he'd meet someone new tonight, someone with the dark and brooding looks he favored, a man who'd resemble a face he couldn't seem to forget.

CHAPTER NINE

JACK STARED at the scenery as the motorcar bumped along the coast road. They were a few miles outside Ballykirk and the closer he got to home the more he wanted to turn around and go the other way. It had been seven years since he'd left Ballykirk for Dublin and four since he'd been arrested outside Aidan's boardinghouse.

"Are ye anxious?" Declan asked, his eyes on the rutted road.

Jack raked his hand through his long hair. He was in need of a haircut and a shave, but he'd left prison with just enough money for the train trip home. "What am I to expect? Have you talked to Mam? She doesn't have a celebration planned, does she?"

"I told her you wanted to keep it quiet. I can't say she'll listen."

Jack had served four years of a seven-year sentence in Mountjoy Prison, the charges stemming from his gun-smuggling activities. The authorities had never connected him to the death of Private Thomas Farrelly, the young soldier killed in the raid. So Jack had carried that crime with him and would for the rest of his life. There were other deaths that plagued his conscience, as well—he'd put hundreds of guns into the hands of the Irish Volunteers, guns that had taken Irish lives, destroyed Irish families.

He'd left Ballykirk full of noble intentions and he now returned humbled by life. Nothing much had changed. The civil war had gone on for a year after he'd been arrested, with fighting fierce in Connaught and Munster. But over time, the army had pushed the IRA forces into the mountains. Irish citizens had grown tired of the constant disruptions in their life and popular support had dwindled. Less than a year after his arrest, the IRA had called a cease-fire and the civil war had come to an official end.

"How was it then?" Declan asked.

Jack shrugged. "It was prison. I couldn't take a walk in the hills or pick a fresh apple or smell the sea in the air." He shook his head and smiled sadly. "I would dream about Ballykirk, about the *Mighty Quinn,* the sound of the water on her hull. There were times I'd wake up in the middle of night and I'd feel my cot rocking, as if I was sleeping on the boat."

"But you're happy to be home?"

"I'm afraid."

"Of what?" Dec asked.

"I'm afraid there's nothing left for me here."

"You don't have to stay," Dec said. "You can come to Cork. I'll find you a job in the factory. You can stay with Gemma and me and the children. We've plenty of room."

Jack shook his head. "I can't be shut up all day in a factory. Too much like prison." He twisted in his seat. "Stop here."

Dec did as he was told. "You all right?"

"I want to walk the rest of the way." Jack jumped out of the car and slammed the door behind him. "I'll see you at home."

Dec shook his head. "Nah. I'm goin' back. I'm still not welcome in Da's house. And you need a chance to settle in without me settin' off our father again. Remember, if you need anything, Jack, you call on me."

Jack waved as Dec turned the motorcar around. He stood in the middle of the road, his face turned up to the sun, his eyes closed. He could imagine what was going on in the tiny whitewashed cottage that overlooked the harbor. His mother was probably making his favorite meal, a savory lamb stew filled with fresh vegetables. And there would be an apple tart baking on the peat-fired hearth.

Even though he'd dreamed about a meal like that, Jack wasn't ready to be around his family. Instead, he circled around Ballykirk and headed up to the hills above the harbor. He knew a place he could go to clear his head, to brush away the last of the cobwebs that had clung to him.

But as he approached the rock, he saw a lone figure standing near it, her face turned out to the sea, her skirts whipped by the wind. He recognized the deep auburn hair immediately and he nearly turned around to walk back the way he'd come. Jack wasn't sure he was ready to see Molly yet.

But in the end, he continued to walk toward her. As if she sensed his presence, she slowly turned to face him. He stared into her eyes, trying to read her reaction. Jack knew he didn't look like the same young man who'd left Ballykirk over seven years before.

"Hello, Molly," he said. "You're looking grand." She was no longer a girl, but a full-grown woman.

"You look tired," she murmured. "And thin. And in terrible need of a barber."

They stood in silence for a long time. Jack cleared his throat. "I'm sorry, Molly. I have to say that right off. I promised I'd come back and I didn't. I got caught up in the fight and I left you waiting for me. That was a selfish thing." He drew a ragged breath. "Tell me you're happy. That you've found someone to love you."

She smiled weakly. "I am happy," she said. "I've been teaching school. And I help my parents at the inn. I still have a few more years until I'm considered a spinster." She reached out and took his hand, lacing her fingers through his in the same way she'd done so many years before. "It's good to see you, Jack. Good to have you home."

He didn't know what else to say to her. Jack

couldn't ignore the guilt that flooded him. Molly had remained faithful to him all these years, yet he'd lusted after Siobhan, images of her naked body drifting through his head every night before he slept.

They'd both written to him at first, Molly with her cheerful letters filled with news of Ballykirk, Siobhan's letters laced with encouragement and promises to find a way to get him out. But Jack had refused to answer any letters. He didn't want either of the women he'd loved to wait for him.

The years had slipped through his fingers. He'd lost a part of his youth, his innocence, and he'd never look at the world the same way again. He wanted to believe that Siobhan was happy, living with a husband and family in some peaceful spot in Ireland. He'd tried to find her after his release, but she'd disappeared, gone from Dublin shortly after her last letter had arrived.

Tears burned at his eyes and Jack fought to maintain control, tipping his head back and drawing a shaky breath. Could he finally find peace now that he'd come home? He'd never once given in to regret in prison, but now that he was out, he suddenly felt more vulnerable.

"Everything will be all right," Molly murmured, reaching up to touch his cheek and wipe away an errant tear. "I promise."

Jack looked away, his attention on the far horizon, where the water met the sky. "Do you believe you could love me again?" he asked.

"I never stopped loving you," she said. "Not for a

single minute of a single day. I knew you'd come back to me and I was prepared to wait forever."

She stepped into his embrace, wrapping her arms around his waist.

"I'm not the person I was when I left Ballykirk. I've done things that I'm ashamed of, things I can't ever change or take back."

"Nor am I the person you left behind. We're stronger and wiser and a wee bit older. But we're both still here and we can begin again."

He had a chance to make one thing right again, to fix a mistake that he'd regretted for years, to do the honorable thing. He owed Molly the same loyalty that she'd given him. "Then we will. And I promise that I will never leave you again, Molly."

"Come," she said, taking his hand. "Your mam is wanting to see you. She has the whole family gathered to welcome you home. And I'm certain the boys at the Speckled Hound will be wanting to share a pint or two with their local hero."

"Can we just stay here a bit longer?" Jack asked. "I'm sure the lamb stew will hold."

She drew him along toward Oisin's Rock. "We can stay as long as you like. I've nowhere better to be."

THE BIG MANOR HOUSE on the Skibbereen road had been closed for nearly three years, the servants gone, the furniture draped with linen sheets. Aidan stepped through the front door, and all at once he felt like the same scared and confused boy he'd been on the day he'd left nearly eleven years ago.

Eamon had died at Christmas in 1924 and been buried in the churchyard beneath a huge monument erected by Aidan's mother. Louisa had stayed in Ballykirk for only a week after her husband's death. Then she'd closed the house and left for Europe, determined to live the life she'd always craved.

Half of Eamon's estate had come to Aidan, including the house and the surgery in town. He'd immediately decided to stay in Dublin. But as time had passed, Aidan had grown more and more disenchanted with his life there. He was tired of leading a double life.

He'd married Maura Sullivan five years ago, just months after Jack had been arrested and thrown in prison. The guilt over what he'd done had begun to poison his life. He'd decided he could have a normal life if he just set his mind to it.

Even on the day of his wedding, he'd known his attraction to pretty men would never really go away. But that didn't mean he couldn't push those desires aside for a time. So he'd married Maura and he'd done his duty as a husband on their wedding night, giving her a healthy son to dote upon. And occasionally, he'd slip away for an evening and seek out old friends, disappearing into a shadow of secrets for just a short time.

"It's l-lovely," Maura murmured, holding on to

Donal's hand, the boy's eyes wide with curiosity. "Larger than I ex-ex—" she paused, smiling apologetically "—expected."

"I think you should take my mother's room," he said. "The nursery is close by and the morning light is better. Of course, you can decorate as you wish. Whatever you need. I'll provide a household allowance."

She stared at him for a long moment, then nodded meekly. They hadn't shared a bed since Donal was conceived, and Aidan had been grateful for the privacy. When the time was right, he'd visit Maura's bed again and they'd have another child. But for now, she had enough with Donal to keep her occupied.

"You'll have to hire a cook and a lady's maid," he continued.

"I thought I would cook."

Aidan shook his head. "No. A special meal now and again would be fine. But we must maintain a certain standing in society and that includes the convenience of servants. I'm sure you'll appreciate the extra time you'll have with Donal."

Again she nodded in agreement, hiding any disappointment she might have felt. Aidan leaned forward and gave her a chaste kiss on the forehead. "I do have something for you. Something to mark the beginning of our new life here in Ballykirk." He reached into his jacket pocket and pulled out a fine leather case. "Eamon had this made for my mother on their wedding day. She never wore it. It was…too Irish for her and she didn't understand the sentiment. He left it to me, to pass along to my wife."

"Me?" Maura said.

"You are my wife," Aidan replied dryly. "Go ahead. Look at it."

He scooped Donal up into his arms and they both watched as she tipped back the cover. Her eyes went wide and she gasped softly. "It's—it's—"

"Lovely," he finished, using one of her favorite words. "It's a claddagh."

"I know," Maura murmured. "The hands are for fr-friendship and the cr-crown is for loyalty. And—and the heart is for—for—"

"For love," Aidan said.

"Do you love me?" she asked.

"What a silly question," Aidan replied. He set his son down and gently steered him toward the stairs. "Why don't you two look around upstairs?"

Maura nodded, then started up the stairs, murmuring to Donal along the way. She never seemed to stutter when she spoke to the child. Perhaps it was because the little boy adored his mother.

Aidan wandered into Eamon's study and sat down at the desk, leaning back in the comfortable leather chair. He'd managed to avoid thinking about one thing as they'd driven back to Ballykirk, but now there was no getting away from it. "Jack Quinn," Aidan murmured.

Jack had served four years of his seven-year sentence. He'd returned to Ballykirk the year before and Aidan would now be forced to face him. Maura had provided a simple solution to Aidan's biggest problem. Any possible rumors about sexual perversions would be immediately discredited by the presence of his loyal wife and handsome son.

But there was still the matter of his betrayal. He wasn't sure how much Jack knew about that night. Had the authorities mentioned Aidan's complicity in his arrest? Or was Jack under the impression he'd been discovered in Aidan's room by chance?

Aidan had even been given a letter of commendation by the government for his part in the capture of an entire network of IRA gunrunners. In some quarters, he might be considered a hero. But Ballykirk had room for just one hero—Jack Quinn.

In truth, Aidan had hoped Jack would never return to Ballykirk. He couldn't regret what he'd done to Jack. He'd done what was needed to protect his own interests, his future. And he'd do whatever it took to protect what was his now—his home, his medical practice and his wife and child.

CHAPTER TEN

THEIR COTTAGE WAS tiny, just two rooms. But Molly kept a tidy house, sewing curtains for the windows and weaving rag rugs for the rough plank floors. They'd married three months after his release from Mountjoy and since then, Jack had tried to rebuild his life.

He and Niall worked together on the *Mighty Quinn,* providing a small income for their parents as they gradually bought out Paddy's interest in the boat. Thomas had saved enough to buy his own boat and they often fished together, Grace's husband, Mick, rounding out the crew on the second boat.

They spent hours at the Speckled Hound, talking about building a fleet of boats—larger, more powerful boats designed to travel farther out to sea. He'd make a comfortable life for his family, and someday Jack's sons would work the boat with him.

He smiled to himself. Molly had found herself with child six months after their wedding. The pregnancy had started out difficult for her, sapping her of her usual energy and often keeping her in bed for most of the day. But the past few weeks, she'd regained her strength and had begun to busy herself with daily tasks around the cottage.

Jack shifted the bucket in his hand, glancing down at the fish he'd brought home for dinner. As he approached the cottage, he expected to find Molly in the garden, enjoying the warmth of the late-autumn sun and awaiting his return. But instead, he found the front door wide open, a basket of laundry spilled on the stone step.

"Molly?" Jack poked his head inside. "Molly, are you here?"

"Jack?" Her voice, thin and weak, came from the bedroom and Jack rushed inside to discover her curled on the bed, her arms wrapped around her stomach.

"What is it?" he asked, bending down to look into her eyes. "What's wrong?"

"Nothing," she murmured. "I—I took a walk and I started to have some pain. It's better now. I just needed to lie down and rest."

"It's too early for the baby, isn't it?" Jack asked.

"It's probably just something I ate." She reached out and took his hand. "I'm frightened."

"I'll go for the doctor," Jack said. He hadn't spoken to Aidan McClain in years, not since the night he'd been arrested. He'd had his suspicions about his friend's actions that night. No one had known he was in the boardinghouse except Aidan and no one had more to lose if the truth of Aidan's life came to light.

He wasn't sure whether Aidan had been forced to

reveal his location or whether he'd gone to the authorities willingly or whether Aidan was innocent of any complicity. It didn't matter. Jack had paid for his actions and now had put his past behind him. Aidan was part of that past.

"No," Molly said. "I don't need the doctor. Go for Grace. She'll know what to do. She's had three babies of her own."

"You'll be all right here? It will only take me a few minutes. Just stay still." Jack backed out of the room, then hurried outside.

He ran as fast as he could, the breath burning in his lungs. He found Grace and her husband in the middle of their supper, their three young children playing on the floor at their feet. "You have to come," he said, gasping for air. "It's the baby."

Grace quickly stood, wiping her hands on her apron, concern etched across her expression. "She still has two more months," she said, turning to her husband. "You'll drive me to the cottage, then go with Jack to fetch the doctor."

"She doesn't want the doctor," Jack insisted.

"Well, she'll have him if I have anything to say about it."

Grace quickly gathered the children and hurried them out to the car, climbing into the rear seat with them. A few minutes later, they were racing back down the road toward the small, whitewashed cottage. When they stopped in front, Grace hopped out, then grabbed the children and swung them down before they all disappeared inside.

"I should check on Molly," Jack said, pushing open the door. "Would you get the doctor?"

Mick nodded, then put the car into gear and started off down the road. Jack entered the house, his heart twisting with every step. He'd just assumed he and Molly would have the family they'd hoped for. Women gave birth every day without complications.

Grace was just coming out of the bedroom and went straight to the hearth. "I need more turf," she ordered. "And you'll need to put the kettle on and heat some water."

"What's happening with Molly?" Jack asked.

"She's bleeding," Grace said, glancing up at him. The look in her eyes told him everything. "And she's weak. I'm afraid the baby might be coming. It's far too early for her to give birth, but I don't think I can stop it."

Jack stood in the middle of the room, unable to move. The room seemed to spin around him, the laughter of Grace's children grating in his ears. Why was this happening? After all the years apart, he and Molly deserved some happiness. Losing the baby would destroy her. "You have to do something," he said. "You have to help her."

"There's nothing to be done," Grace replied, "except wait."

"Aidan will help her." Jack walked to the door,

searching the road for Mick's car. "He'll know what to do. He worked at a big hospital in Dub—" A shrill cry of pain stopped the words in his throat.

"Go to your wife," Grace said. "Keep her calm. I'll watch for the doctor."

Jack strode to the bedroom, but he took a moment to gather his courage before he stepped inside. He'd done many things in his life that had been considered dangerous, but he'd never been truly frightened until now. Molly was his life, his future. She'd loved him despite everything he'd done to her and now he had to find the words to reassure her.

He walked to the bed and sat down beside her, taking her hand in his. "Mick has gone for the doctor."

"I'm going to lose the baby," Molly said, her eyes filled with tears.

"No." Jack smoothed her hair back from her face. "You mustn't think that way. Aidan will know what to do."

"But what if he doesn't?" Molly asked, her face contorting in pain. A low moan slipped from her throat and her fingers squeezed his.

"God is watching over our baby," Jack said. He leaned over and kissed her cheek. "You'll be fine, Molly girl."

He sat with her a long time, talking her through the pain, knowing that she was weakening and nothing he did could stop it. He wanted to gather her in his arms and give her his strength, but he was afraid to touch her.

Finally, after nearly an hour, Aidan walked into the room. They stared at each other for a long moment, the years rushing back along with the questions and the accusations and the anger. "Help my wife," Jack said.

"Leave us," Aidan ordered. "And send Grace back in."

"You have to help her," Jack insisted.

"I'll do my best."

Jack left, motioning Grace to return to Molly's bedside. The sun had already set and he walked through the front door into the garden, drawing a deep breath of the crisp evening air.

He hadn't prayed since before he'd left Ballykirk for Dublin, well aware of his sins and knowing they'd never be forgiven. But he was desperate. He dropped to his knees and clasped his hands together, turning his face up to the sky. "Hail, Mary, full of grace," he began. The words came uninterrupted, one prayer after the next, a rosary interrupted only by private pleas of his own.

Somehow, he sensed that God was seeking retribution, that Jack's sins had somehow come back on Molly and the baby. What price would she have to pay for the things he'd done? Anger bubbled up inside of him and he cursed himself and his decision to leave her.

"Take me if you will," he murmured. "But don't take the baby. And don't take Molly. They don't deserve this."

AIDAN STARED down at Molly Quinn's face, her eyes closed, her features finally at peace. Grace tugged at the bloody bed linens. Her eyes were red from weeping and her voice clogged with tears. "Will you tell him, then, or must I?"

Aidan swallowed the lump of emotion in his throat, staring out at the sunrise that had just begun to paint the sky with pink. "I'll do it," he murmured, turning away from the bed.

He slowly packed his supplies, tucking them into his black leather grip, grateful for the time to gather his thoughts.

Outside, he found Jack sitting on the front stoop, staring out into the garden, his face haggard. He glanced up at Aidan, then quickly tossed aside the cigarette he'd been smoking and stood. But the moment he caught Aidan's eye, he froze, his expression turning to stone.

"I'm sorry," Aidan murmured, meeting his gaze directly. "There was nothing I could do. The child was stillborn and she had lost so much blood by then. Had this happened at hospital, the outcome probably wouldn't have been any different, but..." He let his words trail off, knowing that nothing would comfort Jack now. "She went peacefully, as if she just fell asleep."

"Stop," Jack warned, holding out his hand. "I won't hear this. You won't say this aloud."

Aidan shifted uneasily, tears clouding his eyes. He

wanted to reach out and touch him, to offer him comfort, but knew it wouldn't be welcome. "I'm so sorry. I did everything I could, but—" He drew a deep breath. "Molly is dead, Jack."

Jack gulped in a breath, then another, as if he had to remember to fill his lungs. He stared at Aidan for a long moment. And then he turned away, a sob tearing from his throat. He sank down in the middle of the garden and covered his head with his arms, rocking back and forth on his heels, wailing his anguish into the dawn. Aidan slowly approached and bent down next to him. "She's in a better place."

Jack's head snapped up and his eyes were wild with grief. "Don't you say that. You've lived your life in sin. This is punishment for what you are. I should never have let you touch her. She was pure and beautiful and you are dark and ugly."

"I tried," Aidan said, straightening and stepping back, Jack's words slicing into him like a dagger. "Sometimes these things just happen. It's no one's fault."

Jack leaped to his feet and grabbed Aidan's jacket, shaking him hard, his body tensed with rage. "Get the hell out of here. I never want to see your face again, you worthless piece of shite. This is retribution for *your* sins. I gave four years of my life so you could keep your secrets and now you'll pay for my loss."

For a long moment, Aidan was sure that Jack would simply snap his neck and have it done. Maybe it was a fair trade, Aidan's worthless existence in return for the woman Jack had loved.

But suddenly, Jack let go of Aidan and Aidan stumbled back. He stared at Jack for a long time, taking in the loathing that filled his expression. They'd once been such good friends and now Jack despised him. Aidan turned and walked to his car.

Had it been an earlier time in their life, Aidan would have tried to talk it out with Jack. But too much had passed between them for any memory of their friendship to survive. It had died that night at the boardinghouse.

Aidan wanted to shout or weep or curse the Fates that had made them the men they were, that had set them down this path. But every emotion inside him had been hardened so long ago. He walked to his motorcar, parked at the edge of the road.

As he pulled away from the cottage, he felt numb with grief. Grief for the friendship he'd lost and grief for the man he'd become. His life had been empty for a long time and he'd been existing, waiting for some semblance of love to touch him again.

Now it never would. In the morning, the gossip would begin and by the end of the day everyone in Ballykirk would believe Jack's claims. Because Jack was a hero and Aidan was the bastard son of an Englishwoman.

He stepped hard on the accelerator, the early-morning air rushing past his ears and blocking out the noise in his head. Nothing he could say would ever quell their doubts about him for the story was too salacious not to be discussed again and again. His wife and child would be a curious footnote to the tale, overshadowed by the sensationalism of Jack's claims.

As he rounded the wide curve on the Skibbereen road, the first rays of sun illuminated the low stone walls on either side of the road. He knew the next turn was coming up fast, but instead of touching the brake, Aidan pressed the accelerator to the floor and then shifted into a higher gear.

Ahead, the ruins of an old stone church loomed in the shadows of the trees, the roof gone, the windows like black eyes staring out at him. God's eyes, he thought to himself as he shifted up again.

He hit the wall at fifty miles an hour and the car became airborne for a moment before it flipped over, crushing his body beneath it. It came to a stop against the wall of the church, the engine steaming and the wheels still spinning. Aidan lay on the ground, half in and half out of the wreck, staring up at the last stars of the night as his life slowly seeped out of him.

Suicide was a mortal sin, he thought to himself, his body growing colder with each painful breath. But then, he'd never really believed in mortal sin. In truth, he wasn't sure that there was a heaven or even a God. For what God could have made his life such torture?

He drew another breath, wondering if it would be his last. As the darkness enveloped him, Aidan asked forgiveness for his sins. Would there be a place for him in heaven or would he burn in the fires of hell? Or would he be left to search eternally for a place where he belonged?

CHAPTER ELEVEN

JACK STARED down at the freshly carved gravestone, an ornate Celtic cross. It had been seven months since Molly's funeral and he hadn't been able to bring himself to visit her grave. Instead, for a long while he'd wallowed in his grief, losing himself in bottle after bottle of whiskey, his profits from the boat disappearing the moment the money hit his pocket.

His family had tried to help, bringing meals, tidying the cottage, providing a constant stream of platitudes. But he'd hardened himself to any show of sympathy. Molly was dead and it was his fault. He'd been so anxious for a child, for a new beginning, that he'd never even considered the risks. Women died all the time in childbirth, but he'd been determined to make the perfect life for himself after four years in prison.

Now he had nothing, no future, no reason to live. He reached out and ran his fingers over her name, then set the tiny bouquet of wildflowers at the base of the stone. "I'm sorry," he murmured. "I promised to watch over you and I failed you, Molly girl. Your father was right. You deserved better."

He slowly backed away from the grave, emotions he'd thought had faded suddenly welling up inside of him again. As he hurried out of the graveyard, he glanced to his left, his eyes coming to rest on a monument marked with the McClain name. Another new gravestone stood in the plot, carved with Aidan's name and date of death.

The authorities had pronounced the wreck an accident, but Jack suspected differently. Aidan knew every curve and bump in the Skibbereen road. They'd walked it hundreds of times as schoolboys. He'd never have missed the curve at the old church, no matter how fast he was driving.

Jack slowly approached the plot. Aidan had been buried next to Eamon. The house on Skibbereen road was still occupied by Aidan's wife and their son. Louisa had heard of her son's death several weeks afterward, Father Timothy finally locating her in the south of France.

No one had ever learned of Aidan's secret life and Jack hadn't intended to reveal what he now knew. In his grief, he'd leveled a threat, words that had left Aidan with only one way out.

Jack bent down and picked up a wilted bouquet at the base of the stone. "I'm sorry. You broke a promise to me years ago and I couldn't forgive you. And now, it's too late to ask for your forgiveness." He traced his fingers over Aidan's name. "I've made a lot of mistakes in my life and I haven't lived it half through yet. But I'm going to try to be a better man. And I'll find a way to take care of your wife and son. I owe you that much."

He straightened, then tipped his head back and closed his eyes. He remembered that day when he and Aidan had stood on the hill above the sea and talked about what they might do with their lives. Aidan had never become a soldier and Jack's life with Molly had been cut short. Life had dipped and risen and twisted and turned, like the flight of a seabird blown by the wind. He'd almost drowned in dark water, as Aidan had, but slowly Jack had pulled himself back to the surface.

He'd stopped with the whiskey, letting his head clear until he could finally face the memories. At first, he'd craved the stupor, the numb emptiness that a good drunk gave him. But every day that had passed without a drink was a small victory and the pain grew less and less until now it was just a dull ache surrounding his heart.

Jack picked up his pace until he was running, the blood pumping through his veins, purging the poison from his soul. As he approached the cottage, he noticed a motorcar parked on the road. A priest, dressed in long black robes, stood at the front gate. A knot of tension twisted in his gut and he prepared himself for bad news. But if it had to do with his family, Father Timothy would have come, not some stranger.

"Hello," he said.

The priest smiled. "Hello. I'm looking for Jack Quinn."

"I'm Jack Quinn," he said.

"Then you're the man I've come for," the priest said. "I'm Father James. James Burnett. I'm Siobhan Burnett's brother."

Jack frowned. "Siobhan? I haven't seen her in years. Over six years. Is she all right?"

"She's well," Father James assured him. "I've come here at her request."

"You've seen her? You know where she is, then?"

He nodded.

"How did you know where to find me?"

"She told me."

"If she knew I was here, why didn't she come herself?" Jack asked.

"She wasn't sure you'd want to see her. Siobhan knows of your wife's death and the baby you lost. She didn't feel it was right to contact you until you'd had an appropriate time to grieve." He paused. "And there's a rather delicate matter she wanted me to discuss with you. A few months after you parted ways, she came to me. I have a parish in Wexford." He studied Jack for a moment, then said, "She was with child. She gave birth to a son—your son. His name is Rory, after our youngest brother who died of scarlet fever years ago."

Jack stared at the priest, unable to comprehend what he was hearing. "I—I have a son?"

Father James waved in the direction of the car and the passenger-side door opened. A young boy stepped out and slowly approached. Jack held his breath as he watched the boy move. His hair, his eyes, every feature proved that he was a Quinn.

"Come, Rory," Father James urged. "You understand why we're here, boy. Come and tell your father hello."

The little boy stood in front of Jack, his face turned up to him. "Hello," he said, holding out his hand. "Is this where you live?"

"I do," Jack said, gathering his wits and squatting in front of him. "Would you like to come inside?"

"Do you have any cakes? My mam lets me have cake in the afternoon."

Jack chuckled softly. "No, I don't. But we might walk into town and see if we can find some for you. Would you like that?"

The little boy nodded, then grabbed Jack's hand and tugged him along to the road. Father James walked alongside them then stopped just outside the gate. "Siobhan has raised him on her own," he said. "She felt it was time he knew his father. She thought, if you were agreeable, you might like to take him for a visit from time to time."

"Where is she? I'd like to see her," Jack said. "Has she come with you?"

The priest nodded toward the car. Jack turned and noticed the figure of a woman sitting in the rear seat. It had been so long, he wondered how she might have changed. She was no longer the fiery young woman he'd met on the beach that night, or the determined soldier with whom he'd shared an afternoon of passion. She was the mother of his child. And suddenly, Jack felt as if he'd been handed a second chance.

Without thinking, he slowly approached the car and opened the door, holding out his hand. A moment later, he felt her fingers come to rest in his palm and he helped Siobhan Burnett out of the car.

She looked up at him and Jack felt the years melt away. She hadn't changed at all, her face still as beautiful as it had been the very first time he'd seen her, her eyes still deep and expressive. "He's a handsome boy," he murmured.

"He looks like his father," she replied.

"He fancies some cakes. Would you walk into town with us?"

Siobhan nodded. He took her hand and tucked it into the crook of his arm as he had so many times in the past. As they strolled toward Ballykirk, Jack watched his son scampering ahead of them in the dusty road and wondered at the sudden turn in his fortunes.

He didn't deserve such happiness again. But with every step he took, he walked toward his future, toward another chance at the life he'd dreamed of living. This time, he wouldn't let it slip away. This time he'd hold tight to his dreams and he'd keep all his promises.

PART TWO
DONAL'S PROMISE

CHAPTER TWELVE

Galway, October, 1941

THE SPRAWLING VICTORIAN hotel was set on Eyre Square in the busy heart of Galway. Rory Quinn stared up at the facade, anticipating the evening ahead. He hadn't seen Kit Malone or Donal McClain in nearly a year. Though they'd written to him, letters could never take the place of time spent together.

After too many weeks apart, they'd finally agreed to meet in Galway, Rory securing a weekend pass from his air station at Rineanna in County Clare. It would be a grand celebration of Kit's birthday and a fitting send-off for the journey Rory was about to begin.

Since war had been declared between Britain and Germany two years before, the Irish Air Corps had stepped up recruitment and training, anxious to provide a defense for Eire if needed. Southern Ireland remained neutral in the conflict, while the north, still under British control, had been forced into the fight. Rory had joined the Irish Air Corps in 1940 along with thirty-one other cadets, anxious to experience the adventure that flying provided and anticipating that Southern Ireland might one day get into the war.

But instead of dogfights over the Irish Channel, the Irish Air Corps pilots had been relegated to shooting down errant barrage balloons and tracking belligerent aircraft—German or British fliers who were forced to land on neutral Irish soil. Rory's Ireland was at war with no one.

It hadn't been what he'd signed on for, but where else could he spend every day behind the controls of a plane, soaring in and out of the clouds, then dipping low over the water like a great seabird? He drew a deep breath. There was one other place for a trained pilot, though far more dangerous than Rineanna.

"Rory!"

He turned and caught sight of Kit on the other side of the street. She waved and he ran across, causing a taxicab to come to a screeching stop. When he reached her, she threw her arms around his neck and hugged him fiercely, then kissed him full on the mouth.

"Oh, you're here!" she cried. Stepping back, Kit stared up into his eyes, her face filled with unrestrained delight.

"Happy birthday Miss Malone," he said.

"Look at yourself," she said. "Don't you look grand in that uniform."

Rory laughed and hugged her tight. He still saw so much of the young girl that he and Donal had met years before, the mischievous twinkle in her eye and the unfettered laugh, her lack of concern for propriety.

Rory noticed the looks Kit drew from the passersby on the street. It wasn't just her breathtaking beauty or the way she wore her emotions on her sleeve. She didn't behave like a proper young lady of eighteen. But Rory didn't care.

Kit was a modern woman, a college student now. And she felt no need to heed societal boundaries, especially when it came to showing her affection for her two best friends. She poked at the extra set of stripes on his sleeve. "And what is this?"

"I've been promoted," Rory said, taking in the details of her face, her long lashes and sparkling blue eyes. Her dark hair fell in waves over her shoulders and he brushed it back, enjoying the feel of it between his fingers. "I'm Lieutenant Quinn now. I won't expect a salute, but I will ask that you call me sir."

"Sir? You'll always be just Rory to me," she teased, snapping off a salute. Kit slipped her arm around his waist and drew him toward the front entrance to the hotel. "Come. We're both a bit late. I'm sure Donal has been here an hour already and you know how impatient he is if he's forced to drink alone. He's expecting a big piss-up for the two of you and I'm sure you won't disappoint." She sighed, then threw out her arms and spun around in front of him. "But I've come to dance. You'll dance with me, won't you, Rory?"

The hotel was the largest in Galway and known for the Friday-evening dances held in the ballroom throughout the summer. Even now, Rory could hear the strains of the big-band music drifting out onto the street, American tunes from Glenn Miller and Tommy Dorsey.

They found Donal seated at a table for four near the edge of the dance floor, dressed in a tidy suit and tie, his red hair slicked back. Kit greeted him with the same unbridled glee that she'd given Rory and Rory shook his best friend's hand.

They fell back into the easy camaraderie they'd always shared. Rory and Donal had grown up together, Rory's father looking after Donal's widowed mother, Maura, and taking care of small tasks around the house on the Skibbereen road. Kit had made them a trio when she'd come to live with her uncle in Ballykirk at age nine and since then they'd been almost inseparable.

Kit grabbed their hands and sat down, excitedly telling them about the train trip from Dublin and the mysterious man she'd met who looked like a German spy. Rory watched her silently, taking in the sound of her voice, the gentle lilt of her words.

He'd always cared for her, but from the day he and Donal had met her, there had been an unspoken pact between the two of them. They'd both known Kit was meant to be shared between them; otherwise, they'd diminish the friendship between them all. But they were all adults now and in the past few years Rory had realized his feelings for Kit had changed.

Kit had written him a letter a week since he'd been gone and he'd grown to crave her words, to lose himself in the sentiments she expressed with such clarity and beauty. Since she'd begun her studies at Trinity, she'd sent him some of her poems, one that was to be published in the college literary journal.

He looked forward to her letters, saving them to read before bed, closing his eyes and imagining her voice speaking to him. Through those letters and poems, he'd fallen in love with one of his best friends, and now that he'd seen her again, Rory knew he didn't want to live the rest of his life without her.

"Who will ask me to dance?" Kit asked, tossing her wrap over the back of her chair. "I've spent my month's allowance on this frock and I want to show it off."

Donal groaned. "Give us a bit of break, Kit. We just got—"

"Dance with me," Rory interrupted. He stood and held out his hand. Kit giggled, then walked with him toward the crowd, the dancers swaying to the strains of "I'll Never Smile Again."

He wrapped his arm around her waist, spreading his fingers over the bare skin at the small of her back. She wore a pale lavender dress that shimmered under the light, cut wide across her shoulders, the back dipping nearly to her waist. As her body brushed against his, he couldn't stop thinking about how perfectly she fit into his arms.

There had been plenty of young ladies anxious to make the acquaintance of a pilot, more impressed with the uniform than the skills it took to put an airplane into the air. But in the past months, he'd lived a monkish life, rereading Kit's letters and struggling to put his own thoughts on paper. "You look lovely tonight," he murmured, his breath warm against her hair. "All grown up."

"Thank you," Kit said. She drew back and stared up at him, a tiny frown furrowing her brow. "And you seem different."

"How is that?"

"You look so…competent. You're not the boy I grew up with. You're a man now. And I'm not sure I know you at all any longer."

"You do," Rory said. He drew her hand to his lips and kissed the back of her wrist. "You do. You're the only one who ever has, don't you know?"

He could tell she was confused by his uncharacteristic candor. He wanted to tell her how his feelings had changed, but his thoughts were interrupted by a tap on his shoulder.

"May I cut in?" the young man asked.

Reluctantly, Rory relinquished Kit to her new partner, then walked back to the table.

Donal cocked his head toward the pair. "That didn't last long."

Shrugging, Rory picked up his Guinness and took a long sip. "She's the most beautiful creature I've ever seen." He paused. "Why has it taken me so long to notice that?"

"Because you're dense as bottled shite," Donal said. "I noticed ages ago." He gulped down the rest of his Guinness and motioned for a waiter to bring him another. "But then, she's never had eyes for either one of us, has she?"

Rory sat down and stretched his legs out in front of him. "There are times when I look at her and see that girl with the scabby knees and the tangled hair. When did she grow up?"

Donal chuckled. "I believe all that education makes her more beautiful, if that's possible. She has opinions now and isn't afraid to speak them. Don't even get her started on The Emergency. Christ, she'll talk your feckin' ear off."

"It's a war," Rory corrected, "not an emergency. And thousands of Irishmen are over in France and Africa fighting, while we're here dancing."

"You won't find me gettin' my head blown off," Donal said. "Like Eire, I've decided to remain benevolently neutral."

"We'd be in this war if de Valera had accepted the British offer," Rory muttered.

"And a fine offer it was. We'd get Northern Ireland in exchange for giving them an endless supply of young Irishmen to throw in front of the German guns.

Doesn't sound like a fair deal to me," Donal replied. "I prefer neutrality to conscription."

Rory kept his eyes on Kit. "And I don't," he murmured. "I'm going, you know."

Donal glanced over at him. "You just got here. I'll agree to stop discussing politics if you will. Then we can all have a fine time."

"No. I meant I'm getting myself into this war."

Donal laughed. "You can't. You belong to the Irish Air Corps and, last I looked, they weren't shooting down Messerschmitts. They were escorting them to a lovely landing on our fair shores." He paused, taking in Rory's serious expression, then gasped softly, shaking his head. "You're going to desert, aren't you?"

"Everyone else is. Thousands of men from Eire have already gone north to enlist and many of them have just walked away from the Defence Corps. I know the RAF needs pilots. Since the Blitz started in April, they're getting shot out of the sky every day."

"And you want to get shot out of the sky with them?" Donal sat up straight, shoving his Guinness away from him and cursing softly. "What if they toss you in an infantry division? You'll be slogging through mud up to your knees and living off canned rations while the Jerries hurl grenades at you. You'll be dead within a month."

"I'm qualified to fly Hurricanes. They'd be fools not to send me to the RAF. Christ, I can fly anything they put in front of me."

"Why would you risk your life for the Brits?"

"It's more than just their war. Nine hundred people were killed in the bombings at Derry and Belfast. Nine hundred Irish men and women. Before long, the whole world will be in it, the Americans included. And do you think Hitler is going to stop with France and Britain? We're a tiny little country with barely an army to speak of. He'd make easy work of us and we'd all be saluting the Nazi flag."

A long silence grew between them, Donal turning back to his drink and Rory watching the dance floor. Another man, this one wearing a British uniform with the insignia of the Royal Artillery, now danced with Kit. She was speaking to him, a serious expression on her face, and Rory knew she was questioning him about the war.

He'd never known a woman to be more interested in world events than Kit was. Though she had her own opinions, she also had the ability to listen to both sides of an issue. She'd understand why he had to go and she'd never think to question his decision. Still, he had no intention of telling her.

"I'm leaving in the morning," Rory said.

"And you won't be changing your mind?"

He shook his head. "No. I need to do this." Rory turned back to Donal. "And I need you to do something for me in turn."

"Anything," Donal muttered. "As long as it doesn't involve bullets."

"I'm in love with her," Rory said, nodding in Kit's direction. "I know we've managed to keep romance from getting between us as friends, but I had to tell you. And I hope you'll understand." He chuckled. "One of us has to marry her, Donal, or she'll go off and marry some silly git neither of us can tolerate."

Donal shifted in his chair as he tugged at his collar. "H-how does she feel about you?" he asked, his expression uneasy.

Rory shrugged. "I haven't asked. As far as she knows, nothing has changed between us." He raked his hands through his hair. "I can't expect her to spend her days and nights worrying about me, waiting for me to come back. I just know that when I do, I'm going to marry her."

"She'll worry in any case," Donal said. "I can't stop her, that."

"But you can watch over her. When she's back in Ballykirk, keep her busy. And try not to let her fall in love with anyone else while I'm gone. I've written a letter that I'll leave with you. If she ever once says she's in love with me, give it to her straightaway. Promise me you'll do that."

"She's goin' to be cheesed off at you once she knows what you're about," Donal warned.

"I'll write to her when I get to England and explain. She knows how I feel about the war—she'll understand." He drew a deep breath. "And one other thing. If anything happens to me, I want you to destroy the letter. Burn it. I don't want her living with any regrets." He reached into his jacket pocket and withdrew the envelope, entrusting it to his best friend. "She'll never need to know how I really felt."

Donal nodded, staring at the envelope for a long moment. Then he tucked it into his jacket pocket. "You should tell her, Rory, so she can say a proper goodbye."

He pushed to his feet. "I don't want to think about the war right now. I'm going to go cut in on that soldier she's dancing with and I'm not letting anyone else take her away from me tonight—except you, of course." He strode out onto the floor, leaving Donal to his drink. Rory quickly dispatched Kit's partner, sweeping her into his arms and easily moving along with the band's rendition of "I'll Never Smile Again."

"There," he murmured in her ear. "That's better. I didn't come all this way to watch you dance with someone else."

"Are you jealous?" she teased, giving him a coy smile.

"Madly jealous." Rory twirled her around, then pulled her back into his embrace. "Now, where were we?"

"I believe you were telling me how fine I looked."

"No," he said, putting on a pensive expression. "I believe I was about to tell you how every man in this room would cut off his right arm for a chance to kiss you."

"And what about you?" she asked, tipping her face up to his. "What would you give to kiss me?"

"I wouldn't give an old penny," Rory said.

Kit stuck out her lower lip in a pout. "And why is that?"

"Because, I'd wait until you asked me. Do you want me to kiss you then, Kit? All you need do is ask and it'll be done."

"Yes," she said. "I do think I'd fancy a birthday kiss from you, Rory Quinn. But mind yourself. Don't be taking advantage of the offer."

Rory felt his heart quicken. He'd kissed his fair share of women, but it had never meant much to him. This moment meant everything. He wanted her to know exactly how he felt without having to fumble over his words. In truth, he wanted to experience a tearful goodbye and a promise of love before he left. He bent closer and then touched his lips to hers.

The music and the movement of the other dancers seemed to fade into the background, and for a long time Rory felt as if he and Kit were the only two people in the world. Her lips were sweet and he risked a deeper taste, his tongue tempting her to open for him. When she did, he knew that everything he'd felt for her had been true. Kit was the only woman for him.

When she finally pulled back, he was satisfied she'd wait for him. Though the words still lay unspoken between them, the kiss had sealed their fate. Rory pulled her closer, gliding with her across the dance floor, his face buried in her fragrant hair.

He glanced over at Donal and found his friend staring out at them, a pained look on his face. Rory nodded in his direction and Donal smiled wanly, then motioned to a waiter for another drink.

For the rest of evening, Kit danced only with him. In between dances, they kept Donal company as he switched from Guinness to whiskey and back again. But nothing could dampen Rory's good time. This would be his last night of freedom, his last night with the woman he loved, and he wasn't about to waste a moment of it.

DONAL STUMBLED slightly as they walked out to the street. His head was throbbing but the whiskey had done nothing to dull the ache in his gut. Christ, this was supposed to be a grand evening, but it had turned into the worst night of his life.

"Steady on there," Rory said, grabbing him by the arm.

Donal yanked away. He'd spent the night watching the woman he loved in the arms of another man, the arms of his best friend. Right now, Donal felt like punching Rory Quinn in the face, pummeling him with his fists until he was black-and-blue. Donal loved Kit and he had since he was sixteen. He'd been first to fall for her and, by rights, she was supposed to be his, not Rory's.

"Why call an end to the night?" Kit said. "The band has stopped playing, but surely we can find another spot."

Rory chuckled. "Donal needs some fresh air and a brisk walk and I have to be back at my station in the morning."

"Right. He has to get on back to the air station," Donal said, his words slurred. "The lad has responsibilities. Well, run along with you, then, Rory." He ought to tell Kit right now about Rory's plans. She wouldn't be staring up at him with that starry-eyed gaze if she knew the truth.

Rory ignored his friend, and firmly focused on Kit. "So this will have to be goodbye, Miss Malone."

Kit threw her arms around his neck and hugged him tight. "I don't want you to go," she whispered. "This has been the most perfect evening."

Donal watched through bleary eyes as Rory gently touched Kit's face. He felt his stomach roil and, for a moment, he thought he might vomit. But he swallowed it back, then cleared his throat. "If—if you'll excuse me, I'll just leave you two alone for a bit."

He stumbled down the street to the corner, then stepped out of sight behind a low stone wall. Leaning back, he slid down to sit on the cool cobblestones. His head spun and he drew in a deep breath and moaned softly. He hadn't been this bollixed in weeks.

He'd always enjoyed a bit of the drink, but lately he seemed to spend more and more time either pissed or hungover. Reaching into his jacket, he found his cigarettes and lit one. The sweet smoke filled his lungs, clearing his head. Donal pushed to his feet and walked back toward the hotel.

He saw Rory and Kit standing under a streetlamp, their arms wrapped around each other, and he stopped cold. Christ, he could barely stand to look at them together. He'd always existed in Rory Quinn's shadow even though Donal had all the advantages over him—wealth, intelligence, good breeding. Still, people were naturally drawn to Rory. He was fearless and unpredictable, a man bent on living his life as if it were a series of great adventures. Next to him, Donal would seem as dull as an old butter knife.

When they were younger, Donal had been happy to exist in his orbit, proud that a boy like Rory had chosen him as a friend. Back then, Kit had treated them as equals, finding something to love in both of them. But as they'd gotten older, he'd watched Kit become more and more fascinated by Rory.

Though Donal could offer her a fine life, she couldn't see past Rory's clever charm. He leaned back against the wall again and closed his eyes. He'd kept his feelings for Kit to himself in deference to their friendship. But Rory had changed the rules and Donal wasn't about to let Kit go so easily.

He strolled back to the pair, drawing deeply of the evening air in an attempt to both banish the nausea and temper his jealousy. "Come now," he shouted. "We can't be goin' on all night with this."

"I know," Kit said. She wiped a tear from her cheek and then shook her head. "Tell Donal goodbye."

Rory reached out and Donal shook his hand. But at the last moment, Rory pulled him close and hugged him. "Remember what you promised," he murmured.

With that, Rory turned and strode down the street, a dashing figure in his Air Corps uniform. Kit slipped her arm around Donal's waist and leaned into him as they watched him walk away. "I'm not sure how many more times I can let him go. I want him to come home to us."

Donal's jaw tensed. "Ah, but you know our Rory. He can't be kept away from a new adventure. He'll never be one to settle down in the same spot for long, that boy."

"But he loves Ballykirk," she said.

"Ballykirk? He'd only love Ballykirk if there were a feckin' airstrip down the main street and an airplane parked in front of the pub."

"You don't think he misses us when he's gone?" Kit asked.

"I doubt it. He has plenty of friends to keep him company. He has his mates in his squadron. And then there're all the ladies."

"Ladies?"

"Ah, I suppose he wouldn't be telling you about them. But I happen to know that our Rory is quite the ladies' man."

Kit stared at a spot beyond Donal's shoulder. "Yes, I suppose that's true," she murmured.

Donal took her hand and tucked it in the crook of his arm. "My car is parked down the street. I'll drop you at your cousin's house on my way home."

"You're too drunk to drive back to Ballykirk. We'll have ourselves a stroll and then I'll drive to my cousin's. I'm sure she'll have a room for you. Promise me you'll stay the night."

Donal had had his fill of promises for this night. He wasn't sure what to do with Rory's, but he knew that he'd promise Kit Malone just about anything she asked. "I will," he said. "And then, tomorrow, I'll drive you back to Dublin."

They walked slowly around Eyre Square, not speaking at first. Then Kit sighed softly and stopped beneath a streetlamp. "Can I tell you a secret, Donal?"

He glanced down at her, only to see tears shining in her eyes. "You know you can."

"I believe I'm in love with him," she said, her voice wavering. "I wasn't sure until tonight. But when I was dancing with Rory, I never wanted to let him go." She looked up at Donal through thick lashes. "You aren't angry with me, are you?"

"Why would I be angry?"

She winced. "We've been such good friends. I don't want this to change anything between the three of us."

Donal reached into his jacket pocket and toyed with

Rory's letter, then pulled out his handkerchief and handed it to Kit. "We'll always be friends. And I never want to see you hurt, Kit. So, I have to be honest with you."

"Tell me what you're thinking."

"I'm afraid Rory is not the kind of man to settle down with a wife and a family. He never has been. Loving him will only bring you heartache."

Her tears flowed freely now and she brushed them off her cheeks with her fingertips. "Do you really believe that? Rory would never do anything to hurt me."

"Oh, no? Do you know where he's gone, then? He told you he was going back to his station, but he's gone to Belfast. He's deserted and he's off to join the RAF."

Kit gasped, the color draining from her cheeks. "What?"

Donal felt a stab of guilt at her stricken and stunned expression. But the guilt passed quickly because he knew he had gained control of Kit's emotions. "He should have told you and I begged him to. But he didn't want you to try to talk him out of it. By the end of next week, he'll probably be shooting at Germans over the English Channel."

"How could he do this to me?"

"How could he do this to himself, I say," Donal muttered. "When he comes back, he'll likely be arrested for desertion. Or perhaps he'll just choose to stay in England and avoid charges. After all, he's fighting their war now. Who knows where his loyalties lie?"

She seemed to crumple before his eyes and Donal drew her into his embrace and gently soothed her as she wept. This was where she belonged, in *his* arms, seeking *his* comfort. And with Rory in England, Donal had plenty of time to convince Kit that she'd be better off with a McClain than a Quinn.

"My car is just there," he said, pointing across the street.

"You're still drunk," Kit said, sniffling into his handkerchief.

"Not nearly so," he said with a chuckle. "Your tears have a very sobering effect on me."

"What will I do?" Kit asked, tipping her face up to his.

"You'll go back to university. And then, you'll come home to Ballykirk on your holidays and keep me company."

"I should write to him and tell him how I feel."

Donal shook his head. "Rory has enough on his mind. And what good will it do either one of you? Rory has decided what he wants and it isn't a future in Ballykirk."

CHAPTER THIRTEEN

Ballykirk, October 1932

"SOME SAY he was gassed in the war. It made him mad and now he goes out at night and eats the heads off chickens."

"That's pure bollocks," Rory said. "I've heard nothing about dead chickens."

"I didn't say dead, did I now?" Donal asked.

"Well, if their bleedin' heads are taken off, they'd be dead, wouldn't they?"

Donal frowned and considered Rory's point. His friend had the knack for seeing things clearly. "I suppose. But there's still something not right about the man. He's never once been to the pub. And he has the grocer deliver his order every week so he doesn't have to come to town."

"He limps and he doesn't have a bicycle or a horse or a car that I can see. It makes sense if you think of it. I'm not afraid of him."

They lay on their stomachs in the grass, observing the whitewashed cottage from a distance. It had been abandoned for a long time, and a few months ago a tenant had moved in, an elderly man with a slight limp and long scar on his face. Rumor had run rampant around Ballykirk, and most of the children did all they could to avoid the cottage.

"I wager I could walk right up to the door and talk to him." Rory sat up. "I'll ask if he has any work for me. No use to pay Eddie to deliver things from the village when he could pay me to do it."

Donal grabbed his friend and pulled him back down on the ground. "Now you're the one who's mad."

"What's he going to do?" Rory scrambled to his feet and started toward the cottage. "Even if he wanted to murder us both, we can outrun him."

Groaning softly, Donal watched as Rory walked boldly through the meadow. He'd never known anyone quite as brave as Rory Quinn. There wasn't a dare he wouldn't take or a challenge he couldn't overcome. He was a born leader and everyone seemed to follow him. Grudgingly, Donal got to his feet and trailed after Rory.

They had nearly reached the house when an apple came flying through the air and hit Rory on the back. He spun around and looked at Donal accusingly. "It wasn't me," Donal said.

They both looked at the apple tree near the road. Suddenly, another apple whizzed out from between the branches and fell at Donal's feet. With a soft curse, Donal turned to run but when he looked back he realized that Rory was heading toward the tree.

Torn between his fear and his loyalty to Rory, Donal froze. In the right hands, an apple could kill a person, couldn't it? He waited and watched as Rory stood beneath the tree and looked up through the branches. A moment later, two bare legs emerged and then a young girl dropped down to the ground, wiping her hands on her skirt. They spoke for a short time, then walked back to where Donal stood.

"This is Katherine Malone," Rory said.

"Kit," she corrected. "No one calls me Katherine, at least not anymore."

"Kit lives here," Rory said, "with her uncle."

She wasn't very tall, Donal mused as he observed her silently. Her long dark hair had been braided haphazardly, but one of the braids had come undone. Her hands and face were dirty and she had leaves clinging to her skirt, but she was pretty enough—not that he'd ever admit thinking that about a girl.

"You were spying on him, weren't you?" she said, leveling an accusing eye at Donal.

"No, we weren't," he replied.

"He isn't a bad man. He took me in when I needed a place."

"Where are your folks?" Rory asked.

She crossed her arms in front of her, hunching her shoulders slightly. "They died. I'm an orphan. I was living with my aunt in Galway, but she couldn't take care of me any longer so I came here to help Uncle Harold. He was gassed in the war. And shot. He has a medal for it, he does."

"I told you he wasn't mad," Rory muttered.

"He is a bit," Kit warned them. "Sometimes he has frightful nightmares. And the other day, I found one of our chickens with his head bit off."

They both turned to look at Donal. Donal's eyes went wide. A few moments later, Rory and Kit burst into fits of laughter. "Aw, piss off," Donal shouted. He turned on his heel and started toward home, but Kit and Rory caught up to him.

Rory put his arm around Donal shoulders. "We were just having you on a bit."

"I'm leaving," Donal muttered. "You can stay and play with the wee girl."

"I found a cave," Kit boasted, straightening to her full height.

The boys both turned their attention back to her, curiosity getting the better of them. "Where?"

"I'll show you, but you have to promise not to tell. It'll be our secret." She held out her hand, the little finger stuck out. "Promise."

Rory quickly hooked his little finger onto hers. "Promise," he said. He elbowed Donal, who reluctantly did the same. "Yeah, I promise."

Kit started off in the direction of the water, striding purposefully through the meadow, her arms swinging at her sides. Rory shrugged and followed her, and Donal had no choice but to do the same. A cave was worth at least a look.

THEY'D HIKED all morning to get to the stone circle. Rory had seen it only once, but he knew exactly where it was, about eight miles cross-country from Ballykirk. They'd cut through fields, following the coast, Donal carrying their canteens and Rory with a rucksack of food over his shoulder. Kit had borrowed her uncle's compass and had copied a tourist map from the wall at the post office.

Since they'd met Kit nearly three years ago, they'd shared countless adventures. But summer had offered almost complete freedom for the trio, a chance to venture out into the countryside in search of new sights. At thirteen, Rory was nearly old enough to work the *Mighty Quinn,* but he'd become so proficient at tying nets for the local fishermen that his father had decided he'd be of better use on dry land.

The times his father watched his work, Rory worked slowly and methodically. But he could tie knots with lightning speed and often worked late into the night so that he might have his days for his adventures with Kit and Donal.

"We have to be careful," Kit said as they stood on the hill above the sight. "It's a pagan place, this is. God might strike us dead for coming here."

"It has to be here," Rory said. "This is where they made sacrifices. It's like a temple."

"No, it's a clock," Donal said. They both looked at him. "It is," he insisted. "It's how they kept track of the seasons. There are circles like this all over Ireland. There's a book in my father's library that explains it all."

Rory glanced over at Kit and saw the look of disappointment on her face. Though Rory and Kit shared a vivid imagination, caught up in stories of druids and trolls and fairies, Donal preferred to look at the world in more practical terms.

Rory loved to tell the tales of his Mighty Quinn ancestors and Kit often composed little verses that kept them amused on their travels. Donal didn't offer much more than a pocketful of money and access to his father's library at the big house.

From the time Donal was young, he'd been considered the man of the house. His mother had carefully groomed him to take over the McClain family business concerns, showing him the books and accounts at the end of every month, requiring him to accompany her to business appointments and meetings with the solicitors.

Donal had done it all without complaint, as if sensing his responsibility and accepting his future for what it was. But Rory already knew his future wasn't here in Ballykirk. He was determined to go out into the world and find adventure. He'd pored over books about Mallory's ascents of Mount Everest, and Byrd and Amundsen's quests for the South Pole. There were adventures waiting for him and he was determined to find them.

"We have to do it at noon," Kit said. "It's the summer solstice so it will make the bond more powerful." They ran down the hill and stood in the center of the circle, Donal clutching the pocket watch they'd brought along.

They all drew a deep breath, their eyes on one another as the watch ticked off the seconds. Rory pulled out his pocketknife and sliced into the tip of his index finger. When a drop of blood appeared, he handed the knife to Donal.

Wincing, Donal did the same, then passed the knife to Kit. She didn't hesitate to draw the blade across her fingertip. "Are you ready?" she asked. They both nodded and Kit held up her hand. *"Trì,"* she murmured.

Rory pressed his finger to hers. *"Cumhachdach,"* he said.

Donal added his blood to the mix. *"Araon."*

"Trì, cumhachdach, araon." They chanted the three words over and over, ten times. Though they'd heard Gaelic spoken by many of the elderly residents of Ballykirk, they'd had to look up the words in the dictionary at Donal's house.

"Three. Powerful. Together," Rory said. They chanted those words ten times and, when they were finished, they turned their faces up to the sun and reveled in the newfound strength of their union. They'd been bonded forever in this ancient spot, vowing to remain loyal and true to their friendship. Nothing could tear them apart.

"Now what do we do?" Donal asked.

"We have to offer a gift to the gods," Kit said. "Something that represents our friendship."

Rory held up his knife. "This made our blood bond," he said. He walked to the altar stone and placed it on the flat surface. "Three, powerful, together," he repeated.

Kit reached into her pocket and retrieved a rock. "This is from the floor of our cave," she said. "It's the place we went on our first day together." She placed it on the altar. "Three, powerful, together."

Donal frowned. "I don't have anything," he said, searching through his pockets. He pulled out a couple of coins and a piece of string.

"Give me your canteen," Kit said impatiently. She took it from him, unfastened the top and took a long drink, then handed it to Rory. He did the same and passed it along to Donal. "We all drank from that canteen today," Kit said. "The water inside purified our bodies for the ritual."

Donal eyed Kit dubiously, then took the last swallow of water and placed the canteen on the altar. This was all just pure bollocks to Donal, Rory mused. But if it made Kit happy, like Rory he was willing to oblige. "Three, powerful, together," he muttered.

They stood for a long time, Kit and Rory's faces turned up to the sun and Donal watching them both uneasily. "What are we waiting for?"

"Shh!" Kit admonished. "We have to bathe in the power of this moment and this place, like the druids did. Let it sweep into your body."

Rory glanced over at Donal, and gave him a shrug. A few seconds later, Rory slowly backed away and Donal followed him to where they'd left their rucksack. They sat down in the grass as Kit continued to commune with the spirits. Donal pulled out the lunch they had packed in his mother's kitchen.

"She's an odd one, she is," he said, biting into a piece of buttered bread. "I think she actually believes in all this pagan shite."

Rory grabbed a hunk of cheese and broke it in three pieces. "Someone has to. I guess I don't blame her. She's had enough bad things in her life. Let her have her dreams."

"What bad things?"

"Well, she's an orphan," Rory said. "My mam heard her folks were killed in a terrible car accident when she was little. She was the only one to survive, just a wee child she was, found in the soft grass beside the smashed car. Mam says it was a miracle, that Mother Mary blessed Kit, and that she was saved for some special reason."

Donal watched her, slowly chewing. "I still think she's a queer one."

"She is that," Rory said, smiling. But he hoped Kit would never change. She was meant to go out into the world just as he was, to find her own adventures and to make her mark. Someday, people all over Ireland would know the name Katherine Malone and Rory would be proud to say that she was his friend.

CHAPTER FOURTEEN

KIT STOOD holding the book out to Rory and pointed to the photograph, the sunlight reflecting off the glossy paper. "They're giant tombs," she said, tracing the outline of one.

Rory stared over Kit's shoulder at the photograph of the pyramids. She and Rory had been fascinated with stories of the discovery of Tutankhamen's tomb. Though the discovery had been made in 1922, before she was born, that didn't keep Kit from dreams of traveling to Egypt and digging in the desert for treasures. Or taking a boat down the Nile into the heart of Africa. Or climbing Mount Kilimanjaro.

They usually sat in the library at Donal's house while they pored over the old books for more information, but the spring day had been sunny and warm and Kit had insisted that they meet at Oisin's Rock.

"Donal gave me this book," Kit said, running her hands over the fine leather cover. Donal had given her a great many gifts, but she tried to temper her delight, knowing that Rory couldn't afford to do the same.

"Look, here's the Sphinx. And this is a map of the Nile. And there's a whole chapter on the animals."

"Someday, I'm going to see that place," Rory murmured.

He'd turned sixteen last December and in a few years, he'd be in charge of his own life, Kit mused. She didn't want to think about his leaving Ballykirk, but she knew it was bound to happen someday.

"And I'm going to visit America and see some Indians," he continued. "And I'm going to China to see the Great Wall and Paris to see the Eiffel Tower."

"And the Parthenon in Greece and the Coliseum in Rome," Kit added. "My parents traveled to Europe on their honeymoon. I have a photo album. Vienna and Venice and Barcelona and Madrid. I'll go to all of those cities someday and visit the places they did."

"And we'll meet," Rory teased, leaning back against Oisin's Rock, crossing his arms over his chest, "in a fancy restaurant."

"No," Kit said. "In a train station…at midnight. We'll pass on the platform and we won't recognize each other at first. You'll be on your way to…Persia. And I'll be on a tour of the great art museums."

"And what will you say to me?" Rory asked.

"I'll say, 'Is that you, Rory Quinn?' And you'll nod." She laughed, caught up in the fantasy. "And then, I'll jump into your arms." She dropped the book onto the grass and threw her arms around Rory's neck, hugging him fiercely. When she drew back, she looked up into his eyes.

She felt her stomach flutter as he looked down into her eyes. It had always been so simple between them. They'd been great friends, sharing everything along with Donal. But things had begun to change. She was nearly fourteen and her girlish figure had filled out, causing the boys in the village to notice her. Instead of childish braids, she now wore her dark hair long and free and she'd begun to care about pretty dresses and shiny shoes.

She swallowed hard. "And then, I'll kiss you," she murmured. Kit pushed up on her toes and pressed her lips to his. He jumped slightly at the contact, but then his curiosity took over and he leaned into her, his hands slipping around her waist.

Kit hadn't planned to kiss him—she'd simply been caught up in the fantasy. But as the kiss went on, she realized it was only proper that Rory Quinn was her first. She wondered if she was his first, or if another girl's lips had touched his.

When she finally stepped back, she found him staring down at her. Her face flamed. "I—I shouldn't have done that," she murmured. "I'm sorry."

Rory frowned. "No. It was—fine. I—I didn't mind."

He didn't mind? What was that supposed to mean? He'd never really looked at her as he did the other girls in Ballykirk and now she knew why—he didn't fancy her at all. "Just forget it," she said, her voice thin.

"I don't think I'll be forgetting it," he said.

She stared at the toes of her shoes. "I know you don't think I'm pretty."

Rory laughed. "What are you saying? I think you're prettier than all the girls in Ballykirk."

"I am?"

He nodded. "And you're smart, too. And I like talking to you more than anyone else in the world."

"You do?"

"I do."

Kit breathed a silent sigh of relief. She could always trust Rory. No matter what kind of mess she found herself in, he always seemed to make her feel better about it. "But I shouldn't have done that," she said.

Rory searched her face. "Why not?"

"Because." She shook her head. "It wasn't right."

"I'm a boy and you're a girl," he said with a grin. "What's not right about it?"

"You know what I mean." She lowered her voice. "Donal."

"I don't want to kiss Donal."

She slapped his arm, then scrambled to pick up her book. "We have our oath. It's disloyal to Donal. I—I can't like you more than I like him. It would be wrong."

"And do you like me more than—"

"No," she lied, refusing to meet his eyes. "It can't be any other way. You can't kiss me again. Promise me you won't."

Rory nodded. "All right. But you're the one who kissed me."

"And I won't be doing that again," she said.

It should have been easy to accept her decision, but Kit didn't want anything to stand in the way of her feelings for Rory. If he wanted to kiss her, then she wanted him to do just that. And if she wanted to marry him someday, she didn't want to have to consider Donal's feelings.

A low whine sounded in the distance. "That's Donal now. We mustn't say anything to him." She drew a deep breath and shook her head. "If he's stolen his mother's motorcar again, I won't ride with him. Since he's taught himself to drive, he's a menace."

"No," Rory countered, frowning. "That's not a car." He looked up at the sky. He gasped softly. "Christ, will you look at that." He pointed to the horizon and Kit followed his direction. An airplane appeared over the hills and swooped down toward them.

"Mary, mother of God," she said.

Rory's eyes were wide and his mouth hung open. They'd both seen photographs of airplanes and had read all about Charles Lindbergh and his historic flight across the Atlantic. Kit knew there were planes all over Ireland these days, but they'd never had the luck to see one up close.

"It's a biplane," Rory said. It was flying so low they could make out the pilot with his leather helmet and goggles. Suddenly, the kiss they'd shared was all but forgotten.

"Can you imagine what it must feel like to fly? To see the world like a bird would? Like God does? I wonder how high you'd have to fly to see the whole of Ireland?"

"Do you think he'll land here?" Rory followed the path of the plane's flight from west to east. "Come on. Let's see where he's going!"

Kit tucked her book beneath her arm and ran along after him. Rory took her hand to keep her from tumbling down the hill and she felt a tiny thrill at his touch. "I'm going to fly one of those someday," he shouted.

Though he'd told her many of his dreams, there was something in his voice this time, something about the look on his face. It was as if he was seeing his future. Somehow, she sensed that this was a dream Rory would make come true.

RORY SCRAPED at the weathered hull of the *Mighty Quinn,* flakes of paint spraying around him as he worked. His father stood a few feet away, doing the same. "We're going to have to pull her out soon," he said. "We made enough last season to overhaul the engine. I figure I can afford to keep her out of the water for a week to get the work done. Jimmy Finn's going to do the overhaul. I want you to help him out."

"What about school?" Rory asked.

"You're sixteen now. You've had enough schooling. It's time you come to work with me on the boat."

He knew this was coming. His father had mentioned it more than once. In truth, only his mother's insistence had kept Rory in school for this long. "I don't want to work the boat," he murmured, averting his eyes.

"What?"

"I said, I don't want to work the boat." Rory stared up at his father. "What about Jimmy? What is he going to do?"

"He'll still work with us. But your grandda has had enough work for one man's life. It's time for you to take your place and give him his rest."

"But fishing isn't for me," Rory said. When his father arched his eyebrow, he continued, "I—I was thinking I might join the army. Or maybe go to Belfast and find a job on a merchant ship. I want to see the world."

Jack Quinn opened his mouth, then snapped it shut. He tossed the scraper into a bucket and sat down on the edge of the dock. Nodding to Rory, he pointed to a spot beside him. Rory settled himself next to his father, toying with the scraper.

"It's fine to have a dream," Jack said. "I had a few of my own when I was a young man. But sooner or later, you have to get on with life."

"What if my life isn't here?" Rory asked. "You left Ballykirk. Why can't I?"

"There was a war to be fought," his father said.

Rory knew his father's story, about his time with the IRA and the prison sentence that followed. He remembered his own childhood, when he'd lived in the country with his mother in a two-room cottage—and then the long trip to Ballykirk to meet the man who was his father.

At first it had been confusing and then, for a long time, he'd put it out of his mind. But as he'd grown older, Rory had begun to understand what his mother had been through, having a baby, unmarried and alone, trying to provide for them both while his father was in prison.

There were times when he felt his father had no right to tell him how to lead his life. Jack Quinn hadn't been there when he was born. He'd been married to another woman, beginning a different family. But that woman and her baby were buried in the churchyard.

"I know you don't think I've lived my life the right way," Jack said. "But I've done the best I can. And I want the best for you."

His father was still a young man. Why couldn't he remember what it was like to have dreams? "Then let me go," Rory said.

Jack stared out at the water, then, after a long while, nodded. "When you're eighteen. Until then, you'll finish school and continue helping out on the boat when you can."

"What was it like?" Rory asked. "The war?" His father rarely talked of it, but that didn't quell Rory's curiosity.

"I thought it was a noble and a just cause, and it was—until I had to stare at a fellow Irishman down the barrel of my gun. And I had to pull the trigger and do my best to take his life. Nothing prepares a man for that moment."

"You killed someone?"

Jack nodded. "I did. And I'm not proud of it. Ireland still isn't free, and until she is, that death will be mine to bear." He looked over at Rory. "So you still think you want to go to the army? Can't see much of the world in the Irish Army."

"I'm not really interested in the Army. The Air Corps. That's where I want to be. I want to learn to fly."

"The Irish Air Corps?" Jack chuckled. "Do they even have planes?"

"Not the Irish Air Corps," Rory said.

Jack frowned, Rory's words slowly making sense to him. Then he shook his head. "I'll allow you your dreams, but I won't give you that."

"They'll teach me to fly, Da. The RAF has always taken trainees from the south. Mick Mannock was a fighter pilot and an ace in the war and he was born right here in Cork."

"He was a fool to fight when he didn't have to. And a fool to fight for them."

"But he did have to," Rory insisted. "Because he

believed what the British believed, that Germany needed to be stopped. Just because we're on opposite sides in Ireland doesn't mean the Brits are always wrong."

"I am not about to discuss politics with you," Jack said.

"Airplanes are the future. Soon they'll fly all over Ireland. There'll be no trains. And they'll fly across the ocean, from here to America and back. I want to be part of that."

Jack levered to his feet. "You have my answer. No son of mine will join the British Army or Navy or Air Corps."

"I will," Rory said.

Jack leveled his gaze at Rory. "Then you won't be my son." He strode off down the quay, his shoulders set.

Rory groaned, cursing softly. Serving for the British would be a betrayal too difficult for his father to forgive. But once he turned eighteen, Rory's life was his to live. And he could do as he chose. He would learn to fly and it didn't matter who taught him.

CHAPTER FIFTEEN

THE WAKE WAS HELD in the tiny whitewashed cottage. Kit sat next to the rough plank table where her uncle's body was laid out, her hands clasped in her lap. Harold Malone had been dressed in his army uniform, adorned by a single medal for the wounds he'd suffered. He'd died of lung fever, never recovering from the gas he'd inhaled on the battlefield.

Kit hadn't expected a large crowd for the wake, but after just a half hour, a steady stream of people had paid their respects. No one in town knew much of Harold Malone, but Ballykirk was a small village and they all knew Kit.

Kit whispered her thanks to one of the teachers from school, then noticed Rory standing in the doorway. Suddenly, her emotions welled up inside of her and tears pressed at the corners of her eyes. He read her distress immediately and he grabbed a chair from near the hearth and set it next to hers, then sat down and took her hand.

Kit smiled, a tear trailing down her cheek. He gave her hand a squeeze. Over the next hour, they didn't say a word, communicating with a silent touch or a quiet look as mourners offered their condolences. Donal wandered in with his mother at his side but left almost immediately.

When the crowd had thinned, Rory pulled her to her feet and they walked out the front door. He drew her along to the apple tree near the edge of the meadow, then took off his jacket and spread it out on the grass.

"I should go back," Kit murmured.

"No," Rory said, grabbing her hand and linking his fingers through hers. "Stay here and talk to me for a bit."

"Where is Donal?"

"His mother wasn't feeling well so he had to take her home. He said he'd stop back later."

Kit nodded as she sat down next to Rory. Just being near him made her feel right again. "He probably wasn't comfortable standing in the same room with a dead body."

Rory chuckled. "He's been afraid of your Uncle Harold for years and now that Harold's dead, he's even more terrified."

She folded her hands in her lap and stared down at them, desperate to contain her emotions but she couldn't stop a teardrop from plopping onto her skirt. "You and Donal have been my best friends. And I love you both so much." She looked up at him through watery eyes. "I wish he hadn't died. Everything is so complicated now."

"What are you going to do?" Rory asked, reaching out to brush a tear away with his fingertip.

She drew a deep breath and put on a bright smile. "My mother's sister will take me in again. I'm to leave tomorrow morning."

He gasped. "You're going to leave Ballykirk?"

Kit nodded. "My uncle left me the cottage but my aunt controls the money from my parents' estate until I'm eighteen. I'll be sixteen in a month. She'd never allow me to live here alone."

"You could come live with my family," Rory suggested.

Siobhan Quinn had been the closest thing Kit had had to a mother and she knew the kind woman wouldn't hesitate to invite her into the Quinn household, but Kit didn't want to burden a family that already had trouble putting food on the table.

"Donal said the same. His mother offered me a position working for her. Mrs. McClain's arthritis has gotten much worse and she said I could be her companion. I'd help her with things around the house, sewing and correspondence. She offered to pay me, but I don't need her charity."

"But you could stay, then," Rory said. "And it wouldn't be charity if you made yourself useful around the house. Then when you turn eighteen, you can move back into the cottage. You always talk about being an independent woman. This is your chance."

"Being an independent woman takes money."

"You want to go to university. And if you combine the money you can make working for Donal's mother with the money from your parents, you could afford a better college. It's a sensible plan. Surely, your aunt would agree to that."

Kit considered the notion for a long moment. It did make sense and her aunt would have to see that. A smile touched the corners of her mouth and she drew Rory's hand up and pressed it to her cheek. "You are my dearest friend," she murmured, closing her eyes.

The heat from his skin warmed her, and for a long moment she didn't want to move. She'd tried so hard to love both Rory and Donal equally, to look upon them as the brothers she'd never had. But Rory had always been her favorite. He would always protect her, no matter what. And in return, he'd have her heart.

Her mind wandered back to the day at Oisin's Rock, the day she'd worked up the courage to kiss him. Kit wished that he'd kiss her now, that he'd touch his lips to hers and banish all the worry from her mind.

She felt his arm slip around her shoulders and he pulled her close. "Father Timothy is standing at the door," he murmured. "I suppose we should really go back inside."

"You don't have to stay," Kit said.

"I will. As long as you need me, I'll be here."

And that was why she'd fallen in love with Rory Quinn, Kit mused. He never asked anything of her.

But she knew that in an instant, he'd lay down his life for her. No matter how far they wandered, he'd always be her knight, willing to ride to her rescue when she called.

THE HOUSE on the Skibbereen road was ablaze with light. Inside, the McClain family cook fussed over the platters of food set out on the mahogany dining table. Donal glanced at his pocket watch, then grabbed the dressmaker's box he'd tossed on the settee and hurried upstairs.

Though Kit had been working for his mother for over a year, she wasn't treated as a servant. She occupied one of the prettiest bedrooms in the house, just down the hall from his. And in addition to her wages, his mother had showered her with gifts.

Donal knew that Maura McClain approved of the match between them, but he wasn't sure how Kit felt. Though they'd been living in the same house, their relationship hadn't changed at all. She still treated him like a kindly brother.

But he was determined to change that. She'd turned seventeen a few days ago and he'd planned a festive party for her tonight. All the young people from the village had been invited and he'd spared no expense to make certain it was an evening Kit would never forget.

Donal rapped softly on her bedroom door, and when she called out he walked inside, the box behind his back. She sat at her dressing table, her slender body wrapped in a pretty silk robe. "I'm not sure what to do with my hair," she muttered. "I'd like to wear it up, but I haven't a clue how to get it to stay that way." She stared in the mirror. "Rory says he prefers it down. What do you think?"

Donal fought a tiny sliver of envy. Why was Rory's opinion always more important than his? "Maybe this will help make your decision." He held out the box and she slowly stood.

"What is this?"

"An early present," Donal replied. "Open it."

"You've already given me this party. I couldn't ask for more."

"And you haven't. Now, open it."

Kit crossed to the bed and set the box on the embroidered coverlet. She threw aside the top and rummaged through the tissue paper, then cried out in surprise. Slowly she pulled the gown from the box and held it out in front of her. He'd been assured by his mother's dressmaker in Dublin that it was the height of fashion.

The pale cream color suited her perfectly and the intricate beading across the shoulders and bodice made for an elegant design. It was cut to hug her slender figure yet still be modest enough for a young woman. "Do you like it?"

"Oh, Donal. You shouldn't have done this."

"Answer my question," he said.

"I love it. It's the most perfect gown I've ever seen."

"Then put it on," he urged. "There are shoes dyed to match inside the box. Hurry now. Your guests have already started to arrive. They'll expect you to make your entrance soon."

She carefully laid the dress on the bed then crossed the room. With a warm smile, she wrapped her arms around his neck and hugged him tightly. Donal closed his eyes as her body pressed against his, the silk robe clinging to her form like a second skin. He'd told himself over and over again to be patient. They were still young and he didn't want to move too quickly. But someday, Kit Malone would be his.

"I'll be back in a bit to escort you down," Donal said.

"Rory, too," Kit said. "I want both of you to walk down with me."

Donal nodded, his jaw tight.

When he reached the parlor, he found his best friend standing near the fireplace, a glass of punch in his hand. As always, Rory managed to look quite dashing in a well-worn suit and an unfashionable tie. As soon as he saw Donal, he crossed the room and grabbed his arm. "I have something to show you," he said, his voice low.

"Did you get the whiskey for the punch?" Donal asked.

Rory scowled then shook his head. "No, I forgot. Besides, your mother would murder me if I dumped spirits into her crystal punch bowl. You know how she feels about the drink." He dragged Donal along to the front door. "Come on. This is more important."

When they got outside, Rory pulled an envelope from his pocket and handed it to Donal. "Read it."

Donal unfolded the paper.

> Dear Mr. Quinn. Thank you for your enquiry regarding the cadet training program of the Irish Air Corps. In order to qualify for consideration, you are required to report to the aerodrome at Baldonnel on or before November 15, 1940 for medical tests. A class of thirty-two cadets will be selected to begin training in the following weeks.

Donal glanced back and forth between the letter and Rory's face. "Christ, you did it then. You said you'd find a way to fly and you did."

"I'm not in yet. And it's not the RAF, but it will make my da happy. They're flying some of the same planes. And who knows when we might decide to get into this war."

"You're to report next month," Donal said.

Rory nodded. "But I'm leaving in a few weeks. I thought I'd go early, get a feel for the place, and get a closer look at the planes."

"When are you going to tell Kit?"

"Tonight," Rory said. "She'll be so surprised. She knows how much I wanted this, she can't help but be pleased."

For such a clever boy, Rory Quinn was sometimes as thick as a plank. He was so set on a life out in the great, wide world that he didn't see what was right in front of his nose. Kit was in love with him and he hadn't bothered to notice. Donal knew she'd be crushed when Rory gave her the news, though she'd put on a show of support. Still, this was the best news he'd heard in ages. For the next year, he'd have Kit all to himself.

"How long will you be gone?"

"Three years with the possibility of more if need be," Rory said. "Once they train a pilot, they're not keen to let him go. But that's fine by me. As long as I'm flying, I'll be happy."

"Maybe you ought to wait to tell Kit," Donal suggested. "I don't want her weeping all night long. You know how sentimental she gets."

Rory nodded. "I'll find the proper time. I can't imagine why she'd be upset. She didn't expect me to sit here in Ballykirk while she went off to university next year, did she? And if she goes to university in Dublin, I'll be close by."

He handed Rory the letter, then turned to the door. "She should be finished in front of the mirror by now. She wants us to escort her downstairs. Are you up for it?"

Rory laughed. "For Kit, anything."

They walked back inside the house together and waited outside Kit's room while she made her final preparations. When she appeared at the door, Donal watched Rory's reaction closely. But there was nothing more he could see beyond the proud smile of a close friend.

"You look grand," Rory said, tucking Kit's hand into the crook of his arm. "All grown-up."

"And I'm glad you've finally noticed," Kit teased. She looked over to Donal, then looped her arm through his. "Shall we?"

"It's your night, Miss Malone," Donal said. "Lead on."

THE PARTY WAS a glorious affair. Nearly every young person within ten miles of Ballykirk attended, the crowd spilling out into the gardens behind the house. Kit reveled in the attention and Rory stood on the fringes, watching her as she moved from guest to guest, dressed in a beautiful gown, her hair swept back from her face and tucked into a knot at her nape.

He'd waited all evening for a chance to talk to her alone, but Donal seemed fastened to her side, never allowing her to stray far, always making sure that her glass was full and that she'd sampled the latest tidbit from the kitchen.

Rory reached into his pocket and fingered the small box he'd hidden there. He'd thought long and hard about what to get Kit, running back and forth from shop to shop, examining every option in the village of Ballykirk. Though he knew Donal would present her with something quite fine and expensive, Rory hadn't the means to do the same. So the gift had to be special—something that would touch Kit's heart.

When he saw Kit wander toward the stairs, he caught up with her and grabbed her hand. "You haven't had a moment for me," he teased. "I'm feeling neglected."

Kit giggled. "And you've had a group of chattering girls around you all night long. I should be the one to feel neglected, Rory Quinn."

"Then take a stroll with me. I have something to tell you."

They walked through the French doors, out onto the wide terrace, then slowly descended the steps into the garden. Festive lights hung from the trees, bathing the garden in a romantic glow. Rory continued on until he found a private spot near the rose arbor. They sat down on a small bench and he pulled his gift from his pocket.

"I wasn't sure what to get you," he said, toying with the box. "It's hard to compete with Donal."

"You don't have to compete with him," Kit murmured.

Rory took her hand and turned her palm upward, then placed the little box in it. "I hope you like it." He watched as she carefully unwrapped the gift and opened the box. She reached inside and withdrew the delicate bracelet, staring at it in wonder.

"It's lovely," she said.

"It's sea glass," Rory murmured as he fastened it around her wrist. "I searched for it on the beach beneath our cave. Remember, we used to hurl bottles with messages off the cliff when we were young? They broke down below and over the years the sand and the water wore them smooth. The green was the prettiest. I had the jeweler in town fashion the bracelet."

Kit stared up at him, her face filled with unspoken emotion. "It's the most wonderful gift you could ever give me," she said. "I'll treasure it always."

She reached out and touched his cheek with her palm then brushed a quick kiss across his mouth. Rory closed his eyes, letting his lips linger over hers for just a moment longer. Then he murmured, "I have good news."

"A gift and good news," she said. "This is turning into quite a birthday."

"Last month, I applied to enter the Irish Army Air Corps. I just received a letter today that said I qualify. I leave in a few weeks."

Kit's eyes went wide. "Just like that? You're leaving Ballykirk? Why didn't you tell me about this sooner?"

"I didn't think I'd get in. I still don't know if I'll be chosen. I want to fly. And short of joining the RAF, there's no other place to do it." He grabbed her hands. "The very best thing is that, if I get in, I'll be stationed near Dublin. So, when you go to university in a year, we'll be able to see each other all the time."

"And until then?" Kit asked.

"I'll be home on leave," Rory assured her. He stared down at her, confused by the conflicting emotions on her face. "Are you angry?"

She shook her head. "I wish you'd told me about this earlier," she scolded. "I know it's what you want, but I don't fancy having to say goodbye to you. It's too soon."

"Then we'll have to make the best of the next few weeks. We'll visit all our favorite spots. We'll hike to the cave and go to the stone circle and visit the old abbey once more. And when I finally leave, you'll be so exhausted, you'll be happy to be rid of me."

"No," Kit said. "I'll never be happy to see you go."

Rory gathered her into his arms and gave her a hug. He felt her tremble and he knew she was fighting back tears. "Do you remember the blood oath we took all those years ago? We may have to spend time apart in our lives, but that won't destroy our friendship."

"How do you know?" Kit demanded. "Everything is changing so fast. Soon, we'll have lives of our own and all we'll be to each other is an assortment of fond memories. Do your parents still see their childhood friends? My parents are dead and all their friends have forgotten them."

"Don't be cross with me," Rory pleaded.

"I just thought we'd be together forever."

"And were you going to pack Donal and me up in

your trunk and take us off to university with you? Perhaps let us live under your bed while you fed us scraps from the dining hall?"

Kit's expression softened into a smile, and then she shook her head. "No. But you must promise that the next time you decide to leave me, you'll give me at least a month's notice so that I can adjust to the idea."

"I'm not certain I can cope with you weeping on my shirt for thirty days," Rory said.

Kit straightened, then carefully wiped her eyes with her fingertips. "I'm better now. And I truly am happy for you, Rory, even though I don't act it."

"Come, let's get you back to your guests."

Kit slipped her arms around Rory's waist and hugged him hard. "Can we just stay out here for a bit longer?"

Rory pressed his lips to the top of her head, so softly she wouldn't feel the kiss. "We can stay here for the next two days if that's what you'd like."

CHAPTER SIXTEEN

THE GALWAY TRAIN STATION was quiet when Rory arrived. He'd left Kit with Donal in front of the hotel on Eyre Square and found himself questioning his decision to leave. He'd returned to the bus station in the early morning hours to retrieve his kit, then shed his Irish Air Corps uniform and changed into civilian clothes in the tiny washroom.

After that he spent the hours before dawn walking along the banks of the Corrib, taking the time to think about his decision. He'd been reluctant to leave her again but Rory knew the more time he spent in her presence, the more he'd come to question his dreams.

On the way to the train station, he'd stopped at a small church and lit a candle, hoping it might give him inspiration or provide divine intervention. He had a long letter to write and words had never come easily.

He closed his eyes and let images of Kit drift through his mind. She had been right. The night had been perfect. And he'd carry those memories with him throughout his time away. If the time came and he found himself close to death, her face would be there in his thoughts, providing comfort.

It seemed that he'd been doing nothing but leaving lately. He'd left Kit in Ballykirk when he'd enlisted in the Air Corps. And then, just a few months after she'd arrived in Dublin, he'd been transferred out to the new air station at Rineanna, where he'd flown coastal patrol. And now, he was moving even farther away, across the Irish Channel to Britain and then on to the war in Europe.

Rory knew it would be the most difficult thing he'd ever done, fighting a war, watching men die, wondering if he'd be the next. He'd always considered himself indestructible, but it was easy to feel that way when no one was shooting at him.

He could have stayed behind and finished out his term with the Air Corps, seeing Kit on the odd weekend leave and returning to Ballykirk when he got out. But flying had become his life and he wanted to be the best. A man couldn't be the best unless he flew with the best, flew in situations that would test his abilities. He had faith in his talent as a pilot. Whatever the situation, he'd find a way to survive.

The Saturday morning train to Dublin was announced and Rory picked up his bag and slung it over his shoulder. If he had any doubts, he'd have to confront them now.

He drew a deep breath, then started for the platform. As he walked, he noticed the young men moving around him and wondered if they were heading for the same destination.

Rory swung up onto the step of the car and then searched for a spot to sit. He found an empty seat next to a middle-aged man, dressed in a tattered canvas jacket and worn trousers. After tossing his bag onto the rack above, he settled in. There was no going back now.

"Where are you off to?" the man asked.

"Dublin then on to Belfast," Rory replied.

"Me too," he said. "I'm gone to enlist." He chuckled, waving his hand. "I know, I'm a wee bit old. But I fought in the first war and it was a grand adventure. I'm bound to fight in this one."

"And what does your family say about this?" Rory asked.

The man shrugged. "Don't have a family. Lucky that, I suppose."

"Lucky," Rory murmured. Was it luck to have no one to wish you home, no one to mourn you if you were lost? He saw his future sitting next to him, an old man anxious to recapture the better days of his youth, idealizing war until the true dangers didn't seem real at all.

Would he become this man? Or had he become him already? The train started to roll and Rory fought the impulse to grab his bag and jump off. He had another two years with the Air Corps. After that, he could offer his services to the RAF—if the war was still going on.

Rory reached into his jacket and pulled out the stub of a pencil and the folded orders for his weekend leave. He smoothed the paper out on his knee and quickly wrote "Dearest Kit" on the back. He ought to begin with an apology, but he wasn't sorry he'd left without telling her. Nor was he sorry he was going to war. With a soft curse, Rory crumpled the paper and shoved it back into his pocket. He glanced over at the man next to him.

"I've heard there are men deserting from the Irish Army every day," the man said. "The Defence Forces didn't want me, but the Brits will. Not for the infantry, but my back is still strong. They'll have a place for me. I can pull a trigger, I can. I'll kill some Germans for them."

Rory stared out the window as the train slowly pulled out of the station. If he expected to live a life filled with adventure then he'd be forced to do his share of leaving. But for the first time, he was separating from the woman he loved and that made the leaving bittersweet.

KIT THREW OPEN the shutters, sending dust motes whirling through the sunlight that poured through the cottage window. She wiped her hands on her apron, then turned to survey the work ahead of her.

The cottage hadn't been opened since her uncle's death. Everything was as she'd left it, save for the thick coat of dust. But the prospect of transforming the cottage into her own home made the task of cleaning it all the more satisfying.

She'd finished the first term of her second year at university just a few days before. Right after she'd written her last exam, Kit had packed her bags, anxious to spend Christmas holiday in Ballykirk. This was her home now; this was where she belonged.

She crossed the room and tossed another piece of turf onto the fire, the scent of burning peat wafting through the room. The teakettle whistled on the stove and she picked it up and filled the small china pot. She hadn't any biscuits, but her first cup of tea in her own house was special enough without.

She'd just settled on the old couch when a knock sounded at the door. A second later, it swung open and she found herself staring at a familiar overstuffed chair. "Where should I put this?"

"Donal?" Setting her teacup down, Kit hurried to the door and helped him inside. With a grunt, he set the chair down in the middle of the room. "What is this?" she asked.

"A housewarming gift from Mother," he said. "It's the one from your bedroom. She thought you might like to have it for your own."

"How kind of her," Kit said. She plopped down into the chair and threw her legs up over the arm. "It still fits perfectly."

Donal glanced around the room and sniffed. "Not

much has changed," he said. "I can't see why you insist on living here when you have a comfortable room at our house."

"Because that's *your* house. And this is *my* house now." She jumped out of the chair and gave him a hug. "I'm glad you're here. You're my first guest. Would you like a cup of tea before you help me move all this furniture to the other side of the room?"

Donal groaned. "I should have known you'd put me to work."

Kit fetched him a cup, then poured the tea. He sat on the couch and she curled up in the chair. "It seems right, this," she said, looking at him over the rim of her cup. "Being back in Ballykirk." She paused. "There's just one thing missing."

"Rory?"

She nodded. "Have you heard from him lately?"

Donal shook his head. "Not since last month. I sent a parcel for the holiday, but I'm not sure if he got it."

"I did, too. Some socks and chocolate bars." She tipped back her head and closed her eyes. "He seems so far away. I wish I could just snatch him from all that and bring him back here to be with us for Christmas."

"He's where he wants to be," Donal said.

Kit's throat tightened with emotion. She'd tried so hard to put Rory out of her thoughts, to deal with her feelings for him in a practical way. There was no chance for a future with him, she knew that by now.

But it didn't stop her from loving him, from scouring his letters for any indication of deeper affection.

But his letters had changed over the past year. The chatty warmth and good humor that had always made his letters from Rineanna such a delight had disappeared. He talked about his mates, the food, the scenery near his air station at Kenley, just south of London, in a detached manner. Occasionally, he mentioned a trip into the city for an evening out, but even then there was nothing of his own thoughts or feelings in the letter.

"Does he ever tell you anything about the war?" Kit asked.

Donal shook his head. "I don't suppose he can. It's surely against regulations—you know, loose lips sink ships."

"I just sense he's in trouble."

"Rory can handle himself. You know him—he's invincible." Donal got up and fetched the teapot from the table, then warmed her cup. "Let's talk about something more cheerful. Now that you're here, what do you plan to do with yourself?"

"Work on my little cottage and do some reading for next term. And I have to select a group of my poems to submit to the Literary journals." She paused. I've been thinking that next year I might want to continue my studies at the university in Cork. Then I could live here..."

"I'd like that," he said, "and speaking of poems, I

have a small gift for you." Donal reached into his jacket pocket and withdrew a small parcel, wrapped in brown paper and tied with a red ribbon. He handed it to her. "Happy Christmas, Kit."

"Donal, you shouldn't have. You don't have to give me gifts all the time."

"And why not? I enjoy making you smile. Now, open it."

Kit untied the ribbon, then tore the paper to reveal a small leather-covered volume. *"The Poems of Katherine Malone,"* she murmured, running her fingertips over the gold-stamped title. She glanced up at him with a stunned expression, then flipped through the pages.

"I took the poems you sent me and I had them put into a book. I've a whole box of these books in the car for you. I thought you might like to give them as gifts, maybe sell them in some of the local shops. Your poems are beautiful, Kit. People should read them."

She pressed the book to her heart and smiled at Donal. Though it was just a vanity publication, paid for by Donal, it was still a book. It made her poems seem... important...enduring. "Thank you," she whispered.

Kit crawled out of her chair and leaned over him, placing a kiss on his cheek. But as she drew back, Donal slipped his hand around her neck and stopped her retreat. Without a word, he touched his lips to hers in the gentlest of kisses. The contact surprised her at first, but it wasn't an unpleasant experience.

She suspected that Donal cared about her, beyond their friendship. But she'd always imagined herself with Rory. He was exciting and unpredictable. Donal was dependable and sensible.

Kit stepped back and smiled weakly. Though she ought to have felt a tiny bit of passion, all she could think about was the thrilling kiss she'd shared with Rory that night in Galway. And the desire that had warmed her blood when he'd held her on the dance floor. She wished that it was Rory who'd brought her the book of poems, Rory sitting here drinking tea, Rory pulling her into his arms.

"I suppose we ought to get to work," she murmured.

Donal grabbed her hand. "Let me call my mother. She'll send over our housekeeper and she'll have this place shining like a new penny in no time."

Kit shook her head. "No. I want to do this myself. But thank you for the offer."

"Well, I have business to do in Kinsale. Why don't I stop on my way back and I'll take you to supper?"

"I think I'd like to spend my first evening here at home," she said. "But come by tomorrow for tea."

Donal nodded, then walked to the door. "It is good to have you home, Kit."

She watched from the window as he drove off. How simple life would be if she loved Donal. He was a good man, a man who'd be able to provide well for a wife and a family. But did she really want to marry?

There were many women who devoted their lives to a career. Why couldn't she be one of them?

Kit poured the last of the tea into her cup and curled up in her chair with her notebook, paging through the bits of poetry she'd put to paper. She came across a letter she'd begun to Rory and took up her pen to finish it.

> Now I'm back in Ballykirk. The cottage is cozy and will make a fine home for me, once I've given it a good cleaning. Donal has already brought me a gift of a chair and I sit here thinking of you. Your letters tell me nothing of how you are or what you are feeling. Do you think of us at all, or are your thoughts occupied with staying safe and alive? I think of you every day and pray for your return every night. I'm sending you a small gift that I hope you'll enjoy. Donal has published some of my poems in a little volume. Please write to me, if only to let me know that you are well.

Kit paused, then signed the letter as she always had. "All my love," she murmured.

She carefully tore the paper from the notebook, then folded it and placed it inside the front cover of the book. She'd post it tomorrow. Though it wouldn't arrive before Christmas, he'd have it before the new year.

Kit smoothed her hand over the cover of the book. It was time to move on with her life. Though she'd still pray for Rory, she wouldn't allow herself to dream of him. She'd already spent too many nights wishing him into her arms, imagining the love they might share, hoping for a future together.

But Rory would never love her the way she loved him. If he had, he wouldn't have gone to war. He wouldn't have left her to wait and wonder.

RORY STRETCHED OUT on his bunk, not bothering to take off his jacket and boots. Exhaustion overwhelmed him and he wanted to sleep, to forget war for just a day. They'd scrambled before dawn, flying a ramrod mission deep into France to destroy a German airfield.

They'd lost one of the four bombers and three of the fourteen fighters to heavy enemy fire. It hadn't been a good day. His closest friend in the squadron had gone down, Rory watching Mac Granley's Spitfire spiral down from the clouds to earth.

He and Mac had arrived at Kenley the same day. A brash Australian, Mac hadn't been the best pilot in the squadron, but he'd made up for it with his good humor.

Rory covered his eyes with his arm, fighting back his grief. Why was this loss any different? Day after day, he'd gone into the air expecting that he'd return without some of the men he'd come to know. For short stretches, they wouldn't lose a single plane and then, just when they began to feel a bit cocky, the Germans would find a way to even the score.

He'd been at Kenley nearly a year, coming there directly from No. 6 Operational Training Unit where he'd qualified to fly Spitfires. His squadron had originally been made up of an odd assortment of flyers, mostly Australians, some Brits, a Pole, a Canadian and two Irishmen.

But over the months, pilots had come and gone, some dead, some injured, some transferred and a number taken as prisoners of war after bailing out over occupied territory. And others had simply disappeared.

Sooner or later, his number would come up. He'd felt it, in every close call he'd had. The flak would hit his plane or he'd have a mechanical failure on takeoff or a Messerschmitt would sneak up on him and blow him out of the air. The clock was ticking, the odds were narrowing, and there was nothing he could do about it.

Reaching up, Rory grabbed the bundle of envelopes stuck beneath the springs of the bunk above. He unfolded Kit's last letter and began to read. His gaze fell to the close of the letter. "All my love."

It was the only thing keeping him sane, the prospect of someday returning to her. But was she waiting for him or had she found another man to occupy her thoughts? Rory rolled over and pulled a packet of stationery from beneath his bed. He grabbed the pen from the binding of his logbook and began to write.

> You've asked me to tell you what I'm feeling and perhaps it's time I tried. I'm lying here in my bed, trying to think of better days, days that haven't been stained by danger or death. There is only one thing I know for certain.

Rory paused, the ink from his pen bleeding onto the paper.

> I love you. I should have told you that night in Galway, but I thought it would make leaving all the more difficult. When I feel as if I can't go on, I read your letters or recall our conversations or relive our adventures, and it gives me strength. Please don't tell me how you feel. If you don't love me, then I won't want to come home. And if you do love me, I won't want to stay here. There, it's been said and I'm glad for it. I'll post this letter and I'll finish my work here and hope that you'll be waiting for my return.

Rory folded the letter and slipped it into the envelope, then wrote out the address in Ballykirk. Just as he was sealing it closed, the siren sounded. Men dozing on the bunks jerked upright and the squadron began to scramble. He tucked the letter into his leather flight jacket then stood up.

They were scheduled to fly another ramrod at sunset, an offensive mission targeted at a German army camp in Normandy. The Spitfires would fly low over the channel to avoid detection, flying into the sun, then swoop down on the camp, strafing the area with machine-gun fire. But if they were going up now, at midday, the sunset mission would have to be scrubbed.

The Germans had given up daylight missions long ago, preferring to bomb at night. RAF planes had been fitted with airborne interception radar to provide a defense against the raids, but Rory's squadron usually ran offensive missions.

Rory passed Al Whitney's bunk and reached over to shake him awake. "Press on," he muttered, the familiar phrase laced with sarcasm. "Press on regardless" had become the unofficial motto of the RAF. To most pilots, it meant flying on through any adversity. But Rory's squadron had been so battered over the past few months that the phrase had been an expression of resignation. They had no choice in the matter. Sooner or later, the odds would get them all.

Rory waited for Al, and then they both grabbed their Mae Wests and pulled them over their heads as they hurried out of the barracks. They stopped when they saw a sprog bent over in the bushes, losing his lunch. The kid had just arrived from training and this would be his first mission. Though he'd practiced dogfighting, practice was nothing like the real thing.

Rory stood over him, patting him on the back. "You'll be all right," he said. "Once you get in the air, you'll know what to do."

"I don't think I will," he said, his face as white as a sheet.

"I didn't think I would either, but when someone is shooting at you, you'll shoot back. Don't worry, I'll keep a watch out for you."

The three of them jumped into a passing jeep and arrived at the airfield a minute later. The squadron crew chief was shouting orders to his men as they prepared the Spitfires for takeoff. Rory watched as the first three planes rolled out to the runway, then one by one, accelerated and took off. The crewman gave him a thumbs-up.

"You checked that sticky stabilizer?" Rory asked.

"Couldn't find anything wrong with it," he said.

Rory climbed up to the cockpit and slid into his seat, his folded chute providing a cushion on the hard metal. He ran through his preflight in quick order, then pulled on his flying helmet and adjusted his radio gear. When his engine had reached proper RPMs, he swung the Spitfire off the line and headed to the runway.

The squadron leader's voice cracked over the radio. "Red group climb to angels twelve. Blue group follow them at angels fourteen. Keep your wits about you, boys. Let's see if we can get a jump on them from the cloud cover."

"Red one climbing to angels twelve," Rory said, taking the plane up to 12,000 feet. He heard Al reply as Red two and the sprog as Red three and glanced around to see them following him. They flew out over the channel, Rory watching through the wispy clouds for the familiar sight of the German Messerschmitts. Suddenly, they were there. "There they are, boys. Eleven o'clock. I count at least sixteen. Red group, follow me down."

Rory pulled his plane into a steep dive and came down on top of the lead ME. He fired on him and the German pilot peeled off from his formation to evade him. Rory caught sight of Red three and watched as the ME banked to come in behind the sprog.

"Red three, you've got one on your tail. I'm on him."

The German took aim on the sprog, but the kid pulled his plane into a dive. Rory followed them both, zeroing in and letting loose with a burst of machine-gun fire from one hundred yards. The German took the standard evasive maneuver, taking his sights off the kid and heading further east.

Rory stayed on the ME's tail, cursing softly as the plane twisted and turned, trying to get around him. "Your arse is mine," he muttered, coming in close for another burst. The German began a steep climb. Rory checked his airspeed and altitude. He knew he was approaching the French coast and if he got too close, he'd take antiaircraft fire from below.

A burst of fire ripped through his fuselage. "Christ," he muttered. He twisted around in his seat and saw another Messerschmitt coming up on him from five o'clock. Another burst of fire hit his engine and hydraulic oil sprayed the interior of the cockpit.

An instant later, the German's plane exploded behind him and Rory saw the sprog coming up on him. He tried his radio, but it was out. His engine sputtered and then stopped. He had enough altitude to keep himself aloft for a while but Rory knew he didn't have nearly enough air to get back across the Channel.

He gave the sprog a thumbs-down sign and the kid's eyes went wide. Rory knew he'd wait and follow him down so he could report his position, but Rory shook his head and pointed to an approaching German plane, telling the kid to get back into the fight.

As he continued to lose altitude, Rory evaluated his choices. He could probably reach the French coast but he didn't relish spending the rest of the war in a German P.O.W. camp. If he ditched, his chances of survival weren't good. The Spitfires weren't made for water landings and if he survived the impact, then he'd probably drown or freeze before someone found him. Bailing out over the water didn't improve the odds much.

He checked his parachute harness, then turned the plane toward the French coast. He didn't want to die today. He wanted to survive the war, go home to Ballykirk and marry Kit Malone. He'd take his chances in France. If he survived bailout, he might be able to evade capture.

But his plane had other ideas. He was losing altitude too quickly, the strong tailwind providing no additional lift. He unlatched the canopy, waiting until the last possible moment. But the sticky stabilizer that had plagued him during his last mission began to act up again. His plane started to spiral down in wide circles, gaining more speed as he lost control.

Rory pushed out of the seat and said a quick Hail Mary. But the canopy wouldn't slide open. He pushed with all his strength, then wriggled out, the forces of the spiraling dive conspiring against him. Just as he slipped all the way out, the canopy slammed closed, striking Rory hard in the chest.

He felt the world go black around him and he thought of Kit. And then he was in the air, tumbling down, barely able to breathe, knowing that he might hit the water before his chute fully opened. He pulled the ripcord then allowed himself to drift into unconsciousness, grateful that he wouldn't have to face death awake and aware.

CHAPTER SEVENTEEN

DONAL TOSSED his jacket over a chair in the entry hall of the house, then loosened his tie and his collar as he walked through to the study. He'd spent the entire afternoon with the family solicitors and he was ready for a few fingers of good whiskey.

As he passed the parlor, Maura glanced up from her book. "Donal, you had a caller."

"I'll take care of whatever it is later."

"I th-think you'd best come in here," she said, motioning for him to sit with her. When he'd settled in the chair across from her, she reached out and took his hands. She must have something very distressing to tell him, Donal mused. She rarely stuttered anymore, and only when she was nervous or upset. "He br-brought a cable from the war office. Your fr-friend, Rory, has been…lost."

"Lost?"

"His airplane went d-down over the Channel. He's presumed dead."

Donal shook his head. "No. He can't be. There must be some mistake."

"I—I'm afraid it's true." Maura's eyes swam with tears as she held out the message. "I wish it wasn't, dear. His family has asked if you'd tell Kit."

Donal raked his hand through his hair as he read the cable, then closed his eyes. His heart twisted in his chest, making it impossible to breathe. He'd wished Rory away so many times over the past few years, but he'd never wanted him dead. He'd just wanted him…gone. He felt the pain of loss well up inside. Rory had been his best friend, his only true friend besides Kit, and now he was gone.

"I'd better go now," he muttered numbly, grabbing his jacket, "before she hears from someone else. Have Kit's bedroom made up. I don't want her to stay at the cottage alone tonight."

Donal strode back out the front door and got into his car. But as he reached for the ignition, his hand trembled. He drew it away and clutched the steering wheel until his knuckles went white. He wondered about Rory's last seconds, whether he'd been frightened, whether he'd known he was going to die.

Donal couldn't imagine having that kind of courage, to be able to put himself in danger and then wake up the next morning and do it again. What drove a man like Rory to sacrifice his life in such a way? Donal had very simple needs—he wanted to accumulate as much wealth as quickly as he could, he wanted to indulge his every whim and live a life filled with pleasure. What was lacking in him? Donal parked down the road from Kit's cottage and walked the last two hundred yards, trying to put his thoughts in order.

He found Kit sitting in her garden, bundled in a warm wool sweater, a fountain pen in hand, her journal open on her lap. She looked up as he opened the gate, smiling at him. But as she waited for him to step inside, her smile faded.

Donal cursed inwardly. She could tell something was wrong. He might was well get it out. "There's been news," Donal said quietly, "about Rory."

She watched him warily, as if afraid to ask. "You have a letter?"

Donal slowly approached, shaking his head. "No."

She drew in an agonized breath and stood, holding out her hand to ward him off. Donal looked into her eyes, praying that he wouldn't have to say the words, hoping that she'd understand. He saw it first in the ghostly paleness of her complexion, and then in her tears, and finally in the way her body seemed to crumple into his arms.

"I'm sorry," Donal murmured, slowly stroking her hair. "God, Kit, I'm so sorry."

"Tell me," Kit demanded, her voice filled with anger. "I need to hear you say it. It won't be real unless you do."

"His plane was shot down near the coast of France.

They say it went down in the water. There's no sign that he survived the crash."

A moan erupted from deep inside of her and she sank to the ground, her arms covering her head as if she were trying to protect herself from the truth. Sobs racked her body and Donal didn't know what to do. Kit had always been so strong. He couldn't bear to see her in such pain.

He bent down and drew her back to her feet, but she was limp with grief, her tears staining the front of his shirt. Donal gently led her into the cottage and sat her down on the couch.

"I shouldn't have let him go," she said. "I should have gone to bring him back from the train station. He would have come if I'd asked, if I'd told him that I loved him."

"Stop," Donal said, grasping her shoulder with his fingers. "You can't do this to yourself. Rory made the decision to leave."

She brushed away his hand as she pulled her legs up to her chin. Donal backed off, knowing that nothing he said would make a difference to her. Rory had always held the key to her heart. And now her heart had been shattered.

Donal went to put on a pot of tea, but then instead searched the cottage for something stronger to drink. He left Kit weeping on the couch and walked out to the car, pulling a flask from beneath the front seat. Tipping his head back, he took a long swallow, the whiskey burning a path to his belly.

How the hell was he supposed to feel? Rory had been his best friend, yet he'd stood in the way of the one thing Donal had wanted—Kit. Now that he was gone, would she finally put her feelings for Rory in the past? Or would he grow to even more heroic proportions in her mind?

Donal took another swallow of the whiskey, then tucked the flask into his jacket pocket. When he returned to the house, he found Kit curled up on the couch, her fingers toying with a bracelet she wore. Like a rosary, she held each green bead and whispered a prayer before moving on to the next.

He bent down and brushed the hair from her face. "I'm going to take you back to the house. I don't want you to be here alone tonight." Kit shook her head, but when he reached down to help her up, she didn't offer any resistance.

As he drove, she stared out the window, softly weeping. Donal wanted to share in her grief, but the guilt he felt was overwhelming. He still had the letter, tucked away in his desk at home. Should he offer it to her now? She'd be angry at his deception, but at least he wouldn't be forced to carry the lie any longer. Kit loved Rory and Rory had loved her. After absorbing that knowledge, she would certainly move on from there.

When they got to the house, Maura was waiting. She gathered Kit into her arms, then walked with her upstairs to her room. When she came out of Kit's old room, Donal stepped inside.

"Can I bring you anything?" he asked, kneeling beside the bed to look into her red-rimmed eyes.

"No," she said in a tiny voice.

"Then I'll see you in the morning," he said. He pressed a kiss to her forehead.

She clutched his shirt, holding him close. "Stay with me."

"All right," Donal said.

She slid over on the bed and held up the blanket. Donal kicked off his shoes, then shrugged out of his jacket. He crawled in beside her and gathered her into his arms. "It will be all right, Kit," he murmured, pressing his lips to her forehead.

"How will it ever be right again?" She drew back and stared into his eyes, waiting for him to explain.

"I don't know," Donal said. "But life does go on. Rory would have wanted us to be happy."

"Promise me, you won't leave," she said, clutching his shirt tightly in her fists. "No matter how bad the war gets. Promise you'll never go."

"I won't leave you, Kit. I'd never leave you." He dropped a kiss on her nose and ventured lower to her lips. She hesitated for a moment and Donal waited, wondering what was going through her mind. Was she wishing that it was Rory holding her and kissing her?

But then, she leaned closer and kissed him back. All the emotion she'd been fighting seemed to come rushing out as she pulled him on top of her. "Make love to me," she murmured, her eyes closed tightly. "I need to be close to you."

Donal knew what he was doing was wrong, that she didn't want him. Through it all, she never looked at him and it was obvious that she imagined herself in Rory's arms, making love to a man she could never have.

And when it was over, she wept, her delicate frame curled against his, her tears warm on his naked skin. When she'd worn herself out from weeping, she slept for a bit. Then began a cycle of them talking about Rory, about some memory that had come to her in her dreams. But inevitably the memory would bring more tears and she'd cry herself to sleep again.

But Donal didn't care. Kit belonged to him now. Rory was gone and he would do his best to make himself the most important man in her life. Sooner or later, her love for Rory would have to fade. And then, Donal would be there, ready to show her that they had been meant for each other all along.

THE VOICES CAME and went with the strange shadows that passed before his eyes. Rory tried to focus, to understand what they were saying to him, but everything was garbled, like a radio signal, fading in and out.

Someone grabbed his wrist and he fought back, fear welling up inside of him. More words, faint, indistinct and then a slow fall into darkness. Was he dead, caught in that limbo between heaven and hell?

He tried to open his eyes, but saw only darkness. He opened his mouth to speak, but his throat was dry and raw. He felt a hand on the back of his neck and a cup at his lips. The water soothed his thirst. But was there water in heaven?

He tried to remember where he'd come from, but he couldn't recall his life before this moment. Had he ever lived or was this all there was to him, this crushing pain in his chest, this throbbing head and dry throat, this ache that felt as if his limbs were being torn asunder?

"Do not speak." The deep voice was barely a whisper, but he understood. "Do you know where you are?"

Rory shook his head. Was he still alive? A memory teased at his brain, the sound of an explosion, the whine of an engine, the rush of wind, his pulse pounding in his head.

"Your plane went down," the man said.

He spoke with an accent and Rory understood enough to know it wasn't German. Was it French? He felt a small measure of relief, but he wasn't sure why.

"You were unconscious when they found you, hanging from a tree by your parachute. You've been asleep for three days. You're in occupied France, at a farmhouse near the village of Guigny. Your plane crashed along the coast south of Calais but the air currents saved you from the water. The underground has moved you inland over the past three nights until you ended here."

Rory lifted his hand and touched his eyes, the memory of the dogfight slowly filtering back into his head. He wasn't dead. He was alive, after bailing out over the Channel.

Gently the man pulled Rory's hands back down to the rough woolen blankets. "Your face is burned a bit, but not seriously. There is a bump on your head and your chest is badly bruised."

"Il faut que nous le cachions. Les Allemands le cherchaient depuis que l'on a trouvé son avion," another man's voice said.

"He can't be moved until he can walk," the man muttered.

Rory struggled to sit up but the pain in his chest made him dizzy. And with no visual guide, he felt disoriented. He fell back against the pillow and listened as a whispered argument began among the three men in the room. He had no idea what they were saying, but he knew it had everything to do with his fate.

He remembered the dogfight now, the bursts of bullets shearing through his plane, the oil spraying into the cockpit and the fire at his back. He remembered the images of Kit that had flashed in his mind as the plane had begun to tumble toward the water. He was in enemy territory now, occupied France, and these people planned to send him home—but to what?

"I—I can't see," Rory said. "I can't see anything.

I—I'm blind." The room fell silent and he waited for someone to say something.

He felt a wave of panic overwhelm him. Even if he did make it out of France, what good would he be once he reached England? They might as well send him into the countryside to be shot by the Germans. At least he'd die a hero, instead of wasting away in some hospital for old and infirm flyers.

"Qu'est-il a dit?"

"Il est aveugle," the man said.

Rory heard a low curse and then footsteps walking out of the room. "The underground has rescued many pilots," the man explained. "We send them south, over the Pyrenees and into Spain. But you cannot make that trip in your condition. It is difficult for even the strongest of men. We will have to make other plans."

"What plans?" Rory asked.

"There has been contact with a British agent in this area. He has been helping the resistance. He might have a way. And there are some men in the next village who have plans to take a boat across the Channel and offer their services to the British Army. Perhaps we can send you with them. But once our plans are made, we will have to get you back to the coast." Rory felt the hand on his wrist again. "Can you tell me if you have any other injuries?" he asked.

"I think I can walk," he said.

"You will have to," the man replied. "The sooner we move you again, the safer we will all be."

"I'm ready," Rory lied. He closed his eyes and drew a deep breath, his chest aching as he did. He wasn't sure he could take a single step. But now that he knew he was still alive, he was going to do everything he could to get out of occupied France—and back to Kit.

If he just prayed hard enough, his sins would be washed away. Then his eyes would clear and he'd be able to look at her pretty face again.

CHAPTER EIGHTEEN

KIT REACHED DOWN and picked up the skirt of her wedding gown. She slipped her feet into the soft leather pumps, then walked to her bedroom door. The wedding ceremony was scheduled for ten a.m. Donal had knocked on her door just moments before to inform her that the car was waiting.

She grabbed her Bible and the embroidered handkerchief that her mother had carried on her wedding day, then headed down the stairs. Donal stood below and as soon as he saw her, he covered his eyes. "I'm not supposed to see you," he said.

Kit stepped up to him and pulled his hands down. "That's just a silly superstition."

"I don't want any bad luck to ruin this day for us," he said, slipping his arm around her waist and kissing her cheek.

"It won't," Kit assured him.

"Well, I'm glad I've seen you then, because I have something to give to you and I didn't think I'd get a chance before the wedding."

Kit sighed. When would he stop trying to buy her

affections? She'd finally agreed to marry Donal after numerous proposals. Since the night they'd spent together after learning of Rory's death, their bond had grown deeper. It was as if she'd taken all the love she'd held in reserve for Rory and given it to him, and he'd eagerly accepted it. Without Rory, they needed each other.

Everyone in Ballykirk had been delighted to hear of their engagement—the poor orphan girl and the heir to Ballykirk's wealthiest family. Kit was the only one with reservations. Was it too soon? It had only been four months since Rory's death. She worried that marrying Donal was just a reaction to her grief. But there had only ever been two men she'd loved in this world and the second one was Donal McClain.

"Don't you want to know what it is?" Donal asked, his question interrupting her thoughts.

She smiled up at him. "I don't need any more gifts."

"This is different," he explained. He pulled a small leather case from his pocket and worked at the delicate clasp. "Mother gave this to me to give to you. My grandfather had it made for my grandmother when they married. My mother wore it and now it's yours."

He pulled out a long chain with a jeweled pendant dangling from it. Kit slipped her fingers through the chain. "It's a claddagh," she murmured.

"A family heirloom," he said. "It's meant to be worn close to your heart. Will you wear it?"

Kit nodded and Donal took it from her. He fastened

it around her neck, then came back to stand before her. "Someday, I hope you'll pass it along to our son to give to his bride."

"I hope so, too," she murmured, rubbing the pendant between her fingers.

"Come," he said, holding out his arm. "Let's drive to the church together. The sooner we get married, the sooner we can enjoy our honeymoon."

Kit forced a smile. She hadn't thought much about the honeymoon. She had always imagined a wedding to Rory, a honeymoon spent at some secluded cottage by the seashore. He'd been the hero in all her fantasies. It was his body she dreamed of touching, his hands that would make her ache with desire. Could she ever feel that passion for Donal, that overwhelming need to be possessed?

He helped her into the car and she watched as he circled around to his door. She owed it to Donal to walk down the aisle with a pure heart, her love for Rory put behind her once and for all. She and Rory had had their chance and the Fates had conspired against them.

Kit clutched the small white Bible in her gloved hands. She would learn to love Donal as a wife should love a husband and they'd have a happy life together. They'd raise a family and grow old together and only occasionally would Rory's name come up in conversation.

"Are you ready?" Donal asked.

"Drive on," she said.

Donal chuckled as he started the car. The drive to Ballykirk passed so quickly that Kit barely had a chance to calm her nerves. She'd wanted a small wedding, but Donal had insisted they invite everyone in the village and make a celebration of the day.

When they arrived at the church, the guests were all milling around outside rather than waiting inside for the ceremony to begin. Donal helped Kit out of the car and almost immediately Siobhan Quinn approached, her hat askew, her color high. The crowd quieted and turned their attention toward Donal and Kit.

"What is it?" Kit said, glancing around.

"We've had a letter," Siobhan replied, pulling Kit into a fierce hug. "Rory is safe. He's been in France, hidden from the Germans. They finally managed to smuggle him out with several other pilots."

Kit felt the breath leave her body. She stepped back and pressed her palm to her chest, gasping for air. "Oh, my God." Her head spun and her legs felt boneless. "Where is he now?"

"In hospital," Siobhan said. "Somewhere outside London. I don't know what's wrong or how long he's been there, but I have an address."

Kit's closed her eyes, tears threatening. She'd never dared believe that he was alive, though every night she'd said a prayer that one day she'd see him again. She glanced at the crowd. There was only one person who understood how deep her feelings for Rory ran and he was standing beside her, a stunned expression on his face.

Her first impulse was to get back into the car and find the fastest way to England, to Rory. But she could never humiliate Donal that way. He'd offered her his love, his loyalty, his entire life. How could she throw that back in his face and still live with herself?

Kit swallowed back her tears and smiled. "How wonderful for your family," she said, giving Siobhan another hug. "We'll have two events to celebrate today."

She'd made her decision. Rory was safe, her prayers had been answered. Now it was time to put her foolish infatuation for him in the past. He'd never loved her the way she'd loved him. If he had, he wouldn't have left. "I'd like to write to him." Kit forced a light laugh. "After the wedding, of course."

Siobhan nodded. "I know he's probably anxious to hear from you and Donal. And he'll be so pleased to learn that you two have been married."

"Yes," she murmured, "I'm sure he will."

As the guests began to move inside, Kit wandered over to the churchyard and stood at the wall, staring out at the weathered crosses that marked the graves. They'd put up a marker for Rory and now they'd be taking it down. In the blink of an eye, he'd returned to the living and his death had been undone. She felt Donal's hand on her arm.

"What do you want to do?" he asked.

"About what?" she asked, her attention still fixed on the stone.

"The wedding. Do you want to postpone? Or perhaps you want to cancel."

Kit turned to look at him, seeing the apprehension in his eyes. He was giving her a choice. A flood of affection overwhelmed her. Donal loved her enough to let her go. How could she walk away from a love so selfless to a love that had never existed at all? "Do you?"

"No," Donal replied, grabbing her hands and giving them a squeeze. "All I've ever wanted was to make you my wife."

"Then I don't want to cancel. Why don't you go in and tell Father Timothy that we'll be ready to start in five minutes?" She pushed up on her toes and gave him a quick kiss. "I'll see you at the altar."

He nodded, then walked off. Kit turned back to the churchyard, focusing on an old Celtic cross. She closed her eyes and said a silent prayer of thanks. She had been given the one thing she'd wanted most in the world. Rory was alive and he'd come home. She'd be able to look into his eyes and listen to his voice again.

But she couldn't ask for more than that. If she did, God might choose to take something else away from her.

"AND HOW ARE YOU feeling today, Lieutenant Quinn?"

The voice came out of nowhere. Rory started, then

twisted in his wheelchair until he faced in her direction. She was Irish. The sound of home wove through her words like a forgotten melody and he suddenly ached for a bit of human contact.

"You're new," he said.

"Not new. Just transferred up from the burn ward."

"Where are you from?" he asked.

"Donegal," she said. "And you?"

"A small village in County Cork. Ballykirk."

"Ah, you're from the south."

"I am. Unless they moved Cork to the north since I've last been home."

She laughed softly. "No. I'm sure it's still where it's always been. It's just that I don't know many pilots from the south." He felt her hands on his lap, adjusting the blanket that covered his legs. "It's damp out here. Wouldn't you like to go inside, Lieutenant?"

Rory shook his head. "The place smells of antiseptic."

"It has to. For the burn victims. They're susceptible to all sorts of infections." She paused for a long moment. "Well, don't stay out too long. When you're ready to go in, just give a shout and I'll come to get you." He heard her footsteps retreat on the stone walkway.

"And who should I call?" he asked. "Surely you have a name."

The footsteps stopped. "My name is Brenna. Brenna Rooney."

"Wait right there, Brenna Rooney." He turned the

wheelchair around and started in her direction. He could see vague shapes, light and shadow, just enough to find her. "Keep talking. If you haven't noticed, I'm having a bit of trouble with my eyes lately."

"What should I talk about?" she asked.

"Tell me what you're doing in a place like this."

"I'm a nurse," she said. "I was needed, so I came."

"All the way from Donegal." He held out his hand, and when she took it he gave hers a firm shake. "Rory Quinn."

"I know," she said. "I cared for you when you first got here. You weren't in the mood for conversation as I remember. You were feelin' quite sorry for yourself, now, weren't you? I'm glad to see that your attitude has changed."

Rory let go of her fingers, then gripped the wheels of his chair. "I believe I deserved a bit of a sulk. I planned on seeing the world once this war was over. I won't be doing that now."

"You can't be sure," Brenna said. "Your sight could return slowly. The doctor believes you may have something called Purtscher's retinopathy. The tiny blood vessels in your retinas were hurt when you injured your chest. They just need time to heal."

"I'm blind," Rory said, his mood darkening. For a moment, he had felt almost normal. He'd forgotten Kit, forgotten the letter from home informing him that she'd married Donal, forgotten that he didn't have a life anymore. But talking about his eyesight brought it all crashing back.

"Yes, you are blind…for now," Brenna countered. "But there's always hope."

"Ah, yes," he muttered. "We'll just pray to the patron saint of blind flyers for intervention. We Irish are good at our prayers, aren't we? Well, you pray double to make up for those I won't be saying."

"A prayer now and then couldn't hurt," she said. She stood beside him, close enough for Rory to feel the heat from her body.

"Maybe you should take me inside. I've had enough fresh air for one day."

Brenna wheeled him back to the ward, but when she tried to help him into his bed, he brushed her hand away. "I'm not a cripple," he said.

"I know that." Her voice was tight, her words laced with frustration. "But you are rude and surly and acting like a spoiled child."

"You have something more to say to me, Nurse Rooney? If not, I think I'd prefer to be alone now." He steeled himself for another round of platitudes, those empty words of encouragement that were meant to make him feel better, to make him try harder.

"No," she said. "I trust you've heard all you need to hear. Until you begin to listen, I'd just be wasting my breath." She walked to the door, then stopped. "I'll come back after you've had your supper, Lieutenant. If you have any letters to write, I can help you with that."

Rory opened his mouth to dismiss her offer, but he knew she was already gone. He leaned back into his pillow and tipped his face up to the ceiling, squinting his eyes, trying to make out the details of his surroundings. His eyesight had improved only a bit. Where there was once blackness, now he saw shadows or hazy light. There was no detail, nothing to give him a compass by which to navigate.

He lay in his bed, listening to the sounds of the patients around him. Most of the men in East Grinstead Hospital were burn victims, fighter pilots and bomber crewmen who'd been caught inside burning planes. He'd been seen by the eye specialist and was told there was nothing to do but wait.

Rory had become quite good at waiting. Hours crept by at a maddeningly slow pace when he couldn't see a clock. He'd guess at the time and find an hour had been only fifteen minutes. Volunteers sometimes came to read to him and the day passed faster, but he'd lost track of how long he'd been at the hospital, unable to tell day from night.

As the afternoon passed, Rory found himself more anxious for supper to be served. Would Brenna Rooney keep her word and stop to see him? He'd already decided to dictate at least two or three letters to fictional relatives. He merely wanted the company and was certain she wouldn't stay without a reason.

He was willing to do anything to get his mind off Kit Malone—or Kit McClain as she was now known. Just the thought of her, living in that big house with Donal, sitting across the dinner table from him, sharing his bed, made him angry. He'd squandered whatever opportunity he'd been given with her. He should have told her how he really felt that night in Galway, instead of giving Donal that ridiculous letter.

To his surprise, supper was delivered sooner than he'd anticipated. He picked at the boiled potatoes and stringy chicken but ate the plum tart in three quick bites. And before he knew it, she was there, beside his bed.

He smelled her before he heard her, the faint scent of lilies breaking through the sterile disinfectant of the ward. "You're back," he said, wiping his mouth with his napkin.

"You didn't eat your dinner."

"I'm not used to the fancy food they serve here. It's a bit rich for my tastes."

Brenna laughed softly. He tried to imagine the face that went with a voice so gentle and sweet. Over the past few weeks, he'd done his best to forget Kit, but thoughts of her had constantly bedeviled his mind. Brenna was a distraction, a way to forget the woman he still loved.

"I thought I might wheel you down to the recreation hall," Brenna said. "They play music in the evenings and it's quite a lively crowd."

"I don't want to stay inside," he said.

"All right. We'll take a stroll."

She reached out and took his hand, leading him to his wheelchair, but Rory shook his head. "I can walk."

"All right." Brenna placed his hand on her elbow and they started toward the door of the ward. They walked down the long hallway, then turned left.

"Where are you taking me?" he asked.

"You'll see."

By the time they stopped walking, Rory was completely confused. They'd gone down a flight of stairs, then down again on a lift, then walked outside for a fair distance, down a long hill.

"What's that smell?"

"Roses," she said. "There's a fine garden of them. Pink and red and white. The scent is more lovely in the evening." She drew him forward. "Come, there's a pleasant spot beneath an oak tree."

They sat on a wool blanket that she spread on the grass, Rory reaching back to feel the rough bark of a tree behind him. The birds sang and the breeze ruffled the leaves and for a moment, he felt as if he were home, back in Ballykirk.

"I've brought paper," she said. "I can write letters if you'd like. To your parents or perhaps a sweetheart?"

"There's no sweetheart," Rory said. "There was, but it's the same tragic tale. She married my best friend. I got the letter a few weeks ago."

"Was it...your accident?"

Rory shook his head. "No. Kit never really knew I loved her. I left for the war without telling her. And she certainly didn't love me. Hell, she married someone else."

"I'm sorry," Brenna said.

"Why should you be? It wasn't your fault. I blame him. If I was up to punching him in the face, I would. But considering my circumstances, I might miss him entirely." He chuckled dryly, then reached out for her hands, fumbling to find them. "Tell me something, Nurse Rooney. And I want you to be honest."

"I will."

"Do I look blind? If you didn't know, could you tell?"

"No," Brenna said. "In truth, you're quite a handsome fellow. You have dark hair and a strong chin and lovely eyes. An odd color, a bit green and a bit gold."

"Tell me about your eyes," Rory teased. "And your hair. I'd like to imagine how you look while we're speaking."

Brenna sighed softly and tugged her hands from his. "I don't think you would," she said. "I'm not very beautiful. I'm not beautiful at all. I'm plain and ordinary, the kind of woman you'd pass on the street and not notice."

"I wouldn't notice a purple elephant if it passed me by," Rory said. "Still, your description can't be entirely true."

"Oh, it is," she said in an earnest tone. "I've got great gangly legs and unruly red hair. My eyes are too small and my mouth is too wide and my nose is a bit crooked."

"You exaggerate," Rory said.

"Not at all," she replied. "I've come to accept that I'll never find a man who'll want me, so I've found myself a career. I'm quite satisfied, you know. I love my work."

Rory leaned back against the tree. "Perhaps we place too much value on beauty. To me, you're quite beautiful, your voice, your kindness, the scent of your soap, the touch of your hand. The rest doesn't really matter now, does it?"

"People who are beautiful always say things like that. Beauty comes from the inside, they say. Or beauty is in the eye of the beholder. Quite patronizing to ugly folk."

Rory raked his hand through his hair and imagined himself looking into her eyes. "I may be beautiful, but I'm also blind. People see me differently, too. They pity me."

"Only if you allow them," Brenna said, reaching out to touch his cheek. Her fingers were there one moment, and gone the next. Rory longed for that touch, the warmth of human contact that seemed so much more important now that his world had gone dark.

"Why don't we write that letter?" she suggested.

Slowly, he reached up and searched for her in the

space in front of him. His hand found her cheek and he gently explored her face, skimming his fingertips over her nose and then lingering on her mouth. "Or we could play cards," she suggested, drawing back out of his reach. "I've brought these along."

She placed a card in his hand and Rory ran his fingers over it. "Four of diamonds," he said, the raised surface simple to read.

"We can play gin rummy," she suggested. "I'll tell you what's discarded and what I pick up. You'll just have to remember the rest." Brenna shuffled the cards, then dealt them, leading his hands to the cards in front of him.

"Do you have any money, then?" she asked. "I think a small wager would make the game more interesting, don't you?"

"How do I know you won't be looking at my cards while we're playing?"

"You'll just have to trust me," Brenna said.

Rory smiled. "I suppose that wouldn't be too difficult to do."

It felt good to relax, to forget about his troubles for a short time and to pretend as if his life might one day be normal again. He knew it would all end the moment he stepped back onto the ward, when he allowed himself to lapse back into self-pity. But for now, his world was right. He'd handle tomorrow when it came.

CHAPTER NINETEEN

HE HADN'T WANTED to return home, at least not yet. But there was nowhere else for him to go. Rory's eyesight had gotten progressively better over the three months he'd spent at East Grinstead and he was deemed fit to be released. The RAF didn't want him back. He was still close to blind in his right eye and a half-blind pilot wasn't any better than a fully blind one in the judgment of the Royal Air Force. He'd been given a choice—more time in a rehabilitation hospital or a full discharge. To him there had been only one option.

In Ballykirk, he might be able to make a living. Perhaps he might find work on his father's fishing boat again. As a teenager, he'd been anxious to avoid such labor, but now the prospect seemed like a welcome relief. He needed to find a way to live and the sea would provide that for now.

Rory had other fears, though. He knew he was going back to a place that held poignant memories and harsh realities. Donal and Kit were living in the big house on the Skibbereen road. There was no way to avoid seeing them in a village as tiny as Ballykirk.

Kit had written to him a number of times at East Grinstead, long, chatty letters signed by both her and Donal. He'd tried to get his mind around the two of them, tried to think of them as a couple. But his heart refused to acknowledge Kit as anything other than his love.

As his sight had improved, his relationship with Brenna had cooled. She'd still been friendly and attentive, but he sensed her insecurities had been tempered when he was blind. Now that there was a possibility he might see her, she retreated, as if afraid of his reaction when he did.

The truth was, Brenna Rooney wasn't a beautiful woman. But that didn't change Rory's affection for her. She'd been a light in his dark world, a beacon shining in the distance and beckoning him back from the edge of the abyss. For that, he would always be grateful.

Rory drew in a deep breath and tipped his face up to the sun. He'd been back for two days, setting up residence in an old cottage a few miles from Ballykirk. The house sat on a bluff above the sea, and in the afternoon he could watch the sun set over the ocean.

The place provided the solitude he needed to adjust to life outside the hospital. It gave him time to make his mistakes, to trip over unseen obstacles, to struggle with small tasks that once had seemed so easy—lighting a fire in the hearth or peeling a potato for dinner.

But there was one thing he could do—and do it with his eyes closed. He could tie fishing nets faster and cleaner than anyone along the coast. The task would occupy his time and his mind until he had the courage to set foot outside the cottage.

Rory made his way back to the door. He could see detail now with his left eye, though everything still appeared as if he were seeing it through the bottom of a whiskey bottle, blurry and distorted. At times, objects nearly came into focus, but mostly, everything was still seen as hazy-edged shapes with vague detail. If he concentrated, he could read the headlines in the newspaper, but he worried he'd never be able to read a book again.

He held his arm out, reaching for the door, ready to face the task of making his lunch. But he was so confident with his movement that he forgot the shallow first step up into the cottage. Rory caught himself against the doorjamb, but he fell down on his knees, slamming one against the sharp edge of the stone step.

"Jaysus, Mary and Joseph," he shouted. A few moments later, he felt a hand on his arm.

"Are you all right?"

Rory froze. He'd heard the voice so many times in his dreams he couldn't help but believe he was still asleep. But the pain throbbing in his knee told him differently. He stumbled to his feet, pulling out of Kit's grip. "I wondered when I'd see you again," he muttered. "Or hear you, as the case might be. How long have you been standing there?"

"Not long," Kit said, the lie evident in her tone. "I just found out you were back. I saw your sister in town yesterday." She paused and Rory stared at her, frustrated that he couldn't see the true beauty of her face.

He'd dreamed of this moment nearly every night since he'd returned from France, all the hours spent lying in the hospital. He'd dreamed about it and yet dreaded it at the same time. They were different people now, one of them ruined by war, the other confined by marriage. How he wished they could return for just an afternoon to the carefree days of their youth, when love was still a possibility.

"I've brought lunch," Kit said, "and supper. I didn't know if you'd be up to cooking."

"I'm not an invalid," Rory snapped. He felt his defenses rise along with his frustration and anger. He didn't know what to say. All he could think about was pulling her into his arms and kissing her, erasing the past few years in a single act. But Kit was in love with another man and he was bound to respect her choice.

"I didn't mean that you were. I—I just thought… well, you were never much of a cook before, as I recall." She cleared her throat nervously. "But if you don't want it, I'll just—"

Rory opened the door and stepped inside the cottage. "Suit yourself."

She followed him inside and he heard her set the basket on the table. "So, how are you?" Kit asked.

"I'm nearly blind." Rory's jaw went tight as he

tried to control his temper. He wanted to hurt her, to lash out at her and inflict the same pain she'd caused him. How could she have married Donal? Rory had loved her for as long as he could remember and she should have known that. "You don't need to stay. I get along quite well on my own."

A long silence descended over the cottage and she drew a ragged breath. "I can't believe you're here," she murmured, her voice trembling. "You're alive and you're safe. When I heard your plane went down, I nearly died. I couldn't imagine the world without you in it."

"But you didn't die," Rory said, his words cool and indifferent, his anger receding. "Instead, you married Donal." He braced his hands on the mantel. He'd have only one chance to come clean, and if he didn't do it now, he never would. "I loved you, Kit." The words came out in a strangled whisper. "I thought, when I got back, that we might marry."

She gasped and he could only guess at the expression on her face. Shock? Horror? Embarrassment?

"I—I didn't know." A moment later, she was at his side, her fingers gently resting on his arm. "How was I to know that?"

"You weren't. I never told you. At least not in words."

"I wanted the same, Rory. From the time I was a girl, I thought that we'd have a grand romance. And that we'd get married at the church in Ballykirk and live in my little cottage."

At first, he thought he'd imagined her words. That he'd wished for them so many times the fantasy had overtaken his mind. Rory slowly turned, reaching out to touch her face. He felt the dampness of her tears then moved down to find her lips curled up in a rueful smile. "I was a fool. I should have told you how I felt that night in Galway. But I was afraid I wouldn't be able to leave."

"I never would have married Donal," she said. "I would have waited for you…forever."

"Christ, it's my fault," Rory said, pulling her into his arms and pressing her slender body against his. A flood of memories raced through his mind and he was taken back to that night they'd danced together, the last night he'd held her in his arms. "I wrote you a letter and gave it to Donal. I told him the moment you expressed the same feelings for me, he was to give it to you. I should have given it to you myself." He felt her stiffen in his arms and he drew back. "What is it?"

"I never saw the letter," she said.

"I asked him to destroy it if anything happened to me. I never wanted you to have any regrets for feeling only friendship toward me."

"That doesn't matter. You're here, you're alive, and that's all I need." She cupped his face in her hands and an instant later she was kissing him, her lips soft and damp against his.

It felt like everything he'd lost had been found again. Rory yanked her against him and surrendered to the taste of her mouth. He didn't need to see her, he could feel her, invading his body and his soul, proving there was still a man inside him. His hands skimmed over her neck and her shoulders, fumbling with the buttons on her blouse, desperate to feel her skin beneath his fingertips.

And then she was gone, pulling out of his embrace and retreating to the other side of the room. "I—I—that's not what I meant to do," she murmured. "I'm sorry."

"I'm not," Rory said, shoving his hands into his pockets. He turned away and walked back to the hearth, staring up at the clock he couldn't quite read. "Now I know you want me as much as I want you."

"Don't say that."

"If I could take it all back, I would. I should have kissed you properly that night in Galway and then never let you go. I thought I knew what I wanted, but I didn't, all those silly heroic ideals. What I really wanted was standing right in front me, within my grasp and I let it go." He turned back to her, and for a moment, Rory could see her face again. He wasn't sure whether his eyes actually focused or whether it was just his memory filling in the blurry spots, but he saw her and she was the most beautiful thing in his world. "I've only ever wanted you. And I still do."

She shook her head, covering her ears with her hands. "We can't do this, Rory. This is wrong. I married Donal. We had our chance and it passed us by and now we have to live with our lives the way they are." She crossed the room and took his hands, folding them between hers and pressing them to her heart. "I will always love you, but we can't make that love real. We can't possibly be together."

She was right, Rory mused, the taste of truth bitter in his mouth. What could he offer her that Donal couldn't? He'd barely be able to make a living for himself, never mind a family. With Donal, she'd have a comfortable life and a good future for her children. Kit deserved that. But Rory still couldn't accept it. "Leave him," he said. "Love me. We'll leave Ballykirk. We'll go to Australia or America and make a life for ourselves."

"I—I can't," Kit said. "He's my husband. I just… can't." She pushed up on her toes and placed a soft kiss on his cheek. "Welcome home, Rory," she said sadly.

With that, she ran out of the cottage, leaving Rory to face the rest of his life alone. He took no solace in the knowledge that she had loved him once and perhaps still did. God had chosen to play a cruel trick on him, to make him pay for some sin he'd long forgotten. Taking his sight hadn't been enough. He'd now taken what Rory had always desired more than anything else in the world.

"Goodbye, Kit," Rory murmured.

KIT FLUNG OPEN the front door, letting it crash back against the wall. She listened for the sound of her husband's voice, but the house was silent all around her. With a soft curse, she strode back to Donal's study. The desk was unlocked and she yanked open the center drawer and began to rummage through the contents.

"Where is it?" she muttered, fighting back tears.

All this time, all the pain and indecision she'd felt, and for nothing. Rory had wanted her, needed her, and Donal had known that. But in his unwavering desire to own her, Donal had stolen the one chance she'd had at true and lasting love.

A sob tore from her throat and Kit sat down in the leather chair and buried her face in her hands. Why had this happened? What had she done wrong? Was this some perverse punishment for not loving them equally? It felt as if the two of them were tearing her apart.

Angrily, she brushed aside her tears and opened another drawer. Her mind replayed that night in Galway, her conversation with Donal after Rory had left for the train station. There was no doubt in her mind that she'd expressed her feelings clearly. *Can I tell you a secret?* That's what she'd said before professing her love for Rory Quinn. But had Donal heard her? He'd been so drunk that night that he'd barely been able to walk upright.

Even if he had understood, why did she expect Donal to act any differently? He'd loved her with the same blinding intensity as Rory had. It seemed they both would have tossed aside their own friendship to lay claim to her. She pulled open another drawer and tossed the papers on the surface of the desk, shuffling through the mess of folders and envelopes.

"Kit, the front door was—"

She looked up to see Donal standing in the doorway. He took in the jumble of papers on his desk and raised an eyebrow. "Are you looking for something?"

She stood up and shoved everything off the desk and onto the floor. "Where is it, Donal? Where is the letter?"

He frowned. "What letter?"

"You must have known I'd find out about it. With Rory dead, your secret was safe. But now he's returned and you're going to have to confess."

"I don't know what—"

"Stop!" She drew a deep breath and tried to calm her hammering heart. Right now, she hated him more than she'd ever hated anyone before. "No more lies. Just give me the letter. Give it to me now and I'll forget you were supposed to give it to me that night in Galway."

He shifted uneasily, his face suddenly ashen. "I don't have it," Donal said.

"You're lying. If I have to tear this house apart to find it, I will. And after I do, I'll never trust you again." Tears streamed down her face and she wrenched open another drawer. "You were supposed to give it to me. You made a promise to him."

"What promise? Do you think I remember anything from that night? Christ, Kit, you know how much I had to drink. He gave me the letter and then I forgot about it. I only found it the next morning and I wasn't sure what I was supposed to do with it."

She looked up at him, shaking her head. "No. No, I don't believe you." She shuffled through the pile of papers on the desk, then screamed in frustration. "Tell me where it is!"

Donal stared at his shoes and Kit waited, sobs racking her body. "It's in the safe." He crossed the room and opened a small cabinet beneath a bookshelf. A moment later, he straightened and held out the envelope. "I couldn't give it to you. I couldn't watch you wait for a man who didn't love you enough to stay. What if he hadn't come back, Kit? You might have wasted your whole life loving him and that wasn't fair—not to you or to me. It would have been so much easier if he'd just stayed dead."

Kit crossed the room and slapped Donal as hard as she could. Donal gasped as his head snapped to the side, then turned back to her, his eyes narrowed.

"I will never forgive you for this," Kit said, and snatched the letter from his fingers.

He nodded, rubbing his cheek. "I gambled and I lost," he said with a casual shrug. "But the prize was worth the risk. And I'd do it all again, Kit. I loved you then and I love you now. That will never change."

She turned on her heel and walked out of the house, slamming the front door behind her. Tears again pressed at the corners of her eyes and she fought them back, refusing to give in to her grief. She'd lost Rory once when his plane had gone down and now it felt as if she'd lost him all over again.

She wanted to run to him, to cast her fate to the wind and take her chances with love. But in the eyes of the church and the Irish Free State, she belonged to Donal and there was nothing she could do about it. Divorce was still illegal in Southern Ireland.

When she'd put enough distance between her and the house, she stopped by the side of the road and took the letter out of the envelope. The breeze whipped at her dark hair as she perched on the edge of a low stone wall and read Rory's familiar scrawl.

My dearest Kit,

I love you. There, it's done. I've wanted to say the words out loud for such a long time. I've written them in countless unsent letters, imagined the sound of them on my lips, but always worried that my feelings wouldn't be returned. You have been my best friend. Dare I wish for more? The time has never seemed right for us but I promise that someday it will be. While we are apart, I will see your face every night before I fall asleep and will wake up each day wondering if the sun is shining where you are. Wait for me and I will come back to you, darling Kit. My heart is yours.

Rory

She traced her fingertip over the phrases, each word stabbing at her heart like a tiny dagger, stealing the breath from her lungs. She could have been happy for a lifetime with Rory. But she'd made her choice that day at the church, the day she'd learned he'd come back from the dead. She'd ignored her heart and now she was left to pay the price.

Kit sat in the same spot for a long time, her knees tucked under her chin, thinking about the events that had brought her to this place in time. If she walked away from her marriage, living outside the church with Rory was not an option she would consider. She'd have to make a life for herself, find a way to make a living. Life wouldn't be easy for a woman on her own.

She pressed her forehead to her knees. Or she could go home and make the best of what she'd been given. She could reconcile with Donal. She could have children and lavish her love on them. And she could dream about Rory for the rest of her days.

The sun was nearly set by the time Kit started for home. Numbly, she walked through the large entrance hall, the letter clutched in her hand, and slowly climbed the stairs. She couldn't imagine sharing a bed with Donal now. She'd move her things back into her old room.

"I didn't expect you back." Donal stood in the doorway to his study, a nearly empty whiskey bottle swinging from his fingers. "Have you come home to pack?"

he asked, his words slurred by the liquor. "Ready to run to your precious Rory?"

"No," Kit replied, refusing to look at him. "I'm not going to leave you, Donal."

"It would be better if you did," he muttered, his words laced with bitterness. He took a long drink from the whiskey bottle. "Put me out of my misery, Kit. I know you love him. And I don't think I can live with that."

"Well, you don't have a choice," Kit said. "And neither do I. We're married, Donal, and there's no way out of that." She started up the stairs again. "I'm going to move back into my room. I'll let you know when you're welcome to visit."

When she reached the top of the stairs, she saw Maura, standing in the doorway to her sitting room. The older woman watched her silently, her expression filled with sadness. Slowly, she turned and walked back into her room, closing the door behind her.

Maura Sullivan McClain had loved just one man in her life and when he'd died at a young age, she'd never once considered marrying again. Why had Kit been cursed as she had?

Two men loved her, yet she couldn't find happiness with either one.

CHAPTER TWENTY

THE TRIP TO East Grinstead Hospital took three days. First the boat from Ireland and then the train from Wales and a bus from London. By the time Rory arrived, he was exhausted from the effort of trying to read train schedules and track numbers and ticket prices.

He'd stayed in London for a day to see a military doctor about his eyes, hoping there might be some new treatment, a way to make reading a bit easier for him. But the doctor could only offer a new pair of eyeglasses and assurance that his sight might still get better over time. Discouraged, Rory had set out for East Grinstead, hoping to speak with the specialist who'd treated him upon his return from France. But his trip back to the hospital in West Sussex had a far more important motive.

Rory was determined to find Brenna Rooney and East Grinstead was where he'd begin. He'd written to the hospital last month, but his letter had been returned without being forwarded. She'd had friends among the staff. Perhaps they might know where she'd gone.

It had been nearly a year since he'd made his escape from France and eight months since he'd returned to Ballykirk. The war had come to an end in Europe, and there was a new sense of hope in the air. How he wished he could have been part of the RAF's raids on Berlin, exacting justice for all the friends he'd lost to the Luftwaffe.

Rory brushed the thoughts from his mind. He'd done his duty and paid the price. And he knew his noble intentions and his lust for adventure had cost him dearly.

He climbed the front steps of the hospital and opened the door. Immediately, the smell of antiseptic assailed him and he was swept back to a time when he'd lived in total darkness. A middle-aged woman, dressed in the tidy uniform of the Red Cross, sat at a desk near the entry. He strolled over and gave her a charming smile. "Hello, my name is Rory Quinn and I'm looking for a nurse."

She gave him a dubious look and clucked her tongue. "So is every other man in this hospital, Mr. Quinn."

Rory chuckled. "You don't understand. I was a patient here and she helped me. I didn't realize how much until I got home. I'd like to write her a letter and thank her. I was hoping to get her address."

The woman's stiff posture softened a bit and she managed a smile. "What's her name, dear?"

"Rooney. Brenna Rooney. She worked on the second floor in Ward six, about this time last year. I'm sure someone up there would remember her. Could you check for me?"

The woman nodded, then hurried off, her heels clicking against the stone floors. Rory waited patiently, guessing at where Brenna might have gone. He'd thought about writing to her in Donegal but couldn't remember her father's name. She could be working in any of a hundred hospitals across Great Britain. The possibility that he might never find her niggled at the back of his brain.

Perhaps that would be best, he mused. He knew he could never love her the way he loved Kit. And maybe there was another woman for him, a woman he'd yet to meet, someone who could erase the memory of Kit from his head and his heart. He strolled over to the window and stared out at the unceasing spring drizzle.

He'd nearly managed to put his life back together, settling into work on the Mighty Quinn, renting a small cottage near the water in Ballykirk and facing the almost daily prospect of seeing Kit and Donal. He'd spoken with Kit on a handful of occasions, but they'd tried to avoid each other as much as possible.

It hurt too much to see her and to know that he'd never be able to have her. She was desperately trying to make her marriage work, though Rory had his doubts about her chances for success. She looked so sad and preoccupied when they'd catch sight of each other at the market or along the docks. And Donal was drinking more than ever, becoming a regular fixture at the local pubs.

But Kit and Donal were still sharing a bed. There had been news of a baby on the way and then just a month later, whispers of a miscarriage. Rory's heart ached for Kit, but he knew there was nothing he could do. She'd made her choice and he'd have to respect that.

As for himself, Rory was determined to find happiness where he could. He remembered his time with Brenna, the quiet conversations, the laughter and the gentle affection. She was a practical girl, with no illusions about love. And she was the type of woman who would be a caring mother to his children and a devoted wife. He couldn't offer her a great passion, but perhaps she'd settle for a good husband and provider.

"Lieutenant Quinn?"

He spun around at the sound of the familiar voice. His eyes came to rest on a tall figure standing in the middle of the lobby. Her curly red hair was tucked into a haphazard knot and her cap was slightly askew. She nervously smoothed her hands over the apron she wore.

He couldn't help a smile as he slowly approached. She hadn't changed. In truth, she looked prettier than he'd remembered, though his memories of her were little more than a blurry image. "Hello, Brenna. I've come to see you."

She smiled hesitantly, as if she couldn't fully believe him. "You've come to see me?"

"And why not?"

Brenna shrugged, her hands clenched tightly in front of her. "You're well. You don't need me." She paused. "You don't need my help anymore. Why would you come to see me?"

"Is there somewhere we could go to talk. Maybe have a cup of tea?"

She shook her head. "I'm working. I have to get back. There are patients to see and beds to change and—"

He reached out and took her hand, then slowly drew her toward a small group of chairs set against the wall. "Just a moment. I won't keep you too long."

She relented and sat down next to him, her spine stiff, her eyes downcast. "You look well," she finally said, risking a glance up. "Have you come to see the doctors?"

"I told you, I came to see you," Rory said. "I've missed you. I wrote you a letter but it was sent back."

"I left East Grinstead for a time. My mother was ill and she needed my help. Why are you here, Rory?"

"I'm here to issue an invitation. I was thinking you might like to see a bit of Ballykirk." He cleared his throat. "And if you like it there, maybe you'd want to stay for a time—and marry me."

Brenna gasped softly, her nervous hands going still. She risked another glance over at him. "You're having me on," she murmured. "Not a very fine joke, that."

Rory reached out and touched her wrist, then carefully turned her palm up. He laced his fingers through hers, his focus on her long, slender fingers. "I'm tired of living my life all alone. I'm asking if you might want to share it with me. I know it's an unexpected proposal, but I'm hoping it's not unwanted."

"Why me? There are far prettier girls for you to choose from."

"You've seen me at my worst and it didn't frighten you off. That means something to me, that kind of… understanding. Devotion, perhaps." His thoughts shifted to Kit, to the betrayal he still felt when he thought of his love for her. Brenna would never turn away from him. He could trust her with his love.

"If you're looking for loyalty, why not get yourself a dog?" Brenna asked.

He recognized the humor she often used to mask her insecurities and he pushed aside a frustrated reply. Would she ever stop belittling herself? She deserved good things in life, the same as everyone else. And he wanted to give them to her. "I want you to marry me, Brenna," Rory murmured. "Just give me an answer. If it's no, then I'll leave and never bother you again."

She looked at him wide-eyed, her expression filled with indecision before the doubt faded. "Do you love me then, Rory Quinn?"

He opened his mouth to answer, determined to be

honest with her. But Brenna quickly pressed a finger to his lips and shook her head, stopping his response. "I don't need you to tell me. If you said yes, I'd suspect it was a lie. And if you said no, it wouldn't make a difference anyway." She met his regard squarely. "Yes, Rory, I will marry you."

He took her hands in his, pressing them between his. "I'll be a good husband," he promised.

"And I'll be a good wife." They faced each other, lost in the awkwardness of the moment. "I suppose you ought to kiss me," she murmured.

Rory leaned close and touched his lips to hers. He didn't crave the taste of her mouth the way he did Kit's. But he couldn't have Kit and there was nothing more to be done about it. From this day on, Brenna was the only woman in his life. If he wanted a happy future, then he'd have to make it happen on his own terms.

"What do we do now?" Brenna asked.

"I suppose you ought to quit your job here. And we should go to Donegal so that I might meet your parents and ask their permission. And then we can publish the banns and get married."

A pretty blush stained her pale cheeks. "My mother will be pleased. I'm sure she thought I'd never marry. That's why she always told me it would be best if I found a vocation."

"And I'm glad you followed her advice," Rory said. "If you hadn't, we wouldn't have met."

She nodded, allowing herself a smile for the first time since she'd walked into the room. He felt a measure of satisfaction that he'd been able to give her that much. Perhaps, with time, he could give her more. Maybe he could fall in love with Brenna Rooney.

KIT SAT at the base of Oisin's Rock, her journal spread on her lap, a half-eaten apple in her hand. She scanned the lines of the poem she'd been working on and frowned. It was as if the perfect words sat on the tip of her tongue yet refused to leap onto the page. With a quiet curse, she scribbled through the last stanza and began again.

She stared out at the horizon, and her thoughts drifted to the past, to the warm summer days she'd spent in these hills with Rory and Donal. Life had been so simple then, attachments so pure.

Tipping back her head, she closed her eyes and let the memories pour over her, images and sounds and scents, until her mind was filled. Then she looked down at her journal and began to write again.

When she looked up again, she noticed a figure climbing the path from the village. Rory. She hadn't spoken to him since he'd returned to Ballykirk with his bride over a year ago, but she'd known the time would come when they'd have to face each other again.

The thought of Rory married to another woman cut deep, bringing all her own problems into sharp relief.

He and Brenna were expecting the birth of their first child in February, yet she and Donal still struggled with their own problems. Kit had miscarried three times in the past year and she wasn't sure she could face the prospect of trying again.

She ached for all the loss she'd experienced in her life—her parents, her uncle, Rory, then her lost babies. Each time, a tiny bit of her heart had been destroyed and Kit wondered if she'd ever be able to love without holding a part of herself back. Though she'd let go of the others, Kit still felt an undeniable connection to Rory. He was alive and, as long as he was, her love would be sustained.

Kit tucked her pen between the pages and closed her journal, then stood and brushed the grass from her skirt. Rory saw her and stopped short. She thought he might turn around and hike back down the hill, but then she held up her hand and waved.

He continued toward her and Kit prepared herself for a casual conversation. She'd have to congratulate him on his marriage and then mention the new baby. She could inquire about his eyesight and his work on the *Mighty Quinn*. Five or ten minutes of conversation should be enough before she could make her excuses and escape.

"Hello," she called, forcing a smile. "Beautiful day, isn't it?"

"Hello, Kit," Rory said.

He stood in front of her, his hands hitched on his

waist. He wore a canvas shirt and faded trousers. His body had recovered from the months in the hospital. He was now lean and muscled, his shaggy black hair brushed back from his tanned face. "You look well," she said.

"I am well. And you?"

"I'm fine, Rory." Kit suspected that he knew the truth, that her marriage to Donal was in a shambles. "One of my poems was published in a literary journal. And I've decided to go back to university in Cork to begin studies for a master's degree. I'll be doing some teaching there." She stopped when she realized how silly she sounded, rattling off the events of her life as if to convince him that she'd moved on.

"You'll have to give me a copy of the journal. I've always loved your poems, Kit. It's a fine thing that other people will be able to enjoy them." He smiled ruefully. "I carried that little volume of your poems with me in my flight jacket. It was like a talisman. I lost it somewhere in France. Just think, some farm boy may have found it and grown to love your poetry as much as I have."

"I'm writing a wonderful epic poem now. Do you remember the story you told me about the *lianhan shee?* My poem is based on that story."

He nodded. "I remember. That was back when we both used to believe in those sorts of things."

"Would you tell it to me again?" she asked as she sat down.

He seemed surprised by the request but then nodded. Kit pointed to a spot on the grass beside her and Rory joined her, resting his back against the rock. "Let me see if I remember. They way my father tells it, this is the story of Ciaran Quinn and his encounter with the *lianhan shee*. I'll skip over the first part because you know what the *lianhan*—"

"No," Kit said. "Tell it from the beginning. The way you told it to me when we were young."

"All right," Rory replied. "Ciaran Quinn lived in a small seaside village in Ireland, back in the time when the Celtic kings ruled over all the land. He was a young man who had a romantic heart and he was restless to find adventure in life. Every day, he would take his small fishing boat out on the water and, while he worked, he would dream of faraway and magnificent lands just waiting to be discovered."

"You tell a fine story," Kit said, her shoulder brushing up against his. She loved the sound of his voice, warm and rich. And there was comfort in touching him again, even if the contact was innocent. She closed her eyes and tipped her face up to the sun, amazed at how perfect the day had suddenly become. Everything she'd ever wanted in life was here with her.

"One afternoon, Ciaran returned from his day of fishing and came upon a small group of village folk gathered near the water's edge. They told him that the *lianhan shee*, the love fairy, had been spotted in a nearby forest. There is only one *lianhan shee* and she is a fairy of incredible power. She wanders Ireland, seeking love and dominion over men. If a man refuses her offer of love, then the *lianhan shee* becomes his slave. And if he accepts, he becomes her slave. But to possess such an irresistible love, the man must be lured through death, into the afterlife.

"Ciaran was determined to find the *lianhan shee,* ignoring the dangers she posed. Once a man loves her, he can love no other. She becomes his one and only. Those who love her, live for her, and the more they suffer for that love, the more they want her and the more she eludes them.

"He set out for the forest, searching for the *sidhe* along the way. Many fairies crossed his path, beautiful creatures with long yellow hair and slender, delicate bodies. But they weren't the *lianhan shee.* On and on he traveled, deeper into the forest, crossing rivers and climbing mountains. He came to a beautiful waterfall and bent to drink from the shallow riverbed below, exhaustion overwhelming him. And when he looked up, he saw her. Ciaran knew it was the *lianhan shee* for this fairy was far more beautiful than the others, her wings glittering like diamonds and her hair like spun silver. She beckoned to Ciaran and he followed her, climbing up a steep cliff to the source of the waterfall. When he reached the top, the *lianhan shee* hovered just out of his reach, her wings fluttering, her arms outstretched."

Kit sighed, slipping her arm around Rory's and resting her head against his shoulder. "'Come to me, love only me,'" Kit murmured. The story had seemed to lull them both into a world of their own, a world where only they existed and Donal and Brenna had faded from their thoughts.

"Ciaran was torn between his ordinary life on earth and the undeniable love that he felt for the *lianhan shee,*" Rory continued. "He took a step toward the cliff's edge and she flittered just out of his reach. Giving over to his desire, he took another step and tumbled down and down, toward the jagged rocks below. But Ciaran didn't die. He landed in a deep pool between the rocks. He was a strong swimmer and he pulled himself to the surface of the icy water."

Kit watched as he spoke, his eyes on the horizon, his handsome profile kissed by the sun. She couldn't imagine a time when her love for Rory would fade. It had become a constant in her life, a wonderful dream that lay just beyond her reach.

"It was then, shivering and aware, Ciaran decided that he would not give in to his desire. He walked out of the forest and back to his life. Legend has it Ciaran Quinn was the only man to be desired by the *lianhan shee* and to resist her invitation to the afterlife. But most believe that the *lianhan shee* isn't really a fairy at all. She is merely the essence of a man's desire, that which he cannot have without surrendering his soul."

He glanced over at Kit and she smiled at him, losing herself. He bent forward, as if he meant to kiss her, then pulled back. Confusion flickered in his eyes and he waited, as if needing a sign from her. When he bent close again, Kit met him halfway and when he touched his lips to hers she forgot to breathe.

"We can't," she murmured, her words soft against his mouth.

"I know," he replied. "But that doesn't stop the wanting."

A moment later, he was kissing her again. All the desire that she'd held in check for so long exploded inside of her and Rory responded, pulling her down beside him in the grass. He was desperate to touch her and she couldn't ask him to stop, for she was just as desperate to be touched. It had been so long since she'd felt such passion for a man and she longed to surrender completely to it.

He gently seduced her, his hands skimming over her body, brushing aside her clothes. Kit reached out and unbuttoned his shirt, smoothing her palms across his finely muscled chest. She knew it would have to stop. If they made love, they'd both be lost forever. There would be no going back.

If it were only Donal to be hurt by her infidelity, she might consider an affair with Rory. But he had a wife and a baby on the way. God would punish her more severely than he already had.

Rory nuzzled her neck, dropping a line of kisses from her ear to her bare shoulder. She shivered and he pushed up on his elbow and looked down at her.

"We can't do this," she said, praying that he'd ignore her words and continue on, knowing that she wouldn't fight him if he was bent on seducing her.

He brushed her hair from her eyes, his fingers gentle on her face. "Are you the *lianhan shee?*" he asked, his brow furrowed. "You hold a dreadful power over my heart, Kit, a power that I'm afraid will someday destroy me."

"Then run away," she murmured. "Like Ciaran did. He saved himself. Surely you can, too." Kit sat up and fumbled with her clothes, trying to cover her naked skin.

"Are you happy, Kit?" he asked, kissing her shoulder.

She shrugged and then shook her head. "I want to be. I try to be, but it seems as if all the things I need most in the world, I can't have." She struggled to her feet and grabbed her journal. "I have to go."

He didn't try to change her mind—he just lay back in the grass and watched her, his eyes still half-hooded with desire.

Kit closed her eyes and fought back a wave of emotion. Why were there only goodbyes between them? "Meet me here tomorrow," she called back to him. Kit didn't wait for an answer. In truth, she didn't want to hear his answer. Tonight, she wanted to go to sleep believing that she'd be with Rory just once more.

Once more would be enough, she told herself as she ran down the hill toward the village. It would have to be.

CHAPTER TWENTY-ONE

"MY MOTHER'S ARTHRITIS makes it difficult for her to get around. She's had trouble walking for a few years now and her hands cause her a great deal of pain. Perhaps there is some type of therapy you're aware of?"

Donal leaned back in his leather chair and watched Brenna Quinn. She'd been the first person to answer his advertisement for a nurse companion to his mother, Maura. And he found it fitting that he was in a position of power over her husband.

It was obvious the family needed money. They already had two children and from the looks of Brenna, there was a third on the way. Since the end of the war, jobs were scarce in County Cork and those around Ballykirk paid very little.

"I worked in hospitals throughout the war and I was involved in many types of rehabilitation. I'm sure I'll be able to help Mrs. McClain."

"I'm sure you will," Donal replied. He studied the woman who shared Rory Quinn's bed. She wasn't beautiful. She was tall and big boned, an ungraceful girl with unrefined features. It was no wonder Rory Quinn found greater pleasure in Kit's beauty than he did in that of his wife.

"I'd expect you to be here by nine in the morning. Cook prepares breakfast for my mother and she's finished by half past. Morning would be a good time for therapy. You'll eat the midday meal here, in the kitchen with the servants. In the afternoon, you might take my mother for a stroll. Do you drive?"

Brenna nodded.

"Good. Then you can take her into town to shop. She naps at half past three and you're free to leave at that time. As for pay, I'm certain we can match what you made as a nurse. Would that be agreeable?"

She nodded again, then opened her mouth to speak, but thought better of it.

"Please, feel free to ask questions."

"My husband's sister has agreed to watch the children for me, but there will be times when I might need to bring them along. Would that be a problem?"

The last thing Donal needed was a pack of Rory's brats running about his house. But he didn't want to lose this chance to get back at Rory—and Kit as well. "I'm certain we can work that out."

"And there is one other thing," she said. "I know there are some bad feelings between you and my husband. But I want you to know that this will not affect the way I do my job. I'm a trained professional and I take pride in my work. Your mother will receive the best of care."

"I'm happy to hear that. When would you like to begin?"

"As soon as possible?"

Donal nodded. "My mother is in her room now. Why don't you go up and introduce yourself? First door to the right at the top of the stairs. I have some work to do down here. Stop on your way out and I'll give you an advance on your first week's wages."

Brenna nodded and hurried out of the room. He listened as she climbed the stairs, then smiled to himself, anticipating what Kit would have to say about the new employee in the McClain household. He knew she envied Brenna McClain. The woman had everything Kit didn't, namely Rory Quinn, but also healthy and happy children.

He and Kit shared a bed once a week and only for the purposes of procreation. Kit insisted that it was Donal's duty to give her a child, but he'd found it more and more difficult to perform. It had gotten so bad that he'd fleetingly wished Rory would just finish the damned task for him. But the thought of leaving his estate to the son of Rory Quinn was more than he could bear.

Donal didn't have to wait long for Kit's arrival. Ten minutes later, he heard the front door open. He waited until he saw Kit pass through to the kitchen before he called out. "Would you come in here, please?"

Kit appeared at the door to the study, bundled in her warmest coat, her cheeks pink from the cold. Her hair was tangled and her skirt dirty. She'd been with Rory again. It was no secret that she met him at least once a week, usually in the late afternoon. Rory would bring the *Mighty Quinn* in early and they'd meet at Oisin's Rock. Donal had followed her once and stayed long enough to see them fall into a passionate embrace. But he hadn't the stomach to watch any further.

"You'll be happy to know that I've found a nurse companion for my mother. I hired her just today. In fact, she's upstairs with Mother right now. You may want to go introduce yourself."

"Who did you hire?" Kit asked.

"Brenna Quinn," he said, maintaining an indifferent tone. He glanced up to catch her reaction and noticed she'd gone pale. "She's an experienced nurse. And I thought the family might do with the added income."

Kit stepped into the room and pushed the door closed behind her. She leveled a suspicious look his way. "What are you about?" she asked.

Donal shrugged in mock innocence. "I'm just doing a favor for your friend Rory. I can't understand why you wouldn't approve. Unless seeing Brenna Quinn every day might make the guilt unbearable?" He chuckled. "Oh, darling, please don't pretend to be shocked. I know what's going on between you and Rory Quinn."

"You don't know anything," she muttered.

"I know you can't seem to get through a week without running off to him."

Kit drew a deep breath and turned for the door.

"Maybe it just grates that Brenna Quinn has given her husband what you can't seem to give yours," Donal called.

Kit froze, her hand on the knob. "And what is that? Unqualified love and affection?"

"No, a child. Two already and I believe there's one more on the way. Your lover manages to keep both women in his life satisfied. What a fine man he is."

Kit turned to face him. "I won't be listening to any more of this." She pulled the door open and found Brenna standing outside. She glanced back at Donal, shooting him a murderous look, then held out her hand to Rory's wife. "Hello, Mrs. Quinn. I'm Kit McClain. If you have any questions or concerns, please feel free to come to me. My husband isn't always as informed as he should be about the way things work around the household."

Brenna looked back and forth between the two of them, then forced a smile. "I'll be here tomorrow morning," she said.

Kit watched her leave, then looked back at Donal. "Have a care, Donal. You're not good at these games you're playing."

After she walked out of the study, Donal pushed up from his desk and crossed the room to a small table.

He pulled the stopper from a whiskey decanter and poured himself a glass. When he turned around, he found his mother standing in the spot Kit had abandoned. "She's an experienced nurse and you need the help," he said.

"I'm not here to complain about Brenna Quinn. She's a lovely girl. But I would like to speak about your marriage." Maura didn't wait to be invited to sit. Leaning heavily on her cane, she moved to one of the upholstered wing chairs in front of his desk. "You and Kit can't continue on in this manner. There're rumors flying all about the village and most don't blame her for the dalliance. It's your drinking, Donal. You're a bad drunk and you're driving her away."

Donal held up the whiskey glass. "It numbs the pain," he said. "My wife is in love with another man." He scowled. "I don't believe she ever really loved me."

"Marriage isn't just about love," Maura said. "It's about choices. Kit made her choice and she chose you. But you're forcing her to make another choice. She'll leave you if you continue on."

Donal drained his glass and dropped it on his desk, the crystal tumbler tipping, then rolling onto the carpet. "Are you about to give me advice on my marriage?"

"Your father didn't love me, Donal. But he gave me a place in the world, and, for that, I will always be grateful. He gave me you and this home. But I had to make some compromises. I forgot my silly dreams about romance and I looked at my choices. It's time you looked at yours."

"Tell me, Mother, what are my choices?"

"Ask her for another chance, Donal. And this time, you do everything in your power to make her happy. If you don't, you'll lose her and you'll have nothing." She grasped her cane and hobbled to the door, casting one last look back at him.

Donal closed his eyes and rubbed the knot of tension from his forehead. He still loved Kit, he had no doubt of that. But he'd grown tired of trying to make her love him. How could he make one more attempt, only to be faced with the fact, yet again, that her heart would always belong to Rory Quinn?

RORY PUSHED open the door to the cottage and swung the bucket of fish inside. As soon as the children heard the door, they came running. Paddy was three and Seamus was eighteen months.

He set the bucket near the sink and kissed Brenna on the cheek then rubbed her swollen belly. "Good catch today," he said, swinging Seamus up into his arms.

"Change his nappie, will you?" she asked as she scrubbed at a pot. "I just got home from the McClains and I've supper to make for Father Timothy and mending to do. Paddy has caught himself a cold and he's passed it to Seamus and he won't sleep tonight."

"Have you caught a sniffle?" Rory tickled Seamus's belly, then carried the baby into the bedroom and laid him on the bed. He found a clean nappie on the pile of laundry at the end of the bed, then quickly changed Seamus before sending him off with a gentle swat on his backside.

He returned to the kitchen and finished washing the dishes, setting them on the drain board. "I'm going to take a walk," he said, wiping his hands on a dishrag. "I'll be back by supper." He strode to the door, but Brenna's voice stopped him.

"I know where you go," she said, her back to him. She pulled a plate from the drain board and dried it, then set it on the shelf above the sink.

"I hike up to Oisin's Rock. Sometimes I walk along the shore."

"You go to meet her."

"It's not what you think," Rory murmured.

She shrugged, her attention on the plate she dried. "I suppose I can't complain. I suspected you loved her when I married you. I was willing to accept that."

Frustration surged up inside of him. "Why do you hold yourself in such low regard?"

"Because you do," Brenna said, her hands trembling.

Rory crossed the kitchen and grabbed her by the arm, spinning her around to face him. The plate fell to the floor and shattered. "I do love you, you have to believe that."

"But you love her more," Brenna said, tears welling in her eyes.

He cursed softly. It wasn't true. He just loved Kit differently. "Kit and I have been friends for years. I won't walk away from her when she needs me. Her marriage is a bloody mess—she has no one."

"And what of your marriage, Rory? You have a wife and a family and another baby on the way. She has her own husband. Let her solve her own problems." She bent down and began to gather the shattered bits of china from the floor. "Do you think it's easy for me? I go into that house every day, and I see what she has. Everything. But it's not enough for her. She wants you, too."

"You don't know what you're talking about," Rory said.

"Don't I? I hear them fighting. I see the empty whiskey bottles."

Rory drew a deep breath. "We'll discuss this later."

"No, we won't," Brenna said. "We'll talk about it now. I want you to tell me the truth. Are you the father of her child?"

Rory frowned. "What child?"

Brenna bit her bottom lip, as if fighting back a fresh wave of tears. "She didn't tell you? She's nearly five months pregnant. She hasn't mentioned a word to her husband yet or her mother-in-law. I found out from Cook. She's been taking her biscuits early in the morning to soothe the morning sickness. Odd that she'd keep such important news a secret. Unless there's some reason."

"She's had so many miscarriages," Rory said, stunned by the news. "I don't blame her for keeping it a secret."

"Or maybe she doesn't want anyone to know she's pregnant with your child."

"It's not my child. We've never—"

"Don't say it, because I won't believe you." She turned back to her work at the sink. "You need to make a decision. You can't have us both. If I have to raise my children on my own, I will do that, but I won't share you with Kit McClain."

Rory grabbed his jacket and walked out of the house. But he didn't walk toward the hills. He couldn't see Kit right now. Brenna was right. She deserved a husband who loved only her, and his children needed a father who wasn't always on the edge of leaving. But before he could say goodbye to Kit, he had to know that she would be safe and happy.

And there was only one person who could make that happen.

CHAPTER TWENTY-TWO

DONAL MCCLAIN WASN'T fussy about his drinking establishments. The three pubs in Ballykirk each catered to specific clientele, but Donal was happy to spend his money at any one them, preferring the cheap whiskey to interesting conversation. He'd taken to doing all his drinking outside of the house, tired of the disapproving glances he'd get from his mother and wife.

As of late, he'd spent less and less time at home. The time that he did was only a stark reminder of his failures as a son and as a husband. Maura had assumed many of the business responsibilities, preferring to handle the family money herself. And Kit hadn't cast more than a few sentences his way in the past three or four months. He might as well have been living alone.

Donal downed the last of his whiskey, then waved at the barkeep for another. After the old man refilled his glass, Donal stared into the amber liquid, searching for a moment of clarity.

She didn't love him anymore and maybe she never had. Over the past year, Kit had grown so distant that he barely knew who she was anymore. She immersed herself in her poetry and in her teaching job at the university in Cork. And when she wasn't working, she was walking the hills around Ballykirk, slipping away to meet Rory Quinn.

Donal had thought he might be able to hold on to her if he'd only been able to give her a child. But they hadn't slept together in almost four months; she seemed to have given up trying to get pregnant. The miscarriages had stolen all her hope and now she'd begun to search for a future without children—and without him.

Donal had been expecting her to leave any day. He knew his drinking had become almost intolerable, and when they did speak, their conversations were laced with bitterness. He wanted Kit to be happy, but he couldn't swallow the notion that her happiness rested with Rory Quinn.

He closed his eyes and lowered his head to the bar. When would he find the courage to let go, to give Kit her freedom and release himself from this torture? He breathed deeply to combat the nausea roiling inside of him.

"Mr. McClain? Are ya all right? Mr. McClain?"

Donal sat up, dizzy, his vision slightly blurred. "Oh, I'm just grand," he muttered. "Just grand."

"Would ya like me to find someone to drive ya home?"

Donal shook his head. "No, I'll walk. Give me time

to sober up." He stumbled off his stool and wove his way to the door. No one bothered to bid him goodbye. He didn't have any friends in the pub, or in all of Ballykirk for that matter. The only friendship he'd ever had, he'd destroyed.

The weather was cold and damp, a nagging drizzle blanketing the village. Donal pulled up the collar of his jacket and hunched his shoulders against the wind, the sting of the rain clearing his head.

As he walked toward the Skibbereen road, he thought about the mistakes he'd made. He'd wanted to possess her, but Kit was like a wild bird. The moment he'd captured her in his hands was the moment she'd begun to die. There was so little left of the Kit he'd once known, the carefree, confident girl with the infectious laugh and the sparkling eyes.

Donal raised his face to the sky, the moisture of his tears mixing with the rain. But when he stared back down the road, he saw a solitary figure in the mist, thirty feet away. Donal froze, recognizing the tall, lean form of Rory Quinn.

The sight of him brought a surge of anger. This was the man who had ruined his life, the man who stood between him and happiness. With a low growl, Donal ran at him, the whiskey coursing through his veins like liquid courage. But Rory reacted quickly and the moment before Donal hit him, he stepped aside, sending Donal into the mud of the road.

A moment later, Rory stood above him. "Get up, you miserable lush. Get up and let's finish this."

"Why couldn't you have stayed dead?" Donal screamed. "She could have loved me. I could have made her happy."

"How? By living a lie?"

"You were so sure of yourself," Donal accused. "Watch over her, you said. As if I were your servant to order about while you went off on your grand adventure. You never once considered that I might be in love with her and that she might love me."

"But she didn't love you, she loved me," Rory replied, slapping his hands against his chest. "And you did everything in your power to keep us apart. You deserve to be punished. But Kit and I are the ones left to suffer."

Donal picked up a handful of mud and heaved it at him. "Do you think I like living like this? Every day, I watch her go to you and every day I have to numb myself to face it again the next day. There are days I wish she'd never bother coming back."

Rory reached down and grabbed Donal's lapels, dragging him to his feet. "Do you want her? Do you, Donal? Then make something of your miserable life or you'll never deserve her."

"I can't fight you," Donal said, refusing to take the bait. "I can't win."

Rory drew back and slapped Donal across the face,

sending him back into the mud. "If she were mine, I would do everything in my power to make her happy."

"She *is* yours, damn it," Donal said, trying to get to his feet. "Don't you see that?"

Rory shook his head. "No. She's your wife. She'll always be your wife. When are you going to be a husband to her? When are you going to stand up and be a father to the child she's carrying?"

Donal slipped, falling back into the mud as if Rory's words had knocked him back over. "Wh-what child?"

"Kit is pregnant," Rory muttered, wiping his damp hair back from his forehead.

The revelation took every last ounce of fight out of Donal. He slumped over, his arms resting on his knees, his head hung low. "It's yours."

"No," Rory said. "The baby is yours."

Donal saw the pain in Rory's eyes—and the truth. "Mine?"

"Brenna says Kit is nearly five months' pregnant. She's probably been afraid to say anything, afraid she might lose another baby." Rory paused. "I wish it was mine. I wish to God that Kit and I would have had a chance together, that I could take her away from this and make her happy."

"Then do it," Donal said, chuckling softly. "Just put us all out of our misery and do it. Take her to Europe or America. Believe me, she'll forget all about her husband once she has you."

"You're her husband," Rory said, "*and* the father of her child."

"I don't think she cares." Donal shook his head, suddenly exhausted with his life. "I can't fix what I've done to our marriage."

"Stop drinking. Pull yourself together and figure out a way to make your marriage survive. Ask her forgiveness every day of your life and promise that you'll be a better husband." He paused. "You made a promise to me that night in Galway and you broke it. Now, I'm going to make a promise to you. If you don't do your best to be a good husband to her, I swear, I will take her from you."

"And I'm supposed to live with that threat hanging over me?" Donal demanded.

"As long as you're doing your part, you don't have anything to worry about." With that, Rory turned and walked away. Donal stared after him, the haze of whiskey now gone, his mind clear.

He'd been given another chance, a way to repair his life and to make a real family for himself. Donal picked himself up off the road and brushed his muddy hands against his sodden trousers.

Could he forget the past and begin again? Or was he doomed to make the same mistakes all over again?

THE RAIN HAD CEASED after nearly five days of damp and clouds. Rory drew a deep breath of the cool, fresh air as he hiked up the hill to Oisin's Rock. He wasn't sure whether Kit would be there, but he hoped she would, hoped he'd have one last chance to speak to her.

Since his encounter with Donal, Rory had thought about Kit nearly every hour of every day, wondering if her husband had decided to accept his challenge or continue along as he had been. Brenna offered little news of what was going on at the big house and Rory didn't care to ask.

His wife had been sullen and silent, as if she were preparing herself for bad news. But Rory had already decided that his future belonged with his family and that his love for Brenna would flourish if given a chance.

No matter how he felt about Kit, he wasn't going to leave Brenna. His threat to Donal had been empty, just a means to an end. But before he could move on, Rory had to settle things with Kit once and for all.

As he came over a small rise, Rory saw her in the distance, the wind buffeting her slender figure and whipping at her hair. He hiked up to her and she turned and smiled at him, giving him a tiny wave. When he reached her, Rory took her hand and they stood in silence, watching the fishing boats chug back to the harbor.

"This has to be the last time we meet," Kit murmured.

"I know," Rory replied.

She turned to him, her expression questioning.

"I know about the baby," Rory said. "Brenna told me."

Kit smiled weakly. "So much for my secret. Donal knows, too. Cook must have told him. I'm nearly five months along, now. And this time I think it might actually happen. I don't want to do anything to put the baby at risk. I don't want to make God angry at me."

"God has been angry at the two of us for a very long time," Rory murmured. "Perhaps we ought to make peace with him."

"Donal came to me a few days ago. He's stopped drinking and he wants to give our marriage another try. I have to give him that chance, Rory. For the sake of our child, for the sake of my mortal soul, I have to try."

"I understand." He drew Kit's hand to his lips and kissed the back of her wrist. "But that doesn't make this any easier. I don't want to lose you."

Kit reached out and pressed her hand to his cheek. "You'll never lose me. I love you, Rory, to the very depths of my soul, and I believe I always will. We're connected in a way that goes beyond friendship and marriage. But we have to accept what our lives have become and stop living with all these regrets."

Rory heard the truth in Kit's words, a truth he'd repeated to himself over and over the past few days. They couldn't continue living in between their marriage vows, telling themselves that if they didn't make love they weren't committing adultery. They'd been unfaithful with their hearts, not their bodies, but it was still wrong.

"Do you remember when we used to come up here as children?" Kit asked. "Everything was so simple then. *Trì, cumhachdach, araon.*"

"Three, powerful, together," Rory said.

"Do you think you'll ever be able to forgive him?" Kit asked.

Rory shrugged. "I don't know. So much has passed between us. But if Donal finds a way to make you happy, then I'd like to try. But maybe that will have to be left to the next generation of Quinns and McClains, to our children."

"Our children," Kit murmured, touching her belly.

She quietly slipped her arm around his waist and Rory drew her into his embrace. He knew this was the last time he'd touch her, the last time he'd enjoy the scent of her hair or revel in the tiny details of her face. As he stared over her shoulder, he noticed a figure hiking toward them.

Reluctantly he stepped away from her. "I should go. Brenna will have supper and she likes me to help with the children." He touched her face with his fingertips. "I'll always love you, Kit."

"And I'll always love you, Rory," she replied.

He allowed his hands to linger on her waist for just a moment, then broke contact and he started down the hill. She would always be his first love, but she would not be his only love. He didn't look back, certain that they'd made the right choice. But when he passed Donal, Rory stopped. "Make her happy," he murmured.

"I will," Donal said. "I promise."

Rory glanced over at him, then held out his hand. Donal's eyes mirrored his surprise, but then he took Rory's hand and gave it a firm shake. "Thank you," Donal said.

Rory nodded and continued on. As he walked down the hill from Oisin's Rock, he smiled to himself, all the pain and longing slowly ebbing from his heart. He would love Kit Malone until the day he died. But that love would always be just a dream and never a reality.

Like Oisin, he would be strong. He would keep watch over all those he loved, guarding them from harm in this life and the next.

PART THREE
FIONA'S PROMISE

CHAPTER TWENTY-THREE

Cork, April 1966

"IT IS NOW THE TIME for the women of Ireland to take their future into their own hands!"

The small crowd, made up of both female students and faculty members, clapped enthusiastically, some of them waving signs. Fiona McClain stood off to the side and silently studied her mother.

Katherine Malone McClain never seemed to tire. When she wasn't teaching poetry at the University of Cork or caught up in putting together her latest volume of work, she was immersed in whatever social causes she deemed important. For the past several years, she'd been speaking out for women's rights, serving on the board for the Irish Housewives' Association.

Fiona couldn't help but admire her. She wasn't an ordinary mother. As far back as Fiona could remember, her mother had always encouraged her to claim her independence. Kit McClain expected great things from her only child. She'd study hard, go to university and have a career of her own. And whether she married or not, she'd make a valuable contribution to society.

Her mother's views on women's rights were considered quite radical, but Fiona shared in her convictions. Why shouldn't she have the right to practice birth control or to divorce her husband? Women ought to have the choice to shape their own lives and not have them controlled by men.

Though Donal McClain didn't fully agree with all of his wife's ideas, it was obvious he was proud of her success. Her parents' marriage had had its share of troubles, but there was no question that Donal and Kit McClain cared deeply for each other. Looking back, Fiona was almost glad there were laws against divorce in Ireland. Even when they were fighting, she'd never had to worry that they'd leave each other.

In truth, her parents had been getting on so well lately that life at the big house on the Skibbereen road had become very…routine. Fiona longed for the day when she'd leave for university, when she'd finally have the opportunity to take charge of her own life.

She'd turned seventeen just last week and Fiona felt the lure of her future, the sense of anticipation. Life would be different for the women of her generation and she wanted to experience all the freedoms that the world offered.

"We must seize the power. We were granted the vote in 1918. In that same year, the first woman was elected to the Dáil Éireann. Almost fifty years ago that was and we still don't hold our fair share of power in the Dáil. Imagine a day when we take our place as equals in this country. We will determine our rights in the workplace, and at home, and in society."

The crowd broke into another round of cheers, but the noise was tempered by jeering from a trio of young men who had wandered in from the street. Cursing beneath her breath, Fiona brushed her tousled hair out of her eyes and started toward them.

She stepped up to the leader of the trio. "What's this? Do the lads have an opinion to share? Go on, I'm sure she'll give you the podium."

The young man glanced down at her, his gaze raking the length of her body. He was a bowsie boy, one of the hundreds of unemployed young men in Cork with no prospects and no future. He took the cigarette out of his mouth and flipped it to the side. "Aren't you a queer bit of skirt." He nodded to his mates, then chuckled. "What do ya think, lads? Is she worth a snog, then?"

Fiona rolled her eyes. "Tell me, do you love your mother?"

He gasped. "Who the feck are you?"

"I'm your sister. I'm your grandmother. Your aunt and the lady down the street who gave you biscuits and tea when you were young. I'm a woman and every time you degrade me, you degrade every other woman who's wiped your snotty nose and washed your filthy clothes. Do you want to be a real man then? Begin by respectin' the women around you."

"Leave her be," the red-haired one said, grabbing the ringleader by the arm. "She's off her feckin' nut." They hurried off and Fiona watched them go, smiling to herself.

"I might have known I'd find you in a bit of runction. Do you never let down?"

Fiona turned to find Alan Carrick standing behind her. Her heart did a cartwheel and she couldn't keep herself from grinning like an idiot. She'd met him six months ago outside her mother's office on campus. He was smart and sophisticated and he had the bluest eyes she'd ever seen. And even more, he found her beautiful and fascinating and brilliant. He was twenty-one—and he thought she was nineteen and she'd done nothing to disabuse him of the notion.

"I knew I'd find you here," he said.

"My mother insisted I come." She smiled shyly. Lord, he was so handsome he took her breath away. "And I'm glad I did."

"How long will she be?" Alan asked, nodding in the direction of the podium.

Fiona shrugged. "At times, she goes on for hours. She hasn't started in on the International Alliance of Women. And then she'll talk about the fight for the Equal Rights Amendment in America and Betty Friedan's *Feminine Mystique.*"

"Come with me, then," he said. "We'll take a stroll. Get a cup of tea."

"I can't," she said. "We're to have dinner tonight with some of her ladies. If I'm not waiting when she's finished, she'll be angry."

He grabbed her hand and laced his fingers through hers. "Meet me, then. Find an excuse to get away. I'll be at the bookshop at half past three."

"I don't know," Fiona said.

Alan squeezed her hand, looking deep into her eyes. "We can be alone. I know this place, it's...private. We can talk."

"I'll try," she murmured.

"And that's all I'll ask," he said. With that, he turned and strode down the walk. Fiona sighed as she watched him leave. He was so much more mature than all those silly boys in Ballykirk. Alan was from a fine family and he was determined to be a famous writer. If she ever married, Alan would be the type of man she'd choose—passionate, handsome, creative.

"Women all over the world are banding together to fight for our rights." The crowd had grown and they sent up a loud cheer, but Fiona's mother held out her hands to quiet them. "Until women have access to information on family planning, we will continue to be second-class citizens. The poor and undereducated suffer as they accept government interference in their reproductive choices while those of us who are educated find ways to subvert the law banning contraception. I say, *all* women in Ireland, rich or poor, deserve the same choices."

Fiona clapped loudly, catching her mother's eye from across the crowd. Kit sent her a smile. She'd explained to Fiona early on about what went on between men and women in the bedroom, urging her daughter to discuss her questions and fears. Sex was a glorious thing to share between two people who loved each other, Kit had said, but it came at a price—nine months pregnant and the next eighteen years raising a child.

She'd told Fiona exactly how to prevent a pregnancy, going so far as to pull out a condom and show her how it worked. At first, Fiona had been mortified by her mother's frank talk—and her flouting of Irish law. But after a time, she'd grown used to speaking plainly about sex.

"The women of the Irish Housewives' Association have committed themselves to real and lasting change in Ireland and we invite you to be a part of it. We want your voice and we need your support. Thank you for coming."

Kit stepped down from the podium and made her way through the crowd, stopping to talk to small groups of women as she passed. When she finally reached Fiona, she looked exhausted. "I'm sorry. I've gone on too long and I promised we'd shop for your commencement dress." She checked her watch. "Your father is going to be here to pick you up in a few minutes."

"I thought I was going to have dinner with you and the ladies," Fiona said.

Kit shook her head. "We won't eat until after our meeting. And who knows how long we'll talk. I'll probably have to stay here in Cork tonight."

"I'll stay with you," Fiona said, thinking about Alan and her date with him at the bookshop.

"You have schoolwork and your father can't do without at least one of us." She leaned over and kissed Fiona's cheek. "Come now, there's your father's car." Kit slipped her arm around Fiona's and they walked to the street. But when they reached the car, they found Seamus Quinn leaning up against it.

"Not to worry," he assured Kit. "Mr. McClain was caught in a meeting and couldn't break away. But he says he'll join Fiona for dinner this evening."

Seamus had always watched over Fiona. Two years her elder, he had often accompanied his mother and younger siblings to the McClain house where Brenna Quinn served as Maura McClain's nurse and companion.

They'd play together in the garden, hike the hills around Ballykirk, and talk about all manner of subjects. Seamus had been and was still her best friend, even though he considered her nothing more than a nuisance.

"I'm surprised Papa let you drive his car," she teased, "especially after the last time you were behind the wheel."

Kit frowned, glancing back and forth between Fiona and Seamus. "What are you—"

"She's having you on," Seamus said. "I'm a fine driver. She's the one who shouldn't be on the road."

Kit shook her head, smiling, then said to Fiona, "Mrs. Burns will take me to the hotel and I'll ring you later to say good-night." She gave Fiona a hug, then hurried back into the crowd.

"And how was the speech?" Seamus asked.

Fiona shrugged. "She was in grand form. They were planning to hand out rubber johnnies to protest the laws against contraception, but one of the older ladies thought it would be unseemly."

Seamus sent her a sideways glance. "You shouldn't talk like that."

"Like what?" Fiona asked. "Would you prefer I call them Johnnie's raincoats? I suppose I should use the proper name. Condoms." She saw the color rising in Seamus's cheeks. Her plain talk often embarrassed him. "Condom, condom, condom," she said. "See, I wasn't struck down dead for saying the word. You know, you really should be more aware of these matters, Seamus. You're nearly nineteen years old now. What if you find yourself in bed with a young lady?"

"It's against the laws of the church," Seamus said.

"Well, there are other methods you can use that get around the church. There's—"

"I don't want to discuss this with yourself," Seamus said.

"Well, if you ever have any questions, you know where to come." She drew a deep breath. "I—I've forgotten to pick up a book that I ordered. The shop is just down the street."

"I'll wait for you here," Seamus said.

"No. Let's meet at five. That will give me time to browse and buy a gift for Papa."

"Your father would not be pleased if I left you on your own in the city."

"I won't get into any trouble," Fiona insisted. "I promise. I'll meet you back here at five and not a minute past."

Seamus shook his head. "I shouldn't trust you, Fiona McClain."

She pushed up on her toes and kissed his cheek. "But you do." With that, she gave him a little wave and started off in the direction of the bookshop. When she rounded the corner, Fiona leaned back against the wall of a building and giggled. She was free. For nearly three hours, she had her life to herself and she was going to live it.

SEAMUS PACED back and forth beside the car, then checked his watch. Fiona had promised to return by five and it was already half six. He'd found the bookstore an hour ago and talked to the clerk, but she'd insisted she didn't remember seeing a girl matching Fiona's description.

He wasn't sure whether to call the gardai or continue waiting. He couldn't have missed her. He'd left the car parked exactly where it had been earlier that afternoon. Seamus cursed softly. What had possessed him to let her go off on her own? Fiona had always been a headstrong and impulsive girl and those qualities hadn't tempered with age. And she hadn't a bit of common sense, either.

He searched around for a phone booth. He'd ring Donal McClain and let him decide what to do next. Seamus jogged down the street, certain that he'd find a phone close by. But he stopped short when he saw a familiar figure coming toward him.

He ran up to Fiona and grabbed her arm. "Where the hell have you been? Are you all right?"

Fiona nodded, a tight smile pasted on her face. "I'm sorry. I didn't mean to be late. I lost track of the time."

Seamus pulled her toward the car. "I never should have let you go." He yanked open the passenger-side door and waited for her to get inside. But she seemed reluctant to do so. "We're already late. Get in." Seamus strode around to the other side, slipped behind the wheel and started the car. Fiona still stood on the curb and he leaned over the seat. "Come on, then."

When she'd finally settled herself inside, he pulled out into traffic. For the first ten minutes of the ride, they didn't speak. Seamus sent a few quick glances her way, but she kept her attention fixed outside her window.

"Would you care to tell me what you were doing all this time?"

"No," she murmured.

"You didn't go to the bookshop. I checked there and the clerk hadn't seen you." With a soft oath, Seamus pulled the car to the side of the road and turned to her. When she wouldn't face him, he gently reached over and hooked her chin, forcing her to look at him. His breath caught in his throat when he saw her eyes swimming with tears. "Ah, Fi, now don't cry. I didn't mean to be so cross, but I was worried for you."

Fiona stared at her fingers in her lap, her dark hair falling around her face. "I—I think I might have made a mistake. I did something I shouldn't have and now I can't take it back."

"Would you want to tell me about it?"

She drew a ragged breath. "Promise you'll listen and not judge? I need to trust you with this."

Seamus nodded. He'd always felt so protective toward Fiona and he was having a hard time accepting that she was becoming an independent woman. He couldn't protect her forever, nor would she want him to. "I'll listen and after, I'll keep my mouth shut."

"There's this boy I met. A man, really. His name is Alan Carrick and he's a student at the university and we've seen each other a few times. I've had a bit of a crush on him and it seemed as if he fancied me, too. Today, I met him. I wanted to spend time with him… alone. I thought we should get to know each other. I—I didn't mean for it to happen." She shook her head. "No, that's not true. I thought it might, and I was ready. But when it did, I wasn't, only I couldn't stop it."

Seamus moaned softly. "Ah, Christ, I don't want to be hearing this, do I?"

"I thought I was in love. I thought he might have loved me a bit, too. Or even more than a bit. And I hoped it might be wonderful and romantic, but then it got confusing and frightening."

"You did it with him?"

A tear ran down her cheek and she brushed it away impatiently, then forced a smile. "I wanted to. And I was prepared. But he crawled on top of me and it all happened so quickly and then it was over and—" A sob tore from her throat and she covered her face with her hands.

Seamus reached out to gather her in his arms. He furrowed his fingers through her hair, holding her close and trying to absorb some of her humiliation. "Well now, there's no need to be so upset. It's not supposed to be good the first time. It never is. You have to give it time."

"I don't think he wants to see me again," she said, her words muffled against his shoulder. She jerked back and wiped her nose with her fingers. "And I never want to see him. I'm so stupid. How could I be so stupid?"

"There are times you tend to be a bit too romantic, Fi. It's all those silly books you read when you were younger. Life is not a fairy tale and not every bloke is a prince, you know."

"My mother brought me up to be a modern woman and then the first man who pays me a compliment, I—I can't wait to shag him."

"I suppose if you'd like, I could beat the shite out of this guy. Just tell me where he is. We'll turn this car around and go get him."

A laugh slipped from her lips. "I just want to forget him."

"You'll never forget him," Seamus said, wiping a tear from her cheek with his thumb. "He'll always be your first." Tears flooded her eyes again and Seamus cursed. "Ah, don't start again, Fi. I was just statin' fact."

"Do you remember your first?" Fiona asked.

"Vaguely," he murmured. He hadn't had a first yet, but he wasn't about to admit that to Fiona McClain. He feared she'd have it all over the county before sunset. "But then men are different from women."

"Do you think I'm a sinner?" she asked in a meek voice.

Seamus shook his head. "Nah. A bit impulsive, you are, and you have questionable taste in men, but if what you did was a sin, then you'll be meeting half of Ireland in hell." He paused. "Just promise me you won't do that again until you're married."

She shuddered. "I never want to do that again. It was horrid and embarrassing. Now take me home."

As they drove toward Ballykirk, Seamus made a mental note to find out more about this guy who'd taken such advantage of Fiona. Once he did, he'd make sure the bastard never came near her again. She was like a little sister to him and he'd continue to take care of her until she found a man she thought she truly loved—and one Seamus thought was good enough for her.

CHAPTER TWENTY-FOUR

Ballykirk, April 1956

"TAKE FIONA WITH YOU. She needs to get out and about. She spends far too much time indoors."

Seamus groaned and shook his head at his mother. "No. She'll just wander off and then we'll have to go find her. She's always daydreaming and making up such silly stories. The other day, she was babbling on about princes and princesses and she ran into a tree. I won't have her with me."

Brenna Quinn raised her eyebrow, sending Seamus a look that meant his complaints would do no good. "You'll take her and you'll be glad to have her company. Do you understand me, Seamus Quinn?"

"Why can't she stay here with Bridgit?"

"Because Bridgit is going to help me do Mrs. Maura's hair. And Mrs. Kit is off to the university. You and Paddy can do your bit to help me today."

Seamus turned away and stomped out the kitchen door, his fishing pole clutched in his hand. Why was *he* always the one to watch over Fiona? He and Paddy were planning to go fishing that afternoon and Paddy would rather fish alone than have silly Fiona McClain tagging after them.

Seamus found her sitting under a tree in the garden, playing with a paper doll, the fancy paper clothes arranged on the grass in front of her. "My mother says I'm to take you with us," he grumbled.

Fiona glanced up at him, her eyes wide, her dark hair curling about her face. "Where are we going, then?"

"Fishing. But if you make a mess of this, I'm going to leave you behind."

She scrambled to her feet, the paper doll fluttering to the grass. "Papa has taken me fishing. I'm quite good at it. He has a very secret spot and there are hundreds of fishes there, just waiting to be caught."

"A secret spot, you say." Seamus feigned indifference, turning his attention to a tangle in his fishing line. "And where is this spot?"

Fiona regarded him suspiciously. "If I tell you, it won't be a secret."

"If you don't tell me, I won't take you with me."

She plopped back down on the grass and picked up her paper doll again. "Then don't take me with you," she said. "I don't care at all."

Seamus cursed beneath his breath, just loud enough for her to hear. Fiona had always been this way, so stubborn and single-minded. If she decided she didn't want to cooperate, there was no moving her. And she was far too bossy. It was a wonder she had any friends at all.

"If you curse, you'll have to confess to Father Thomas," she said, plucking at the dress on the paper doll. "And he's worse than Father Timothy was with handing out the Hail Marys and the Our Fathers."

"Well, I'm going—and I don't care if you stay here or come with me or climb that *feckin'* tree over there." Seamus started for the road, knowing that the balance of his day rested on a calculated bluff.

He was nearly a hundred yards down the road when she skipped up beside him. "I know how to put the worm on the hook, you know. I'm not afraid of worms like the other girls are."

Seamus had to admit that Fiona was awfully brave for a girl her age. Once, he'd stepped on a broken bottle and she hadn't thought twice about propping his foot up on her lap and picking out the glass. And he'd once found her at the very top of the old oak tree in the garden, studying a bird's nest. Even he would have been a bit dodgy climbing that high.

"It's my birthday soon," she said. "In a couple of weeks, I'm going to be seven years old. I was born on April eighteenth, 1949, on the very day that Ireland became a republic."

"Do you ever stop talking?" Seamus asked.

"Good conversation is an art. That's what my mother says. Although it is a bit difficult to carry on a conversation when only one person speaks. You're supposed to do your part as well or you'll be thought quite rude. Would you like to say anything?"

"Yeah," Seamus muttered.

"Well, have at it."

"Shut yer gob," he shouted. Seamus picked up his pace, hoping that she might decide to turn around and go home. He'd probably get the switch from his mother, but it would be well worth it to have a bit of peace. Someday, he'd finally rid himself of Fiona McClain and her irritating chatter. And that would be a day to celebrate.

CASH'S WAS the finest department store in all of Cork. Fiona had been excited about spending an entire Friday afternoon strolling the aisles and examining all of the merchandise. But her mother seemed to have other ideas.

"Hurry now," Kit McClain said. "We have to find a dress quickly. And then I have to stop at the bookstore and give them a list of my textbooks for next year. And then we have to drop these papers at your father's solicitor."

Fiona stood in front of the long rack of white dresses. "Why do I have to wear white? I'd rather have red. Or blue."

"Because red or blue won't do," Kit said. "If you walked into your first communion wearing a red dress, Father Thomas would have your mother excommunicated. And I've enough troubles with God already—I don't need more."

"Didn't God make red and blue?"

"That's not the point," Kit said. "Now, pick out your favorite and let's check the fit."

Fiona couldn't understand what all the fuss was about. The other girls at school could barely contain their excitement—the pretty dress, the gloves, the parties and gifts that came after. Fiona had paid close attention in class to everything they'd learned about the Eucharist and the bread and the blood, but she still couldn't understand why Jesus Christ wouldn't want her to wear her favorite color.

"Father Thomas says Jesus tells us to share our riches and feed the hungry. I think we should give all our spare money to the Quinns."

"Why?" Kit asked.

"Because they're poor and their clothes are shabby. And they live in a tiny little house with hardly a garden to play in. And whenever I give sweets to Seamus he acts like he's never tasted sweets in his whole life."

"The Quinns are not poor," Kit said, examining the dresses more closely. "And it would be wrong to think of them that way."

"We could buy them all new Sunday clothes. Or send Cook to their house to make them a fine supper."

"It's very kind of you to be so charitable, Fiona. But just because they don't have new clothes or a nice car or a fine house doesn't mean they're poor. They are rich in many other ways. Our family just has more material wealth than theirs."

"You mean we're just lucky?" Fiona asked.

Kit shook her head. "Your great-grandfather Eamon had a lot of money and he gave that money to your grandfather Aidan, who gave it to your father. The Quinns have always been fishermen and it's a hard living. So they don't have as much money. For some people, money is important. For others, it makes no difference. For you, it mustn't ever make a difference. We are all equal in God's eyes." She wagged a finger at Fiona. "Now that's enough of that subject. Choose a dress."

Fiona reached out and pointed to the dress on the end of the rack. It really didn't matter what she was going to wear. Her thoughts were entirely occupied with her mother's revelation.

Fiona had always known she was a bit different from the other girls in the village, but she'd always believed it was because she was especially smart. Now she realized that it was because her family had money. No one in Ballykirk had a bigger house than she did, or a shiny new car or servants to clean the house and cook the meals.

Suddenly, everything made sense—the way her schoolmates and their parents treated her, and her teachers at school and the shopkeepers in town, and even Father Thomas. They were extra nice to her because they hoped she might share her money with them. Or they were very nasty to her because they were jealous.

Fiona sighed as she took the frilly white dress from the rack. When she had money, she was going to give it all to the Quinns. Then she would be penniless and they would be well-off and people would see that it didn't make a difference at all.

CHAPTER TWENTY-FIVE

SEAMUS ROSE with the sun nearly every summer morning, anxious to begin the day. The long school holiday was far too short for his tastes, so he tried to take advantage of every free moment. But the sun was already well above the horizon when he pulled on a faded shirt and a pair of ragged trousers. Paddy and Colm were still sprawled in the old bed they all shared, and Bridgit and Maggie were curled up together in theirs.

His mother was already awake, the scent of toasted bread drifting back from the kitchen. Each morning, she prepared breakfast for his father before dawn, waking the children when she got up and expecting them washed and at the table by the time she dished out the porridge.

But this morning was different. When Seamus walked into the kitchen, he found his father still sitting at the table, a serious expression on his face.

His mother was seated next to him, her eyes red, as if she'd been crying. The last time he'd seen his mother cry had been three years ago when his grandfather Jack had died. Seamus swallowed back the lump in his throat. "What is it? Did our grandmam die?" he asked.

"Sit down," his father said.

Seamus did as he was told, the chair scraping against the rough plank floor and splitting the ominous silence in two. He swallowed back the lump of fear in his throat.

"Today, you're to stay indoors," Rory Quinn said. "You and Paddy are to keep your brother and sisters in the house. No one must go outside and you must let no one inside."

"Why?" Seamus asked.

"There's been a case of polio in Ballykirk."

He frowned. "What is polio?"

"It's a very bad sickness," his father said. "It can kill you or it can do terrible damage to your legs and arms. If you feel sick then you must tell your mam or myself right off."

"I feel fine," Seamus murmured.

"You may have caught it and not yet know that you're sick."

His mother quickly rose from the table and went to tend the teapot she'd set to boil on the cooker.

"Who is sick with it?" Seamus asked.

"It's Fiona," his mother replied. He could tell she was weeping, her shoulders shaking as she bent over the cooker, and Seamus knew in an instant how difficult it was for her. Brenna Quinn treated Fiona like one of her own.

Seamus got up and went to her, reaching out to touch her arm. "I'm fine, Mam," he said. "I'm not sick at all. You needn't worry about me. And Fiona is as strong as a horse."

Brenna turned and pulled him into her embrace, wrapping her long arms around him and holding him close. "Do you promise that you'll stay inside?" she asked.

Seamus nodded. He looked up at her. "Is Fiona going to die?"

"I don't know," she replied, smoothing his hair back from his eyes. "No one really knows. Cook stopped by just before dawn to tell us the news. She's been with the family all night. They've called in a specialist from Cork. Mrs. Kit refuses to take her to hospital. They'll put the poor child in quarantine, she says, and Fiona would be terribly frightened. Mr. Donal is beside himself."

"Maybe I should go visit her," Seamus suggested.

"No," his father warned. "You'll stay here at home until the danger is past."

"When will that be?" Seamus asked.

His mother sighed. "We don't know. For now, we must be patient and pray for Fiona."

Seamus nodded, then wandered over to the back door, staring out into the garden. Though he usually thought of Fiona as a right muzzy, he didn't want to believe that she'd die. His father pushed away from the table and took his mother's hand, whispering to her softly. Then he tipped her chin up, dropped a kiss on her lips and walked past Seamus through the door.

"I could go with Da," Seamus suggested.

"No. I'll need you at home. Mrs. Maura sent word that I didn't have to come to work today, but I think I ought to see if there's anything I can do." She dabbed at her nose with her handkerchief. "There's no treatment, but I've read that moist heat and physical therapy can help." The last was said as if she were talking to herself.

"Should I pick some flowers from the garden for Fiona?"

His mother smiled. "Yes. You do just that. I'll go wake the others."

Seamus walked outside and gathered a handful of violets springing up near the base of the stone fence. But his concern for Fiona wouldn't be calmed by sending flowers. He looked back only once, then hopped over the fence and ran to the road. He'd see for himself what all this worry was about. He'd be able to tell how sick Fiona really was and then, if it was necessary, he'd say a few good prayers.

As he ran to the McClain house, Seamus didn't see anyone about. It was as if the world had come to a full stop. A car passed him on the road and he kept his head down, hoping that he wouldn't be caught along the way.

It took only fifteen minutes to reach the house. Seamus hurried around to the rear and then slipped into the kitchen. Cook was busy polishing silver in the butler's pantry and didn't notice as he tiptoed to the servant's stairwell. He and Fiona had gone up and down the stairs so many times that he knew each creak and groan.

When he got to the top, he ran into the playroom and hid behind the thick draperies at the window. The sound of angry voices drifted across the hall and he listened closely.

"We should take her to hospital," Donal McClain shouted. "They've set up a special center at Saint Finbarr's to treat the sick."

"No! I won't let you take her from this house. Don't you try, Donal. If she goes out that door, she'll never come back. God will take her from me."

"There are things they can do for her, Kit."

Seamus crossed the room and stood behind the open door. He could see past the hinges, to the sitting room across the hall. Dark circles smudged the skin beneath Mrs. Kit's eyes. She sat on the edge of the couch, her hands clutched in front of her as she wept. Seamus knew it was serious.

"I will care for her," Kit murmured. "The doctor said the disease has to run its course. All we can do is make her comfortable and wait. If she takes a turn for the worse, I'll reconsider." Kit closed her eyes. "This is my fault. I took her to Cork with me last month and she was playing with some children in the park. She had such a good time, but I should have known. There are so many children sick there now. They're calling it an epidemic."

Donal pulled Kit to her feet and gave her a gentle shake. "You stop this now. There is no way to know where she got this. We're not even sure it is polio." He drew her toward the hall and Seamus stepped back. "We'll have Cook make us a pot of tea and you'll calm yourself. You'll be no good to her like this."

Seamus waited until they started down the stairs, then hurried to Fiona's room. Maura McClain sat beside the bed, her Bible resting on her lap, her wire-rimmed spectacles tangled in her fingers. Her eyes were closed but as he approached, she sat up and looked at him. "Hello, Seamus."

He held out the flowers. "I've come to see Fiona."

"You shouldn't be here. She's very ill."

Seamus stared at the bed. Fiona's face was flushed and damp with perspiration. She looked so tiny amongst all the pillows. Her eyes were closed and her breathing was shallow. "Should I speak to her?"

Maura nodded. "Just don't get too close."

Seamus stood at the side of the bed. "Fiona," he whispered. "Open your eyes. Fiona!"

The little girl's eyelids flickered and, a moment later, opened. She smiled weakly. "Hello, Seamus. I'm sick."

"I've heard. But you'll be well soon. And then we'll go fishing."

"My Papa has a secret spot," she said. She tried to

move, then winced. “My legs hurt. And my neck. I feel like I fell out of a tree.”

“Not you, Fi. You’re the best tree climber I know.”

“I am good,” she said. “Better than you.”

“Yes. Better than me.”

He reached out and touched her arm, giving it a gentle pat. “I’ll come back another time. Get well, Fi.”

“I will,” she said, closing her eyes.

Seamus glanced at Maura and saw tears in her eyes. “She’ll get well,” he said.

“Yes,” Maura murmured.

Seamus handed her the flowers then walked to the door. He managed to sneak back out of the house and ran all the way home. When he got to the cottage, he found his mother waiting outside, a worried expression on her face. “I played with her yesterday,” Seamus said. “All of us were at the house the day before, except for Da.”

Brenna nodded. “I know,” she said in a soft voice. “Now run along and see to your brother and sisters. And mind Paddy. He’s in charge.”

Seamus gave his mother a quick hug, then watched her walk down the road. She worked so very hard at home and then at the McClains. Someday, when he was grown up and very wealthy he would buy his mother a grand house and servants to wait on her day and night. And she would have the kind of life that Fiona’s mother and grandmother had, full of pretty dresses and fine food.

FIONA SPENT the entire summer of 1956 in bed. Though she hadn't suffered the worst effects of polio, the virus had weakened her so completely that she could barely walk from one side of her bedroom to the other.

It hadn't been the worst thing, to spend her days snuggled against her down pillows with piles of books to read and a tray of biscuits and tea on her bedside table. Her mother had bought stacks of stories from her favorite bookseller in Cork, romantic tales and exciting adventures with handsome heroes and daring heroines. Fiona had barely watched a minute of telly.

But as the school term neared, she made a special effort to get out of bed and recapture her strength. She ate all the healthy foods that Cook prepared for her, she tried to spend just a bit more time each day walking through the house, and she passed each afternoon in the playroom with Seamus.

Since she'd gotten sick, Seamus had become her only true and loyal friend. In the early days of her illness, he'd sent her small presents to cheer her up and written her little notes with funny stories or jokes. And when she was able to get out of bed, he'd stand outside her window and do silly tricks to amuse her. After she was well enough for visitors, he'd sit in her room for hours at a time, telling her stories of his brave and noble ancestors, the Mighty Quinns.

The rest of the children in the village had avoided her, even after she was allowed visitors. They were fearful that they could still catch the dreaded disease. No one else in Ballykirk had gotten polio, but there had been four cases in Skibbereen and two in Schull. Everyone had said that she'd been lucky, but Fiona couldn't see the luck in being sick.

A knock sounded on her bedroom door and Fiona hopped back onto the bed. A moment later, the door swung open and her mother stepped inside. "Have you had your rest?"

"Yes," Fiona lied. She stretched her arms above her head and yawned. "I slept for a long time." In truth, she'd spent the afternoon rearranging her paper dolls and her big box of crayons.

"You have a visitor." She swung the door open to reveal Seamus Quinn.

He grinned at her. "Hello, Fi."

"Hello, Seamus."

"Your mam said you could come outside today."

Fiona looked at her mother and she nodded. "For a time. But you must stay in the garden and there'll be no running about."

She jumped off the bed and rushed to the door. But she stopped when she reached Seamus's side. "You've grown taller," she said, frowning.

He shrugged. "Maybe you got shorter laying about for six weeks."

They walked out to the garden and found a spot beneath the rose arbor, Fiona settling herself on an ornate iron bench and Seamus sitting on the grass at her feet.

"My mother said that you're lucky to be alive."

"Am I?"

"Some of the children who got sick have to live inside an iron lung. I heard her telling my da."

"What's that?"

Seamus shrugged. "I don't know. But it doesn't sound very good."

"The doctors were very worried that my legs wouldn't work, but they work fine now. I bet I could climb that tree over there."

"You'd better not. If you fall, you'd have to go right back to bed."

"Now that I'm not sick, are you still going to be my friend?" Fiona asked.

Seamus examined the toes of his shoes. "Girls and boys can't be friends, Fi. Boys have to be friends with boys and girls have to be friends with girls. Unless you're old and you want to be in love. Then you can be friends."

"I don't want to be in love with you," Fiona said. "But I do like it when you're nice to me."

"I suppose I can still be nice to you," Seamus said grudgingly. "But that's all. I'm not taking you fishing."

"You promised you would when you thought I was going to die."

"I did?"

Fiona nodded her head. “I remember.”

“Then I guess I’ll have to take you fishing.”

Fiona reached over and patted Seamus on the shoulder. “Maybe I could show you Papa’s secret spot—if you promise not to tell.”

CHAPTER TWENTY-SIX

FIONA CLUTCHED the steering wheel with white-knuckled hands. She glanced over at Seamus, who sat in the passenger seat, rubbing his forehead as if it pained him. She'd seen that look so many times before.

As young children, that look had come when Seamus had been stuck watching over her or dragging her along on one of his adventures. But they were teenagers now, Seamus seventeen and Fiona two years younger. And he still was far too impatient with her.

"We'd better give up," he said. "I'm not sure the transmission can take any more of this abuse."

Fiona's spirits sank. "No," she said. "I know I can do this."

"Maybe you can't," Seamus said. "Maybe you're not meant to drive a car. It's not a bad thing, that. You'll just have to live in the city so you can take the trolley or the train or walk."

"I have to learn to drive," Fiona said. "Now, explain it once again. I let the clutch out and I push on the accelerator and the car will go forward. Why is it when I do that, the car stops?"

"You have to do those two things very slowly and at the same time," Seamus instructed. "I'm not sure that you've ever been able to concentrate on two things at once, so our efforts were probably doomed from the first."

"What are you saying? That I'm somehow inferior to you because I'm a female?"

Seamus groaned. "I'd be a right fool to say that now, wouldn't I? You'd bite my feckin' head off if I did."

Fiona ground her teeth. They'd had these arguments again and again. But he never seemed to understand her point. Just because she was smaller and weaker didn't mean that she was any less competent than he was. "And just because you have a penis doesn't make you better than me," she muttered.

He gasped. "What did you say?"

"You heard me. Are you shocked at the sentiment or at the language?"

"I don't have to listen to this," Seamus said, reaching for the door.

"No, no," Fiona cried. "I'm sorry. I promise to behave. Just let's please finish the lesson. And I'll try to take your advice."

"This always happens. You're always running off, doing things all arseways, Fi. You got caught smoking in the churchyard before school. And they nearly expelled you after that paper you wrote about legalizing prostitution. And then, you nearly beat Frankie

Carlisle unconscious with your shoe after he called you a slag. You can't be so impulsive, Fi."

"How is this impulsive? I'm asking for a lesson."

"You decide you have to learn to drive and expect to have it accomplished by supper."

"I just have to learn quickly," she said.

"Why?"

Though she and Seamus could say almost anything to each other, there were some feelings she kept hidden. Such as the fact that she'd tried smoking to fit in with the popular girls, or that she'd read the paper out loud on a dare, or that she was tired of Frankie making fun of her. School was not an easy place when you were an outsider.

"Some of my mates from school have planned a picnic at Mizen Head and they asked if I could get my father's car and drive them all. And I said yes."

"Even though you can't drive?"

"But they invited me," she said softly. "They never ask me to do anything. They all think I have fancy friends and posh parties to attend, but I don't. I want to go to their party. It sounds like fun." She shrugged. "I thought I could sneak away with the car and not be found out until the next morning."

Maybe if she'd had an older brother as Seamus did, he might have paved the way for her. Or perhaps it would have been easier for her if her parents had chosen to send her to a proper finishing school rather than the village public school. But Kit had insisted that Fiona have the same education she'd had, not realizing that Fiona wouldn't be accepted by her classmates.

"What do you reckon to do if you can't learn to drive?"

She smiled at him. "I thought you could take us."

"I'm not your chauffeur, Fi."

A frown wrinkled her brow. "I've never thought of you as a servant. But Papa would consider you a good chaperon. You are older and much...wiser."

"Ha! So you admit it, then," Seamus crowed. "I'm smarter than you." He nodded, looking satisfied. "I'm happy that we have that straight. Let's try it again."

Fiona clapped gleefully, then put the car in gear, glad her ploy of flattery had worked. Closing her eyes, she tried to focus, then slowly played the clutch against the accelerator. The car jerked forward and suddenly, they were moving down the road. Fiona screamed then laughed. "What do I do now?"

"Shift!" Seamus said. "Push in the clutch quick." He reached over and put the car into second gear. "Now let it out."

Fiona did as she was told and to her surprise, the car moved smoothly from one gear to the next. It began to pick up speed and she grew a bit frightened.

"Shift!" Seamus shouted.

She pushed in the clutch again and suddenly they were flying down the road, the steering wheel wobbling in her hands, the wind whipping through her hair. "I think we're going too fast," she shouted.

"Then slow down," Seamus said.

"How?"

"Touch the brake. It's just on the other side of the clutch."

Fiona looked down at the floor, trying to make sure she found the right pedal. Instantly the car drifted to the side. She looked up to see them riding along the edge of the road. Fiona yanked the wheel to the left and they crossed the road, then drove right into a shallow ditch. The car came to a jarring stop.

"Oh, dear," Fiona said.

Seamus groaned. "Ah, Christ. I knew this was bollocks. Women just shouldn't be driving."

"If you say that again, I swear I will run you down with this car," Fiona warned. "And since I'm a silly, incompetent woman, they'll never suspect I've done murder."

Seamus crawled out of the passenger seat and walked around the front of the car, examining it for damage. "I don't know why your father ever gave you permission to take his car. Though I wager this will give him an excuse to buy something new."

She cleared her throat and stared at him through the windscreen. "He didn't give me permission."

His head popped up from below the bonnet. "Please tell me your mother gave you permission."

"No, she didn't."

A vibrant string of curse words erupted from Seamus's lips and he kicked the front tire and started down the road. Fiona scrambled out of the car and raced after him. "Just help me get it back on the road," she begged. "I won't tell them you were with me, I promise."

THE HUGE BONFIRE SPIT sparks into the night air and, from a distance, it looked as though a tribe of pagans had gathered for a midnight ritual at Barley Cove. But the Beatles tune blaring from the car radio and the laughter of teenage girls echoed through the night instead of the chants of the ancient druids.

Seamus sat in the front seat of Donal McClain's roadster, his long legs stretched out over the leather upholstery. He'd brought Fi and three other girls out to Mizen Head earlier that evening and since then, a small crowd had gathered. He'd kept to the edges of the party, watching over his charge from a distance.

Was that really what Fiona was to him? he mused. Just a responsibility? For such a long time, she'd been like a little sister. And then, she'd become a friend. But he'd had to stop himself from thinking of her as anything more. She was pretty and smart and funny, and no one in Ballykirk really understood how wonderful she was. But Seamus knew she could never be his sweetheart.

Fiona was meant for so much more. Her family had the money to give her anything she wanted. She'd go to university and maybe become famous like her mother or wealthy like her father. There was no way she'd settle for a common fisherman like him.

But Seamus had dreams of his own. He'd been putting a bit of money aside every month and he and Paddy had been making plans. The *Mighty Quinn* was old and outdated and didn't have the power to travel miles offshore to catch the big fish. If they could invest in a bigger boat, and then another and another, they could build a whole fleet. His father had mentioned that Quinn men before him had coveted the same dream, but Seamus planned to make that dream a reality.

In a world where an Irish Catholic had become president of the United States, anything was possible. And maybe, a bird like Fiona would look twice at a bloke like him if he had something to offer her.

He searched the crowd for Fiona and saw her sitting on the bonnet of a battered Austin-Healy. She wore a pretty flowered dress and had tied her long dark hair back with a colorful scarf. Though she hadn't thrown herself into the midst of the party, she did seem as if she were having fun.

Seamus glanced at his watch. It was nearing eleven and he'd promised to have her home by midnight. The party had grown more boisterous since some of the boys had brought out a bottle, but Fi had steadfastly refused their offers of a drink.

He watched as Billy Boyle approached the Austin-

Healy, then sat down next to Fiona. He was a strapping sixteen-year-old who had gained notoriety on the local hurling team. But Billy had a temper and an ego that didn't appreciate a good prick. Fiona rarely left home without her pins and if Billy was stupid drunk then he might be on the receiving end of her jabs.

Billy grabbed her hand, pulled her off the car and began to lead her away from the party and the light of the fire. Seamus sat up straight, squinting into the night to see where they'd gone. When he couldn't find them, he jumped out of the car and made his way through the crowd to the beach.

He found them lying on a blanket, Billy wrestling with Fi and Fi trying to shove him off. With a low curse, Seamus grabbed the boy by the scruff of the neck and hauled him to his feet. Fiona scrambled to straighten her clothes, her fingers fluttering to her hair.

"Hey there, Billy boy," Seamus said. "I've been looking all over for ya."

Billy wiped his mouth with the back of his hand and Seamus felt a surge of anger at the thought that he'd slobbered all over Fiona. He fought the urge to pummel him.

"Whaddaya want, Quinn?"

"The boys were just sayin' in that last match against Bantry you scored three points, but Robby says it was just two. They've put a wager on it and they need you to declare a winner."

"It was three," Billy muttered. He gave Fiona a dismissive shrug and stumbled back in the direction of the fire.

Seamus held out his hand and helped her to her feet. "I think it's time we be going."

"You needn't have done that. I could have taken care of him."

"How so? He has at least six inches and sixty pounds on you. Were you going to just toss him over your head and dust yourself off? You have to take care with men, Fiona. They aren't all as nice as I am."

"How am I supposed to experience anything of life if you're constantly hovering over me?"

"You're the one who asked me to drive you to this party. I didn't want to come. But I'm lucky I did—so I could save your pretty little arse from that goon with ten hands and a tongue."

"What right do you have to—"

"I don't have a right," Seamus said, tossing up his hands. "None at all. I'm not certain why I even care. Live your life the way you want and I'll just stay clear." With that, Seamus headed back to the car, leaving her on the beach without a snappy comeback.

Five minutes later, she slipped into the passenger seat. "We can go now."

"What about your friends?"

"They aren't my friends," she murmured. "I have no friends. And they'll find their own way home."

The time it took to drive back to Ballykirk passed

in uneasy silence. But just before they drove through the village, Seamus pulled the car over to the side of the road. "I can't be your friend and not care about you," he murmured. "And I can't care about you and not interfere in your life every now and again. So if that concerns you, then I suppose we can't be friends."

"That's fine by me," she muttered.

"All right," Seamus said. "Say no more."

Seamus threw the car into gear and pressed the accelerator to the floor, turning back out onto the road. If that's what she truly wanted, then he would stay out of her life. After all, she was fifteen. She was old enough to make her own decisions. And it would be a fine relief not to have to spend another minute worrying about Fiona McClain.

CHAPTER TWENTY-SEVEN

"WHERE ARE WE GOING?" Fiona asked. She checked back over her shoulder, certain she'd find Seamus or her mother lurking just around the previous corner. She'd promised Seamus that she'd return by five and if she and Alan wandered too far, she'd never get back in time. "Is it nearby?"

"You'll see," Alan said, holding tightly to her hand.

They rounded another corner and Fiona dragged her feet, trying to slow his pace. If they were going to run across Dublin, then they ought to just hop on a bus. The pretty shoes she'd put on that morning were beginning to pinch and if they walked any faster, she'd barely be able to catch her breath.

Fiona glanced into the window of a small restaurant and pulled Alan to a stop. "This looks like a nice spot. Why don't we stop here?"

"It's not far," Alan said. "Just there." He pointed to a butcher shop on the opposite side of the street.

"Are you sure they serve tea there?"

"Positive," Alan said.

When they reached the shop, Alan opened a battered door that led up a narrow stairway. Fiona followed him, wondering what kind of tea shop would have such an unappealing entrance. At the top of the stairs, he unlocked another door and they stepped inside a small room. "What is this?" she asked.

"It's mine. I live here."

She'd never known anyone so young to live all alone. He drew her over to the bed and quickly straightened the tumble of blankets and linens. "Sit."

"I don't know if I should—"

"Sit down," Alan said. "You've nothing to fear. I'd have thought a sophisticated young lady like you would have visited a gentleman's flat before this time."

"Of course I have," Fiona lied. "I just have to make sure to get back soon."

Alan sent her a charming smile. "Don't worry. I'll have you back in plenty of time. I'm going to have a whiskey," he said. "Would you like one?"

"I—I thought I might have tea," Fiona replied.

"Tea is for old ladies and Englishmen. Besides, I'm fresh out."

"Perhaps just a bit of whiskey would be fine." Fiona surveyed the tiny room. There were books everywhere and piles of clothes on the floor. She noted a poster of the Eiffel Tower. "Have you been to Paris?"

"Not yet," he said, sitting down next to her on the edge of the bed. "But I plan to go. All great writers have to go to Paris. James Joyce lived there. My teachers tell me that my writing reminds them of Joyce. They say I have a bright future ahead of me."

"That's wonderful," Fiona said, enthralled by his handsome face and deep voice. "I'm going to go to Paris as well. Maybe I'll be a painter, or a poet like my mother. I haven't decided yet." He handed her a glass half-filled with whiskey and she took a small sip, the drink burning her throat.

"Perhaps we'll go together."

He leaned forward and kissed her, his tongue probing softly. Fiona had never been kissed so boldly before, at least not by a grown man. She hadn't realized it was supposed to be so...enjoyable.

"Did you like that?" Alan asked, his lips trailing to her neck. She nodded and he pulled back to look into her eyes. "Here, have some more." He hooked his finger beneath her glass and drew it toward her lips.

Fiona took another swallow of the whiskey, enjoying the warmth that seeped into her bloodstream. She felt happy and relaxed and a bit daring. Leaning into Alan, she kissed him again, this time testing his lips with her tongue.

Gently, Alan pushed her back onto the bed. His hands slid over her body, her shoulders, her waist, her hips, sending secret thrills racing through her. Fiona knew she ought to take care, but it didn't matter. This was love, this wild, exhilarating, frightening feeling. And she wanted to experience it all.

He seduced her at a lazy pace, kissing and touching her, innocently at first, pouring her another whiskey and encouraging her to drink, then whispering sweet words into her ear.

"So do you believe all those things your mother preaches?" he asked as he slowly toyed with the buttons of her blouse.

"Of course. I think women in Ireland should have the same rights as men."

He ran a finger along her cheek, then dipped between the buttons of her blouse. "And what about sex?" he murmured.

Fiona swallowed hard. "What about it?"

"Well, if women are allowed birth control, then they won't be so sexually inhibited. Are you inhibited, Fiona?"

"No," she said.

"Good. I'm glad to hear it."

In a heartbeat, he rolled her beneath him, pinning her against the lumpy mattress. His hand skimmed down her thigh and he pulled her leg up along his hip. Fiona felt his erection pressing against her and a wave of fear raced through her. Perhaps she oughtn't be here.

"I'd better go," she said, twisting against him. Alan grabbed her wrists and caught them above her head, his mouth fastening to hers. "Stop," Fiona cried, turning away.

"Don't play coy," he said, his voice ragged. "I know you want it."

"I don't," Fiona said. "Now stop!"

But he was past worrying about what she wanted. Shifting his weight, Alan reached down and unbuttoned his trousers, shoving them past his hips. Then he yanked her skirt up and her knickers down and began to touch her between her legs. Fiona cried out, twisting from his grasp. But the more she struggled, the more excited he became. His long arms and legs trapped her, anticipating her every move.

He entered her violently, pain shattering her fear and stealing her breath. Her instinct to survive overwhelmed all other emotion and she fought as hard as she could, scratching at his face and kicking her legs. Fiona sobbed as he pushed against her, grunting his pleasure into her ear, whispering foul words of lust. And then, he was done just as quickly as he'd begun, rolling off of her to lie sprawled on the bed beside her.

Fiona tried to control her weeping as she adjusted her clothes, wincing at the sticky moisture between her legs. When she sat up, he didn't try to stop her and for that she felt a measure of relief. She found her shoes and tugged them on, then tucked her blouse into her skirt. "I should go now," she murmured, buttoning her jumper up to her neck.

"You'd better. It is getting late."

She risked a glance back at him and found him staring at the ceiling. Brushing at her damp cheeks, Fiona walked to the door. Her knees wobbled and regret made her stomach roil. She wanted to fall to the floor and scream at her naive stupidity. How could she ever have believed that this would be romantic?

"I've got exams coming up," Alan called, "so don't be surprised if I don't see you for a time."

Fiona slipped into the hallway. When she'd pulled the door closed behind her, she let out a tightly held breath. Her body felt numb as she descended the stairs to the street. All she could think about was how disappointed her mother would be at her reckless behavior. And how angry Seamus would be when she arrived late.

SEAMUS HEAVED the nets back onto the deck of the *Mighty Quinn,* then stepped on board. He'd been working the boat with his father and Paddy for almost a year now and had come to love the business of fishing.

Their Uncle Niall had recently bought an old boat and, since his boys were still too young to work it, Paddy and Seamus went back and forth between the *Alice Ann* and the *Mighty Quinn.* Two boats certainly didn't make a fleet, but it was better than one. And before long, if their plans came to pass, there would be another boat tied to the Quinn family dock.

"Seamus?"

He glanced up to see Fiona standing next to the boat. He straightened and tugged off his gloves, smiling at her. He hadn't talked to Fiona for a while, not since that drive home from Cork a few months before, after her unfortunate afternoon with Alan Carrick. He suspected she was avoiding him on purpose, too humiliated or embarrassed to face him after what had happened. "Hello, Fi."

"Are you finished with your work?"

He nodded. "Nearly so. Is there something I can do for you?" She avoided his gaze and he could tell she was upset. "What is it? You haven't seen that Alan bloke again, have you?"

When she looked up at him, her eyes were filled with tears. "I think I may be pregnant."

Seamus stared at her, stunned by the news. Of course, he knew it was a possibility. But he'd hoped that Fiona had been sensible enough to use one those methods that she knew so much about. "Oh, Fi, I'm sorry. Christ, that's terrible news. Are you certain?"

She nodded. "And you shouldn't be sorry. It's my fault, not yours. And now I have to deal with this."

"What are you going to do? Have you told your folks, then?"

She shook her head. "I need money. My mother once told me there are doctors in England that will—take care of these things. I can wait until I leave for university. Once I'm in Dublin I'll take a quick trip across the Channel. It's probably going to cost a lot and I was hoping you might make me a small loan. If I ask my parents for that sort of money, they might become suspicious."

Seamus frowned. "I can't give you money for that,

Fi. It's wrong. It's against the law, here and in England. And it's against the teaching of the church. It's murder, it is."

"This is my life."

"And the life of your innocent baby."

"Alan's baby," Fiona countered. "Do you think he'll want to marry me when he finds out? He doesn't care about me. If he had, he wouldn't have forced himself on me."

"Is that what happened?" Seamus asked, his expression growing dark.

"I didn't want to, but he wouldn't stop." Fiona's voice grew thick with tears. "I can't raise this child on my own. I have to take care of this before anyone finds out."

Seamus jumped off the deck onto the dock, taking her hands in his. "There are other ways," he murmured.

She turned her tear stained face up and looked into his eyes. "What? Are you going to marry me, Seamus Quinn?"

"Yes," he said, nodding. "I'll marry you."

Fiona laughed at the notion and pulled out of his grasp. She walked a few feet down the dock and stared into the water. "I appreciate your attempt to make me smile, but I'm not in the mood for fun."

"I'm serious. I'll marry you, Fi. We'll tell everyone that the baby is mine and that will be the end of it. It happens all the time and once you're married, it won't matter."

"You'd do that for me?" she asked.

"I aimed to marry sometime. Why not now?"

"But we don't love each other," Fiona said.

Seamus shrugged. "We're friends. Maybe that's more important than love. And we've known each other for a lifetime already. Surely it will work, don't you think?"

She considered his offer for a moment before shaking her head. "No, it won't."

"There is no other way," Seamus said.

She closed her eyes. He watched her weigh her choices, knowing that the option he offered wasn't what she really wanted. But Seamus was certain he could make a good marriage with her and that was enough for him.

"All right," Fiona finally said.

"You'll marry me?"

She opened her eyes and met his gaze. "I will marry you, Seamus. And thank you."

He took her hand and gave it a squeeze. When he got up that morning, he hadn't expected to end the day engaged. But now that he was, it wasn't such a bad thing—though his attitude might change once Fiona's parents learned who was to be their new son-in-law.

CHAPTER TWENTY-EIGHT

"I'M GOING TO BE MARRIED," Seamus said.

Maggie and Colm looked up from their game of checkers, their eyes wide with surprise. They both glanced over at their mother, who stood holding a freshly baked loaf of soda bread, then turned to their father who was reading the evening paper with his magnifying glass.

"Who would you be marrying?" Brenna asked, as if Seamus was playing a joke. "I understand Queen Elizabeth is already taken."

"Fiona McClain. I expect we'll post the banns next week, as long as her parents don't object. She's going to have a baby so we're in a bit of a hurry."

Brenna gasped. "Oh, Lord. Fiona is with child? Tell me you're having on me on, Seamus."

He knew it would come as a bit of a surprise. He was still having trouble adjusting to the notion himself. He'd only just learned Fiona was pregnant four days before. "I'm not having you on. There it is and now everyone will have to deal with it."

"Deal with it?" Brenna said, her tone sharp. "Is that

all you have to say? How could you do this? Fiona is barely seventeen. How could you take advantage of her like this? The McClains have been good to our family and you're like a brother to her. This is a terrible betrayal."

"I'm not her brother, Mam. But I'm going to be her husband."

"Rory, say something!"

Seamus looked at his father, waiting for him to weigh in with his own shock and disapproval.

"I suppose that Seamus is old enough to make his own mistakes. He's doing right by her, so that's all that matters now."

Brenna tipped the bread onto the table, then tossed the tin into the sink. "How can you be so calm? Do you not care for the poor girl's position in this?"

"I know exactly what her life will be if she isn't married," Rory said. "My mother had me out of wedlock. She didn't marry my da until I was nearly six years old. I well remember how difficult it was for us, the gossip and the rumors. She fought side by side with men during the Irish civil war, yet that one mistake defined her life. I don't wish that upon any young girl."

"Nor do I," Brenna said. "But I—"

"It doesn't do to dwell on what has already happened," Rory insisted. "That horse is out of the stable now. I'd like to know what Seamus plans to do."

Seamus sat down at the table, facing his father. He

hadn't expected enthusiastic acceptance, but his father's reaction did surprise him. He seemed almost pleased by the news. Rory had always been fond of Fiona, yet he'd often told Seamus that a girl like Fiona was bound to marry well.

"We'll have to find a place to live," Seamus began. "I won't ask her family for money, and I don't think they'll be offering. Paddy and I have been discussing our future and we've been thinking about buying a boat of our own, a big boat. Colm is fifteen. He'll be ready to work the *Mighty Quinn* by the time we've enough saved. And once we go for the big fish, we'll make more money and buy another boat. We could turn Ballykirk into a commercial fishing center. Other boats will come, and maybe a processor. The harbor will expand and the business will be good for us all."

Rory seemed surprised that Seamus had put so much thought into his future. "That's an interesting notion, that. Duddy Kavanagh has an old boat he's been trying to sell. It would take a fair job of work, but you and Paddy could buy it, fix it, then trade it in for a bigger boat in a year or two."

"Who will work the *Mighty Quinn* with you?" Seamus asked.

"Your cousin James has lost his job at the mill in Cork. He wants to move his family back to Ballykirk. He'd take your spot. Niall will have to find someone to work the *Alice Ann,* but I think your cousin Marcus might be ready."

Seamus smiled. "That would work, Da."

"All these grand plans," Brenna said. She stood against the sink, her arms crossed beneath her breasts, her expression sullen. "It takes more than dreams to support a wife and a baby."

Seamus pushed out of his chair. "Well, Mam, you may have to wait a few more years until I can buy you that fancy diamond necklace and that mink jacket, but I *will* get them for ya."

He gathered her into a playful embrace, but she pushed him back. "You aren't married yet," she muttered. "I'd hate to think what Donal and Kit McClain are going to have to say about this bit of news."

Seamus's smiled faded. Fiona had planned to tell her mother that very night. Seamus had offered to be there with her, but she had insisted on doing it herself. He suspected Donal and Kit McClain wouldn't feel very kindly toward the Quinn family after hearing the news.

But Seamus could take solace in the knowledge that no matter how angry Kit and Donal were, he was doing a right and honorable thing in marrying their daughter.

FIONA'S MOTHER HELD UP a pale blue cardigan. "This would be lovely for those chilly days around the quad. I think we might need to buy some more jumpers for you. These are all a bit tatty and not the latest fashion."

“I can buy new clothes in Dublin,” Fiona said, picking through a stack of old blouses. She crawled onto her bed and hugged her pillow to her chest. Her stomach fluttered as if she’d swallowed a flock of jays and she wished that she could just stop time and avoid the conversation she had to have with her mother.

“Are you feeling all right?” Kit asked, reaching out and pressing her palm to Fiona’s forehead.

Fiona shook her head. “I’m knackered. All this talk about leaving Ballykirk is wearing me down.”

Kit smoothed her hand along Fiona’s cheek. “I don’t want you to think I’m looking forward to your leaving, because I’m not. I’m just so very excited that you’re going to begin your life with such promise. Trinity is a wonderful college and you’re going to learn so many things that will make you the kind of woman I know you can be.”

“What is that?” Fiona said quietly. “Someone like you?”

“Of course not. I want you to find your own talents. But whatever you do, I want you to do it well and with passion.”

“And what if I decided to leave university to marry and have a family?” Fiona asked. “Would you be terribly disappointed in me?”

“I suppose I would,” Kit said. “You can marry later, after you’ve discovered more of the world. There’s always time for that. And for children, too. Once you’re married, it’s very difficult to make a life for yourself.”

"You did," Fiona said.

"There was a time when I was lost, I didn't know where my life was leading. It seemed wherever I turned, there was something I could never have. So I made something for myself, something no one—no man—could take away from me." Kit stared out the open window of Fiona's bedroom, lost in her memories. "It wasn't easy."

"Mama, I think I'm going to have a baby."

Kit froze and, for a moment, she didn't breathe. When she turned, Fiona could see the shock and utter sadness in her eyes. "I—are you—I didn't know you were—"

"I wasn't. It was just once and…it happened."

"Who?" Kit asked.

Fiona swallowed hard. Her mother had always been able to tell when she was lying. She prayed that she'd be able to fool her now. "Seamus Quinn."

Kit froze. "What?"

"Please, don't blame him. It was me. I wanted to see what all the fuss was about and he was—" She cleared her throat. "He was swept away by my beauty, I suppose."

"I don't believe you," Kit said. "Seamus would never do that. He's always watched over you. He'd never take advantage like that."

"I'm the one who took advantage. And now Seamus has offered to marry me. And I've accepted."

"You won't marry him," Kit said, jumping to her

feet. She began to pace the room, back and forth in front of Fiona. "You can't marry him. You're only seventeen."

"And I'm going to have a baby."

"You won't marry him."

"Why not? He's a good man and you know he is. Grandmam says that you and Papa and Rory Quinn were the best of friends once. You ought to be happy I'm marrying him."

"He'll never be able to give you the life you deserve."

"But you taught me that money doesn't make a difference. Since when did that change?" Fiona sighed. "He'll take care of me. I know that."

"You'll have an abortion," Kit countered. "We'll go to London tomorrow and have it done with."

"I can't. It's against the laws of the church and I won't commit a mortal sin just for the convenience of it. I'm prepared to do this, Mama. I'll make Seamus a good wife and I'll make our child a fine mother. Now, you can support me or not. It makes no difference to us. We're going to post the banns next week. We'll be married by the end of the month."

"I won't give you my permission," Kit said. "I won't. You're still a child. You have your entire life waiting for you. Why decide your future so quickly?"

"It's already decided. I made a choice," Fiona said, "and now I have to live with the consequences."

Kit stared at her for a long time, her lower lip

caught between her teeth. Then she turned and walked out of Fiona's bedroom. Fiona released a tightly held breath. She hadn't expected it to be easy, nor did she enjoy lying to her mother. But she hadn't had a choice.

"Choices," she murmured. "I made the last of my choices when I climbed those stairs with Alan Carrick."

CHAPTER TWENTY-NINE

THE DAY WAS GLORIOUS, the sky a brilliant blue with a gentle breeze blowing in from the Atlantic. Seamus jumped over a low stone fence, then grabbed the picnic basket from Fiona before he helped her over the loose stones.

"I think my parents have finally accepted the notion that we're going to get married," Fiona said. "Mama doesn't seem nearly so sad when I talk about it. And she's already told me I can take my first term at Cork. We'll drive together every day and I'll be home by the time you come in."

Seamus caught her around the waist as she stumbled, then set her back on her feet. She looked so pretty, her dark hair blowing in the breeze, her summer dress clinging to her slender body. He'd had to remind himself over and over again that she was going to be his wife.

"I think that's a fine idea, Fi. And after the baby is born, we can find a way for you to continue. Perhaps my mam would take care of him while you go to university."

"Him?" Fiona asked. "What if it's a girl?"

"Then my mam will take care of her."

Fiona giggled, but her smile gradually faded. "Sometimes, I forget that there's a baby growing in me. It's not that I don't want it, but I wish I could forget how it got there."

"You will, over time," Seamus assured her.

"I hope so."

They found a spot near Oisin's Rock and Seamus spread the blanket over the grass. Fiona unpacked the lunch, removing a loaf of crusty bread and two foil-wrapped packages, one of ham and the other of cheese. She arranged their meal on a plate, then handed him a bottle of Guinness and an opener.

As they ate, they spoke of the wedding and their plans for a honeymoon. Seamus had decided to ask Paddy for a loan, hoping that he'd have enough to take Fiona to Dublin for a long weekend. He thought about choosing a romantic honeymoon location, but he didn't want to pressure Fiona to pretend to feel something that she didn't. He would give her time to want him.

When they finished the meal, Seamus lay back on the blanket and stared up at the sky. Fiona sat beside him, weaving her fingers through his. "Tell me a story," she said, "Like you did when I was sick."

"A Mighty Quinn story?"

"Yes," Fiona said. "My mother once told me that your father used to tell her stories of the Mighty

Quinns. Do you think they sat in this very spot when they were young?"

"I suppose they did," Seamus said.

She sighed softly. "Sometimes, I catch her looking at your father and she looks so sad. I don't understand why they aren't friends anymore. Maybe if I knew the reason, it might explain why she's so against this marriage." She smiled and shook her head. "Tell me a tale, Seamus."

Seamus searched his memory for a good story, then decided that an ordinary tale would never do. "I'll tell you the story of Tirlogh Quinn. Tirlogh was a young man who was fascinated by the creatures of the forest. Every day, he wandered into the deep woods searching for fairies and gnomes and elves and leprechauns. One day, he stumbled upon a fairy mound and he hid behind a huge tree and watched the beautiful fairies with their hair of gold and their gossamer dresses.

"We all know that fairies sometimes take mortal men as their lovers, luring them to their raths and treating them to glorious banquets. Once they'd taken their pleasure from the men, the fairies would send them off with no memory of their night together. Tirlogh was always curious about that part of the legend. How did the fairies make the men forget, for he would certainly remember a night with a fairy, wouldn't he? He noticed that before each man walked from the forest, the fairies would sprinkle them with petals from an unusual blue flower that grew only from the center of the fairy mound."

"These fairies sound like real scrubbers," Fiona commented as she lay down beside him. "Ladies of very loose morals."

"Fairies aren't bound by the same moral code as humans are. There isn't a Fairy Father Thomas watching over their immortal souls and keeping them on the straight and narrow." Seamus rolled onto his side and stared down at Fiona as he spoke, taking in the tiny details of her face. "Tirlogh waited until all the fairies had taken their gentlemen callers into the rath that night. Then he crawled over the fairy mound and gathered some of the blue flowers. He thought he'd test them, so he sprinkled some petals over his head. The next thing he knew, he was standing in the middle of the village square and he wasn't sure how he'd gotten there. He'd forgotten all about the fairy mound and the blue flowers. Days passed and Tirlogh began to wander in the woods again and he found the fairy mound and the blue flowers. But this time, he took the flowers home for he knew they were powerful magic. He decided to test them on the local moneylender. Tirlogh borrowed a fair sum of money from the old man, and as he left, he sprinkled some of the petals over the man's head. The moneylender didn't remember the loan. Tirlogh began to use the flowers for many dubious reasons. But word got back to the fairies that their magic had been stolen. When Tirlogh returned to the fairy mound for more flowers, the fairies were prepared and they sprinkled him with so many flower petals that his mind was wiped clean of all his memories. He wandered about the woods for days, lost and afraid, and when he found the village, he didn't recognize a single soul. They took Tirlogh to his house and taught him all those things that he'd forgotten. But he never returned to the woods again, for the woods were a place that he feared more than death itself."

Seamus reached over Fiona's head and grabbed a handful of wildflowers, then plucked off the petals one by one. She watched him, smiling. And when he sprinkled the petals over her head, she laughed, the tiny bits of color clinging to her lashes and lips.

"Did you make that story up?" she asked.

"No," Seamus lied. "It's a true story."

She watched him for a long moment, looking for the truth in his eyes. Reaching up, Fiona slipped her hand around his nape, pulling him closer. She touched her lips to his in a kiss so gentle and sweet that Seamus felt his heart ache with it.

At that very moment, he knew that he loved Fiona McClain. And that he would always love her.

THEIR SUNNY AFTERNOON had been spoiled by dark clouds that rolled in from the Atlantic. Fiona had quickly packed the basket and they'd headed back toward Ballykirk, hoping to get to shelter before the rain began.

But Seamus had other plans and he led Fiona along a rutted road. They stopped in front of an abandoned cottage, set on a hillside above the village. Seamus had been to the cottage several times as a young child, though he barely remembered his visits. The white-wash had long faded and the thatch was old, but the home was well built.

"Whose cottage is this?" Fiona asked.

"It's ours to rent, if you like it." He took the picnic blanket from her arms and opened the lopsided gate.

"Ours? Really?"

"My Uncle Jamie and Aunt Mavis own it. They lived here after they were married fifteen years ago. She grew up in the place and her father left it to her when he died. She couldn't bear to sell it when they moved to Kinsale, so they rented it for a time. But when the renters left, they didn't keep it up. Would you like to go inside?"

"Yes," Fiona said, excitement filling her voice. "I assumed we'd live with your parents for a time. I never thought we'd be able to afford our own cottage."

Seamus reached for the doorknob. "Now don't expect a palace. It needs a good scrub and some paint. And new glazing in some of the windows. But it's nothing I can't fix." He opened the door and Fiona stepped inside, anxious to see her new home.

Sunlight filtered through grimy windowpanes and dust motes swirled in the air. A huge hearth dominated one end of the main room and a sink with modern plumbing was set below the window on the rear wall. Two small bedrooms were carved out of one end of the cottage and there was a small water closet in between. As Fiona wandered through the door between the bedrooms, she smiled.

"This could be the nursery," she said.

"I thought so, too. It's not big, but we won't need much room to start."

"Is the rent reasonable?"

"Very," Seamus said.

"Then I love it." She walked back into the main room and grabbed the blanket from beside the front door. She carefully spread it over the dusty plank floor and sat down.

"What are you doing?"

"I'm trying it out," Fiona said. "I want to see how it feels."

Thunder rumbled outside and Seamus peered out one of the windows. "If you want to get home before the rain, we're going to have to run."

"We are home," Fiona said.

Seamus sat down next to her and listened as the storm moved in from the west. Minutes later, the rain started and what began as a gentle shower soon turned to a downpour. Through the broken windows, they watched the water sluice off the old thatched roof. Fiona stared up at the ceiling and smiled. "It's cozy. No leaks."

Seamus nodded. "Except through the windows."

"And that can be fixed. I like it, Seamus. It's a close walk to the village and not far from my parents. And if I hike to the top of the rise, I can see the *Mighty Quinn* come in at sunset. I'll know when to have supper ready."

They sat in silence for a long time, listening to the sounds of the rain and the thunder. Seamus was amazed by the utter contentment he saw in her expression. "Aren't you nervous, then?"

"About what?" Fiona asked. "The roof?"

"We're going to be married."

"Yes, we are. But I know you'll be a good husband. You're my friend, Seamus, and I trust you. You've always taken good care of me and I expect that won't change once we're married."

"It won't. I promise you that."

"There is one thing," Fiona said, toying with the fringe on the edge of the blanket. "I was wondering if you might want to kiss me again. It's not necessary, but we are to be married. And I'd like to know that you do think about things like that from time to time."

Seamus chuckled. "I do. I've been thinking a fair bit about kissing you again."

"Then stop thinking about it and do it."

Seamus hooked his finger under her chin and tipped her face up to his. She was the most beautiful woman he'd ever known and he couldn't imagine refusing an invitation to taste her lips. Fiona closed her eyes, her lashes dark against pale, flawless skin.

The moment their lips touched, everything became so clear. Perhaps he'd only just begun to love her today. Or perhaps he'd loved her all along and just hadn't realized it. But as he tentatively touched his tongue to hers, Seamus thanked God that they'd been brought together.

He didn't care that he'd raise another man's child as his own, or that Fiona didn't come to the marriage as a virgin. Or that she'd accepted his proposal out of desperation. He considered himself lucky that she'd said yes.

They kissed for a long time, learning from each other, testing their desires. Seamus had kissed enough girls to know what to do. But this wasn't just a frantic meeting of lips and tongues. Kissing Fiona was like talking to her without saying a word. He understood her responses, knew when to gentle his assault or kiss her with more abandon.

When he finally drew back, her face was flushed and her eyes bright. He held his breath as Fiona reached for her blouse and began to unbutton it. When she'd finished, she shrugged it off her shoulders. Slowly, Seamus reached out and ran his palm over her naked shoulder. He couldn't take his eyes off her, his heart slamming in his chest, his head spinning.

"Make love to me," she murmured.

She took his hand and placed it on her breast, and Seamus gently caressed her nipple through the soft cotton of her bra. "Are you sure?"

"If you make love to me, then this baby will be yours," she explained. "And all the mistakes of the past will be made right again. I want the feeling of you, not him, to fill my memories."

She didn't wait for an answer. Instead, she reached out, unbuttoned his shirt and smoothed her hands across his chest. A shiver raced over his body and suddenly he was afraid.

"I've never done this before," Seamus said, ashamed to admit his inexperience.

But Fiona smiled and ran her fingers through his hair. "Neither have I."

They slowly undressed each other, taking time to enjoy the process. Seamus marveled at the beauty of her body, the gentle curves that seemed to fit his hands so perfectly, the skin so smooth he couldn't bear to stop touching it.

But touching her wasn't enough. He tasted her as well, the soft skin at the base of her neck, her dusky-pink nipples, and the hollows above her hips. He could spend years exploring her body and never know all its mysteries.

Unfortunately, his body held no mystery. His desire was more than evident and when Fiona wrapped her fingers around him, Seamus had to hold his breath. He fought back wave after wave of pleasure, determined not to give in. And when he couldn't fight it anymore, he gently pulled her on top of him.

She seemed surprised and, at first, wasn't sure what to do. Seamus knew it would be better this way, with Fiona in control. He would erase the memory of that first time by giving her back her choice, her power as a woman. She moved against him and he shifted beneath her and then he was inside her.

Fiona's eyes went wide and Seamus smiled at her, waiting, keeping his desire well in check—easy as long as she didn't move. Once she began to rock above him, Seamus knew he couldn't hold on. He grabbed her hips and gently slowed her pace and, when he'd regained control, allowed her to move again.

Their lovemaking was slow and sweet, both of them enjoying every sensation. He talked to her softly, telling her what felt good, allowing her to take an equal part in the seduction. And when he touched her where they were joined, her eyes snapped open and her breath caught.

He continued, watching her response, unsure of what he was doing but certain it was right. She looked frightened and he stopped, but Fiona shook her head, drawing his hand back to her. She began to move again, her eyes closed and her head angled back.

Her pace increased and then she froze above him. A tiny cry slipped from her throat, and he felt her heat close in around him. The sensation was too much to bear and Seamus found his release.

When the last shiver had left his body, he drew her into his embrace, holding her tight. There was nothing he wouldn't do to make Fiona happy. She was his now and he'd spend his life keeping her safe from harm.

CHAPTER THIRTY

THE SUN BEAT DOWN on Seamus's back as he dragged the nets across the deck of the *Mighty Quinn.* Gulls hovered above, hoping for scraps of the fish they'd caught that day. His father worked beside him, clearing away the gear so they could unload the day's catch.

"I know you haven't been too keen to talk about what went on," Rory said. "But if you have something you'd like to discuss before you get married on Saturday, I'll be happy to listen."

"I think I know what to expect on the honeymoon," Seamus said, chuckling softly.

"Considering Fiona's condition, I'm certain you do. But how do you feel about being forced to marry her?"

"I'm not being forced," Seamus replied as he jumped off the deck onto the dock. "I want to marry Fiona."

Rory hooked the winch to one of the barrels filled with fish. He lifted the barrel off the deck of the *Mighty Quinn,* and Seamus guided it down to rest on a small cart. "I would have thought you'd know better than to get mixed up with Fiona McClain."

Seamus wondered if he ought to tell his father the truth. He wanted him to know that he hadn't done wrong, that he hadn't sullied the family name, but he'd also promised Fiona they'd be the only two to know the real story of their child's parentage.

"Is it another man's child?" Rory asked.

Seamus glanced up, surprised. He nodded. "It was some man she met in Cork. But that makes no difference to me and I trust you'll keep our secret. I want to marry her, Da. She doesn't have anyone else."

Rory shook his head. "You've been protecting that lass for her whole life. And she'll probably never appreciate you for it."

"She may someday," Seamus said. "I'm willing to wait."

Rory stepped off the boat to join Seamus and they dragged the cart down the dock to the waiting truck. "I once loved her mother, you know. I didn't tell her and then she married Donal." He sighed. "After a time I realized we weren't meant to be together, but there are times when I see her and I wonder what might have been. Maybe you and Fiona are meant to experience the love that we could never have."

They carefully rolled the barrel off the cart and started back down the dock to retrieve the next. But Rory stopped suddenly. Seamus looked over his shoulder to see Kit McClain stepping out of her car near the quay. "What do you suppose she wants?" his father asked.

"Maybe she's come to say she'll be attending the wedding after all."

They both waited while she walked toward them, her expression grim. "Hello, Rory," she said.

Rory nodded. "Kit."

Seamus watched the looks that passed between them and he wondered at the relationship they'd once had.

"Have you come for a reason, Kit?" Rory asked.

She turned to Seamus and a sudden fear gripped his gut. "What is it?" he asked.

Kit drew a deep breath. "Fiona had a miscarriage late last night."

"Is she all right?" Seamus turned to his father. "I have to go to her. Can you get Colm to help you unload the rest of the catch?"

"She doesn't want to see you, Seamus," Kit said. "She's very thankful for your offer to marry her, but now there's no reason for you to marry. She'll be going to university as planned."

"I still want to talk to her," Seamus said.

"She'd rather not talk to you and you'll have to respect that. We're leaving tomorrow morning. We're going to stay with my aunt in Galway until it's time for her to go to Dublin. She'll be fine, Seamus. She has a grand future ahead of her now. Please don't get in the way of that."

"And she didn't when she was planning to marry me, is that what you're saying?" Seamus cursed softly.

"You have to understand," Kit said.

"Oh, I understand," Seamus muttered.

He stalked off, certain that if he stayed he'd break his promise to Fiona. Seamus had been good enough to sit by Fi while she was sick with polio and kind enough to drive her about the countryside when Kit was busy with her own work. Kit McClain would think differently of him if she knew the truth—that he'd offered to raise another man's child just to save her daughter's reputation.

He stopped at the first pub he found and ordered a whiskey. Though he wasn't one to drink, Seamus felt it was the only way he could control his temper. Just this morning, his life had been in such fine order. He'd been about to become a husband and a father all at once, to begin a new life with a woman he loved.

And now, in a heartbeat, it was over. Everything he'd dreamed for himself and his family was gone. He was alone and there was nothing he could do about it.

He wasn't sure how many whiskeys he downed over the next hour. But by the time his father arrived, he was well on his way to getting pissed.

Rory sat down next to him and poured himself a measure from the bottle sitting in front of Seamus. "Maybe it's for the best," he said.

"How is that, Da?"

"She didn't love you, Seamus. If she had, she would have married you anyway."

"The truth is Fiona McClain doesn't need me anymore, Da. She has more important things to do with her life than waste away in Ballykirk, raising a bunch of babies and working her fingers to the bone. I don't blame her."

"Do you love her?" Rory asked.

Seamus shook his head. "No, and I never really did," he lied. "I expect I imagined myself in love with her. It made the prospect of marrying her a bit easier to swallow."

Rory nodded, but Seamus could tell that he was unconvinced. "Kit only wants the best for her daughter. Can't blame her, that."

"Like a university education and a wealthy husband and a fancy house?"

"Life is simpler when you don't have a lot to lose," Rory said. "The choices are easier to make."

"COME ON, FIONA. Close your books and come with us. We're going to eat Chinese food at that new restaurant in Temple Bar. Then the lads are going to play rugby and we're going to cheer them on. What could be better? Chow mein and handsome, sweaty boys. I know Danny O'Donnell would be chuffed if you'd come."

"I should study," Fiona said, forcing a smile.

"You'll never meet a man if you stay locked up in

your room," Fiona's roommate whined. "As my older sister told me, there are only two things you need do in college—make good grades and kiss a lot of boys."

"I've got one hidden away in my closet," Fiona replied. "I'm going to take him out as soon as you leave, and have my way with him."

"I'll bring you back a fortune cookie and maybe you'll join us for the rugby match?"

"Maybe," Fiona said. She waited for her roommate to close the door, then sat back in her chair and sighed softly. Parties and dances, socials and concerts, sporting events and academic competitions, they all seemed so silly.

Just a few months ago, Fiona was pregnant and planning to marry. Her mind had been occupied with making a home for her husband and sewing clothes for her baby. Now her head was filled with Renaissance paintings and irregular French verbs.

She leaned forward and cupped her chin in her hand. There were times when she wished she were seeing her new surroundings with the wide-eyed exuberance of her peers. For them, life seemed full of endless possibilities. But Fiona knew how quickly a girl's fortunes could change. A glass of whiskey, a quiet room and a man bent on seduction was all it took to transform a bright future into a bleak existence.

Fiona's mind wandered back to the moment she'd realized she'd lost her baby. It was as if a part of her heart had died, the part that she'd allowed to want the child inside her. After she and Seamus had made love, Fiona had felt differently about her pregnancy. It had no longer been an inconvenience. It had become the promise of a family and a future.

She felt her eyes fill with tears and she cursed. Women lost babies all the time. Her mother had miscarried again and again before she'd given birth to Fiona. Why did the thought of her baby bring such a flood of emotion? Perhaps it was because that time in her life would always remain a secret and if she couldn't talk about it, someday she'd forget.

Fiona longed to share her feelings with someone. Her mother refused to discuss it and her father didn't know what to say. The only person she could ever trust had been pushed out of her life. Seamus would understand. He'd know exactly what to say to soothe her grief.

Sniffling, she wiped the tears from her cheeks and tore a sheet of paper from her Art History notebook. Maybe if she wrote a letter to Seamus, she'd feel better. She rummaged through the mess on her desk for a pen, then chewed on the cap as she tried to put her thoughts into words.

Dear Seamus,

I've wanted to write for such a long time, but I couldn't decide what to say. All that comes to mind is...I'm sorry. I'm sorry I went to Alan's room that day and I'm sorry I accepted your proposal and I'm sorry I lost the baby. But most of all, I'm sorry I left without telling you how very grateful I am to have a friend like you.

I'm supposed to forget about the baby and move on with my life. But again and again, my thoughts return to that afternoon we spent in our little cottage and the life we might have shared. My mother says I'm young and I'll forget. But I hope I never ever forget those very few days of happiness we found together.

All my lo—

The pen dragged to a stop as she tried to complete the word *love.* The word came so naturally to her when she thought of Seamus. But did she love him? Or were these emotions just a mixture of gratitude and affection? Fiona slowly crumpled the paper and tossed it into the rubbish bin beneath her desk.

Maybe she just needed a bit more time to adjust. She would forget—the baby, the cottage, Seamus. There'd come a day when she wouldn't think of any of it and her life would begin again.

Fiona pushed out of her chair and grabbed her jacket. Until then, an evening of chow mein and rugby would be just what she needed. But as she walked down the hallway and out the front door of her dormitory, she couldn't help but think about Ballykirk—and the man she'd left behind.

CHAPTER THIRTY-ONE

A COLD RAIN PELTED the deck of the Siobhan B as Seamus steered the boat into the harbor at Ballykirk. He wiped the droplets from his eyes and peered through the haze that had enveloped the village. It was nearly Christmas and the weather had been chilly and gray, adding to his bleak mood.

Last Christmas, he'd held out hope that Fiona would come home from Dublin and he'd get a chance to see her. But Donal and Kit had swept her off to Rome for Christmas and then to Wales during her Easter holiday. She'd spent the summer touring Europe with a group of her friends. Seamus knew her parents were hoping that time away would make her forget him.

After Fiona had left Ballykirk, Seamus had thrown himself into his work, spending long hours on the water, determined to save enough to buy Duddy Kavanagh's old boat. He and Paddy had launched the *Siobhan B* two months after his grandmother's death and, since then, the fishing had been good.

He'd decided to rent the cottage from his uncle

anyway, and whatever time he had left beyond fishing and sleeping he'd wasted away at the pub, numbing his pain with Guinness and whiskey. Almost a year passed, Seamus doing anything he could to banish thoughts of Fiona from his head. But gradually he realized that he couldn't live the rest of his life in a drunken haze. He began to avoid the pub entirely, occupying his mind and body with refurbishing the cottage.

Seamus wanted to believe he'd someday bring a bride to his home. But he still couldn't imagine himself with anyone but Fiona McClain. In comparison to the other girls of the village, she was smarter and kinder and prettier and had more passion for life. And when he was with her, he felt himself a better man.

Though he hadn't heard a word from Fi, Seamus managed to get bits and pieces of news from his mother. After all that had passed, Brenna had assumed she'd be fired from her position at the McClains. But once Fiona had gone to Dublin, the tensions between the two families had eased and life had returned to normal.

Seamus was amazed people had forgotten so quickly. They'd settled back into the same old routine and no one mourned for the baby Fiona had lost—except him. Maybe this had all been God's plan, to tempt him with happiness and then snatch it away. Or perhaps Fiona hadn't been meant to carry the baby of a man who had hurt her.

Before the miscarriage had changed everything, he'd expected to spend his first Christmas holiday in the cozy cottage, with a Christmas tree and presents and a peat fire blazing on the hearth. Instead, he'd spent it with a whiskey bottle, all alone in his empty cottage with his empty heart.

Seamus hunched over against the rain, drawing the collar of his mackintosh up around his neck. He wasn't about to do that again. He'd decided to accept his Uncle Jamie's invitation to join him and his wife, Mavis, for the holiday in Kinsale. Anything to get him away from memories of Fiona. If he stayed in Ballykirk, he'd spend the whole holiday waiting to run into her in the village or wondering where in the world she was or whether she ever thought of him at all.

Paddy came up from the cabin, a wrench in his hand. "The bilge pump is working again," he said. "Though I can't say how long it will last. I heard of a bloke over in Kinsale who sells reworked pumps. We could get a spare from him."

"I'm going to Kinsale for the holiday," Seamus said. "Give me his address and I'll go take a look."

"Does Mam know you won't be here?" Paddy asked.

Seamus nodded. "I need some time away."

"You'd feel better if you'd get out a bit more. You're like an old hermit, living in that cottage all alone. What do you do up there?"

"I read. I think. I patch the cracks in the plaster and fix the leaky plumbing."

"I've got a date tonight with Ellen Buckley. And she has a younger sister, Colleen, who has quite a high opinion of yourself. I believe when your name was last mentioned, she smiled and said in a dreamy voice, 'Now there's a queer bit of talent.' Why don't you come with us?"

"I'll consider it," Seamus said. "But I won't promise anything."

Paddy clapped him on the back and grinned. "See there, that wasn't so difficult." He walked to the bow and grabbed the line as Seamus steered the boat through the harbor. When they got closer to the dock, Paddy pointed to a lone figure standing on the end. "There she is. Ellen Buckley can't live a moment without me."

"I don't think that's Ellen Buckley," Seamus called. As he remembered, Ellen Buckley was a much larger girl. He wiped the rain from his eyes. As they approached, he recognized the slender form, the long dark hair and delicate features. He felt his heart begin to beat a bit faster.

"Oh, Christ," Paddy said. "Now I see who that is."

A smile touched Seamus's lips. He was glad Paddy had confirmed it. Had Seamus been alone, he might have thought she was a vision or a mirage.

The *Siobhan B* bumped against the dock and Seamus shut down the engine. Paddy jumped off and looped the line around the piling. "Hello there, Fiona McClain," he said. "Nice to see you back."

"Thank you, Paddy. It's good to be back."

She glanced up at Seamus and their gazes met and held. Seamus was afraid to breathe, afraid she might disappear in front of his eyes like the early mist on a sunny day.

Paddy looked back and forth between the two of them, then cleared his throat. "I'm just going to visit one of our local pubs and have myself a Guinness. When you're ready to unload, you come and fetch me, Seamus."

Paddy's footsteps faded on the dock as Seamus scrambled for something to say. "You haven't changed at all," he murmured.

"You have," Fiona replied. "You're a grown man now."

"I have my own boat," he said. "And I'm doing quite well with it. The fishing's been good. The Quinn family has a regular fleet now. Three boats and more to come."

"I'm happy for you," Fiona said. "I always knew you'd make a success of yourself."

Seamus began to toy with the keys to the boat, trying to collect his thoughts. There was a time when he used to practice what he'd say to her, entire conversations to use if and when he finally saw her again. But he'd given that up long ago, about the same time he had stopped getting gee-eyed every night. "I didn't expect you'd be back for the Christmas holiday."

"My father put his foot down. He managed to convince my mother I was over you and that I wouldn't be tempted to run off and get myself pregnant again if I saw you."

Seamus studied the toes of his Wellies. "Are you over me?" He risked a look up. "Was there ever anything between us to get over?" He watched her eyes, searching for a clue to her feelings.

"There was," she murmured. "Perhaps there still is."

Seamus frowned. "What are you saying, Fi?"

"I don't know." She shook her head, then laughed softly. "I'm just happy to see you, Seamus. And I'm glad you're well." She checked over her shoulder. "I should go. My mother just stopped for a moment at the post and she'll be watching for me. I don't want her to worry. If she suspects I've talked to you, she'll drag me off to some foreign capital to look at the architecture and I'd prefer to spend my Christmas in Ballykirk."

She turned and hurried back down the dock, but Seamus jumped off the boat and ran after her. He grabbed her arm and spun her around to face him. "Meet me later," he said, lacing his fingers through hers, desperate to keep her just a moment longer.

"Where?"

"I don't know. Anywhere. Name a place and I'll be there."

"I've got some Christmas shopping to finish tomorrow morning. I might be able to get away for a time."

"Meet me at the cottage," Seamus said.

"All right. I'll try."

He reluctantly let go of her hand and watched her walk away. Hell, he thought he'd managed to put her out of his life, but all it took was one look, a few words, and his heart was lost again. There'd be no going back now; there'd be no other women for him.

If he couldn't have Fiona, then he'd spend the rest of his life alone.

"I DON'T THINK I'll be back before lunch," Fiona said, gathering her jacket and her gloves.

Kit glanced up from the dining-room table. "You're just going to the village."

"I thought I might drive into Cork. I won't find a gift for Da in Ballykirk."

"Why don't I come with you, then?" Kit suggested, pushing aside her work. "We'll make a day of it."

"No, we won't. I have to shop for you, as well. And I'm never good at finding gifts for you. It may take me all afternoon and still, I might come home empty-handed."

Kit studied her for a long moment. "How are you feeling?"

"I'm fine," Fiona said. "Why wouldn't I be? It's pleasant to get away from my studies for a time."

"That's not what I meant." Kit carefully rearranged the papers in front of her as she spoke. "I know it must be difficult for you, the prospect of seeing Seamus

Quinn again. But I think enough time has gone by that you've both been able to put the past in the past. And I'm sure you'll agree, you're better off without him."

Fiona felt her temper flare, but this time she didn't stop herself. "I don't want to hear another word spoken against Seamus Quinn. You don't know him the way I do. And you have no idea what went on between us. I'd be lucky to find someone like him to marry. He's a good and honorable man."

An uneasy expression crossed Kit's face. "You haven't seen him again, have you?"

"Whether I have or I haven't is none of your business, Mama." Fiona reached out and picked up the keys to the car. "I'll be back before supper."

When she got outside, Fiona stood next to the car, trying to calm her anger. She knew how her mother felt about Seamus and she'd been sorely tempted to tell her the truth. She couldn't stand that anyone, especially her parents, thought poorly of a man as good as Seamus Quinn. Or that their opinion had formed because of a lie she'd perpetuated.

"I'm a coward, I am." But Fiona was so eager to recapture her mother's faith in her that she was willing to sacrifice Seamus's reputation. How would Kit McClain, defender of women's rights, feel if she knew her daughter had allowed herself to be seduced by a near stranger?

Fiona climbed into the car and steered it out of the driveway. Just before she reached the village, she turned onto the road leading up to the cottage. It was the perfect place to meet, quiet and isolated, with no gossips about to speculate on the state of her relationship with Seamus.

The car bumped up the hill and as the cottage came into sight, she was surprised at how much it had changed. The stone fence surrounding the garden had been repaired and a fresh coat of whitewash had been applied to the facade. Fiona got out of the car and walked through a new iron gate, then realized that someone was living at the house.

Had she misunderstood Seamus? What other cottage could he have meant? The front door swung open and Seamus appeared, his broad-shouldered form outlined by the light inside. "I have the kettle on," he said. "Would you come in for a cup of tea?"

Fiona glanced around. "Do you live here, then?"

Seamus nodded. "I've done a fair bit of work around the place. What do you think?"

He stepped aside, allowing her to enter. The single room that she remembered had been transformed. Though the decor was simple, the interior was spotless. The furniture was a bit tatty, but well chosen. A potted violet sat in the middle of the dinner table and striped curtains draped the window above the sink, adding to the cozy look.

As if Seamus were reading her mind, he said, "My mam made the curtains. And my sister Maggie gave me the plant. There's no one I've been seeing, if that's what you're wondering. Although I've been told that Colleen Buckley fancies me."

Fiona smiled. She'd wanted to believe Seamus had mourned the end of their short engagement as much as she had. But it was impractical to think he couldn't easily find another woman to take her place. Still, her heart ached to think that he might have been as lonely as she had. "You've done a fine job here, Seamus. It's…perfect."

"Can I get you tea?"

"Maybe we could take a walk." The memories were thick inside the cottage, making it hard to keep herself in the present. The afternoon they'd spent together Fiona had felt so safe and so treasured in his arms and it would be easy to seek out that feeling again.

"Let me get you another jacket," he said. "The one you're wearing won't do against the weather."

He reached for a spare mackintosh that hung from a hook near the door and held it out for her. Fiona slipped her arms into it and Seamus smoothed his hands over her shoulders, allowing his touch to linger for a long moment.

As they started up the rutted path into the hills above the cottage, Seamus took her hand. A slow drizzle continued to fall and the chilly temperatures nipped at her nose and ears. "It feels good just to walk and see nothing but green hills and endless sky. Dublin can be so dreary in the winter."

Seamus smiled at her, then turned his attention back to the path. Fiona knew that she didn't have to speak for him to understand what she was feeling. But she wanted to tell him anyway. "I'm sorry, Seamus. I'm sorry I wasn't brave enough to speak to you before I left."

"You don't have to explain," Seamus said.

"But I do. I owe you at least that much. When I lost the baby, I was so sad. It's silly, because I didn't want the baby to begin with. But our afternoon in the cottage changed that and I thought of the baby as ours. As yours."

Seamus gave her hand a squeeze. "I did, too."

"You offered me so much, and then it was over. I was the girl I was before all of this started. Before Alan Carrick."

"I understand, Fi. There was no reason for us to be together without the baby."

"I thought so, too. But it wasn't just the baby I'd lost. It was you and our life together."

"But now you have the life that your parents have always wanted for you."

"I can't go back. I'm not that girl anymore. But I can't seem to go forward, either. I'm caught in this queer limbo and I can't find my way out."

"Perhaps it will just take more time," he suggested.

Fiona stopped walking and turned to face him. "I feel as if I don't have the time. That every moment I spend in Dublin is keeping me from something. But

I don't know what it is. Sometimes I ache, as if it's left a great gaping hole in my heart."

He reached out and touched the spot above her heart. "Does it ache now?"

She shook her head. "No, I suppose it doesn't. Not this very minute at least."

They hiked higher into the hills, until they stood well above Oisin's Rock. Below, they could see the sea surging toward the low cliffs and the calm harbor at Ballykirk.

The rain still fell, but Fiona didn't feel the cold or the damp. A great burden had been lifted from her soul. For the first time in ages, she was able to be herself, to say the things that troubled her heart and to have someone understand. She'd always thought of Seamus as her friend, but until this very moment, she hadn't realized what an important part of her life he'd become.

"What are your plans then?" Seamus asked. "How long do you intend to stay?"

"The next term begins in early January. I have about three weeks to be home, unless my mother spirits me away for another holiday in Europe. And she will, you know, if she learns that I've seen you."

"Why?"

"I think she believes that what happened between us once might happen again."

Seamus nodded. "Would you like to see me, Fi?"

A smile broke across her face. "I would. Very much. I've missed you, Seamus."

"Then I suppose we oughtn't let your mother know we've gone for this walk. Or that we're planning to have supper together tomorrow. You will join me for supper, won't you?"

"I would love to."

They spent the early afternoon walking and talking, falling back into the easy friendship that they'd shared their entire lives. When they both got too cold to continue, they went back to the cottage.

The late afternoon was spent in front of the fire, Fiona curled up in an old chair, a woolen blanket wrapped around her and a cup of hot tea in her hands. Seamus sat on the rag rug in front of her, his long legs stretched out before him, his feet warmed by the heat from the hearth.

As she drank her tea, Fiona distractedly toyed with Seamus's hair, twisting the dark strands between her fingers, needing the physical contact with him. She was amazed at how content she felt in his presence. This was what it would have been like had they married, she mused. This gentle quiet between them at the end of the day.

The rain continued throughout the afternoon but inside the cottage, they'd found a cozy escape. As the sun began to set, Fiona knew she'd be expected home soon. Seamus had dozed off and she was reluctant to wake him. Instead, she pressed a soft kiss to his forehead. But when she pulled back, she found him looking up at her.

Without a word, he reached up and slipped his hand around her neck, drawing her toward him. Their lips meet in a soft kiss and Fiona felt emotion well up inside of her. All the desires she'd put aside in her life suddenly came rushing back. She was only eighteen, but for such a long time she'd felt ages older, as if the passion of youth had passed her by.

And now it was back again. A sigh slipped from her lips as he pulled her down onto his lap and raked his fingers though her hair. He was so gentle with her, yet Fiona knew the need that bubbled just below the surface. She wanted him as much as he wanted her.

Seamus finally stopped kissing her, pressing his forehead against hers as he caressed her face. "You'd better go."

"I think that would be best." She kissed him again, and this kiss lasted longer than the first. "I'd better go," she murmured against his mouth.

"Then go," he challenged.

His mouth found hers again and Fiona could feel the need growing inside them both. There would come a point where she wouldn't want to stop, where she'd want to escape into the pleasures they'd shared once before.

"Now you really should go," Seamus murmured, his voice ragged with desire. He stood and pulled her up along with him, then walked with her to the door.

Wrapping her in her jacket, Seamus pressed a kiss to the top of her head, then opened the front door.

A damp wind blew through the cottage and a shiver raced through her. Though she knew she would return the next day, it still felt wrong to leave.

"Then you'll come for supper tomorrow?" he asked.

"I will." She walked out the door and hurried to the car. When she got inside, Fiona could see him standing in the doorway, watching her.

A thrill raced through her and her heart skipped a beat or two. As the car bumped back down the hill toward the village, she smiled to herself. She finally felt as if she'd come home.

FIONA CURLED UP against Seamus and nuzzled her face into his chest. They were spending a lazy afternoon lying on his bed, reading and talking. They couldn't seem to get enough of each other and the cottage had become a haven for them.

Though they hadn't made love, Seamus had never felt closer to Fiona. Just to touch her every day or to listen to her voice was enough for him. But he knew the clock was ticking on their happiness. The next term would begin at Trinity in four days and neither one of them had brought up the subject of her leaving.

"What time is it?" Fiona asked, pushing up on her elbow.

"Time for you to go."

She scowled. "Why am I always leaving you?"

"Because I live here." He chuckled softly and kissed her forehead, then pulled her up from the bed. "Come on, it's getting late. Your mother is going to wonder where you've disappeared to. Where did you tell her you were going?"

"I told her I wanted to visit a friend from university in Tralee. It wasn't a lie. I did want to visit her—I just wanted to see you more. And Tralee was far enough away that I could be gone for most of the day, yet close enough that she won't worry that I'm late."

"Clever girl."

"Maybe we should stop sneaking about," Fiona said, her expression suddenly turning serious. "I'd like to be able to go outside without worrying about being seen. And sooner or later, someone will see the car parked here and wonder what's going on."

"There's no chance your mother will drag you off on holiday now."

"But what about my next holiday?" She sighed softly and dropped a kiss on his lips. "Will you be taking the boat out tomorrow?" she asked, slipping on her coat and then knotting a wool scarf around her neck.

Seamus nodded. "We'll be back by sunset."

"Then I'll see you tomorrow night. We can go to Cork and have supper, perhaps see a picture. We'll have a real date, we will."

Seamus smiled. "I'll meet you here." He tipped her chin up and brushed a kiss across her mouth, then opened the door. He watched her drive away, then waved when she turned to look back at him.

After he closed the door, he surveyed the room. There were reminders of her all over the cottage—a pretty scarf she'd worn in her hair, a book of poetry left behind on the table, and the scent of her perfume on his pillow. How would he ever go back to living without her? Would he fall back to numbing his loneliness with whiskey?

He walked to the hearth and tossed another block of peat onto the fire, then settled into the overstuffed chair, closing his eyes. He'd often dreamed about having her back, but now that she'd come, all he could think about was losing her again.

Fiona wasn't meant to live the life of a fisherman's wife and he loved her enough to want more for her. But there had to be a way to untangle this knot that had become their relationship. She could stay in Ballykirk and go to university in Cork as her mother had originally suggested. If the university there was good enough for Kit, why couldn't it be good enough for Fiona?

When a knock sounded on the door, Seamus smiled. He crossed the room, grabbing her scarf along the way, glad that she'd come back for it. But when he opened the door, he found Kit standing outside in the rain. He glanced down at the scarf, then shoved it in his back pocket.

"I know she meets you here," Kit said, walking past

him. She took off her gloves and held them in her hand, gently slapping them against her palm.

"Yes, she does."

Kit twisted the gloves in her hands. "I want you to let her go. I know if you'd ask her to stay, she would. She's been happier these past few weeks than I've seen her in a long time. But she's too young to know what will ultimately make her happy. And I know it won't be a life here in Ballykirk, having your children and keeping your house."

"Don't you think that Fiona should make her own choices?"

"She doesn't know what those choices are. She fancies herself in love with you and she can't see beyond that. You took advantage of her once. Please don't do it again."

"And what if I love her?" Seamus asked.

"Then let her go. You know I'm right. You know she deserves more."

Seamus couldn't disagree. He'd tried to convince himself differently over the past few weeks, but he'd seen how special Fiona was. She was bright and clever and determined. Who could know what she might accomplish if given the chance?

"Please," Kit said. "Let her go. Break it off before you break her heart." She nodded, then tugged her gloves over her hands. "Well, I've finished what I've come to say and I know you'll consider my words carefully."

Seamus walked her back to the door. "I do love her," he said.

Kit glanced up at him. "I know you do. But sometimes love isn't enough."

As he closed the door, her words echoed in his head. It wasn't anything he hadn't told himself a hundred times a day. How could he trust Fiona's feelings? She was only eighteen and had gotten it into her head that he was her hero, a white knight who'd ridden to her rescue once upon a time.

She'd never told him that she loved him. And Seamus was convinced she didn't yet know exactly what love was. The best he could do was to let her find her own way. If they were meant to be together, then she would come back to him someday.

He hung his head, his eyes downcast. Kit was right. Sometimes love wasn't enough. And sometimes it was too much.

CHAPTER THIRTY-TWO

THE DINNER TABLE was laden with all of Fiona's favorite dishes. Cook had outdone herself, but unfortunately, Fiona hadn't much of an appetite.

"I have work to do at my office tomorrow, so I'll take you to the train," Kit said. "Have you finished your packing?"

Fiona nodded, picking at her dinner. Time in Ballykirk had passed so quickly and she'd dreaded this moment. She'd seen as much of Seamus as she could in the past nineteen days, but it wasn't enough. "I want to take my new typewriter with me, but I don't think I can carry it along with all my bags."

"Your father will have it shipped to you," Kit said. "Won't you, Donal?"

He glanced up from his meal and smiled at Fiona. "Of course, darling."

"Or perhaps you could bring it yourself on one of your business trips?" Fiona asked. "You have to visit me at least once a term, Papa."

"I have a trip scheduled for the first week of February. Will that be soon enough?"

"That would be perfect." Fiona pushed away from the dinner table, setting her linen napkin beside her plate. Then she circled around to her father and gave him a kiss. "I'll see you both later."

"Where are you going?" Kit asked. "Cook has made dessert."

"I already feel like a Christmas goose," Fiona said. "Some old friends asked if I wanted to join them down at the pub. I thought I'd go for a bit."

"I thought you'd want to spend your last night at home with us."

"Oh, let her go, Kit. She hasn't had much chance to see old friends. She certainly shouldn't have to sit here and entertain us."

"I might be a bit late," Fiona said. She kissed her mother, then hurried upstairs to change. She'd promised to meet Seamus at the cottage by eight and it was already half past.

Fiona grabbed a pretty wool miniskirt from her closet and tugged on a soft pink mohair jumper. Though most girls were wearing dramatic eyeliner these days, she preferred a simpler look for herself. She added a touch of pale lipstick and bit of perfume, then headed for the door. But she found her mother waiting at the bottom of the stairs.

"I know you're going to him," Kit said, her hand gripping the newel post.

Startled, Fiona wasn't sure what to say. "Who?"

"Seamus Quinn. I know you've been meeting him

nearly every day for the past two weeks. You've been lying to me and your father and sneaking off to be with him."

"I didn't want to lie," Fiona said. "But I didn't have a choice."

"You have more choices than you can imagine. I didn't have a choice. Things were different for women when I was your age. But everything's changing now and you have so many opportunities. And you're throwing them all away."

"What opportunities? I don't know what I want to do with my life. I'm not a great poet like you are. I won't ever be an artist or a musician. I like history, but that won't make me famous. So what is so special about my future?"

"It's yours. It doesn't depend on a man to make it a success. You can do that yourself."

"But what if I don't want to?" Fiona asked. "What if I want to get married and have children?"

"Don't be naive. Do you honestly think you can be happy with Seamus Quinn? Living in that little cottage, having ten children, growing old before you have to?"

"Why do you hate him so?" Fiona asked. "He's a good man."

"He seduced a seventeen-year-old girl," Kit countered.

Fiona drew a ragged breath. "But he didn't."

"I don't care if it was your idea, he still—"

"I slept with a boy I met outside your office at the university. His name was Alan Carrick and he was in one of your poetry classes. Do you remember him? I thought I was in love with him and I hoped he was in love with me. It was a silly infatuation that ended horribly in a ragged little room above a butcher's shop."

"I—I don't understand," Kit murmured.

"When I thought I was pregnant, I confided in Seamus and he offered to marry me. He offered to raise another man's child with me, Mama, without giving it a second thought. Just to spare me the humiliation. So don't you dare say another word to disparage his character. I'm lucky to have him in my life."

With that, Fiona brushed past her mother and walked to the front door. She grabbed her jacket on the way out, tugging it on as she headed to her car. But when she got there, she found Seamus leaning up against it.

"What are you doing here?" she asked. "I was just about to drive to the cottage."

"I thought we might say goodbye here," Seamus said.

"Here? In the cold?"

He nodded. "You know you have to leave and I know you have to leave. And if we go to the cottage, there's a chance I might not let you go. Right now, I'm fairly certain I'd say anything to convince you to stay. So we'll say goodbye here, where our goodbye will be much simpler and easier to bear."

He reached out and she hesitated, then stepped into his embrace. "I don't know what I'll do without you," Fiona murmured. "I won't have another holiday until Easter and that's only a few days."

"Time will pass quickly," Seamus assured her. "Before you know it, you'll be home for your long holiday in the summer. Unless your mother takes you to Europe."

"She won't," Fiona said. "I'll refuse to go." She looked up at him. "I told her about Alan. I thought it was time."

"Maybe it is."

He bent close and gently kissed her, leaving Fiona to wonder how she'd go for months without touching him or kissing him. "I don't want to go," she whispered.

He gave her a fierce hug. "Goodbye, Fi. Take care."

She didn't want to let go, afraid that if she did, everything they'd shared would be forgotten. But did she want him merely because he made her feel safe? Or did she truly love him? How was she supposed to know? "Come inside for a bit," she pleaded.

Seamus shook his head. "I don't think that would be a good idea." He smoothed his hand over her cheek. "Tell me goodbye now, Fi. And promise that you'll come back. That's all I ask."

She took his face in her hands and kissed him, squeezing her eyes shut to ward off the tears. "I will come back. I promise."

Seamus stepped away from her, allowing his hands to drift down her arms to her fingertips. The moment he broke contact, she felt an emptiness settle over her, an ache that couldn't be ignored.

He smiled at her. "I love you, Fi. I always have and I always will."

She swallowed back the lump in her throat and nodded, then watched as he turned and started for the road. Fiona prayed he wouldn't look back, that he wouldn't see the tears running down her cheeks. And when he was out of sight, her knees buckled beneath her and she sat down in the middle of the driveway and wept.

He loved her. His words hadn't come as a surprise. Maybe she'd known all along, even from the time they were children, that they were meant to love each other. She drew in a sharp breath, the chilly air clearing her head.

"I love you, Seamus," she whispered. And neither time nor distance was going to change that.

"Fiona?"

She looked to see her mother standing in the front door.

"What are you doing out here?" Kit asked.

"I love him, Mama. I can't help myself. We belong together. I don't want to go back to Dublin. I belong here, with Seamus. And if that makes you angry or hurt or disappointed, I'm sorry. But I'm going to be with him and I'm going to be happy."

Fiona got to her feet and dusted off her knees, waiting for her mother's reaction, prepared to plead her case or to walk away from her family forever if she had to.

"You'll regret this someday," Kit warned.

"Maybe I will. But I'm willing to take that risk."

Kit shrugged, defeated. "Then go to him. Maybe this was the way it was meant to be all along."

She stared at her mother for a long moment, Kit's expression of resignation dimly visible in the faint light from the house. And then Fiona turned and ran to the end of the driveway.

"Seamus!" she shouted. "Seamus!" She stared down the road, squinting through the harsh light from the lamps on either side of the drive.

A moment later, he appeared out of the dark, breathless from running. Fiona rushed into his arms and he gasped in surprise. "Fi, what is—"

"Take me home," she murmured, kissing him frantically, her fingers skimming over his face.

"You are home."

"No, take me to the cottage. Take me to our home."

He wove his fingers through her hair and drew her back so he could look down into her eyes. "What are you saying?"

"I love you, Seamus. It's as simple as that. I don't want to go back to Dublin—I want to stay here and marry you. I want to live in our little cottage and have your children and grow old with you."

He stared into her eyes for a long time and a sliver of worry shot through her. She'd just proposed marriage to him. Though she was a modern, independent woman, Fiona knew that Seamus preferred to approach matters like these in a more traditional manner.

"You do want to marry me, don't you?" she asked.

"I don't know," he said. "That wasn't a very proper proposal now, was it?"

She saw the glint of amusement in his eyes and the hint of a smile at the corners of his mouth. Fiona grabbed his hand and dropped down on one knee. "Seamus Quinn, will you marry me? I promise to take care of you and make a good home for you and give you strong, happy children. And I promise to love you for the rest of my life."

"And what about a ring?" he asked. "Shouldn't there be a ring?"

"I don't care about a ring," Fiona said, rising to her feet, her hands holding tight to his.

"Then yes, Fiona McClain. I'd be glad to marry you." With a deep laugh, Seamus reached down and scooped her up into his arms. "Come on, let's go home."

"Are you going to carry me the entire way?" she asked.

"I am," he said. "I don't intend ever to let you go again."

Fiona wrapped her arms around his neck and kissed his cheek.

A broken promise had nearly torn them apart and now a promise kept would tie them together forever. And when they were old, with grandchildren of their own, they would look back at these days and know that their promises had become the foundation of a life well lived and a family well loved.

EPILOGUE

County Cork, Present Day

A LOW WALL SURROUNDED the churchyard at Ballykirk, setting it apart from the rest of the bustling seaside village. Fiona Quinn stood in front of a stone bench, staring at the inscription that had been carved into the back. "In loving memory of Katherine Malone McClain," she murmured. "Wife, mother, poet."

It had taken Fiona nearly a week to work up the courage to visit her parents' graves. The memories of Donal and Kit McClain had been so vivid to her while in Ireland that it was almost as if they were alive again.

She traced her fingers over the inscription and smiled. Her mother might have changed the order had she been in control of the chisel. She'd always considered her poetry her greatest accomplishment, not her marriage or her daughter. Fiona sighed. It was a difficult thing to be the ordinary daughter of an extraordinary woman.

She turned and faced the headstones neatly

arranged in the McClain plot. There was old Eamon with his ornately carved Celtic cross, the best that money could buy, looming above all the others in the cemetery. And Aidan to his father's right, his life tragically cut short. And an empty spot for Louisa, who had been buried far away in Italy alongside her fourth husband. Maura had been buried next to Aidan, her simple stone a testament to her enduring strength.

Fiona slowly walked to the other side of Eamon's grave and knelt down in the grass. Tears burned in her eyes and she fought back a flood of emotion. Her mother had been only fifty-eight when she'd died, succumbing to the aftereffects of a stroke she'd suffered two years before.

Her father had died just nine months later, a broken man, the McClain family fortune nearly gone. He'd spent it all after Kit's stroke, trying to find a way to bring back the wife he'd loved. When Maura had passed away, the house had been sold to pay the last of the debts. All that was left of the McClain name in Ballykirk was here, in this tiny plot in the churchyard. The tombstones would weather over time, the names would be erased and then forgotten completely.

"I wish I had known you better," Fiona said as she stared at her mother's stone. "Known what made you the woman you were. Maybe then we could have understood each other a bit better."

Her father had begged Fiona to come home to Ireland after her mother's stroke in 1979. But Fiona had been preoccupied with problems of her own. Besides, she'd always assumed that Kit would recover, her spirit too indomitable to be crushed by something as minor as a stroke. And she knew her presence would only remind Kit of the disappointment her daughter's life had been.

Now, with years of perspective on raising a daughter, Fiona had come to understand her mother's high expectations. The world could be a cruel place for a woman without dreams of her own. Fiona had pinned her dreams to those of Seamus and when he failed, she had failed with him.

She'd been trapped in her marriage almost from the moment they'd set foot in America, poverty and alcohol and gambling destroying whatever hope she'd had for happiness. Overwhelmed with raising six sons virtually alone, she had finally had enough, escaping for what she'd thought would be just a week or two away.

"I suppose if you were here now, I'd allow you at least one I-told-you-so. Everything you predicted for me came true. Life with Seamus was more difficult than I'd ever imagined. So many promises broken and so many dreams destroyed."

A gentle breeze rustled the trees above her head and Fiona looked up to see the sky clearing. "But it wasn't just his fault. I made a mess of my life and I've only just begun to fix it."

Kit had lived the last seven years of her life with her only child an ocean away and her grandchildren just a series of photos sent by post. Fiona remembered the pain in her mother's eyes when she'd told her of Seamus's plan to take the family to America. It was as if her heart were being broken in two. Fiona had been so anxious to leave, to prove to her mother that Seamus could be a great success in the land of opportunity.

Fiona felt a hand on her shoulder and realized Seamus was standing behind her. She squinted against the sun and for a moment Fiona saw the young man that she'd fallen in love with, his dark hair and his boyish smile, the odd-colored eyes that twinkled with humor or darkened with passion.

"I thought I might find you here," he said, squatting down beside her.

"I've left it to the last minute and now there are so many things to say, I'll barely have the time."

"You don't have to say anything, Fi. Your mother and father already know." He took her hand in his and kissed the spot below her wrist. "They know."

"Do you ever wish we could go back and do it all again? And get it right this time?"

"Would you do it the same? Or would you have taken that train back to Dublin?"

"I would have married you, Seamus. I've never regretted that. But I would have taken more care with our marriage. I left it all to you to make me happy and I realized too late that that wasn't your job."

"But it was," he said. "I made so many promises to you and when things began to fall apart, I didn't know what to do. I felt as if nothing I did was right. I wanted so much to give you the life you had, all the very best. When I couldn't, I looked for excuses and found them in a whiskey bottle." He drew a deep breath. "I don't blame you for leaving, Fi. I wasn't a good husband—the drinking and the gambling." He helped her to her feet and sat down next to her on the stone bench. "Still, I thought you'd come back. Why didn't you, Fi?"

"I was so angry. When you pawned the claddagh necklace my mother had given me, it was like a knife to my heart. It was the only connection I had left to her and then it was gone, sold for money you gambled away."

"I went back to get it, but the pawnshop had sold it. I didn't realize it was you who'd bought back the necklace." He stared into her eyes. "You don't know how I came to regret what I'd done. But was that all it was? The necklace?"

Fiona shook her head. "I suppose I wanted to test you, to see if you still loved me. But after I left, you didn't seem to care. The housekeeper you hired, Mrs. Smalley, told me that you never spoke my name. It made me feel so insignificant. A few weeks turned into a month and then two. And when I heard you'd told the boys I was dead, all my fears came true. I knew if you could say that to our sons, then you had no love left for me at all."

"I was angry with myself for my failures," Seamus said, "but I blamed you. In my heart, I knew none of it was your fault."

"I always believed I'd come back and get the boys and give them a better life. But I could barely provide for Keely and myself, let alone six hungry sons. For a time, I kept in touch with Mrs. Smalley and she always told me how well they were doing. And then one day, I realized the boys were grown and even if I did go back, they wouldn't need me." She shook her head, refusing to give in to her tears. "I made a lot of mistakes, too. But leaving you and our children is the one mistake that's unforgivable."

"Why didn't you ever ask for a divorce?"

"Because I was married to you. And I still loved you. There was no other man for me."

"And do you love me now, Fi?"

Fiona smiled softly. "Since that rainy afternoon that we first spent at our cottage."

Seamus squeezed her hand. "For me, I think it was when I learned you were sick with polio. I couldn't imagine losing you. At the time, I thought it was just friendship between us, but looking back, that's when I realized I loved you." He slipped his arm around her shoulders and pulled her toward him. "So have you said what you've come to say, Fi?"

She nodded. "I have."

He kissed her forehead. "I've been sent to fetch you. The children have some sort of surprise for us. Conor is waiting on the road with the car."

"We do have wonderful children, don't we?" Fiona said, smoothing her hand over the front of his shirt. "I'm not sure I deserve them."

"Nor I," Seamus added. "But they seem to want us around."

They walked back to the road, hand in hand. As Conor drove them through the village, he was oddly silent about their destination, but when he turned the car toward the hills above the village, Fiona knew where they were going.

Conor watched her in the rearview mirror and grinned. "We thought we'd like to see the old cottage just once more before we leave."

"I'm sure the owners are starting to get sick of these pesky Americans who keep showing up on their doorstep," Fiona said.

"Oh, I don't think they'll mind just one more look, Ma. We've traveled such a long way."

When they arrived at the end of the rutted driveway, Fiona saw the entire family, everyone except Conor, waiting in front of the cottage—her six other children, all seven spouses and her two grandchildren. "Oh, this is too much," she said. "We can't continue to put these people out like this."

"See there, Keely has her camera set up," Seamus said. "We'll just take a pretty picture of the old home place and then leave."

But when they got out of the car, their children had other ideas. They gathered around their parents, chatting excitedly. Conor cleared his throat and everyone fell silent. "When we planned this trip to Ireland, we all thought we'd be coming on a relaxing vacation.

But after just a few days here, I think all of us have felt a special connection to this place, to this home we left so long ago. A connection we didn't want to break."

"Tell them," Keely urged.

Seamus frowned, then glanced over at Fiona and shrugged. "What are you about, Con?" he asked.

Conor reached into his jacket pocket and handed Keely a thick envelope. "I think I'll let you do the honors, little sister, since your husband worked out all the details for us."

Keely took a deep breath, in irrepressible grin on her face. "It's yours," she said, handing Fiona the envelope with a flourish.

Fiona looked down at it. "What is?"

"Open it," Keely urged. "Daddy, come and see."

Seamus stood next to Fiona and watched over her shoulder as she pulled an official-looking document from the envelope. Her breath caught in her throat and she glanced back at her husband. "It's a deed. For this cottage."

Seamus gasped and took the papers from Fiona, examining them closely. "How can that be?"

"We made them an offer they couldn't refuse," Conor said, chuckling. "We all chipped in. A family our size could use a vacation home."

"Oh, my," Fiona murmured. "I can't believe this." She turned and threw her arms around Seamus's neck, hugging him tightly. "We have our little cottage back."

"Not quite yet," Conor said. "The old owners needed some time to find another place to live. But by the summer, it will be empty and you can come back and enjoy it."

"Thank you," Fiona said, her eyes filled with tears. "I'm not sure any of you know what this means to us."

She turned and looked at the pretty whitewashed cottage, at the window boxes that Seamus had built so long ago, now filled with spring flowers, the familiar iron knocker on the front door, the rosebush she'd planted the day before her first child was born. Life had such an odd way of twisting and turning and then bringing people right back to where they began.

"Here it is," Seamus whispered in her ear, his eyes surveying their children. "Here's your success, Fi. I think your mother would be proud, don't you?"

Fiona nodded, smiling through her tears. And as they arranged themselves for Keely's photo, she glanced at each of her children. Though she'd made terrible mistakes in her life, she'd been given a second chance. And now, surrounded by memories from the past and hopes for the future, Fiona realized what a rare gift a second chance was.

She closed her eyes and made a silent promise to herself that she'd never have need for a third.

*Everything you love about romance...**and more!***

Please turn the page for Signature Select™ Bonus Features.

Bonus Features:

BONUS FEATURES

EXCLUSIVE BONUS FEATURES INSIDE

Quinn Family Tree

The descendants of Seamus Quinn

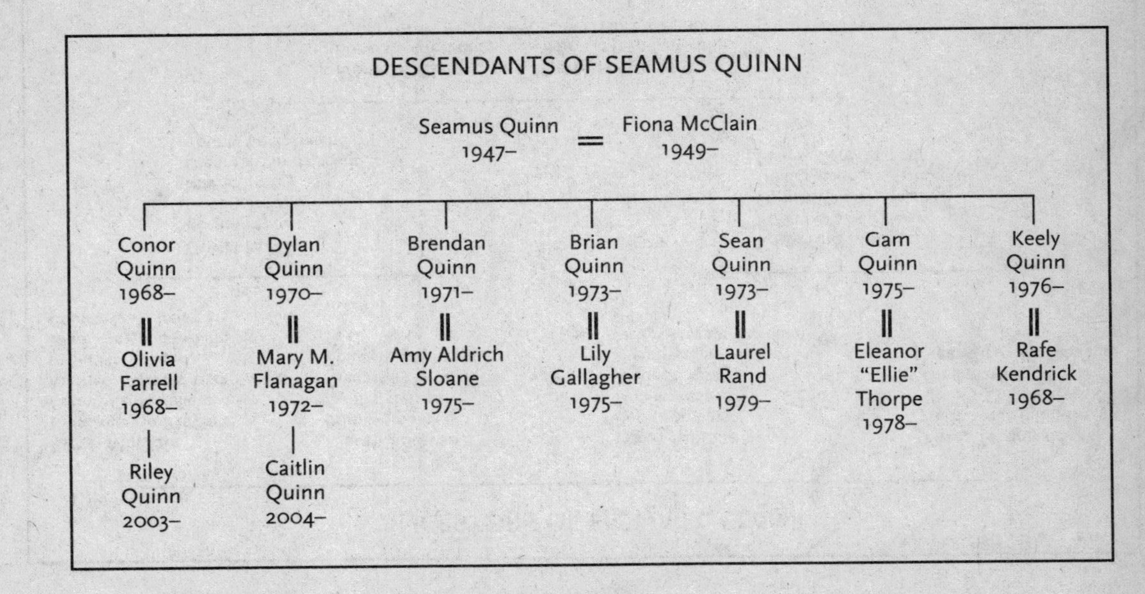
DESCENDANTS OF SEAMUS QUINN
Seamus Quinn 1947–
=
Fiona McClain 1949–
Conor Quinn 1968–
Olivia Farrell 1968–
Riley Quinn 2003–
Dylan Quinn 1970–
Mary M. Flanagan 1972–
Caitlin Quinn 2004–
Brendan Quinn 1971–
Amy Aldrich Sloane 1975–
Brian Quinn 1973–
Lily Gallagher 1975–
Sean Quinn 1973–
Laurel Rand 1979–
Gam Quinn 1975–
Eleanor “Ellie” Thorpe 1978–
Keely Quinn 1976–
Rafe Kendrick 1968–

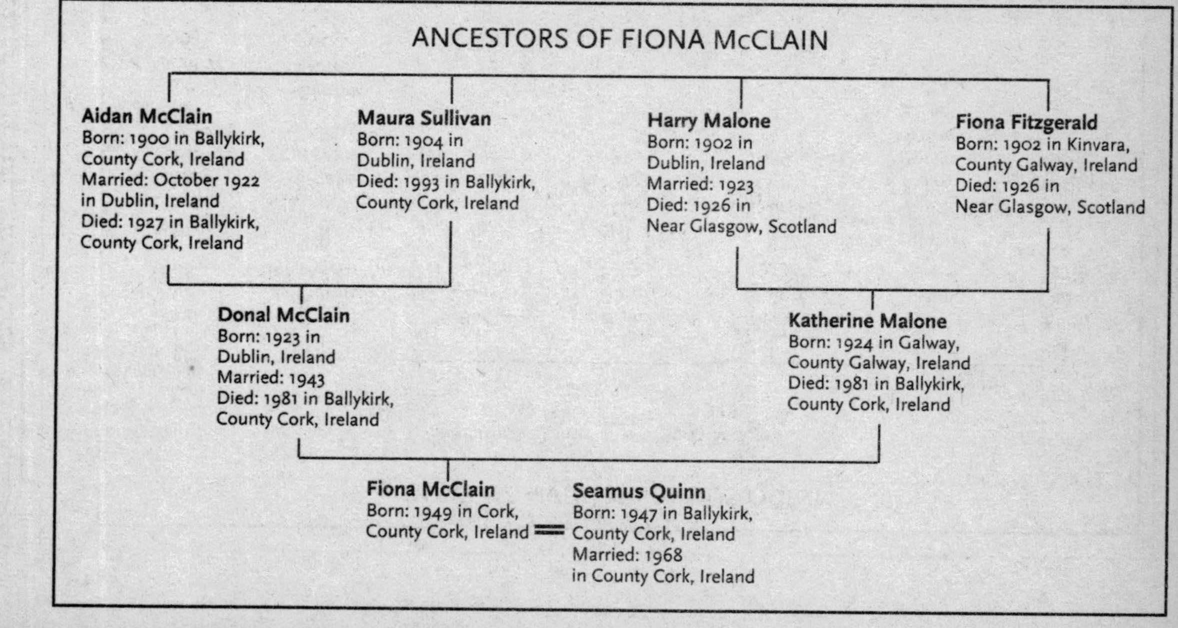

ANCESTORS OF FIONA McCLAIN
Aidan McClain
Born: 1900 in Ballykirk, County Cork, Ireland
Married: October 1922 in Dublin, Ireland
Died: 1927 in Ballykirk, County Cork, Ireland
Maura Sullivan
Born: 1904 in Dublin, Ireland
Died: 1993 in Ballykirk, County Cork, Ireland
Harry Malone
Born: 1902 in Dublin, Ireland
Married: 1923
Died: 1926 in Near Glasgow, Scotland
Fiona Fitzgerald
Born: 1902 in Kinvara, County Galway, Ireland
Died: 1926 in Near Glasgow, Scotland
Donal McClain
Born: 1923 in Dublin, Ireland
Married: 1943
Died: 1981 in Ballykirk, County Cork, Ireland
Katherine Malone
Born: 1924 in Galway, County Galway, Ireland
Died: 1981 in Ballykirk, County Cork, Ireland
Fiona McClain
Born: 1949 in Cork, County Cork, Ireland
Seamus Quinn
Born: 1947 in Ballykirk, County Cork, Ireland
Married: 1968 in County Cork, Ireland

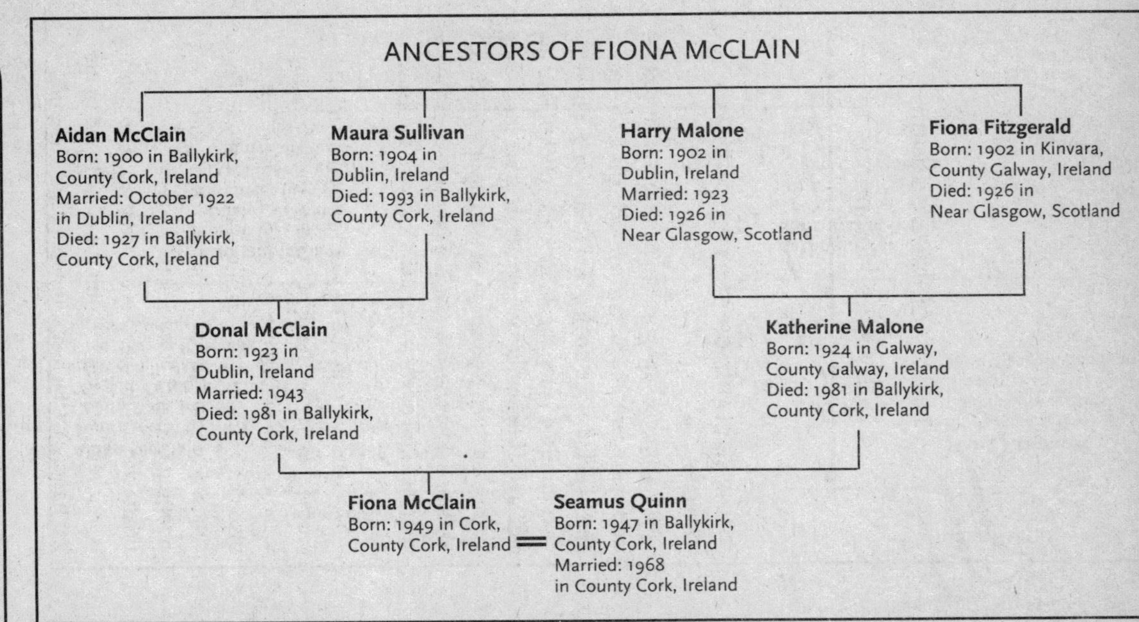
ANCESTORS OF FIONA McCLAIN
Aidan McClain
Born: 1900 in Ballykirk, County Cork, Ireland
Married: October 1922 in Dublin, Ireland
Died: 1927 in Ballykirk, County Cork, Ireland
Maura Sullivan
Born: 1904 in Dublin, Ireland
Died: 1993 in Ballykirk, County Cork, Ireland
Harry Malone
Born: 1902 in Dublin, Ireland
Married: 1923
Died: 1926 in Near Glasgow, Scotland
Fiona Fitzgerald
Born: 1902 in Kinvara, County Galway, Ireland
Died: 1926 in Near Glasgow, Scotland
Donal McClain
Born: 1923 in Dublin, Ireland
Married: 1943
Died: 1981 in Ballykirk, County Cork, Ireland
Katherine Malone
Born: 1924 in Galway, County Galway, Ireland
Died: 1981 in Ballykirk, County Cork, Ireland
Fiona McClain
Born: 1949 in Cork, County Cork, Ireland
Seamus Quinn
Born: 1947 in Ballykirk, County Cork, Ireland
Married: 1968 in County Cork, Ireland

History of the Claddagh
by Kate Hoffmann

THE IRISH CLADDAGH: THE ETERNAL SYMBOL OF LOVE

Many symbols have come to represent Irish culture and sentiment: the lucky shamrock, the Celtic cross, the Irish harp, the Book of Kells. But for the past four hundred years, the enduring symbol of love and fidelity has been the Irish claddagh. A claddagh ring combines three elements—a heart, topped with a crown, held by two hands. The hands represent friendship, the heart love and the crown loyalty.

A claddagh ring can be worn by both men and women, either on the right hand or the left. Many wear it as an engagement or wedding ring, but it also can represent friendship. Traditionally, if the ring is worn on the right hand with the heart pointing outward, it means the wearer is unattached. If the heart is turned inward, the wearer is in love or spoken for. And if it is switched to the left hand with the heart turned inward, then that love has been returned by another, usually in marriage. Tradition also holds that it is improper for a person to buy the ring for themselves—it must be received as a gift.

The word *claddagh* originally referred to a village near the seashore. An ancient village outside the walls of Galway had its origins in Celtic times and soon the name *Claddagh* became associated with this specific place. In the sixteenth century, Richard Joyce, a native of Galway, was on his way to the West Indies. Algerian pirates captured his ship and sold the passengers into slavery. Joyce was sold to a wealthy Moorish goldsmith who instructed Joyce in his art. Over time, the Moor took a liking to Joyce and in 1689 released him from his bonds. Joyce returned to Galway to set up his own shop in the Claddagh. It was there that he created his first rings, some of which still exist today. The design for the claddagh may have come from Algiers or it may have originated with Joyce. But some believe that the design came from an ancestor of Joyce's, a woman known as Margaret of the Bridges.

Margaret Joyce was first married to a Spanish

merchant. After his death, she inherited his vast wealth and later was married again, to the mayor of Galway. While he was on a long voyage, she occupied herself by building bridges. Most of the bridges of Connacht were built at her expense. Legend has it that one day, as she was surveying her work, an eagle dropped a gold ring into her lap. Her family believed the ring was a reward for her charitable work and it was passed along as an heirloom. This ring could have been the first claddagh ring and an inspiration for Richard Joyce's design.

The claddagh ring became popular outside of Ireland as Irish emigration spread through the U.S. and Australia. And claddagh rings made in Ireland
10 were worn by both Queen Victoria and King Edward VII. Today, the claddagh ring is worn worldwide, not just by those with Irish blood, but by those who believe in the ideals of friendship, love and loyalty.

BONUS READ

The First Mighty Quinn

by Kate Hoffmann

12

In Ireland, the lines between past and the present are often blurred—and legends take on a life of their own. The Quinn family lives in a modern world, far from the magical land of druids, faeries and Celtic kings of their past. Yet the blood of Ireland still pulses through their veins and the legends still influence their daily lives. For if a Quinn surrenders to the power of a woman, then he is lost forever...just like Connla, the first Mighty Quinn.

CONN CETCHATHACH was a powerful king, known by many as Conn of the Hundred Battles. He had fought hard for control over his kingdom and had to guard his lands with great vigilance, lest they be seized by his enemies. But all of his power and riches could do nothing to save his eldest son from the power of a woman's charms.

Connla, son of Conn, was a bold warrior and heir to all that his father ruled. But though he'd fought in many battles, Connla was an idealistic young man. He imagined a world without war and suffering, a place where beauty and peace ruled the land.

One day, as Connla stood on the hill of Usnech with his father, he saw a woman approach. She wore a flowing dress made of fabric as thin as the morning mist. "Who are you?" he asked. "Where do you come from?"

The mysterious woman smiled, her beauty stealing the breath from Connla's chest, her gaze drawing him closer. "I have come from Moy Mell," she said. "There is no death in our world, no need and no sin. We live in peace and know nothing of war."

Connla was intrigued and began to question the woman about this wondrous land. But his father interrupted him. "Who do you speak to?" he demanded, for the king could neither see nor hear the faerie maiden.

"Come with me," the maiden said, holding out her hand to Connla. "With me, you'll never know death or sorrow or longing. You will always be as you are today, young and beautiful and happy."

The king grew angry and summoned his most powerful druid, Coran. Coran could hear the woman's voice and told the king that a faerie maiden had bewitched his son. The king ordered Coran to cast his most powerful spell against the faerie maiden's wiles. Coran made the faerie invisible to the young warrior, silencing her voice and banishing her image. But before the spell took effect, the faerie tossed a golden apple to Connla.

Connla could not erase the sight of the beautiful woman from his mind. For a month, he refused to eat anything but the golden apple and with each bite he took, the apple became whole again, feeding his hunger but never quelling his longing for the faerie maiden.

A month passed and the king believed his son was safe

from the faerie maiden's power. One day, as they walked together on the Plain of Arcomin, the faerie maiden appeared to Connla again. "Come with me," she called. "Do not live here among mortals, awaiting your death. With me, you will live forever."

The king immediately called for his druid, but the faerie maiden said, "Conn Cetchathach, cling not to druid powers. Their magic is not righteous and their power is false."

The king looked at Connla to see how the faerie maiden's words had affected him, but Connla seemed not to hear. "Have her words touched your heart?" the king asked.

"I love you, Father, and I love our people, but my longing for this woman has captured my soul. I must follow her." Connla rushed away from his father and followed the faerie to her curragh, a boat made of crystal.

The king and his men watched as Connla sailed away, disappearing into the blue of the sky and the sea. From that day, Connla was never seen again. And when the king returned, he summoned his younger son, Art, and told him of the faerie's power. "You must never trust a woman," the king explained, "for their powers can overwhelm your own and make you weak."

And thus was the first tale of a Mighty Quinn told, by the powerful king, Conn Cetchathach, to his only son, Art mac Cuinn.

THE END

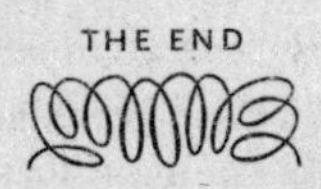

The Future Widows' Club

by

Rhonda Nelson

Jolie Marshall's husband Chris is definitely no good. He conned Jolie into "I do" and her mother out of her life's savings! Now Jolie is sticking out the marriage—with a little help from the Future Widows' Club—while she gathers evidence to send him to prison. But when Chris ends up dead, Jolie's the prime suspect. And her only hope is Detective Jake Malone—the man she should have married in the first place....

PROLOGUE

"IF EVER A WOMAN needed to be a widow, it's that one," Sophia Morgan said from the side of her mouth with a significant look across the crowded dining room.

Bitsy Highfield and Meredith Ingram leaned slightly back in their chairs and followed her line of vision. Meredith instantly recognized the woman in question and her mouth curved knowingly. She shot Sophia a shrewd look.

Bitsy, as usual, wore her typical vacantly bewildered expression. "What woman?" Her penciled eyebrows formed a wrinkled line. "I don't see a woman."

"Jolie Marshall," Meredith hissed. "There." She pointed. "See her?"

Bitsy adjusted her bifocals. "Ah, yes. I see her. But if you ask me, her husband looks near enough to death as it is." Her wrinkled brow folded into an exaggerated frown. "Rather pasty-looking fellow, isn't he?"

Sophia swallowed a beleaguered sigh. "Not him, you idiot. *Her.* The young woman in the cream suit. And that guy's not pasty looking, for heaven's sake," she said with an exasperated snort. "That's a statue of

David." And a poor one at that, but it was in keeping with the owner's taste. George Brown fancied himself an expert on all things Greek. His restaurant, *Zeus'*, was crammed with Greek statuaries and pictures of mythological gods, murals of Prometheus, Athena, Persephone and Zeus. Which might have been appropriate were it not a steak house. Sophia sighed, resisting the urge to roll her eyes. But it was the best Moon Valley, Mississippi, had to offer, so she ignored the tacky decor and carved off another bite of her filet.

Meredith snickered as Bitsy's blank look turned to one of dawning comprehension.

"Oh," she murmured. "*Oh.* Why she's just a child!"

"Not a child, but a young woman," Sophia clarified. She harrumphed under her breath. "Too young to be shackled to that bastard of a husband of hers, that's for sure."

Meredith quirked a brow. "That's Christine Caplan's girl, right?"

"Oh, I've heard that story," Bitsy piped in, her voice pitched to the tenor reserved for sharing a significant secret. She was notoriously scatterbrained and clumsy, was blind as a bat—but her memory and hearing were sharp, both of which made her a valuable asset to the Club. "I heard Sadie talking about it a couple of weeks ago down at The Spa while I was getting my hair set."

That was hardly surprising, Sophia thought. Sadie Webster owned The Spa and the trendy-hair-and-nails boutique, as in most small towns, was the hub of Moon Valley's gossip wheel. In order to satisfy her addiction to gossip and aerosol fumes, Bitsy kept a standing appointment.

"She and that Jolie are friends," Bitsy continued with a covert look at the woman in question. "I only caught part of the conversation—mind you, I was under the dryer—but apparently, from what I was able to piece together, she met that rounder on a vacation. She fell hard for him and he convinced her that he could take the proceeds from her daddy's life-insurance policy and triple it."

Meredith calmly sipped her sherry. "I take it he didn't."

"No. That's what makes it so interesting. From what I gathered, he *has*—they own that new software company down on the square. He just refuses to give the money back. Somehow, despite the fact that they're partners, he's stashed it in one of those off-shore accounts."

"Still," Meredith hedged, the perpetual voice of reason. "I don't understand. If she's a partner, then why doesn't she do something about it? If the company is so successful, why doesn't she just hire a good divorce attorney and take half?"

"What good would that do if he's hid the money from her? If he can show that the company doesn't have it?"

Bitsy inclined her head. "I know that she's talked to Judge Turner about it. There's also a shady prenup, though I don't know the particulars."

"So what's she doing?" Meredith asked.

Bitsy smiled and a determined glint flashed in her faded blue eyes. She leaned forward, as though sharing a another juicy secret. "Now that's the real mystery. If the rumors about her temper are true, then she definitely wouldn't sit idly by, but no one seems to know what she's doing about it. All anyone knows is that she is doing *something*. She's got a degree in accounting, she's on the board and has signature authority. My bet is that she's working that angle."

Sophia shifted in her seat. "Meanwhile, he's making her miserable. He's a cheat and a liar. He's not the least bit discreet about his affairs and seems to delight in embarrassing her." She lifted her shoulder in a negligent shrug. "He's a bastard." Her gaze drifted significantly between the two of them. "And we all know what's it like to live with one of those."

Bitsy and Meredith both frowned, evidence of the truth of that statement.

Meredith gave Sophia another probing look. "So she's the reason we're here?"

Sophia nodded. "I want to issue The Invitation." As founding members of the Club, they all had to agree. "Do either of you oppose?"

Bitsy snorted indelicately. "I certainly don't. She's young. She could use some widow training, and from the sounds of it, the poor girl is going to need all the help she can get."

Never one to make snap decisions, Meredith's focus slid to where Jolie Marshall sat across the room, seemed to take her measure. After a prolonged moment, she nodded. "I agree."

Sophia nodded, pleased. She lifted her glass, waited for the other two to do the same before readying their standard toast. The three shared a conspiratorial look, a secret smile. "To The Future Widows' Club."

Welcome to the Future Widows' Club—a secret society of women who've been treated like trash by their no-good husbands and prefer waiting for widowhood over divorce. But sometimes waiting can be murder...

Look for The Future Widows' Club by Rhonda Nelson on sale April 2005.